BEYOND THE RIM

Borgo Press Books by S. Fowler Wright

Arresting Delia: An Inspector Cleveland Classic Crime Novel
The Attic Murder: An Inspector Combridge & Mr. Jellipot Classic Crime Novel
The Bell Street Murders: An Inspector Combridge & Mr. Jellipot Classic Crime Novel
Beyond the Rim: A Lost Race Fantasy
Black Widow: A Classic Crime Novel
The Capone Caper: Mr. Jellipot vs. the King of Crime: A Classic Crime Novel
Crime & Co.: An Inspector Cleveland Classic Crime Novel
Dawn: A Novel of Global Warming
Dead by Saturday: An Inspector Cleveland Classic Crime Novel
Dream; or, The Simian Maid: A Fantasy of Prehistory (Marguerite Cranleigh #1)
Elfwin: An Historical Novel
The End of the Mildew Gang: An Inspector Cauldron Classic Crime Novel (Mildew Gang #3)
Four Callers in Razor Street: An Inspector Combridge & Mr. Jellipot Classic Crime Novel
The Hanging of Constance Hillier: An Inspector Cleveland Classic Crime Novel
The Hidden Tribe: A Lost Race Fantasy
The Jordans Murder: An Inspector Combridge & Mr. Jellipot Classic Crime Novel
The King Against Anne Bickerton: A Classic Crime Novel
The Mildew Gang: An Inspector Cauldron Classic Crime Novel (Mildew Gang #1)
Murder in Bethnal Square: An Inspector Combridge & Mr. Jellipot Classic Crime Novel
The Police and the Public
Post-Mortem Evidence: An Inspector Combridge & Mr. Jellipot Classic Crime Novel
The Return of the Mildew Gang: An Inspector Cauldron Classic Crime Novel (Mildew Gang #2)
The Rissole Mystery: An Inspector Combridge & Mr. Jellipot Classic Crime Novel
The Screaming Lake: A Lost Race Fantasy
The Secret of the Screen: An Inspector Combridge & Mr. Jellipot Classic Crime Novel
Spiders' War: A Novel of the Far Future (Marguerite Cranleigh #3)
Three Witnesses: A Classic Crime Novel
Too Much for Mr. Jellipot: An Inspector Combridge & Mr. Jellipot Classic Crime Novel
The Vengeance of Gwa: A Fantasy of Prehistory (Marguerite Cranleigh #2)
Was Murder Done? A Classic Crime Novel
Who Murdered Reynard? A Classic Crime Novel
The Wills of Jane Kanwhistle: An Inspector Combridge & Mr. Jellipot Classic Crime Novel
With Cause Enough?: An Inspector Combridge & Mr. Jellipot Classic Crime Novel

BEYOND THE RIM

A LOST RACE FANTASY

by

S. FOWLER WRIGHT

THE BORGO PRESS

An Imprint of Wildside Press LLC

MMIX

CHAPTER I.

IT was three years ago—three years last February—that Franklin Arden missed his train at Victoria, and wandered into the Ricardo Restaurant. He was not concerned by the delay, having no wife to consider, and his housekeeper being used to his irregularities. He had an hour to wait, and a meal was indicated.

So he ordered dinner and sat down alone in a quiet corner, but the room began to fill, and the three other places at his table were soon occupied one after the other.

The man who came in first and sat opposite to him really originated the whole matter, and changed the lives of the other three whom chance had gathered; yet he was of the least importance, and though Franklin retained a vague memory of his appearance, and a keen one of his manner, he did not learn his name, and might not have recognized him had they met a week later with a different background.

The man who took the seat on his left, whom he was afterwards to know as Captain Sparshott, was short and spare, with a very brown and furrowed skin, and puckered wrinkles sound eyes that were small and bright

The fourth place was taken by a lady whom a waiter directed to the only seat left vacant, with some apology, to which she replied that it would do quite well, "unless these gentlemen wish to be private." She could not know that they were all equally strangers.

It might have been difficult to recall how the conversation started. Doubtless a request for mustard or the menu, a barren courtesy of convention, and then—somehow—an allusion to broadcasting by the man opposite Franklin Arden, the one who had come in second, and whose name he did not learn.

There had been an article in the *Evening Telegraph* advocating the inclusion of more controversial subjects in the broadcasting programmes, to which he alluded, and Franklin gave it a word of casual approval, at which the man broke out into a somewhat unmannerly disagreement.

"If you once begin that sort of thing, you'd never draw the line," he said dogmatically. "You'd soon have the Anti-Vivisectionists, and the Anti-Vaccinators, and all the other cranks wanting a go, and end up with someone telling us that the earth is flat."

Franklin didn't think that the earth was flat, any more than most people do, but the man irritated him. He hated cant phrases like "draw the line." He knew them for a sign of a mind that accepts everything orthodox, and sneers at originality in thought or conduct. So he said quietly: "I suppose that could be argued."

"It might among lunatics."

"I hope I'm not that bad."

The man stared at him incredulously.

"You don't really—" he began, and the contempt in his tone annoyed Franklin further.

"No," he interrupted, "I don't. But I say it could be argued quite sanely. The arguments commonly put forward would satisfy no one who was not convinced already—or perhaps I should say prejudiced—by previous assertion."

"What arguments do you mean?"

"Well, I once read—actually in a school textbook, adopted by a leading educational body—that the earth is round *because it casts a round shadow on the moon*. A soup plate would do the same. It was almost as silly as the answer I got myself when a small child, from a maiden aunt. 'It's round,' she said vaguely, looking for something to illustrate her assertion, and seeing a water-bottle on the table, 'round like a water-jug.'

"Another frequent argument is that a ship's hull may pass out sight while its masts are still visible. This is true enough, but how do we know that the textbooks for the next generation will not offer a different explanation of this optical peculiarity?"

The man answered as one who restrains impatience with difficulty at a child's persistence. "There are some things too evident for dispute, when once we know them. The science of astronomy—"

"Got on very well when it was convinced that the earth was a fixed globe in the centre of the universe. I've no doubt, if it were convinced tomorrow that the earth is flat, it would adjust its theories without much difficulty. The theologians have shown us a score of times what can be done by such mental gymnastics."

"If you really mean to argue such a thing seriously," the man answered with an increased irritability, "there is one proof which even you must admit to be final. The earth being a sphere, the distance between its extremes of longitude must be greatest at its equa-

tor, and diminish equally with each degree of northward or southward latitude, declining at last to nothing at the poles. If it were otherwise—if, as you appear to suggest, it were a flat disc, with the
North Pole at its centre—could those who live in the Southern
Hemisphere, or those who sail its seas, be unaware of the immense
distances that would divide them, or which they would have to traverse? Would not our maps reveal it? Should we not have a centre of
all parts of the world at the North Pole, from which they would be
spread out, so that their southern portions would be of vast extent, or
separated by enormous distances?"

It is discourteous to laugh at a chance-met acquaintance, but
Mr. Arden could not avoid a smile as he answered. "Then look at
any map, and your case is ended. *That is exactly what you'll find.* I
remember discovering this as a child, while my mind was still confused by the water-jug. I that if men who lived on a flat earth persisted in saying that it was round, the map we have is just what they
would be obliged to make it—crowding continents round the North
Pole, and showing immensities of ocean in its Southern Hemisphere.

"I looked at that map twenty years ago, and though I don't say
that the earth is flat, I think I've kept an open mind ever since."

The stranger was less concerned than was Franklin Arden to observe the amenities of such a discussion; or, perhaps, he felt that the
intellectual provocation that he was receiving was unusually great.
His upper lip rose in an open sneer as he asked: "Would you tell me
what shape you really suppose the earth to be, and whereabouts you
would put the poles in your own map?"

"I've told you I don't assert that it's one shape more than another. I keep an open mind. But the shape I've indicated is quite
easy to understand. It's like a plate, with a patch of ice in the middle
which we call the North Pole, and a rim of ice all round the edge,
which isn't a pole at all. It's just the vague immensity of ice and water which we call the Antarctic region."

"What nonsense."

"Probably it is. But you've got to recognize this. You could
draw a map of the earth on those lines, and it would be much like
what we know it to be. But suppose you tried to put the South Pole
in the centre, you'd find it wouldn't work in the same way. Instead
of a real centre, from which the continents spread, you'd have a
vague immensity in the midst, with the continents—well you just
couldn't place them at all."

"I think it's too silly for words." The stranger called for his bill.
He hadn't finished what was before him, but he seemed to have lost

his appetite in irritation at the conversation which he had himself initiated.

Franklin watched him with some amusement. It would have been impossible for him to lose his temper in discussing theoretic possibilities. He thought the man was a fool, and the man had thought he was mad.

It might have ended there if he had not caught the glance of the lady upon his right, and seen that it was alight with amusement akin to his own. Laughter rippled to the surface as their eyes met.

"You didn't ask him," she said, "about the stars."

The voice was friendly and confident, neither bold nor shy. The speaker was young—probably not more than twenty-five—with clear frank eyes in a sun-tanned face. She seemed assured, and therefore unconscious of herself, and to accept Franklin Arden without thought as one of a kindred kind. She was well-dressed, but rather as though it were routine than preoccupation. Feminine enough, but not aggressive in femininity. She would have been unattractive to those men who require womanhood to override personality, as such men would have been to her. Franklin answered without realizing that it was a stranger who had spoken. They might have been friends for years.

"Oh, you mustn't take that rot seriously. I've no doubt the stars would have blown the whole nonsense sky-high, if he'd understood what he was talking about well enough to know how to bring them in."

"I didn't quite mean that," she replied. "I remember I had the same sort of argument with a governess when I was young, and I put a question to her which may have a simple answer, but she didn't know it, or was too impatient with a child's difficulty to try to understand.

"I'd been shown the North Star, and told that it was always in the same place, and all the other stars—except, of course, the planets—move round it: and I said: 'If the earth's really round, mustn't there be a South Pole star on the other side, and all the stars on that side move round that in the same way? And if not, why not?' And when I heard you bringing out so many arguments for the earth being flat, I half-expected to hear that too."

"Yes," he said, "I hadn't thought of that. It is curious that if you once imagine the earth as a flat plate, and the Arctic Circle making a central pattern of ice, with the North Star overhead, and the sun and all the stars moving round that point, and then an outer ring of ice that makes the rim of the plate—it's curious how everything seems to fit in, just as you'd expect it to if that were the real truth."

"It's queer to think of us," she said lightly, "as cheese-mites running about on a plate that we can't get off; and yet when you come to think of it, it fits in again. I mean, if we wanted to keep some cheese-mites on a plate, we should make the rim so that they couldn't get over it, and that's what the Antarctic is. And we should put the cheese in the middle, and that's just how it is, with the continents crowded round the North Pole, and great oceans everywhere dividing us from the rim of the plate. It seems so much like it would be when you think it over that I almost begin to convince myself," she concluded, as one who smiles at her own foolishness.

"Oh, you mustn't do that. I was only pulling his leg, as he might have guessed. If I really thought there were any doubt, I should be starting to find out before the end of the week."

"So should I," she said unexpectedly. "Like a shot."

The third man, who had sat silent, but listening with a curious intensity of interest to this conversation, suddenly ejaculated: "Ma'am, if you meant…."—and then stopped as their eyes turned to him in a common surprise.

His accent, slightly nasal and slightly marine, did not belie the evidence of the form of address he had used, or the appearance that met their glances. It might be Boston or Baltimore, but they did not doubt that they were companioned by a seaman of the Western world.

The lady hesitated for a second, as though she might ignore or repulse this unexpected address, and then said, coolly enough, as one who will not venture too far to withdraw easily, though with a smile that softened the words: "And what of that, if I would?"

"Because," he said, with an impressive earnestness, and yet with the tone of one who anticipates incredulity: "*I'm the one man living that knows the way.*"

The girl did not answer, looking at him with sceptical and appraising eyes.

Franklin said, as one who humours a joke: "Meaning you've looked over the edge?"

"Meaning I know the way through. And a bad day it was for me."

Franklin looked at his watch. He had already missed his next train. He thought there was a tale to be had here, for amusement if not belief. He said: "But you came back alive."

"Yes, sir. I'm a live man. But I left the *Maryland*, and not a man of her crew survived. That was six years back, and I've not had a ship since."

He spoke the last words as one embittered by a monstrous wrong, and fell silent, so that Franklin asked, to rouse him to speech again: "Do you mean they blamed you for losing the ship? In those regions—"

He was about to speak of the violence of the Antarctic storms but the man interrupted him to say: "No, it wasn't that. I'd been whaling there, mate and master, for fifteen years, and a clean bill. It was nigh two years from when the ice shut us in to when the *Falkland Lass* picked me up in an open boat, and we'd been given up for lost long enough.

"No, I'd found land, and I'd found coal. Coal in thousands of tons lying close to the water-side, to be taken out with a pick, and a water swarming with whales, that had never heard siren blown, and when I'd said that, they'd have given me the best ship in the fleet. Only, I said too much."

"Too much?" The mariner had fallen silent again, and Franklin must stir him to resume his tale.

"Yes, I said where I'd been, and how long it took, and what I'd seen at the end, and they stopped talking about that ship. They looked at each other and me, and said: "'Captain, you had a hard time. You sure did. You're needing a rest now. Here's five hundred dollars. Just you go away and forget.'

"So I had the rest, though I was fitter than them. Fitter than the best on the day I went. And I came back, 'What about that ship now?' But they said that times were worse than they were, and they'd got two boats lying up, and better let it be for a time."

"And that was six years ago?"

"Six years come March, and I'm for Norway now for a last chance, with the last two hundred dollars of the bit of money I had, and then it's the forecastle for me, or a job on shore."

"You mean you told them something they didn't believe?"

"Yes. I did that. But I'm not blaming them overmuch. No one would."

The girl asked: "What was it you saw?"

"I can't say that. I've learned that I can't say that and be counted as a sane man. 'Oh, yes,' they say, 'and you came back alive?' and then they shift their chairs a bit further away."

She did not press for an answer which she felt she would not get. She asked: "Would you go again?"

Sparshott looked at her with a sudden hope in the small bright eyes, which died as it rose. What could it be more than the idle question of a curious girl? But he answered eagerly enough. "Would I go again? Ma'am, when you've been called a liar for six years, and seen men winking behind your back—men that used to run when you spoke—and been hanging round for that time for a job that you couldn't get...."

"He left the sentence for her to end as she would, and she reached down a hand to where her bag lay beside her on the floor. She took out a card, and passed it across the table. "Could you come to see me at eleven tomorrow morning?"

Franklin read the name as he passed the card: *Eleanor Blanche D'Acre*. It was a known name. Why had he not guessed it was she? But the press photographs gave her a harder, a more masculine face.

"Yes, ma'am, I'll be there." The seaman rose at the word, rather as one who had been dismissed, or it may have been that he was unwilling for further questioning.

The two others remained seated. The curious incident seemed to have drawn them together in a natural intimacy. Franklin said: "You'll take coffee?" as one who speaks to his own guest, and then: "I wouldn't trust that man further than I can see."

"No?" she said, smiling. "I wonder.... But it ought to be a good tale."

"Oh, yes. If you're wanting that." He knew her as one who had won fame by an expedition into Arabia, and a daring penetration into the monastic privacies of Tibet. One also who wrote of her adventures, and sometimes would contribute tales to the magazines. She was reputed to be almost fabulously wealthy, since Lord Dagsworth's death. Of course, if she thought she could use the man for some good copy, and doubtless pay him well for her whim.... Well, there was no reason to interfere.

They rose to go without further words on that subject. But when he used her name at parting she said: "You ought to let me know your name, as you know mine. It's only fair that you should." And then added, as she took his card: "I'll let you know if it's anything really good."

CHAPTER II.

FRANKLIN ARDEN waked early next morning, and his mind reverted to the dinner of the night before. But it was not concerned with the geographical area of the Antarctic regions. Whatever that might be, it had been so for a long while, without any alarming consequences to the world which it encircled or rounded off, as the ease might be. It could look after itself without any help from him.

His mind was on a more intimate and more urgent problem. How could he renew acquaintance with the companion who had sat so casually at his right hand? He could be nothing to her. He remembered the frank, impersonal, friendly gaze. He could not delude himself that it had implied any interest except in the subject to which the talk had turned. Should he thrust himself upon her, taking advantage of that fortuitous intimacy? To what end could it lead? She was, so he had heard, one of the richest women in England. He was a consulting engineer who had not been consulted during the last three weeks. He had qualified six months ago, and had not earned enough since then to pay his office rent and the wages of his single clerk. Beyond that, he had an income of five hundred pounds. Enough to make him comfortably independent, but not enough to make him anything better than the financial satellite of a wealthy wife. For his thought went so far. The girl's face with its unconscious beauty, its indifferent frankness, would not leave his mind. And common sense told him to forget. To treat the incident as one of those pleasant disconnected interludes with which every life is occasionally punctuated. And then he thought of Stimson, who was on the Baltic Exchange, and knew all the nautical gossip of the two hemispheres.

He got Stimson at the third attempt, at 9:48 A.M., and talked to him till 10:03, and then had to cut off rather abruptly, for Stimson was one of those men who start talking more than they stop, and at 10:07 he was in a taxi for Cadogan Square. It might be foolish for his own peace, but he told himself that he was doing no more than duty required. How could he consider his own feelings, immediate or remote, as being of any consequence, beside the duty of the warning he had to give?

At 10:38 he was shown into a room where Miss D'Acre was already seated. The Yankee skipper had not arrived.

She received him with a politeness that approached cordiality, and yet left him with a faint discomfort. She did not ask him why he had called at that early hour, but she made no effort to develop conversation, leaving him to feel that such an explanation was necessary.

"I had a friend on the telephone this morning," he began. "Stimson. He's on the Exchange—the Baltic, of course, not Stock Exchange—where they know everything about...."

"Yes," she interrupted, to assure him, "I've heard of the Baltic Exchange."

"Yes, of course. Well, I asked him if he knew anything of a Captain Sparshott of Baltimore, and I thought you might like to know what he told me before he called."

"It's very good of you, but I'm not quite sure that I should."

Franklin might have felt less resentment at this rebuff had he been more indifferent to the lips from which it came. Actually, it was not offensively spoken. The girl seemed to utter a genuine doubt, with no implication of blame, but equally with no thanks for the offered help. The trouble was that he had anticipated a different reception. He rose from the chair which he had taken a moment before as her hand indicated. "Of course," he said coldly, "if you feel like that. I'm sorry I interfered."

He was halfway to the door before she looked at him, or appeared to be aware of his intended withdrawal. Then her eyes met his with a sudden smile. "No, please don't go," she said, in a tone that assumed compliance. "Have I been rude? I'm afraid I wasn't thinking of what you said. And that's being ruder still! The fact is, Mr...Arden, I'm a little intrigued about that man. I don't *want* to hear he's a fraud, as, of course, he is. I was just wondering when you were announced whether he'd turn up this morning. I suppose it's ten to one that we shall never see him again."

"No. I think you'll see him. But...."

"Then do you mind if I ask you not to tell me any more till I've talked to him myself? I've always had a fancy for forming my own opinions. If you wouldn't mind staying, if you can spare the time. Thanks, I'm glad of that, if you're sure it's not asking too much. You can hear what passes, and if I arrange anything with him, you'll be able to judge what a fool I am, knowing whatever you do."

"Arrange? You don't really...?"

"Probably not. I expect it's no more than a wild tale. But if I thought there were half a chance that it's something more...that there's something worth finding out. Yes, I'd start tonight, if I could."

Franklin heard this surprising declaration with mingled feelings. It is true that it was no more than had been implied the night before. But there is a difference in the morning hours. Also, he realized sharply the freedom that wealth confers. And it was a wild idea— wild and reckless in the cold light of day. What did she know of the uncharted terrors of the Antarctic ice? And at the calling of such a tale!

He said: "It wouldn't be much like Arabia."

"No. Quite different. You mean that I've no idea what the Antarctic's like? I've never been there, if you mean that. I don't suppose you have either."

"No. I've done a little Alpine climbing. Just enough to know what cold means, and to help to imagine the rest. But, of course, that's nothing to what has to be faced there."

"Probably not. I don't suppose it's quite as bad as people make out. Few things are. I've felt cold in Tibet. Well, I believe that's he, by the voice."

Captain Sparshott entered the room.

CHAPTER III.

THE quick eyes of Captain Sparshott glanced from one occupant of the room to the other, and brightened at what they saw. He might be dreamer or cheat, but he was of an alert intelligence. He had seen that these two had been strangers yesterday. He had left them together. That they were together now seemed to imply that he was being taken seriously, in which he was as nearly right as such deductions are likely to be.

Miss D'Acre showed a more positive cordiality to Captain Sparshott than she had done to her earlier visitor. She encouraged him to the comfort of a fireside seat (for the morning was not warm), and the earliness of the hour did not deter her from an offer of liquid refreshment. But Sparshott did not drink. Neither would he draw on the contents of the cigarette-box which she held out toward him. If he preferred a pipe, she suggested, he must not hesitate. But he said no to that also. He assured her that he did not smoke. Fact or pose, he presented himself as an abstemious man, and there was nothing in his appearance to deny it. It was no more than fair to recognize that if he had been unemployed for six years, he appeared to have faced adversity without moral disaster.

"I wish," she said, as they were comfortably seated around the fire, with the Captain in the middle, "I wish you'd tell us the tale in your own way. How you lost the ship—I mean how it got lost—and how you got back alone."

It was neatly put, giving him the opportunity, in the intellectual sobriety of the morning hours, of telling a tale that need be of no more than credible disaster in South Polar seas, or of going further at his own will if he were disposed to do so. But it appeared that the alternatives were alike unwelcome.

He shook his head as he answered, "No, ma'am. I couldn't do that. I couldn't tell you how I lost that ship. I've learned better than that. You'd show me out for a crazy man."

"But if you won't tell anyone...."

"I've told a-many before now. I talked of it and couldn't stop when they picked me up. And they listened and smiled, and the doctor said: 'Let him sleep all he can, and he'll come round. It's just a question of time.'"

"Yes," she answered with sympathy, "I know the feeling myself. I saw three things in Tibet that I mentioned once, and learnt that lesson for life. But you needn't be afraid here. We know what a queer place the world is."

He looked at her gratefully, even with a moment's doubt, and then shook his head more resolutely than before.

"Ma'am," he said, "I want to make people believe I'm a sane man. *I want a ship once again.* I'll tell you all you'll believe, and perhaps a bit more. But what good's it going to do me then? I don't want money. I've still got enough to last me a few weeks. *I want a ship.* If I don't get it in that time, it's the lower ratings for me."

"No," she said, "I don't say I could get you a ship. I'm not going to promise that. I'm not going to promise anything. But when someone comes back from a strange place, and tells me of what he's seen, I always think he's more likely to know than anyone else, and I believe what he tells me, unless I've got a good reason not to."

She saw that he must be drawn in, if at all, with a gentle line. She added: "Tell us just as much as you like, and stop as soon as you think we've had as much as we're fit to hear. I suppose you got caught in the ice at the start, and drifted the wrong way?"

"No, ma'am, it wasn't that. Not, so to speak, at the start-off. There'd been two bad whaling seasons, and no prospect of better, and more ships on the ground every year, and I got secret orders from my firm not to waste time fishing, but just to slip away to the Enderby quadrant, and see what I could find. I don't know whether you know...."

"Yes," they both said, "we understand that." (Had they not both been busy last night with Antarctic maps?)

But he pulled out one of his own, spreading it on his knees, and pointing as he went on.

"The fleet made for the Weddell Sea, but I slipped off in the night, with Coat's Land a hundred leagues on the starboard bow, bearing south-by-east as the pack-ice would let me through. The *Maryland* was the stoutest ship of the fleet, and they'd given me a picked crew, sober men who could be trusted to keep a shut mouth

15

over what we found, if it were made worth their while. I wasn't looking for new lands, or caring how far south I could get. The less ice the better for me. All I wanted was whales, and I looked to find a fresh feeding-ground there, if there were any left in the world. Well, I found that right enough.

"I found it when I was further south than was over-safe with the season as far gone as it was, and I in the worst part of the Antarctic, as all the records show it to be, though there's not many of them, for the ships that have gone east of Coat's Land since 1830, when Enderby's sent John Briscoe, could be counted on one hand, and it's little but battered hulls that they could have brought back.

"Well, I'd been dodging the pack-ice for about ten days, keeping dear enough, but being forced south all the time. That was the queer thing. The winter was coming on, and the ice thickening everywhere, but there'd always be a lane to southward, and perhaps a broader one beyond that, till we came at last to an open sea.

"That was the first of the queer things I had to tell when I got back. Not that they doubted that. And whales! We saw more in three weeks than I'd set eyes on for the ten years before. They were the big blue whales mostly, and some of them a size that I'd never hoped to see, except in a dream. And all the water was pink with the diatoms on which they fed.

"I thought it was fortune for the owners, and a bit for me and the crew, and we were in good spirits enough, though the ice wouldn't let us through. It kept closing in, and we kept feeling our way, east or west as we best could, but always trying to get out to the north, and it ever heading us south, till it brought us to land at last."

He paused here, as though hesitating how to go on, and it was more to rouse him to speech than with any purpose of questioning the tale that Franklin said: "Your firm believed that?"

"Yes. It wasn't hard to believe, more or less. You see, the Enderby quadrant, as it's called, has never been penetrated very far. It's been supposed that the Antarctic continent extended further on that side, and the few who've tried to sail along it have met such weather as did little to tempt the next. But no one's really known how the land lay. It's been fog or blizzard or snow, and the ice-pack round the bows, and to south'ard here and there a loom of land or a wall of ice, which may be island, if it's land at all, and the mist closes again. No, they listened to that. It was just what they'd hoped to hear."

"Then it's hard to see why they didn't give you another chance. Did they send other ships to find out if the report was true?"

"They wouldn't say, if they had. But I don't think they ever did. I guess I know all the boats they've got, and where they've been since then. I said they believed all right, and so they did at the first, but when I went on. Well, they thought it was the mad-house for me."

"And you could get there again?"

"Yes. I know where it is. I could find it, if I could get through."

"And there's no reason you shouldn't," Miss D'Acre interposed, "with a good ship?"

"Yes. It's likely enough. But, ma'am, I don't want to tell you wrong. It was the mildest summer down there that year that's been known since the first whaler went south. When Kemp sailed that way in 1833, he didn't get within miles of where I got through the pack."

"But you know the way if you could get through?"

"Yes. There's only ice in the way." He spread the map on his knees, and his two auditors bent forward from either side, as he laid his finger on a spot about 500 miles east of Coat's Land, where a space as large as Europe was shown as an unexplored vacancy crossed by no more than the dotted line that marked the limit of the doubtful land—land that did not exist at all, or, at least, continuously, if Captain Sparshott's tale were true.

"Couldn't you expect to get through," Miss D'Acre asked again, "if you took full advantage of the summer months?—I mean, got on the spot by when the summer starts, and went prepared to stay the winter there if there weren't time to get back?"

"No, ma'am, I couldn't promise for sure. I expect you could. It all depends on how the ice breaks, and the storms that you'd have to face."

"But I thought that the summer—I know it's short, but I've heard that the Arctic summer's a lovely thing, when the sun never sets. It's all sunshine and flowers."

"But, ma'am, this isn't the Arctic. The south is another tale. There's no flowers there at any time of the year. There's not a tree in a thousand leagues. There's no foxes or bears. It's what you said last night. It's like the rim of the dish. There's one point here"—he laid his finger on Ross's Sea as he spoke—"where you can go deeper in. It's like a crack in the edge. But you come to the ice-wall there. You come to that if you go on long enough anywhere. It's ice or rock, eight or ten thousand feet high. Hard as iron, and barren and cold. There's no summer there like there is in the Arctic lands. There's no summer, and there's no life of man, or bear, or tree. There's a bit of moss, at the best, and even that making a hard fight. And the weather's hell. I've seen storms in the Behring Straits, but the wind was like a cat purring at home to what you meet there."

"If there's a wall of rock or ice everywhere round the Arctic pole—or rim, if that's what it is—" Franklin persisted, "I suppose you'd have come to that sooner or later if you'd gone south by the way you went?"

He had his own reason for doubting Captain Sparshott's tale, and he kept to his point of drawing him further on as persistently as Miss D'Acre held to that of the practicability of repeating his expedition

There was a short pause, as though the man feared that if he said more he would be led further than he had a mind to go, and then he answered:

"You're right in that. We came to that just as you'd think we would. There's a cliff there like a wall—a cliff that's ten thousand feet high. But it isn't that, it's the way through." He fell silent again.

"You mean there's a way through the cliff?"

"Not through. There's a way between. There's lower land on the coast. It's there you can shovel up coal from the water-side. And there's a river that flows out. It's a river that doesn't freeze. We steamed up it at last, when the ice closed from the north, and kept heading us in. There was the great wall, and the canyon split it through, and the river came out of that."

"So I suppose you went up? Was it wide enough for the ship to go?"

"Yes. We went up. We steamed up that canyon with the new coal we'd picked up on the beach. *We steamed three weeks and it never changed*…and you could see the stars all the time."

"But the sun wouldn't have gone by then," Franklin objected.

"You mean it was so deep?" Miss D'Acre asked. She was leaning forward with her hands clasped round one knee, and her eyes on the seaman's face. He seemed to have gained one convert at least, and her tone may have given confidence to his own speech, for he answered as one who sees again, and whose eyes are fixed on a distant thing.

"It was wide enough for the ship to steer through, and it never altered its width, and the wind blows up it, cold and steady, like a draught that never stops, and it's smooth and deep. There's no rapids nor shallows, nor any change in its depth. And the cliffs are so high that there's little light down below. They're…." He seemed to feel the lack of any word to interpret the vision that held his eyes, and ended weakly, "…So high." If he were an actor, he was a very good one, Franklin thought as he watched, but he remembered what had been told him scarcely two hours ago.

His thought was interrupted by an unexpected question from the girl. "Are you married, Captain?"

"No, ma'am. That's to say, not to matter."

"I mean, is there anyone who is dependent upon you—who would be worse off if you were to die?"

"No. Not to matter, that is."

"Then I'm going to make you a sporting offer. I'll tell you first that I shan't alter a word. It's just to take or leave. Is it worth your while to try for £10,000?"

He made no answer to that. Perhaps he thought there could be no need. The small bright eyes in the puckered face did not leave her own as she went on.

Franklin had a fear that she was going to involve herself in a reckless gamble, from which a word would have saved her. If only he had been resolute to speak before! He gave a half-articulate protesting sound, the meaning of which must have been plain enough, though it had no influence, for she made a motion of silence, and threw a "please" in his direction before she went on.

"I'm going to offer you that. You must guide me to that canyon, whether it takes twelve months or twelve years, and I'll pay every expense, but not a penny beyond that. If we find it, and you come back alive, there'll be £10,000 for you at my London bank whether I'm living or dead. And I won't ask you a word more as to what you found at the end of the three weeks, or how you came back alone. I don't want you to tell. I'm not one to glance at the last chapter before I begin the book."

Captain Sparshott's eyes lit as with a sudden satisfaction as this offer commenced, but before it ended they had fallen to the hearthrug. He had the look of a troubled man. But he said: "Thank you, ma'am. It's a big sum. What if I don't come back?"

"It will be paid to whoever you direct."

"And if none of us comes back?"

"In that case, at the end of three years, it shall be paid in the same way."

He seemed satisfied at that, and his mind turned to the practical issues of the expedition which had been so casually determined. "At this time of year...," he began.

"Oh, I'll see to all that," she said. "I'll do it now, not to lose any time." She picked up the telephone from a little table at her left hand.

"Miss Collinson, please get through to the Stores, and ask them for a quotation for equipping an expedition to the Antarctic for two years. It must be timed to reach Enderby Land, or thereabouts, as the ice breaks. A good whaler to sail from Cape Town I should think, but I leave that to them. There'll be equipment needed for two women—yes, of course, and three men. Tell them if they overlook anything that matters, it's the last order they'll get." (That seemed likely enough!)

She laid the instrument down, as she added, "It costs more doing it that way, but it adds ten years to your life. Miss Collinson says if I wanted to marry, I should ring up the Stores. 'I want a husband at St. Margaret's at twelve-thirty on Tuesday next. A short mild-mannered man, with blue eyes.' Or something of that sort. I've no doubt they'd have him there, if I did."

She rose, saying: "You'd better let me have your address, Captain." The men rose also, her manner and words giving the impression that the interview was at an end.

Captain Sparshott said: "It's the Beaver Hotel, ma'am. Off Moorgate. I'll be at hand any time." His eyes still had a look of preoccupation, as though the plan of returning to the scene of his strange adventure had brought back some sight of wonder or horror too vividly to be put aside. He said: "I don't know but you ought to know before then." But he spoke rather to himself than her. Then he went out.

Franklin would have gone too, but she held him back with a glance, which he was quick and willing to understand. He felt bewildered by the display of an efficiency which did not require his help, and strangely saddened by the thought that his day-old acquaintance would disappear from his life as completely as the confines of the earth allowed. Yet there was one warning that he ought still to give, though he might have no thanks for giving it.

But he met the unexpected again. The door had scarcely closed on the seaman's exit when Miss D'Acre reseated herself, and said: "And now tell me the lurid tale."

CHAPTER IV.

"THERE'S nothing definite against the man," Franklin said, "so I'm told, except that. But, in this connection, it's a good deal. He's nick-named 'Tell It Sparshott,' and they called him that years before he came back alone from his last cruise. Stimson says he believes he had it from a boy. If his mother sent him round the corner for a quarter of tea, he'd come back with a tale of a runaway racehorse, or a house on fire with the flames a mile high.

"His owners knew this, but they didn't mind, for he's allowed to have been a good sailor, and a steady man, but this last time it was a bit too much. He came back having lost his ship, and he wouldn't tell what happened. Not a sensible tale that anyone could believe. They even had to make a compromise on the Insurance, as they daren't have taken such a tale into court. Stimson knows some underwriters who held part of the risk, so he had it at first hand."

Miss D'Acre listened to this tale in a thoughtful silence.

"It does rather queer the pitch," she said at last. "But it doesn't really prove anything. A queer thing might happen to a man who'd been inventing them all his life; and then, of course, no one would believe a word."

"The question is whether you'll ever see him again."

"Oh, I don't.... Do you really think that? Well, there'll be an amended quotation needed for one man less."

"You mean you'd go all the same?"

"Rather. Think how I should have wasted the morning if I dropped it now! I've got a feeling that there'll be something interesting in the Enderby quadrant, and, after all, he hasn't given us any very definite assurances as to what it is...but, of course, if you feel differently, it would be for two less instead of one."

"You mean that the three men were to include me?"

"Well, of course. I thought we settled that yesterday." Franklin Arden was conscious of a bewildering confusion of feelings that delayed reply. He was aware of a very pleasurable excitement; perhaps aware also, however subconsciously, that the event was certain, and that he would follow this cool and masterful young woman to the world's end (or even further!) if she would permit him to do so; but he was conscious of the bewildering, almost casual speed of the decision, and resentful of the way in which his coming was unconditionally assumed. And the last feeling, though not the deepest, was the most active upon the surface of his mind. And while he hesitated, the telephone-bell rang.

Miss D'Acre heard the voice of her secretary. The Stores wished to know whether they should estimate for sledges only, or Siberian ponies. It was a question at which to pause. If the programme were to be the sailing up an endless canyon to an unknown end, the utility of either was less than certain. She realized that it might be difficult to obtain a satisfactory outfit without a larger measure of confidence than she would be willing to give. But she was not one to show indecision. She said: "Tell them if they're in any doubt about anything, they'd better estimate both ways."

She put the receiver down, and repeated the inquiry she had received. She added: "We shall need a few more words with Captain Sparshott about this equipment."

Franklin had had a vague idea during this moment of interruption, He would not be dragged at her tail in this way. He would follow to protect and rescue! Then he had rejected it instantly on financial grounds. He had an indistinct recollection of reading that Shackleton had raised £20,000 for his expedition, and had then been embarrassed for lack of means. Then he became very sure that it was not a thing to be attempted by a woman at all. Even the ordinary perils of the Antarctic—if ordinary they could be called—were something that no woman had ever faced. Why should he not go alone, and bring back report of the unknown? She could finance the expedition. That would be glory for her. He had an illogical feeling that he would not mind her financing it, if she were not there. But if she were both to finance and control.... Besides, it was not a woman's work. Arabia was a very different thing. So was Tibet. The question about the ponies made it more real, more definite, than it had been previously.

He said: "I wonder whether you've got any idea what the Antarctic's like. I don't know that a woman ought to go there at all. I don't believe one ever has."

"Then it's time one did," she said lightly, "if not two." And then added, in a more serious tone: "You're not backing out, are you? If there's any difficulty about getting away...." Her hand reached instinctively to the cheque-book which removed so many impediments.

"No, thank you," he said, his eyes following her hand. "I can look after my own affairs."

"Sorry. But when I'm dragging you away suddenly like this...."

"You mentioned five. May I ask who are the other also-rans?"

Miss D'Acre might have an impetuosity that was her own, and an imperiousness that wealth and beauty are apt to give, but she was no fool.

"The also-rans? Oh, I see. Mr. Arden, I want you to come as Leader of the Expedition. Of course, you'll be in control. You'll have Captain Sparshott as guide. The also-rans will be my cousin, Bun Weldon—you'll like Bunny Weldon well enough—and two women to sew the buttons. Of course, you'll name your own fee. Whatever's reasonable for engaging a Consulting Engineer for two years, and leaving a practice to go to pot. But I hope you won't be rude to me by putting it too low. I know when I've got the best, and I like to pay for it."

Her eyes met his as she finished, in a very feminine, almost pleading way. He thought, as he had done last night, that her beauty was softer, more alluring, than her pictures showed. Illogically again, the thought made him determine that he would take no fee. His little capital could be realized, and his office closed. He would have ample means for his personal equipment, and his independence would remain. He said: "Of course I'll come. But we won't talk about fees, or leaders for that matter. You can finance the expedition, and I'll just come along and pay my own expenses. That doesn't mean much. We shan't put up at hotels."

"Mr. Arden," she answered seriously, "you can have it your own way about the fee. Anyway, we can leave it till we come back, if we ever do. But I've seen enough to know that someone's got to lead in a thing like this. Only Communists don't know that, and that's why they'll come croppers until they do. So if I put up the money and you lead, it's a fair deal."

He said no more on that point, though he might have noticed that she was having her own way, even then. He was becoming conscious of an exhilaration of excitement, hard to control to his usual quiet manner, as he committed himself to the wild folly of this adventure. He only asked: "You said two ladies. May I ask who is to be the other?"

He had a thought that she might not easily secure a companion on such a voyage.

"Oh, I should have told you. Miss Collinson, my secretary. You'll like Gwen too."

"Does she know her fate?"

"Yes. She's known it for half-an-hour. Didn't you hear me tell her to get the estimate? She wouldn't think I'd be mean enough to leave her behind."

CHAPTER V.

DOVE-GREY sky, and a sea of silver and lead: a cold wind from the south, and a distant glint of pack-ice on the starboard bow. So they came to seas which had been unknown of man except that once, a hundred years ago, the white wings of Briscoe's brig had glided through the mist—glided and gone.

Ahead, even if geographers were right as to the nature of the earth's extremity, even then, to right and left there were three thousand miles of icebound coast which was not even outlined on the maps of men. An iron coast, it was said, from which there came a blizzard, often at a hundred miles an hour. A blizzard that never ceased. That, at least, was the explanation given by explorer and whaler for the fact that there was, even now, no clear continuous map of the outmost edge of that side of Antarctica.

Blizzards there might be, but it seemed that the *Bergen* came on a quiet day. Quiet, and lifeless too, except that once a flight of Antarctic petrels had crossed the stern, and a slate-blue albatross hovered below the clouds.

The *Bergen* was an ice-breaker from the Arctic seas. It was the best of its kind that the world held, unless for one which is Russian-owned, and that even Miss D'Acre's purse could not have secured. Its owner, Captain Ericson, was to navigate it to the Antarctic Circle, when the command was to be taken over by Captain Sparshott. So the charter had specified, and Sven Ericson did not like the idea. Sparshott might be a good seaman, but of that he had no proof. He might also be mad, of which he had heard tales enough.

The terms of the charter had been too liberal to reject, but it had the sound to him of a crazy cruise. And with women, too! Not that he objected to them. He would have been pleased to see more. But the women messed apart. The ship had settled that for them. It was not designed for passengers, nor for a large officers' staff. There were two small cabins, in which, if cubic capacity had ruled the decision, they would have messed three and three. But Miss D'Acre had vetoed that, with discretion. Had she given that preference to Bunford Weldon, he would have burst his skin with conceit, and how Mr. Arden would have taken it she could not say. Probably he would have given no sign. But if Bunny had been put out, and Franklin preferred, he would have sulked like a whipped dog. Besides, he was her cousin. No; she couldn't do that. The men must manage as best they could.

The two captains had sat together when the mate was in charge above and the others had turned in. Ericson had tried with deliberate purpose to loosen his companion's tongue with the rum-bottle. Not that he intended to make him drunk while he kept sober himself. Captain Ericson was a gentleman, and he knew that there are things that a gentleman does not do. But to get your companion tight, and remain just a little more under control yourself—that is a permissible cunning. To finesse is not to cheat.

Whatever may have been the ethical basis of this experiment is the less important, as it had no success. Tell it that Sparshott was an abstemious man. The rum that he took was moderate in quantity, and it had no visible effect whatever.

Apart from that, he belied his name. It was not only that he was silent upon the object of the voyage before them. He didn't tell anything. He had become a silent, preoccupied man. He seemed to live in the shadow of some approaching moment. Was it merely that he expected to be revealed as the liar that he most probably was? Suppose that the bones of his ship might still lie, not up some canyon of a hundred leagues, but on the shore of the coal-strewn bay?

That was a wonder which came at times to Franklin's mind. Captain Ericson might have thought the same, but that he knew less. All he knew was that he was to navigate his ship to the Antarctic Circle at Longitude 16° east, and then hand over its direction to Captain Sparshott, only to resume its control on written instructions from Mr. Arden; and that he was to be prepared to winter in the ice or to return to Cape Town, and take in fresh stores for a relief expedition as he might be required. His charter was for two years, with the right of renewal for a further year if required, and he had received the first year's money before he sailed.

Beyond that, there was the evidence of the motor-boat which was lashed down on deck. A new boat, beautifully built and appointed. And the evidence of the stores he carried. Was it to be a new try for the Southern Pole? With two women to drag along! And the Enderby quadrant too! He had never been in the southern seas, but everyone knew that the Antarctic was unapproachable from that side. Well, after all, Captain Sparshott's ideas didn't matter much, as long as he understood how to handle a good boat, because what *would* happen was plain enough. There would be some weeks, prolonged to months, during which they would be sailing through fog and blizzard and dodging ice, with perhaps a glimpse of high inhospitable rocks, or perhaps not. And then they would be steering north again, or locked in the ice with six frozen months to think it over in the Antarctic night.

With such thoughts in his mind, Sven Ericson had brought his ship to the Antarctic edge, sailing south-by-east, until this morning, when he had handed over his charge to Captain Sparshott, who had put the helm due south for the polar seas.

CHAPTER VI.

THE expanse of water which lies south of Africa and India is the largest, loneliest ocean that the earth holds. Southward of New

Zealand or the Falkland Islands, there may be traffic north-and-south, and the whalers have made precarious footing on the barrier-ice. But here were seas where they might sail eastward for ten thousand miles and see neither steam nor sail, or south a thousand, more or less, till the ice should challenge their further way. Perhaps ten million square miles of storm-held waters, where not a dozen ships had crossed since Cook had first adventured in his tiny vessels— Cook first, and then at different points Briscoe and Kemp and Bruce and later Mawson. All to come back with the same report of ice that spread further north than on the other sides of the Antarctic, and of more dreadful storms.

Steaming south, day after day, across this lonely ocean, it was easy for Franklin to imagine that his jest was true, and that the Antarctic was really the outer rim of the world, rather than a terminal extremity. Here, said the geographers, the earth began to narrow towards its southern end, and yet here more than anywhere was a sense of vastness which had defied the explorations of men, of an interminable ocean surrounding a barrier of unexplored immensity, a barrier which had even defied the efforts of men to follow around its edge. There was no such expanse of ocean around the North Pole. No such unexplored barrier, such impenetrable continental vastness of land, as the Antarctic held. Franklin had a feeling that there would not be space for these around the North Pole. Suppose after all…suppose *really*…what wonder might they be the first to see? Or, rather, the first after the crew of Sparshott's ship…who had not come back.

He mentioned the idea to Captain Ericson, making it half a joke, to see what he would say, but Sven Ericson had no use for jokes. He was a literal-minded man. He answered with some argument about longitudes and observations which was conclusive to him, and which might have been so to Franklin had he understood it more thoroughly.

As to why there was more ocean in the Southern Hemisphere, he had an explanation also, though it was less clear than his knowledge of navigation. It was something that he had read. Something about the moon.

Franklin said no more to Captain Ericson on that subject, but he resumed it with Miss D'Acre as they bent together over the Antarctic map. Even as it is conventionally presented, its contrast to the North Polar regions is beyond concealment. Vague immensities of ocean, vague and vast suggestions of uncharted land—land which no man has trodden, no man has seen. There was one white blank on which all Europe would have lain, and it would have remained uncovered. Ice bound, mist-hidden barriers, that is all we know, and the rest is guessing.

It was true that there were two widely separate points where some penetration had been made, and which were represented as approaching one another at a southern pole. But the position of these was obviously determined by the fact that New Zealand and South America approach most nearly to the outer rim of the world. The points of landing had been opposite these extremities. They had penetrated some distance over the icy barriers, each to be confronted at last by a high plateau of barren frozen land, of more than Arctic severity. A land where summer never came. Where no beast lived. Where no flower ever grew. Surely the rim of the world!

They might claim to have approached the same spot, but what proof was there in that? It was what they had supposed that they must inevitably do. They could not have considered the evidences with impartial minds, for prejudice was too strong. Even if they had walked straight, what did it prove? You can reach the same place from two points on a flat surface, as well as a sphere.

They looked at the records of Antarctic voyages, and the growing doubt that possessed their minds was increased when they failed to find any ship that had circumnavigated the Antarctic. There were voyages that had been made round the world in more temperate regions, which were claimed as evidence of its rotundity. But, in fact, they proved less than that, as a child—an unprejudiced child—could see. It was strange that such a fact should be accepted as serious argument. Could you not sail round a plate?

But a close encircling of the Antarctic regions it did not appear that there had ever been. Here and there men had nibbled along the edge.

"Yet it seems strange," Franklin said, "if there be a rim to a flat world, that men have never made a more resolute effort to look over the edge."

"I don't know that it does, when you consider the extent of ocean that surrounds it, and the nature of the icy rampart itself, as it has been described by those who have ventured its exploration. We've got to remember that sailing-ships have their limits of capacity. It's wonderful what was done in those times; and since the time of the steam—and, of course, long before—it was assumed that there was nothing to cross."

"Besides that," he added, "we don't know that no one ever has. They might not have come back. They might not have—been allowed."

"They might not have wanted to," she replied more cheerfully. "But there's another thing that might help to account for it, if any further explanations were needed. It's the fact that men can't walk straight if they try.

"I was thinking about it last night, and remembered an experience I had in the Arabian desert. But it's a thing everybody knows. We all begin to walk in a circle if there's no landscape to help us to keep straight.

"Of course, it doesn't prove anything, but it's curious how all the evidence seems to fall into one scale as soon as you examine it with an open mind. If we had made a world of cheese mites, and meant them to live on a plate, what should we have done? Shouldn't we have put the cheese—that's the land—in the middle of the plate? And if we'd let them think that there wasn't any way off, wouldn't it have made it a lot simpler? And if we'd made them so that if they got away they'd just run round in a circle while they thought they were going straight on, wouldn't it have been a good thing to do? I suppose that's where Captain Sparshott's canyon scores—it keeps you straight whether you will or no."

But Franklin scarcely heard what she said. He was directed by the colour in a girl's hair. Hair that had been very close, as they had bent over the chart together

She became conscious of his eyes as he answered: "Well, we shall find out before long. It would be fine if we found that there really is a rim to the world, and we were the first to look over the edge. There's a line of verse I can't get out of my mind. '*Beyond the utmost purple rim.*' I must have learnt it at school. We had to do poetry there. I've always hated it since. I've no idea where it comes from, or what it's about. Have you?"

Miss D'Acre gave him an enquiring and slightly self-conscious glance. Was it a genuine ignorance? She knew the context quite well. If he didn't, she wasn't going to complete the quotation. And yet, why not?

"No," she said deliberately. "I never heard it before." Yet she was a girl who very rarely lied.

CHAPTER VII.

TOWARD evening there were signs of thicker pack-ice to starboard, and Captain Sparshott altered his course a point or two to the southeast for the clearer sea. He seemed more cheerful, more confident, now that the time for action had come, and he was once more in command of a good ship, and showed willingness to talk, when Franklin halted beside him, leaning against the rail.

"I understand you can't often expect to find a clear sea at this time of the year," Franklin said. "We seem in luck so far."

"Maybe, yes," was the cautious answer. "But it's not always the best start that gets soonest there." Still, he admitted cheerfully, every mile southward was a mile gained.

He was in a mood to be optimistic, though he knew that the most probable meaning of the clear water was that the ice was breaking late, and that there would be delay further south, if there were nothing worse. But even that wasn't sure. He went on at greater length than it is needful to follow, explaining how there is a barrier of ice that stretches out from the land for hundreds of miles, two hundred feet high, and twice as deep underwater. It is a floating continent of frozen water, behind which rises the Antarctic land, to the highest table-land on the earth: twice as high as the great Asiatic plateau which we call the roof of the world. And from this high continent, where there is no life of beast or insect or tree, enormous glaciers move slowly, inexorably, down its valleys, and push the ice-field further out to sea, so that it splits at times under these pressures, and huge fragments, sometimes larger than an English county, are floated loose. Always, ice is forming on the high plateau, and round the winter coasts. Always, with the coming of the milder severity which is miscalled summer, it breaks away, and is driven by current and tempest to be dissolved in the warmer seas. But how much will break away is an uncertain thing, and so, to a less degree, are the directions in which it drifts.

Franklin had read this before, but it had an increased reality coming from the lips of a man to whom it had been a familiar knowledge, and a continual sight. Anyhow, as Captain Sparshott said, they were moving freely now, and every mile was something gained; and the weather, though the wind had a biting quality, was fine and clear. So it seemed to him, but the Captain had a more doubtful mind. He looked to the southeast, toward which they steered, and he ordered that there should be no loose raffle about the deck. Franklin noticed that two of the crew had been detailed to test and strengthen the lashings that held the motor-boat down. Sven Ericson noticed it too, and decided that the madness of Captain Sparshott was not of a dangerous kind. He was not familiar with Antarctic weather, but he was also looking at the horizon in a thoughtful way.

Then Miss Collinson came on deck to ask if Mr. Arden would make a fourth at bridge, which he was very willing to do.

We have not seen Miss Collinson previously, though we have heard of her at the other end of the telephone. She had been supplied—need it be said?—from the Stores, in response to a request for the best secretary in London, and she had justified the description. She was slightly plump, it is true; but there is no social or national law which forbids it. Had there been, there is no doubt that the extra stone would have been quietly and efficiently done away with. She was attractive in appearance and manner, but not sufficiently so to rival or eclipse her employer. She had a clear and pleasant voice and a ready wit, which only appeared when it was needed. She was of good birth and well-educated. Of good health, and good at games, either of brain or muscle. She showed no objection to departing at short notice for Thibet or Arabia, and had been unperturbed and efficient under the variety of disconcerting circumstances which are liable to arise in such wanderings. She had other qualifications which it would be wearisome to detail. In the course of four years, the business association had developed into an intimate friendship, and the two women were Eleanor and Gwen to one another, except in their most official and public moments.

To reach the ladies' cabin you had to pass through that which the men occupied. Captain Ericson, now relieved of official duties, sat there in conversation with Bunny Weldon. Bunford had been reading about the Antarctic regions, and was uneasy in mind. They seemed to him to be very unpleasant places, where, in the intervals of being frost-bitten and having your toes sawn off without an anæsthetic, you fell into hidden crevasses, usually with fatal consequences. It was a place where even Siberian ponies came to a violent end. He might prove to be as hardy as a Siberian pony, but it seemed unlikely. The deduction is obvious. He did not like it, and decided that it was getting time to turn back.

It was just like Eleanor to want to visit the Antarctic. He would not have been surprised if she had set out to visit the moon. Nor would he have refused to follow. But he didn't *want* to visit moons or glaciers. He hadn't wanted to visit lamas and sheiks. He didn't suppose that anyone (except Eleanor) really did. But if she wanted the Antarctic, well, here it was, with a horribly cold wind and ice in the water. Lots of ice. Even Eleanor ought to be content with that. It was getting time to turn back.

He put this view before Captain Ericson with some vigour. It appeared that when the night came in this region it went on more or less for six months. No one wanted to stay indoors for that period. On the other hand, it did not appear to be a country in which a lady should be out after dark. Clearly, it would be best to turn back while they still could. He thought that Captain Ericson would support this view, but that gentleman was in a contentious mood.

With an aspect of judicial impartiality, he considered the problem. He pointed out that women are better swimmers than men, or, at least, that they float more easily, having more adipose tissue. Adipose tissue is just what the Antarctic requires. Are not women therefore better equipped by nature than men for such explorations? He was inclined to think that the North Pole would have been discovered much earlier, if the women had undertaken the enterprise.

Confronted with this unexpected theory, Bunny remarked desperately that Miss D'Acre was of a thin build, to which the Captain replied that she had been laying on fat for the past three weeks like a prize pig.

Mr. Welford was shocked at this metaphor, and was also inclined to dispute the fact, and an absurd quarrel was on the horizon when Franklin and Miss Collinson entered, and led the indignant gentleman into the next cabin to complete the required quartet.

Franklin looked at Miss D'Acre, and decided that the seaman was right, however objectionably he might have stated the result of his observation. She might still be of a slim figure, but the good appetite which had come with the cold brightness of this southern voyage had certainly given a somewhat more rounded softness to her attractive contours.

Gwendolen Collinson had been, as we have remarked, of a reasonable plumpness before she started. But though he observed the fact, he was unwilling to recognize the logical consequence of the suggestion which he had overheard, and send the ladies forward alone. Besides, the programme (as far as he knew) would not involve the traversing of glaciers, and the climbing of icy slopes. He said: "Oh, beg pardon, three diamonds. No, four."

For the next two hours he was sufficiently occupied in supporting Miss Collinson's very capable game, and then, just as he had declared two spades with a pleasant consciousness that the rubber was in his grasp, Captain Sparshott put the helm over, and the engines back, and the litter of the card-table slid smoothly into Miss D'Acre's lap.

CHAPTER VIII.

MISS D'ACRE reached out an unhurried hand for her cloak. "I think we might see what's happening up above," she said, as she led the way. Up to now she had shown little interest in the voyage, and

even the beauty of its horizons had received an unwilling or perfunctory regard. It was an attitude which had puzzled Franklin, till it
had been illuminated by Miss Collinson's remark. "She wouldn't let
anything rouse her now. She always saves herself up for the real
time." Well, the real time might be getting near.

They climbed up through a slopping of water, and to the sound
of the running feet of the crew, but the peril of the moment, if it had
amounted to that, was already passed.

They looked out on a sight such as might be common enough in
the coming days, but is seen by few of our kind. Seen, indeed, by
few creatures that live, except the snow-petrels and the albatrosses
and the skua-gulls. They were in the midst of the pack, and the low
sun, skimming a horizon below which it would not sink, made a
dazzling splendour of berg and floe that tossed on a swelling sea.

Far to northward, by the way they had come, the ice-pack
ground and heaved. Far to the western horizon it showed alike in the
light of a reddened sun. Far ahead was the same, but here and there a
larger block, scarcely of size to call a berg, rose twenty or thirty feet
out of the sea.

It was one such which had overbalanced as the *Bergen* passed,
and rolled over, as they sometimes will, almost falling upon the
deck, which it had deluged with the wave it raised.

But when they looked to the east, they saw a different and
grander sight. There there were actual bergs, not towering in irregular grandeur as those of the Arctic do, but flat-topped, and of an
even height. Straight-sided too, for the most part, and floating with
lanes of water, more or less narrow, between them.

There was a mass of hurrying cloud overhead, though it was
still clear along the sunlit west, and a southeast wind blew in rough
gusts, and was very bitterly cold.

Sven Ericson stood beside Captain Sparshott, surveying a scene
so like and yet so different from those he had known in the arctic
north.

Captain Sparshott looked at the sky, he looked into the wind, he
looked longingly at the clear lanes of water between the bergs, he
looked at the lifting sea.

"They can't be much, by the swell," he said, as one who speaks
half to himself, and with a note of doubt in his voice. Captain Ericson answered, "Ay, she should win through." The ship's head came
round slowly to port among the grinding floes.

Captain Sparshott's doubt was a simple thing. The clear lanes of
water could be passed at a good speed; could, indeed, only be passed
with reasonable safety in that way. He knew the pace at which ice-

bergs move, and he did not wish to be crushed between two of those floating walls. He thought a blizzard was near. There might be clear water beyond the bergs. He did not wish to be among the ice-floes when the blizzard came. Still less did he wish to be among the bergs. But he looked at the swell which came from the direction where the bergs were, and he decided that they did not extend very far. Yes, it was worth the risk. So he ported his helm, and the ship was soon steaming at the greatest pace it could make in narrow lanes of sea, between high walls of ice that might unite to crush it should it delay too long.

The sky darkened, and the wind screamed through the bergs with a scatter of sleet. The blizzard was already upon them when Captain Sparshott saw open water through a gap which was so narrow that there would scarcely be space for the *Bergen* to pass between the icy walls. It looked to be a desperate chance, but he was a man of courage on his own deck. It was already hard to see ahead through the driving sleet. The way between the bergs, lying northeastward, was sheltered from the direct force of the storm, and could be seen clearly enough. There are times when boldness and caution are the same word. Captain Sparshott steered for the gap.

Ten minutes later the *Bergen* was facing the fury of an open sea.

CHAPTER IX.

THE next fortnight was a hard time alike for those who fought their way half-blindly through a blizzard that never ceased, and those who seldom ventured upon the storm-swept decks.

It was toward the end of January when the wind fell for a time, and then came steadily from the north, and the sky cleared, and a sun which was still high in the summer sky set the ice dripping from the shrouds.

They looked round on a sea where no pack-ice showed; a sea that tossed and sparkled, and with a school of whales blowing astern. They went ahead now at full steam, wishing to take every mile's advantage of a calm that the next tempest might wake at any moment to a further fury. So they steamed for three days, and were then hindered again by a drifting ice-pack, which they skirted eastward for forty miles before a southern passage opened to let them through. A week later they sighted land, and came to the low beaches of which Captain Sparshott had told them.

And, so far, it had become evident that his tale was true. They had sailed through a sea of whales—whales of every variety that is known in the southern Hemisphere, but with the blue whales predominating. They came to a coast that was barren and bleak enough, but which showed less of the barrier ice than had been recorded in any part of the Antarctic land. A few miles inland at some places, at others almost close to the tide-line, basaltic cliffs rose too straightly for ice or snow to find any permanent lodgement upon their sombre sides.

They found the beach where the crew of the *Maryland* had landed, and where relics of their camping were still scattered about. The lower cliffs showed sandstone here, and coal out-cropped from the sloping beach and could be taken with no more toil than the handling of pick and shovel. There was nothing strange in this. Such outcrops have been found before in Antarctic lands. But it confirmed again the accuracy of the Captain's narrative, so far as he had told it to them.

The beach was of a dull brown colour, being mingled with volcanic sand, which at some places predominated, blown there by the wind, or, it might be, washed up by the water.

For there was a current here that was almost fresh, and that gave a surprisingly high temperature to Franklin's thermometer. Following this current along the coast, they came to the final confirmation of the Captain's tale in the opening of a great gap in the cliffs, through which the river of which he had told flowed black and rapid into the bay.

They saw the mouth of this river from the ship's whale-boat, for the motor-boat was still lashed on the deck. They looked up a canyon of black precipitous walls that rose so high that they narrowed the river's actual width. Its sides washed the cliffs, leaving no space on which a man might walk either right or left. It stretched straight inward, showing neither turn nor change of character as far as sight could reach. Only, it seemed that the black, close-closing cliffs rose ever to a greater height.

Franklin stood that night with Eleanor—they had all dropped the formalities of address as the days of confinement lengthened in the narrow cabins—alone on deck.

They looked on the desolation of the barren coast and to the black heights of the cliffs which no man had ever scaled, over which the moon shone. The sun still showed its light beneath the western horizon, paling the stars. In the water there came the sudden flurry of a frightened seal, and the plunging rush of the killer whale that pursued it. Then the silence resumed. The air was cold. There was perhaps thirty degrees of frost, perhaps more, but they were well clad and well fed, and felt it little in a still air. Even now, they knew little of the Antarctic in its moods of terror. It seemed that, so far, it had contemptuously let them through.

"You still want to go on?" he asked in a voice which he endeavoured to make as toneless as possible. He knew that the moment of decision had arrived. A decisive moment, even to life itself. If they went back now, they had done much. Their names might be recorded forever after. Even financially, the knowledge of that sea of whales meant fortune if it were sold judiciously to those who would bring wholesale daughter to its quiet peace.

If they went on to the unknown—well, all they knew was that the *Maryland* had not returned.

She looked at him with a surprised questioning that was baffled by the passivity of the eyes that met her. She said: "I thought that was understood. I was to leave everything to you. But we were to go on till we were turned back."

"Then don't you think it's time we made Sparshott tell bit more?"

"If you like; but I shouldn't unless he offers. He's either a fraud, or he's got something he's sure we shan't believe, and that he wants us to see for ourselves. Of course, his difficulty may be that he's told the truth to this point, and invented whatever went further. If he's never been up the river before, you can see his difficulty. If he says anything, he's almost sure to give himself away. But if he keeps a shut mouth, we can come to Heaven or Hell, and he'll just say: "Yes, I knew that all the time.""

"If we make him talk, we shan't know whether to believe him or not, and we may be worse off than we are now."

"Yes," he said, "I've thought much the same myself. I half-expected to see the ribs of the *Maryland* sticking out of the sand."

"It isn't only that," she added frankly. "I told you that I'm not one who likes to read the last chapter first. It might make it all like a stale show. It's the unknown for me."

"Very well," he said. "I shan't raise the question again. There'll be some of us feeling tired by tomorrow night."

Half-laughing, half-seriously, she held out a fur-gloved hand. "It's for you to order from now," she said. "I've no more to say beyond this. Life or death, we go on."

He took the slim strong hand, and his tone answered to hers. "It's the unknown for us. Life or death, we go on." But the contact roused another thought, stirred within him a more immediate passion. The unknown for her! Was there an unknown country that she would always miss? Not if he could guide her to it. But he saw that the time, if ever, was not now.

CHAPTER X.

IT is one of the greatest difficulties of the penetration of the Antarctic that the ice does not break immediately when the spring comes. The summer light will be half over before the invading keel can push inward through berg and floe to its goal of the frozen land. And when it reaches land, it will be already time to turn on its backward course, if it would win free before the new winter's ice will gather and close it in.

Franklin's plans had been ready, only waiting for the sight of the river-canyon of which Sparshott had told, and next morning word was given which changed the quiet scene into one of fevered activity that scarcely slackened when the short darkness came.

There were huts, which had been brought out in sections, to be carried up the beach, and erected where a bend in the cliff wall would give wind shelter when the winter came. There were great quantities of stores to be landed. There was the motor-boat to be launched and equipped.

For three days the solemn penguins lining the beach watched the incessant activity, only scurrying aside with a squawk of protest if some erratic movement of these strange invaders threatened to overrun them. Then the wind rose again, and, for four days, a blizzard swept land and sea, such as no man could face and live. Fortunately the anchors held, and crew and passengers emerged from under hatches at last to the sight of a blue sky that was still crossed by flying clouds, and a beach on which their piles of timber and tinned stores were buried in new-frozen ice. For the storm had driven the water upward along the beach, and it had frozen over the lumber, making fantastic hummocks, from the centre of which the tins must be extracted with axe and pick.

Then the unrelenting toil was resumed, for it was a task which was shared by all. Captain Ericson was to take his ship back to Cape Town, and return next season with further stores. Every hour that he could save increased the probability of easy passage through the soon-gathering ice. Franklin's party were equally anxious to have their winter quarters prepared, and to make a start up the river-canyon while yet the light endured, and they might hope to go far and return before the falling of the Antarctic night.

They might, it is true, have left at once, and trusted to Captain Ericson for the erection and equipment of the base on which their lives might depend, but it was not a risk that Franklin was disposed to take. It was a position in which any oversight might be a dangerous, or even a deadly thing. Not to be lightly trusted to men who worked in a haste to go.

Captain Sparshott superintended these operations on shore, and Miss Collinson fulfilled her secretarial duties with a notebook and pencil, checking everything with unremitting oversight, and accepting no assurance, even with the picturesque oaths that the seaman knows, till she had verified its accuracy or exposed its guilt. Bunford Weldon took his part also in this activity, and did well enough, till he slipped in landing on a frozen rock, and must nurse a sprained knee for a few days in the ship's cabin, while Franklin and Eleanor made expeditions right and left, beneath the cliffs on foot, or rowing in a small dinghy that they had brought to be towed after the motor-launch, seeking a place where the high cliffs might be scaled; for it had come to Franklin's mind that as they ascended the river-canyon they would see nothing of the country through which they passed, and it would be well to have some idea of its character. But they gained nothing by these expeditions beyond some increased knowledge of the coast line, for the cliffs were an impregnable barrier. Franklin's alpine experience could do no more than assure him that they could not be scaled by any resources at his disposal. They must ascend the river with no knowledge of the country through which they would have to pass.

CHAPTER XI.

THE *Blanche* was moored in a little rock-bounded cove near the river mouth. When she came back from its exploration, if come back she did, it was where she would have to lie in the frozen water through the winter months, for, even unballasted, it was too heavy for them to drag it ashore.

She was a boat which had been first built for a millionaire's whim, and was a model of comfort and speed. She was half-decked, with cabins fore and aft, the better of which, in the bows, was assigned for the ladies' use, while the three men were to make the best of the accommodation at the stern. They loaded her with all the equipment suggested by Captain Sparshott's experience, or the advice that they had received. They took, as a precaution, six weeks' provisions, though they did not expect to be away many days. At the boat's speed they could go far in a short time, and Franklin resolved that, whatever they might find before them, they would be back again when the long darkness closed, in the security of their winter quarters, and with their stores safely anchored around them. If there were a temptation to go further, it should be put forward to the spring, when they would have three months of increasing light and warmth—if that word were not too complimentary to the efforts of the Antarctic sun—before the *Bergen* could force its way once more through the breaking ice. So he planned, as a leader must, but how many plans are for the derision of the watching Fates?

Looking at the instruments and apparatus which were being handed down for accommodation in the stern cabin, as the loading of the launch proceeded (while the *Bergen* still lingered, taking on some extra coal from that which the shore offered so freely), Miss D'Acre observed a couple of sporting rifles and a large box of cartridges which she knew to be the cherished property of Mr. Bunford Weldon.

"Gwen," she said, "who put those on the list? I should have thought even Bunny would have been content with one. We're not going to shoot the Antarctic, and everyone knows he won't find any animals here."

Miss Collinson looked doubtful. "You'll break his heart if you don't let him take them," she answered. "I asked Franklin, and he said: 'Oh, yes, they won't sink the boat. You can throw them in.'"

"So I did," Franklin added, coming up at the moment, and overhearing the words. "You never know, and it's always best to be on the safe side, though I don't expect he'll get any crocodiles here."

Eleanor had accepted without protest a limitation of weight which had obliged her to leave many personal comforts in the huts which she would have preferred to bring, and a moment's annoyance was natural enough, but it was a question for his decision. She said no more.

He did not explain that he had had a similar hesitation. He had not handled a rifle himself since he had been a school cadet, and whatever might be before them, he did not propose that they should engage it in violent combat. They were too weak for that. It must be retreat, or an effort for peaceful passage.

He was not surprised at her protest, for he knew that she held the opinion that a show of weapons increases the dangers of wandering in the wild places of the world. She had said that, once at least, she had owed her life in Tibet to the fact that her escort carried no arms of aggression. "And once," she had said very sensibly, "is a good deal."

Besides that, he had not thought of Bunford as a man of war. But the fact was that that gentleman's favourite sport had been the stalking of red deer in the Scottish forests, and though it is not an occupation for which any courage is needed, it does teach familiarity with the long-range rifle and some skill in its use. Mr. Weldon was in a panic at the frozen solitudes into which his somewhat doglike devotion to his cousin, and the fear of her contempt (complicated by the fact that he was financially dependent upon her), had led him on this occasion. He was in real need of the moral courage which the presence of his rifles gave.

But Franklin had not been influenced by these considerations. Captain Sparshott, if he told the truth, had been up that canyon before. He had seen him looking carefully to the loading of a revolver which he had dropped into his hip-pocket. Franklin said nothing to that, but he had armed himself with a similar weapon. He let the rifles go.

As to the Captain, being asked nothing, he offered no further information. Since he had handed the command of the *Bergen* back to its owner, he had become as morosely is silent as he had been earlier. That he had some doubt or trouble on his mind was a certain thing. But, beyond that attitude, he did his part in the work of preparation, and made no protest.

So they came to the day when the *Bergen* hauled up its anchors and steamed out to a misty sea. It was early morning of March 3rd when they watched it go, and as its hull became lost in the mist, the little party turned, not without some feeling of desolation, toward the motor-launch which was in readiness to take them to a destination which, to four at least of their number, was beyond their guessing.

The *Blanche*, as Franklin had renamed it, before he became sufficiently familiar with Miss D'Acre to know that she preferred the earlier of the names which her parents had bestowed on her, had been specially adapted for the journey which was now before it, and refitted with new air-cooled, four-cylinder engines, as water-cooling would have been unless in those frozen regions. They could drive the boat at perhaps five times the speed at which the *Maryland* (if Captain Sparshott's tale were true) had steamed up the narrow gorge. And the river offered a straight passage, with no hint of shallow or rapid, running smooth and swift between its confining walls. They looked right and left, and the cliffs were further off than they had expected them to be. They looked up, and the strip of sky was so slight and far that it seemed that they were closed by walls too narrow to let them through. It was never too light for the stars to show in that ribbon of distant sky.

So they went on, and the hours passed. The cliff walls grew higher yet, and the gloom deepened. The entrance through which they came dwindled to a point of light, and went out, but they could not see that they bent at all either to right or left, and the canyon still opened ahead. Except for the rising height of the black basaltic walls that confined their course, there was no difference at all.

CHAPTER XII.

IT was the second morning. Franklin steered, as he had done most of the time, but there had been little sleep for any of the five. Four who watched for they knew not what, for something that never came, and one who might know more, but who found no comfort in what he knew.

So Franklin judged, observing a furtive restlessness which Captain Sparshott controlled with difficulty, and which appeared to increase as the days passed. Yet what was there to fear? Franklin, feeling that the lives of all were in his hands, went ceaselessly over the question, imagining many fantastic and some impossible things. The way back was clear at any time. That seemed certain. They had encountered no difficulty of fall or rapid. With the current's aid, they could return even more quickly than they had come. Even should the engines fail, they would drift down at a pace which would return them long before their provisions would be exhausted.

Nor could he see that anything could cut off their retreat. All the time he had watched for any opening in the rocky walls, and when the need of sleep had become imperative, he had charged others with the same duty. But they were all tense with expectancy of what this canyon would show at last.

For it could not go on forever. Already they might class it with the greatest wonders that the world contains. A wonder that might be doubtful if they should return with no proof to show. And, so far, there would be nothing at all.

It was the second day, and there had been no change except that the walls had increased in height, the sky was narrower and further yet, and the gloom had deepened, so that they had lighted a lamp from the acetylene outfit that the boat carried, and the white glare was thrown forward on the black water, and the blacker cliffs.

Once the narrow strip of sky had shown a vivid crimson for several hours. They could not tell what that might mean, but it had ended at last, and some time later there had been a thin falling of frozen snow.

But it was not intensely cold. Twice Franklin had taken the temperature of the water, and had found it slightly warmer than it had been at the river's mouth.

He had not made any set rotation for the steering of the boat. He had a vague distrust of Sparshott, and was unwilling either to give the helm to his hands or to make a disposition which would pointedly exclude him from his natural turn. Yet the man had done nothing on which suspicion could fix. Only, once he had shown concern as to the security of the rope that towed the little dinghy behind the launch. Franklin remembered that he had been active in suggesting that this smaller boat should be brought along. Did he know of some narrower passage which they must take, where the *Blanche* must be left behind? Franklin did not like to think of the five of them in that little boat, depending on oars alone, and with such provision as it would carry. He would think twice—indeed, many times—before he would agree to that.

So he had kept to the helm himself as long as he could command the alertness of mind which the situation required, and then handed it over to one of the women or Bunford for a short time, telling them to watch incessantly for any change in what was before them, and to slow up and wake him instantly at any happening of whatever kind. For at the pace at which they advanced it would not do to doze at the helm on that narrow and unknown way.

And then he had resumed his charge, and still nothing happened, and so, once again, he called Bunford to take the helm, and settled down for the short sleep which he could not safely defer. Bunford steered with a loaded rifle beside his hand. He had a timidity which was unashamed. He said that place gave him the jumps, and if he hadn't got something handy that could give the other fellows what for. Franklin said he hoped he wouldn't do anything rash, but may have found some confidence also in the loaded weapon. Not knowing what was before them, who could tell what was best?

So he dozed for a time, and was awakened by Bunford's frightened voice. "*Damn you, you swine*," and then, as Franklin sat up quickly from where he lay, "Sparshott's off in the skiff. He whacked me across the head."

Franklin was conscious of a moment of hesitation. The man had bolted, meaning doubtless to drift down in the dinghy. He would have the run of their stores. But he could not use everything. He would be unlikely to do any wanton damage. Why not let him go? Or was he so sure that he would never see them again? That he

41

would not want to see them again was a sure thing. He would have to wait until Ericson's return, and then make the best tale that he could. He might say that they had left him in charge, and had not returned. Who could blame him for that? But he would not want them to return before Ericson's arrival, and his explanation of that cowardly flight. Suppose he removed enough of the stores for his own use to some secret hiding-place, and set fire to the huts and all they held? That would make their fates sure.

All these thoughts came as Bunford brought the boat round, and the white light shone down the narrow canyon. Bunford passed him the helm. He went forward, rifle in hand.

"Bunford, you're not going to shoot?" he called, and got for answer: "You don't want him back here, do you?" Even as the answer came, the light settled on a man who was sculling desperately down the stream. He could not have seen Bunford, who was behind the light, but he must have had a fear of what that pursuing light would mean, for he dropped the sculls and crouched down in the boat. Bunford saw no more than the top of his head, but it was enough for him. He fired once, the shot sounding like thunder in that narrow space.

"You can turn her up again, unless you're wanting the boat," he called, as he laid the rifle down.

Gwen Collinson, who missed little, noticed how his hand shook, though it must have been steady enough as it pressed the trigger. She said: "You'd better let me tie up that wound. You've got blood all down the side of your head."

It was an episode of two frightened men. There is nothing more pitiless than fear.

Eleanor said only, as the *Blanche* turned upstream again: "Franklin, hadn't we better go slow? It looks as though there's something about here that he wasn't anxious to meet."

Franklin said yes to that. He added: "They can't say we've called on the sly. I mean, not without knocking. That noise might have waked the dead."

He was hardly conscious of what he said, and was annoyed to feel that his own excitement was not easy to control. Then Gwen said quietly: "I think there's something on the cliff on the left. We've passed it now. I couldn't see what it was."

CHAPTER XIII.

THEY brought the *Blanche* to the cliff face and found no more than a metal ring, bolted into the rock. The ring was thinned and corroded with age. They threw the light of the lamp upon it, and Franklin scraped it with his knife. He said: "It seems like bronze. It must have been here for a long time." And then, as he lifted it: "I think there's an inscription on the underside." It was less worn underneath. There were faint marks which it would be hopeless to try to read. They might be Aramaic or Hittite for all he knew, but they were inscribed in no modern tongue. He tried to turn it round to get a better view, and the worn bolt slipped from the rocks. He was not quick enough to tighten his grip, and the ring fell into the water with a loud splash.

"Well," he said, "it's a long while since any boat could have been tied up by that ring. Sparshott didn't run from that."

No one spoke in reply. A sense of mystery was upon them. There was a remote antiquity when this far place had been known to men. How had they come here? How lived? What did it mean? What was before them now?

There may have been more than one of them who would have lacked courage to protest if the boat had turned downstream at that moment, though there was none to be the first to propose it. Yet they had seen nothing but an old ring, and even that was no longer there.

But very soon they saw more. It was on the left-hand side still. A great gap in the cliff face, through which a liner could have steamed in without lowering its funnels. They threw the light inward, and had an impression of an enormous natural cave. But the sides of the entrance were of mortised stone. Here, again, however distant, was the work of man.

Franklin said: "Shall we go on, or go in?"

Eleanor answered: "It's for you to say that."

"Then we'll have a look round. I don't like leaving anything behind that we don't understand. So far, we've got a fast boat, and a safe rear. Bunford, you can keep that rifle ready, but don't fire unless you're sure it's the right thing to do. You girls had better go into the cabin. We'll call you out if there's any show."

"I think, if you don't mind, we'd rather stay where we are," Eleanor answered. He said no more. It was unlikely that they were entering anything more formidable than a long-empty cave. He steered the boat inward at a crawling pace. Gwen had moved to the light.

She threw it upward and round. The roof rose as they went inward to a height which the lamp could not penetrate, nor could they see anything but black water ahead. On the right hand the cave wall rose sheer from the water. On the left there was a shelving ledge, and black openings, as of dry recesses, above it. They kept along the left-hand side. There was no sound, nor any sign of life, till Gwen said, with an unusual sharpness in her voice: "What's that over there?"

There was no doubt of the answer. The shifting light settled on a vessel's name. It was the *Maryland*, lying half out of the water, heeled over on her side, an empty, abandoned wreck. Franklin let the boat come to a standstill while they gazed in silence at this evidence of the truth of Sparshott's tale. But what did it mean? What had been the fate of its crew when their captain had fled in an open boat, once before, as he had attempted to do again? There was no answer in the darkness of the silent cave.

And then, shrill in the silence, sounded a baby's cry.

Gwendolen was the first to speak. She said: "That's a child."

Bunford added: "With its mother's hand over its mouth, or wringing its neck by now." He had a vision of hidden enemies that watched them from every side, and that would bring them to the same end that had befallen the crew of the ship they had just seen. He said: "We're best out of this," and his voice shook with the words. And then the child's cry came again.

Certainly it did not sound as though there were any effort either to silence or comfort it. It was like the cry of a child that is hungry or alone. Franklin had a thought that it might be a cunning lure, such as had drawn the *Maryland's* crew to their fatal end. He had read somewhere that there are creatures that can cry like a human child. He could not remember what they were. But his instinct agreed with Bunford's protest. They would be best out of this. On the other hand, they had said that they would go on until they were turned, and what was there to turn them here? An empty wreck and a child's cry. He pulled out his pistol as he said: "We don't know that it's a child at all."

Gwen said: "But it is. Anyone could tell that. Any woman I mean."

It was continuous now.

Eleanor spoke at last. She shared Franklin's doubts, but she had come to see, not to turn from an unsolved cry. She said: "We can't gain by delay. We'd better have a look, as Gwen is so sure. We can't go without finding anything out." She reminded herself that Miss Collinson was not often wrong.

44

Franklin said: "Bunford and I will go. You girls had better stay in the boat, and be ready to take us in."

"I'd rather come, if you don't mind." That was from Gwen. Eleanor said: "Then I'll stay. We can't all leave the boat. It's not far, by the sound."

Gwen led the way, the two men following with ready weapons, not knowing to what they came. She had a flash-lamp in her hand, but it was of little use, for Eleanor swung the boat's light round upon them so that they saw where they went, except as their own shadows obscured their way.

But it was only a few paces ahead that they found the source of the cry, where a pile of fragments of rock made a semi-circular hollow against the wall, and as Gwen's flash-light illuminated the interior, they gazed down on two young creatures that squirmed in a nest of dried water-weed of a pallid unfamiliar kind.

She reached down and brought one up for a clearer view. "Yes, they're babies right enough. But the poor thing's blind." They saw what looked to be a human child, with a long, slim, well formed body and exceptionally long fingers and toes, showing starkly white in the glare of the acetylene light, but the eyes were closed and very tiny, hardly developed at all.

"I wonder whether the other's like it," she was saying, and bent down to look, when there was a warning cry from the boat. "*Look out! She's coming for you.*"

They turned round at the cry, and saw the figure of a woman, if such it were, that had risen from the water with some kind of fish in her mouth.

She had run crookedly at first, as though confused by the light, and in a useless fury, but when she had her back to it, and was guided by her child's cry, she sprang snarling at Gwendolen's throat.

Gwen had the child on one hand, which she did not drop, but her left arm came up with a quick instinct to guard her throat. Strong projecting teeth met in a well-covered elbow, and there it ended for her, for Bunford fired, and the woman fell at their feet.

"Oh, Bunford, you shouldn't have done that. She's a woman."

So she seemed to be, of a queer kind, with a projecting, long-toothed mouth and rudimentary eyes, but otherwise well-favoured enough, lying still now, and very white in the acetylene glare.

Bunford's teeth chattered as he tried to answer. "She's not a woman, she's a horrible thing." He looked with expert eyes to see where the bullet went. "She'll get over that," he said with assurance.

"She'll be up again in five minutes, making another rush, and then you can deal with her in your own way."

Gwen made no answer, for they were suddenly aware at once of Eleanor's warning cry, and of a score of forms swimming swiftly toward them, rippling the water as they came, or running with a barefooted silence along the edge. The noise of the rifle had done its work.

It was the light that saved them then, for there was an instant's delay after Bunford leapt into the boat. Gwen turned to put the child back into its nest, and Franklin stood aside for her to go first. But those who came were plainly blinded by the glare that met them as the boat's head slid along the side.

Then, as Eleanor brought it round to the cave's mouth, and the light shone outward, the rush came upon them. Franklin, beside Eleanor now, used his revolver-butt to beat off a clutching hand, but the boat's speed, though they could not let her go as she would till they had turned at the cave mouth, was too great for those that followed.

Eleanor heard Franklin's low voice at her side: "Have you had about enough now? Which way is it to be? Up or down?"

It was a decision which must be made in five seconds. There was the clear course backward down the river, too swift for pursuit, as Captain Sparshott had doubtless taken it in a slower boat seven years ago; or they might go further on to the unknown, leaving this peril to bar their return. How could they know how many caves there might be from which similar creatures would swim out to seize them? How they might return later through waters alive with hundreds to drag them down? How did they know what resources for their destruction they might possess? Only the crew of the *Maryland* could have answered that.

Franklin called out: "Don't shoot again, Bunford. There's no point in that," and as he did so, he heard Eleanor's answer. "We're not going Sparshott's way." She brought the rudder about, and the boat turned up the river with a foaming wake.

CHAPTER XIV.

"I OUGHT not to have brought him," Eleanor said. "I see that now. But he's been all right other times."

"More or less," Gwen admitted. She had a very private dislike of Bunford Weldon, which she believed to be unsuspected of any. He was her employer's cousin, and it was an opinion best kept to herself. But he was not her cousin, and he did not wag his tail like a dog if she patted his head. Perhaps she saw him with clearer eyes for these differences. She added: "Anyhow, I'm not the one to complain this time. It was my silliness in wanting to look at the child that made all the trouble, and she was in a bloodthirsty mood. She'd have had a few drops more if he hadn't fired when he did."

Gwen had bared her elbow beside the stove in the tiny cabin, and showed tooth-marks that had broken the skin, though little more. "It's a good thing we go well clothed in this climate," she said cheerfully. "But I'm not sure we oughtn't to have brought a doctor along. There's Bunny's head already, and this elbow, both of which might have been worse, and I've got a feeling that we're in for a livelier time than we've had yet."

"I thought you knew everything."

"Well, I don't. All the surgical knowledge we've brought along is in Bunny's head. He knows what a bullet doesn't or does, and there's no one better able to tell us when we're quite dead, but that's the limit with him; and I know just that much less. Don't you remember about Aleppo?"

But Eleanor did not want to remember about Aleppo, and it is a tale which it would be unkind to tell, there being no need. She returned to their first subject, saying: "It wouldn't be so bad if Franklin'd make him give up those guns. He shoots first and thinks afterwards."

"It wouldn't matter if he'd only shoot when he's asked. A shot's sometimes a useful thing." Gwen was a fair-minded girl, and she saw that her elbow might have been worse. It was throbbing quite enough now.

But they both knew the folly of going into strange lands in an attitude of offensive violence. It is just the way to get killed. Gwen went on: "He'll hate Franklin if he makes him give up those guns. It's only you can do that without a row."

"Yes, I suppose I must. What do you think they were?"

Gwen knew that, as the best secretary in London, it was her duty to have her head furnished with any information which her employer might require. She had just admitted her deficiency in regard to the repair of the human body, and it was much too soon to do so again. She answered confidently: "Oh, I suppose there was a time when ships of some old civilization used to come here. Perhaps it wasn't as cold then as it is now. And then something happened, and they didn't come any more, and the people who had been left here had to live in the caves, and penetrated further in, because there wasn't anywhere else to go, and so they've gradually lost their sight, and grown teeth that can catch their prey in the water.

"When you come to think of it, it's the only thing that could happen. There wouldn't be any wood in the caves to build another ship. There isn't any wood in the whole Antarctic, for that matter. What a ghastly place it seems, when you think of that! And the only food they could get would be underwater, so they'd soon learn to pursue it there. When you think it out, it's just what would be sure to follow."

"Sounds simple," Eleanor answered sleepily. "But how many million years do you think it would take to get eyes like that? To say nothing of the teeth. Even the babies...."

But Gwen held her own theory, as a competent secretary may be expected to do. "I don't ever take those millions of years very seriously. Think of the last five or ten thousand, and of how much we know has changed in that time. It's easy enough for scientists to say anything took a few thousand million years. It's only adding a few noughts, more or less. If they had to live through it, they might be a bit more moderate in their ideas."

"Yes. I expect they would." Eleanor was more interested in the facts around her than in their problematical origins. She yawned as she added: "Anyway, they're a ghastly sight. But what makes you so sure they came up the river? We haven't seen what the ships were like. Why not down?"

Gwen had to admit to herself that it was an idea. "Yes," she said thoughtfully, "there is that."

They knew little, and could guess as they would. All they knew was that the straight river continued, and the high cliff walls, for Franklin had promised to call them if there should be change, of whatever kind, and the engines throbbed, and the water swirled from the stern, and they went onward to a goal which they could not guess.

"Suppose we smash up the boat," Gwen suggested, with her usual cheerfulness, "and the skiff's not exactly lost but gone before, as the tombstones say. It looks rather like a life sentence for us. I wonder how long we should take growing such useful teeth. I expect when we got hungry enough we should do it in about a week."

"Don't be ghastly," Eleanor said, even more sleepily than before. "You ought to know that Franklin'd manage better than that, and I've got a useful secretary, too. Besides, I've told the Stores they're to send for us if we're not back in two years, and they won't forget. It's about the best order they've ever had."

"Well, I hope they won't have to make out the invoice. It wouldn't matter to you. You've got the devoted Bunford, but there'd be nothing better than Franklin left over for me." Miss Collinson watched her employer's face as she said this. She, at least, was not in a sleepy mood. Eleanor's eyes half-opened, as though there were something in the last remark which might have stirred her at a livelier time. "Bunford?" she said. "If you'll just sling over that cushion, you can have him, rifles and all."

Gwendolen considered this answer. It gave her no pleasure, and no surprise.

CHAPTER XV.

FRANKLIN was a tired man, but he kept the lookout himself, for he felt that the women needed rest, and he would trust Bunford if he must, but not otherwise.

He had a more definite anxiety now, watching for further openings in the cliff wall, and wondering, with a too active imagination, what means of communication might be known to the dwellers of the subterranean caves. He had a vision of vast populations that the dark interior of the mountains held, and of a sudden swarming forth of thousands of these amphibious men, to surround the boat. He saw them rise in the water from all sides. What would be the use of speed? They clutched at the boat's bows. The body of one of them jammed the propeller. They clambered aboard from every side. What was the use of resistance? To kill a few before they themselves were torn asunder with bloody teeth?

But as the time passed, and the cliff walls showed unbroken fronts, his thoughts went forward again to what must be the end of this endless-seeming way. Did it really go beyond the confines of the earth we know, to some unimagined mystery? Would it ever end?

Yes, it was ending now. He called to the others as he had promised, and they looked together on a prospect of lessening cliffs, and to what they could not yet distinguish as more than a blackness that barred the way.

He noticed that Bunford Weldon had picked up a rifle, as though to defend himself from some visible foe. Bunford was in an evident fear.

He was aware himself of an excitement which was half apprehension of what the next hour might bring. He had not had such a feeling since he had approached the noticeboard to see the result of the examination on which his future depended. It steadied him somewhat that the women took it in a more casual way. Not that they were indifferent. Who could be so, having penetrated by such a route to a country that no man might have trodden since the dawn of time? Yet it was likely that it might be no more than a frozen waste, already threatened with the iron severity of the Antarctic night. What more was there to hope? What else to fear?

"I wonder," Eleanor was saying calmly, "what we're really expecting to see?"

"If we all said that, we should know some things that won't be there," Gwendolen answered. "Life's always different. That's the one sure thing. What you expect is just what you never get."

"And we mostly expect too much."

"The only way not to be disappointed is not to expect anything."

Perhaps the exchange of these platitudes told a tale of suppressed excitements, which they would not show.

Bunford said irritably: "There's no sense in rushing on at this rate, before we know what's ahead. We might at least slow up a bit, and wait till it gets dark."

It was afternoon, and as the cliffs diminished the light increased. Franklin had already switched off the light in the bows. He answered Bunford: "I think we're all rather inclined to expect to see more than we shall, when we get clear. It's the way Sparshott told us about it first. But we've seen what scared him, and that's behind us now. If there's nothing here but a frozen plain, we'll be turned round, and going back before night. We can come again in the spring, if we think it's worth while, to look around a bit more."

His words influenced his own mind, as much as those others who heard them. They had been excited beyond reason, and with an unspoken apprehension that was more foolish still. But they kept their eyes upon the forward prospect, and the lessening walls. "It seems a long time."

"It looks like nothing more than a blank wall."

"It can't be that."

"Suppose it's only that the river turns?"

"That would be an event, after the time it's kept straight."

"It must be a thousand miles."

"Scarcely that."

"No. A lot more."

"It can't be only that the river turns. Look at the way the cliffs have come down."

The last was a fact that could not be significant of less than a great change in the land above them. They had run on hour after hour between walls that might have been ten thousand feet high, or more than that, through the Antarctic heights, of which it was known already that they would reduce Mount Everest to a little hill, but now these walls were not of a height of more than five hundred feet either to right or left, and the far distance, which had been before them so long, had changed to a darkness which they quickly neared.

Franklin put down the glasses with which he had been examining that approaching shadow. "I think," he said, "the river flows underground."

CHAPTER XVI.

THAT was how they found it to be. Before them, and on either side, the straight rock rose for five or six hundred feet, and, smooth and dark, the river flowed from a hollow that arched it with a roof that was not ten feet high.

Franklin cut off the engines as they approached, and the boat lost way rapidly against the current. He looked at the cliff walls on either hand and before. They were straight beyond hope of climbing. It was a case of return, or advance beneath the gloom of that low roof from which the river flowed.

It was not an inviting prospect, so soon after the adventure of the cavern in which the *Maryland* lay. He had a mind to say that they had come far enough. Perhaps in the spring.... But there was one of the four who could not endure the suspense which his silence held.

Bunford said: "We've had too much of this. If you're thinking of going under there, it'll save time to tell you that you think wrong."

Eleanor said sharply: "Bun, don't be a fool."

Franklin saw the panic the man was in. He saw the rifle that was beside his hand. He was dangerous in such moods, one whom it was best to answer discreetly, though it must be plain that he was not taking orders from him. He said: "You shouldn't cry out before you're hurt. I haven't decided yet whether to go on or not."

But the answer was not sufficient to quieten the nerves of a frightened man. He answered with a sudden truculence. "No. But I have. This damned folly's gone far enough. I've got the ladies to think of, if you can't. You'll put this boat downstream in ten seconds, or I'll put a bullet where it won't be worth while cutting it out." He lifted the rifle as he spoke, with a finger on the trigger. Franklin knew that his life was in a deadly peril if he should fail to obey. A word of refusal or even argument might have been answered with an instant shot. Yet he was unwilling to give way to such an order, and the seconds passed as he sat inactive, wondering what could be the word which would reduce this frightened madman to reason. What might have happened is hard to guess, but the two women interposed in their own ways.

Gwen said, in her most casual tone: "Mr. Welford, if you wouldn't be so melodramatic, we might get back quite as soon." Eleanor did not trust to further speech.

She was immediately behind him as the threat was spoken. She reached forward suddenly, striking the rifle from his hand.

"Bun," she said, "you'll give me both of those silly things, and you'll do whatever Franklin says." She picked up the loaded rifle, and passed it backwards to Gwen, who put it into their own cabin.

He made no movement to retain the weapon, but broke into excited protest. "Eleanor, you don't understand! If we go under there, there'll be the same creatures again I We shall be eaten alive. And it's all for nothing at all. And, besides, it's too low. We shall get upset more likely than not, and what shall we do then? Aren't we in mess enough, all alone for the next six months, without making it more?"

"Where's the other one?"

"It's more than six months. It's eight or nine, more likely than not."

"Where's the other one?"

Franklin said: "It's in here." He got the other rifle out of the stern cabin, and passed it along.

"Any pistols, Bunny?"

"You know I haven't. They're no use to me. They've got no range."

"Very well. And now perhaps you'll listen to what Franklin's going to say."

Franklin had made up his mind by now. He said: "I don't like to turn back without knowing a bit more, and I don't suppose anyone does. But I don't like the look of going under those rocks. I expect we all feel the same about that. But it's very likely there isn't enough space to go far, and we're quarrelling about something we couldn't do if we tried. I say we'll take the boat just a few feet in, and see what the searchlight shows. If we couldn't get through, there's no more to be said, and we'll go back at once. It won't be any use coming here again, unless we're prepared to climb the cliffs, or blast a way underneath But if the roof's high enough, we'll go on, if we can see that there's a way out, and if you ladies want to, but not if you don't. We've taken risks enough, as Bunford says, and we know we're done for, if anything goes wrong here."

Eleanor said: "Haven't we come rather too far to turn back, unless we're obliged? Bunny, I wonder what you think it's cost me to get here?"

Gwendolen moved towards the stern. "We'll look after the engines and steer her in, if you'll manage the light, and call if you want to back out." She took Franklin's place, and he went forward. Bunford sat muttering in the well of the boat, following Eleanor with sullen eyes, which changed, if they met her own, to those of a scolded dog.

The *Blanche* moved slowly up to the cavern mouth, and its head went under. Franklin threw the light far forward into the blackness. It showed space sufficient to go on, if they took care of their heads—space to pass, but no more. Then he switched off, but could see no point of light, distant or near, such as might have shown had there been a place within range of sight at which the river entered the cavern, with space above it for the boat to pass. He called back that it was useless to enter.

But the boat continued to move slowly forward. He heard whispering in the stern. Then Eleanor called: "I don't want to go back. We've come too far for that. You know the bargain we made. (Be quiet, Bunford. There's no danger at all.) Gwen feels just the same."

Her voice sounded strangely loud under the low roof, and the walls echoed it back.

"Very well," he said, switching the light on again. "But go slowly. I don't want to go far enough to lose sight of the way in. Not unless we can see a way out at the other end."

"We needn't worry about that," Eleanor answered. "The current will show us the way we came."

That was true, and made his last condition sound a needless timidity. But the responsibility was his—and with no better than Bunny to share it!

Yet the same thought stilled him from any further protest as they went on under a lowering roof, through a darkness which gave no glimmer of distant light, and at a speed that Gwen increased is the minutes passed. Were they to think that they had come here in the protection of two men, and that *both* were cowards?

There was no further sound from Bunford. He was a dim figure crouched in the well of the boat, not to be seen clearly as the two women gazed forward into the light that was thrown ahead, and by which they steered.

Gwen wanted badly to turn back now, but it was for Eleanor to say. She thought the air was getting harder to breathe. Was it fancy only that made the black roof seem even lower than before? Gradually, steadily, declining to crush them? She had a sudden panic of unreasoned fear that it was descending upon them, and that she must push it off with her lifted hands. She wanted to scream, and repressed the weakness to control her voice to the question: "Isn't it about time to turn?"

But the answer was: "We'd better go on a bit more." And after a pause: "It may be shorter forward than back." Eleanor thought she answered naturally enough, but Gwen heard the fear in her voice. It was then that she increased the pace at which they drove into the darkness. She must get somewhere where she could breathe! There was no doubt that the roof was lower now. There was scarcely room to pass beneath it.

Eleanor said nothing, but Gwen knew that it would be useless now to tell her to turn. She was ready with an answer that repeated itself in her own mind. "I'm too scared to turn. I daren't go back that endless, endless way."

Franklin, gazing forward from the bows, and watchful for the first sign of any change that the light would show, thought that there was a difference in the blackness ahead. Did the roof close down to the water's level? He called to Gwen to go slow, but for the moment there was no change in the speed at which the boat drove through the water. Had the women gone mad? Had Gwen lost her nerve? He called sharply *"Eleanor, for God's sake!"* It was a matter of seconds now. He wondered what chance of life there could be if they wrecked the boat on the rocky wall. In those seconds of time he saw himself diving into the black rushing water. He might rescue one. Scarcely both. Could they reach the overturned or shattered wreck, and cling on as it floated down? Would they ever find it at all in the black darkness that would be theirs when the light failed? No, it would be death for all if the boat crashed...and crash it must.

Gwen had acted quickly at the second call, but she had had too much speed for safety in that narrow darkness. She could turn neither to right nor left. Head-on they crashed into the black wall—and did not recoil.

The bows drove forward into something that gave way with a cracking sound, and remained wedged. Franklin, regaining balance from the shock of the impact, looked at the wall against which they had collided, and cut off his own light. Daylight showed through a wide crack. They were conscious of a blessed freshness of inrushing air.

Bunford's frightened voice came from the well of the boat: "What's the matter now?" Less imaginative than the others, after his first frightened protest he had sullenly fallen asleep in the midst of his angry fears.

Franklin answered: "Anyhow, we've come through. They're nothing but rotten boards."

CHAPTER XVII.

"YOU mean it's been boarded up?" Eleanor asked, incredulously.

"Yes. But a good while ago. The wood's rotting. It looks like oak, though I'm not sure. There's a heavy framework and boards across it. It looks as though it's been meant to prevent anything floating down. You'd better back a bit, and come on very gently again. It looks as though it would give way at a push. Wait a moment, I'll come and do it. Bunford, you might come forward, and be ready to help clear the way through."

There was ten minutes of cautious ramming and breaking up of the screen, and then, going dead slow, they came out into the sunlight of the failing day.

The banks of the river were quite low, and became lower as they advanced. The left one remained too high for them to see beyond it, but the right—the one on their left—became lower until it sloped gently to the water level, showing an orchard of apple trees now laden with ripened fruit, and beneath them the deep swathes of unmown autumn grass.

"Of course," Eleanor said quietly, "we know that it isn't true."

"Yes, we know that. There isn't a blade of grass in the whole of the Antarctic continent. I suppose we were drowned five minutes ago, in which case Heaven isn't as bad a place as we've been taught to believe." So he said, only half in jest, for they had come on an unbelievable thing; but he looked round keenly the while for sign of human life, or other indication of the nature of the country to which they came.

Eleanor answered with a lighter tone, being less conversant with the limitations of the Antarctic flora, or less impressed by unexpected idiosyncrasies it might exhibit. "If we did drown, it doesn't follow it's that. It's more like the other place, if you ask me. Just look at that sky. There's no sunset there."

They looked ahead to a horizon of mighty hills, showing a whiteness of snow or rock in the evening light upon their northern sides, but beyond them the whole of the southern sky was lit with a bronze-red glow.

Gwen had said nothing till then. There are conditions under which the best of London secretaries may wish to look round for a time, before she distributes wisdom or information to those about her. She was conscious also of a sick and shocked reaction from the panic which had almost overcome her in that hateful cavern. She was proud of her nerve, of her self-sufficiency and self-control. Now she dipped a boat-hook overside to capture a floating weed which the water showed. She looked up to say: "That isn't sunset, that's fire." And then added: "Do you know that the water's warm?"

So it was. Not hot, but so that the hand could be dabbled in it and not be conscious of any chill. So it must have been for some time, but they had had other things to occupy their minds.

"We'd better land," Franklin said, "and see more of what kind of place we're in, while it's still easy to make a quick retreat if it seems likely to prove unhealthy."

"Not that way," Gwen interjected, and then regretted the exclamation. Of course they must go back by that way, if danger threatened here. Her efficiency told her that. Where had her nerve gone? In any case, they must go that way again, sooner or later. She could not foresee that she, at least, would never again enter that dark cavern, in which there was no sound but that of the broken water through which they drove, and no light but the acetylene glare upon black water and black rocks ahead. To retrace that perilous way might be for others of that party, but not for her.

Eleanor said: "Don't you think we'd better have a meal first? There'll be time for that before dark." Her words made them all aware of a neglected hunger. They tied the boat to a tree that was near the shore, and picnicked under such conditions as they had not hoped to know for a year's space.

Silently, a girl came with a basket, picking wind-fallen apples from the thick grass. She came close behind them before she saw a sight at which she started in wonder, but stood still, showing no fear.

They did not look round till a cock crowed from a fence at the orchard top, and then were silenced by the astonishment of what they saw.

She was a young girl, rather buxom, with pale gold snooded hair, and dressed in homespun clothes that gave a vague suggestion of Stuart days. She looked at them with a fearless wonder that seemed in no haste for speech.

56

"What we should like you to tell us," Franklin said, without rising, lest he should scare her to flight, "is whether we're in Heaven or Hell?"

She looked startled at the question—or was it shocked?—but she answered with simple directness: "You're in Norfolk County on Abel Trustwell's farm. But I'm a-wonder of where you came."

She spoke a clear English, though her accent and construction had unfamiliarities which were not of any dialect or period that they knew.

Eleanor rose as she answered. "We're strangers here. We came by the boat that's tied up on the bank. Is Mr. Trustwell a friendly man when strangers look in?"

The girl seemed more puzzled at Eleanor's speech than they had been at hers. Or she may have been additionally amazed as they rose up, at the strangeness of the clothing they wore. But she answered simply: "Master Trustwell could give you supper and beds if you're meaning that. Peradventure, you'll be going on at the dawn?"

"Yes," Franklin answered, "that's the idea." She looked uncomprehending, and he altered the phrase to, "I expect we'll go on at the dawn." It might prove to be the best thing to do. To slip away at the dawn, into the cavern where no pursuit would be likely to overtake. Who could tell? But Trustwell sounded a friendly name.

"What about leaving the boat?" Bunford asked. He still had the air and tone of one who was dragged into a dangerous folly against his will.

"We've got to do it, soon or late," Franklin answered. "I don't suppose we shall be far away."

"Well, we won't leave it. I think I'll stay."

Franklin controlled a movement of irritation, an impulse to treat the reply as an insubordination against the authority which had been conferred upon him. But he did not wish a disparaging quarrel to expose itself to the stranger's silent regard. He did not feel any fear that Bunford would try Sparshott's game. He would not venture the cavern passage alone. Neither was his disloyalty of that order. His devotion to Miss D'Acre, of its own kind, was a certain thing. He suspected that Bunford would have made difficulties had he been asked to do that which he now offered. After all, they would be much better without him. He said: "Yes. That's a good plan, if you're willing."

Bunford went back to the boat, and they followed the girl up the orchard, and along a path of dark-brown dust, to a house that was built of solid timbers and unshaped cemented stones.

CHAPTER XVIII.

ABEL TRUSTWELL sat at his evening board, with a platter of buttered barley bread and a cup of goat's milk before him, expecting his niece's presence, but not waiting for her (for in godly households the old do not wait for the young), when he heard a sound of strange voices, as of men and women who came in through the byre-yards.

Abel was a vigorous man, though in the evening of life. He was not uncomely, though his eyes were strangely bloodshot and over-hung by brows that could not cease to frown. That came of the snow-blindness that he had suffered from many times, as those must do whose substance is in the mountain goats. Of late years he trusted as much to his ears as to his eyes, for their hearing had become more acute as his sight failed. Now he listened with a strained look, for the voices had a strange sound, and his eyes went to the heavy broadsword that hung on the further wall. A thought had come to his mind that they must be of the Anabaptists who still lingered on the lips of hell. But he put the thought away, seeing its folly. And, be-sides, the voices had a pleasant sound. They might be angels of God, such as are known to call at times at the dwellings of men. That was a more likely thing. In any case, he was not one to fail in the duty of hospitality, unless for a good cause.

He rose and went toward the door, letting the sword be, as Paradise led the strangers in.

"Uncle," she said, "Here are three who have come from the great world." For so they had told her as they came up through the orchard trees.

He looked them over with peering eyes. "You come in a good time, and Michael God's-Truth will be a thankful man. It is likely that you were sent of God?"

The last words were a question, which Franklin felt should be answered in the right way. He had an instinct of peril here. Peril of a kind that he had not expected to meet. "We have been led here in a strange way." The answer did well enough.

"Came you through the great ice?"

"We came through a great ice, and then by the river gorge."

The man looked puzzled at this reply. He said: "Our fathers were three years in the ice."

Franklin would have replied, but the man had turned away to give the service of hospitality. "Paradise, bring butter and loaves and such milk as remains. I will set stools." In a few minutes they were seated round a table of very solid wood. A table meant to endure.

They had taken off the heavier of the furs and woollens that the Antarctic requires, for it had not been cold without, and was warm here,
and showed an open hearth where a wood fire burned.

They did not say that they had just fed, for they had a common
instinct to be wary of speech, but sat and ate the buttered barley
cakes and drank the milk, finding them good after the preserved
foods that they had eaten for many weeks.

When they were seated, Franklin was quick to continue the conversation. He had a natural curiosity, and a feeling also that they
might be safer if they understood more. And yet they had been well
received, and it was hard to say why he should feel as he did. He
asked: "You say your fathers came through the ice. Was it long
ago?"

"It was more than two hundred years. They fled from the persecutions of the ungodly, seeking a new world, but not this. They were
driven long by storms, so it is told, and their ship was frozen at last
for three years in a great ice, which was of the guidance of God, so
that they came here."

"They must have had a rough time. I mean, they must have had
much hardship to endure."

"They were saved of God."

"Were there many of them?"

"By the judgment of God, there were but eight alive when they
were held in the great ice. For He slew with plague all who were not
of a pure faith, all but one, whom he left alive for a chastening of the
righteous in the days that followed."

It was in this way that the conversation continued. Abel Trustwell neither offered information nor refused it. Answering each
question without apparent reluctance, but adding nothing beyond the
required reply. He spoke as one who had not been reared in a chat-
tering school.

The two women sat silent, leaving it to Franklin to bring out the
tale. They may have been the more disposed to this attitude by the
fact that Abel did not address them, nor look their way. There was
no impression of any conscious rudeness. Women were of subordi-
nate importance. Let them chatter among themselves, and sit silent
when men are talking of weighty things. He simply recognized facts.

And as the narrative by interrogation proceeded, they gained a
clear impression of how this strange Antarctic colony had come into
being, and something also of its natural features and climate, some
idea of the disposition of its present inhabitants.

They saw the *Morning Star*, a small, stoutly-built, two-masted
brig, putting out from an English quay, crowded with the households

of some scores of stubborn-hearted dissenters who would not conform to the Acts which had been passed to oppress them. They and their families, and a store of weapons, tools, and seeds, setting out for the founding of a colony in the new world. And then weeks of stormy seas and opposing winds, and disease in the crowded cabins taking them off, till the despairing remnant found themselves caught in the fierce grip of Antarctic tempest, and frozen at last in an ice field which had drifted slowly southward—further southward each summer as the sun's heat had given it leave to move—until at the end they had come to land. But by what road they had come could not be learnt more nearly than this: that it was clear that it had not been by the river gorge.

The pestilence that had appeared to be their destruction had been salvation to the surviving remnant, for it was the smallness of their numbers which enabled many needful things to last which would otherwise have been consumed long before the passing of the three years in the grip of the ice. As to it having been so long as that, there could be no proof beyond the tradition of those who survived, so we may think as we will.

But there had come at last three men and four women, and a child of a few months, who had been kept alive with goat's milk, they having carried some of these hardy animals, and fodder for their provision, for the sake of the children that the brig held when it put out from the Yarmouth pier. The children had died, except the one that had been born to the Antarctic cold. But there were some fowl, and a goat and a kid or two that still lived when they had landed on something more hospitable than the glacial ice.

The goats had flourished in the new land, and had multiplied rapidly. So had the human population, which now consisted of over two thousand souls, apart from an outcast crew, the descendants of one of the original immigrants, and these had inherited from his obduracy the amazing heresies of the Anabaptists, and had been expelled from a community of saints in which the Creator had shown a natural interest by guiding them to this isolated security, where they could practise their religion at the mouth of Hell.

For they found that this country was on the very threshold of Hell, from which, indeed, it derived the measure of genial temperature which enabled crops to be grown and brought to a swift maturity when the sun shone in the summer days. And because of the colonizing purpose with which the brig had been equipped, there had been a store of seeds and other necessities which had enabled them to make full use of this fertility. And grass and weeds had sprung up, the seeds of which must have been mixed with those of a better sort, or brought in the soil in which some plants had been carried. And the grass had spread over the land, as rapidly as water runs downhill. "Has there been no effort," Franklin asked, "in all these years, to go back to the larger world?"

"It has been tried twice by those who set themselves against the Divine Will. When I was young, there were nearly twenty men who set forth over the great heights and frozen snow, and when no news came as the years passed, there were those who said that they had gone back to the strange hot lands where the Lord walks among men. Others said they had perished, or they had surely returned, or others come out of curiosity to see how we did, had it been told. And these last were right, for ten years later there was another party who would go out by the same way, but having travelled for certain days they found the bones of those who had gone before, whereon they came back, being already in evil wise. There have been none since this. Nor was it likely that such should have been again, for it has been held of late years that God destroyed the world after leading His elect to this secure place, even as He destroyed Sodom in a like case. It is for denying this that Patience God's-Truth is even now waiting trial of the Elders who heard the testimony of her accusers. Wherefore I said unto you that Michael God's-Truth will be a thankful man, and that you are sent of God, lest one be condemned, being without sin."

"We certainly came by a strange way," Franklin answered, still feeling that he must move carefully, as though there were pitfalls around his feet, "but it is a long tale. Nor would it be easy to tell in a clear speech until much else had been understood."

Abel Trustwell accepted this answer without curiosity, and as it was not of the nature of a question, he remained silent.

The girl, having attended upon the needs of her guests, was now seated with them, eating in a primitive style, but without vulgarity. Without seeming to look, she saw all, in a woman's way, and her thoughts were busy with problems that did not enter her uncle's mind.

Not that his was idle, or that he was of any natural stupidity. His attitude was the result of a definite purpose, controlled by the requirements of his own code.

He knew it to be the settled policy of the leaders of the community, which he also approved, that there should be no communication with the outer world, if such world were still in existence after its saints had fled. The desire to discourage efforts by the more adventurous of the younger men to re-establish connection with it may have fostered the theory that it had ceased to be.

His thoughts, from the first moment of the appearance of the strangers, had been concentrated upon this aspect of the problem. It would be his duty to see that they did not return by the way they came (whatever that might be) till they had been examined by the Elders, and their fate decided by a higher authority than his own. But there was no force to seize them in his own hands. And having these thoughts, religion and personal character combined to control his attitude. He would not alarm them with any show of hostility, but neither would he entice them with friendly words. He gave the hospitality which the occasion required, and he answered the questions that were put to him. More than that, even the thought of Jael (who was on his mind during that mealtime more than either of the ladies who had called upon him) could not incline him to do.

But Paradise Trustwell had better eyes, and a less preoccupied curiosity. She observed the strangers, and considered that, if they were typical of the people from whom they came, the outer world must be of a finer kind than she had been taught to believe. As to which she erred in a very natural way. If all the people of the quality of her visitors were deducted from the population of Britain, it might still be a well-peopled country. But she could not know that.

She looked at their physical condition, and at the state of their clothing, with a different wonder. They wore the best that experience of Antarctic travel and unlimited money could surly, and it had been new when the *Bergen* sailed, and when they had stepped into the *Blanche* a few days before. She knew enough of the iron cold of the heights, and of the barren plateau beyond, of the toil of making way over glacier, crevasse, and moraine, and of the many bruises that come to those who climb among granite rocks, to be amazed at the condition of those upon whom she looked. The keen purity of the Antarctic air in the unsetting sun of its summer days had given a clear brilliance to the complexions of her feminine visitors, which had rendered them independent of the cosmetics of which they had not been entirely innocent a few weeks earlier, and which, had they worn and she perceived them, would have led her to classify them at once with Aholibah, and other ladies of similarly abandoned habits, such as were without examples in her own community, but the knowledge of which had been maintained by the reading of the Hebrew scriptures, and who, she had been told, walked wantonly with the oppressors, in the world from which her fathers fled.

When the conversation between her uncle and Franklin ceased, she said timidly to Eleanor, who was seated at her left hand: "You must have come by a hard way?"

"It has not been hard for us. We came in a ship, and then by the boat you saw."

"Were you long in the great ice?"

"We were not frozen in. We sailed through the pack-ice in the summer days, and then landed, and came up the river in the boat."

"But the boat had no sails?"

"No. Nor did the ship really. We say sailed, because it is the word which has always been used, but we have found another way of making ships move."

"I had never seen a ship with sails. But we have pictures of what they were. Are there none in the world now?"

It is a penalty of bad sight that a man does not recognize clearly the expressions of those about him. Being unaware of such reactions, he may become less careful himself in the extent to which he reveals his feelings by gesture or change of look. Abel Trustwell had been on his guard, but as this conversation developed he not only listened with keen ears, he turned his blear-sighted eyes towards the speakers, and an expression crossed his face which showed clearly to Franklin his distaste for the curiosity that the girl's question indicated.

Gwen saw it also, and intervened before the next answer came. "Don't you think we ought to go back to the boat? Bunford'll wonder where we are for so long."

The question drew Eleanor's attention the more surely, because, spoken at random as it was, it had a quality of unreason. Bunford had heard the invitation given that they should be entertained for the night. He had preferred to remain. If they did not return till morning he had no grievance, and no cause for surprise. But she had been with Gwen in strange and difficult situations before. It did not occur to her that her companion might be talking nonsense.

"Yes, we ought to let him know what we mean to do. We could go and be back in a few minutes."

She saw no cause for alarm, but if Gwen had noticed something which had escaped her, she felt that that was the right thing to say.

So it was. Let their hosts think they were returning, and if, when they had talked it over, they decided differently, they would be very quickly beyond danger, and beyond pursuit. Franklin thought thus, and would have spoken a confirming word, but Abel Trustwell was quicker than he.

"You have another with you?"

"Yes. There are four of us."

"He also will be our guest?"

"I don't think we need burden you with him. He likes to stay with the boat."

"He is your servant?"

"No, he is one of ourselves."

"Then if you will let him know that we can find sleeping quarters in comfort for him also, he can come or stay as he may be led to do. And the ladies can rest here the while."

"I'm afraid we can't do that, Franklin," Eleanor interposed quickly. "There are things we shall need to fetch. Besides, it's no distance to go."

Abel was on his guard now. He gave no sign of his thoughts. He had a suspicion, born of the lack of goodwill in his own mind, that they might not intend to return. But he did not see how he could prevent their going. Nor did he see that anything would be gained if he should attempt this in a violent way. For if they had a companion in the boat, he might flee by himself on being alarmed, and the evil would be complete.

He felt that he could do no better than to reassure them before they should go, if that were possible. If he could have detained the women on any pretext, without appearance of constraint, he supposed that Franklin's return would have been certain, but he could not see how to do this. Nor was he one who could lie with ease. So they went without further words.

When they had gone, and Paradise was busy with preparations for her amazing guests, Abel took a small piece of linen rag (for he had no paper) and wrote upon it with a piece of lead, *The Sword of the Lord and of Gideon*. He went out into the barns, and found a boy who was working there.

"Timothy," he said, "you will go at speed to Master Michael God's-Truth, giving him this clout, and saying that I would have him here by four hours after the sun sets, with all the aid he can bring, for Satan walks in the land. You can return with him."

Abel acted with more discretion in this than we may quickly see. Timothy was a slave. That could be told by his name, for slaves were named from the latter part of the Sacred Book, which was used only for them. Being a slave, being so young, showed that he had been taken as a child from the Anabaptists. This was according to the policy of the Elders, who would save the souls of these children, and who reduced the number of the Anabaptists in this way without of shedding of blood. And there may have been mothers among the accursed ones who were half-willing to let their children go rather than attempt to rear them amid the hardships of the mouths of hell.

But the fact of their origin could not be concealed from the children, and while they were little likely to make voluntary return to a life of hardship (with perdition to follow), their loyalty was never trusted in matters of strife between their new masters and those from whom they came. The words on the rag, which the boy could not read, were the warning signal of Anabaptist raid. That would puzzle Master God's-Trust, who would not see how it could be possible for them to have come so far through the land without detection. He would conclude that they could not be a large party, if they were there at all. He would come at once, with his sons, and others that were within call.

Abel wrote that message so that the boy should not know what he said. He sent warning in that way, because he felt that it would be difficult to write the truth convincingly in a few words. He had a conflicting thought that this might be a visitation of God for the special benefit of Michael God's-Truth. Let him and his household know before it should be spread through the land.

The written word and the spoken message would bring him quickly, and so prepared that he would be able to secure these witnesses, either by force or goodwill. The only question that remained was whether they would return from the boat, and he had little doubt of that, for he thought that the purpose of God was plain.

It may be thought that he did not show much curiosity about the conditions of these strange visitors, or to inspect the vessel in which they came. That is true enough, but he was a man whose imaginations were little set on material things. He herded his goats among the lower hills, and the narrow rising gorges that gashed the mountains far up into the icy heights, but, while he did this, his thoughts were on the things of the spirit, and the dealings of God with man.

CHAPTER XIX.

THEY made their way back to the boat with a doubt in each mind which might have hardened into determination not to return had it received a more decided support. But when they spoke they found a difficulty in expressing any adequate reason for these feelings of disquiet. Having no verbal support from each other's words, they were stillborn and quickly superseded by a more confident spirit.

Indeed, when they spoke it was to recognize the good fortune they had encountered beyond any reasonable expectation. Where they had looked for a land of Antarctic severity, they had come to a temperate climate, and the fruiting of orchard trees. Where they might have expected to find either a desolation or a population hostile or suspicious, and of alien and probably repellent habits, they had come on men of their own race, and even of their own language, a sober, God-fearing folk of English stock, who had welcomed them with hospitality, and the offer of their own roof.

Franklin did, indeed, say: "Well, it's our chance now. You can do a bolt if you will."

But Eleanor, who was the least perturbed of the three, and perhaps the keenest in the desire of exploration, said definitely: "No, thank you. After two nights in the cabin, I'm not going to miss the chance of sampling Mr. Trustwell's beds. Besides, if we went now, we shouldn't have the face to come back. It would be rude. And we've got to get something better than this apple-core to take home, or we shall be worse liars than Sparshott. Suppose we got Miss Paradise to come along? We might persuade her in a few days."

"Or perhaps a bit longer than that," Gwen suggested. Her thoughts had veered to compare the climate and comforts of this new-found land with the ice-bound cabin in which the winter must be spent should they return to the coast. No doubt it would be dark here, and not so warm as it was now, but still. Might they not find sufficient friendship to enable them to remain till it should be near the time when the ice would break, and the *Bergen* would come again?

"I wonder how it is," she said, "that it's so much warmer here."

They discussed that till they reached the boat. The low-lying land watered by warm streams from the great volcanic range which appeared to be in continual eruption, giving a dull-red glow to the width of the southern sky: the abrupt rising of the hills to the great Antarctic table-land to the north—the barrier through which they had found so strange a way. They speculated as to where the ice-field could be which avoided the barrier and by which the ancestors of these people must have drifted here. Was it to east or west?

Bunford met them on the bank. He had got to the rifles, and had one on his arm. He had glasses also, with which he was sweeping the slopes of the northern hills.

"Wild goats," he said. "You should see them leap! I'll have a go after them in the morning, and you shall have tome fresh meat."

"They're not wild," Gwen told him.

"Not wild?" His face showed annoyance and incredulity. "Well, they'd make good sport anyway. They look wild enough to me. You'd better ask them if they don't want one or two shot. What kind of Johnnies are they, anyway? Just louts, I suppose? Usual farming sort."

Mr. Bunford Weldon took the presence of these people in a more casual way than the others were able to do. They seemed more natural than not. It was the endless Antarctic desolations that had confused his mind. But, after all, the world was more or less what you'd expect it to be.

Eleanor said: "They're not the sort of people to take liberties with. I wish you hadn't got that rifle out. We don't want any trouble now. We want to make friends. I daresay they don't know what a gun is."

There might be a doubt about that, but all voices were joined in persuasion that he should do nothing rash, and that the rifle should be put away. There was no trusting Bunny with a gun in his hand. They had learnt that already.

Well, he said, rather sulkily, they needn't make such a fuss. He was going to stay where he was. He wasn't going to interfere with them.

They got out a few things that they might want, and went back to the house.

It was already twilight, for with the coming of March the days had begun to shorten rapidly, and Abel met them with the assumption that they would retire immediately.

"Master Franklin," he said "—oh, Arden, is it? I crave pardon for that error. Paradise will show you and Mistress Arden to the best chamber we have. I would it were better garnished than you will find it to be. The other lady will share Paradise's own room."

"I beg your pardon," Franklin said. "This is not Mistress Arden. This is Miss Eleanor D'Acre." It was rather awkwardly put, and he had a following thought that the next moment might provide him with another wife. So he added hastily, "And this is Miss Gwendolen Collinson."

Abel Trustwell considered this information in a moment of grim and disconcerting silence. Franklin tried to relieve the position by saying: "But the arrangements you have kindly made will be quite satisfactory. The two ladies will sleep together, and I can...." He stopped as he realized that the arrangements could not be so simply adjusted, and that he was allocating himself to the society of an earthly Paradise.

Gwen caught his eye, and felt it to be a position at which even a secretary might be allowed to smile.

She saw that Eleanor was maintaining her usual serenity, but she thought it was not over easily done. She looked as though she could have appeared confused without much difficulty, from which Gwen drew an inference which was not new to her mind.

It was all in no more than a moment's pause before Abel said: "The ladies will share the chamber, as you propose. I will find other harbour for you."

Franklin found himself in a little room which had a window too small for human exit, and a single door which led through Abel Trustwell's own chamber. He reflected that it was a very natural thing that the house should be designed in the Elizabethan manner, and a very possible one that he might not be trusted over-much.

He came to a feather-bed, raised on a wooden frame. There were linen sheets, with goatskin blankets. He observed that there must be a climate here which would grow flax. The bed was warmed with hot stones, inserted in goatskin bags. He should have slept well.

But instead of that he stayed awake, thinking of Blanche. Not of the boat of that name, nor yet of Eleanor D'Acre. There was a distinction here. Eleanor was a very wealthy woman whom he might love, but could never wed. If he made love to her in this isolation, while they were so inseparably together, it might make a very embarrassing position, and he was unsure that it was one that his code allowed. Had she been a poor girl, one that he could marry on their return, he might have looked at it differently. Miss Collinson, for instance. A delightfully pretty girl, and blessed with unusual brains. One who certainly did not dislike him. Who read his thoughts very easily. Who met his eyes with a quick smile. He was half-conscious that he might have won Gwen if he had really tried. But his choice was Eleanor, of whom he must never think, either now or when he returned. Not, at least, unless he should find gold in this new land lying about as freely as the coal on the landing-beach. It would have to be almost like that. He knew something of the amount of Miss D'Acre's wealth. So much for Eleanor.

But Blanche was a different matter. Eleanor did not like Blanche. She did not like the name. So he had heard her say. Well, he did. Much better than Eleanor. So he separated them in his mind. Eleanor was an inaccessible young woman, with whom he was obliged to travel, but avoiding any exceptional intimacy. Blanche was a girl he loved.

Had it been Blanche who had come here, how different it would have been! They would almost certainly have been married at Cape Town. Or if not there, on the *Bergen*. Is it not well-known that any captain can perform a marriage at sea? And then there would have been no occasion for embarrassing explanation. Eleanor might be inaccessible, but Blanche would have been in his arms now.

His thoughts were interrupted by the sound of movements in the next room. Not many movements. He thought that Abel got up, and went out. He thought he heard the stairs creak, though there were two doors between him and them. The clearness with which he heard these sounds reminded him that he had heard little from the next room after Abel had shown him in. And he had not been asleep. Abel must just have lain down in his clothes, and now got up again as softly as he could.

Well, there might be nothing in that. Nothing to cause alarm. Abel might have duties with his livestock which called him out in the night, and have been anxious not to disturb his guest. He might always lie down in his clothes. Some men do. The habits of these Antarcticans would be sure to show some divergences from those of their English cousins. It was foolish to get flurried at every sound.

There is no earthly stillness like that of the Antarctic, beyond the oceans edge. The remotest desert, the loneliest ocean, have sounds under the stars. But there are no birds in Antarctica. There are no animals of any kind. Scarcely the most rudimentary form of any insect life. Only in the water, and beneath the blue roofings of ice, the marine life teems, waiting for the change of climate which the ages will surely bring, so that it may invade the land. Petrel, penguin, and albatross may use the shore at the ocean's edge, or further inland at times, but the water is their real home.

There was life of sorts that had come through the ice in the hold of the Puritans' brig. Life of animal, bird, and plant (and of some insects, too, which had been plague enough), but they were not of kinds to change the silence of the midnight hours.

Franklin thought he heard movements of men. He thought he heard voices, though they were low and far-off, being beyond the byres. He would have liked to rise, but saw the folly of showing suspicion or alarm. It was a night of moon and stars, and a faint light came through the little window. He got up quietly, taking the revolver from beneath his pillow. He knew the way to the women's room. He felt sure that his door was not secured, and that Abel had gone. He could go to them very quickly if there should be real cause. But he did not want to do anything foolish. What could be more likely to cause suspicion than for him to be found wandering about the house in the night? And then nothing happened, but he was too wakeful to sleep, and was still alert when, an hour later, loud and sharp, a rifle-shot broke the silence, and then another.

CHAPTER XX.

MICHAEL GOD'S-TRUTH stood with his two sons and with three men that were his in the moonlit space on the farther side of the barns. Michael was a tall man and broad, with a great beard which would have been grizzled-brown in the daylight. He stroked this beard, as his way was, while he listened to Abel's tale.

He and his sons wore high leather boots and belted doublets which, with their heavy swords, gave them the look of cavalier rather than puritan stock. That may have had its root in the character of Gabriel God's-Truth, the most dominant of the three men who had landed from the ice-locked brig. He had been a man of a fine front, and one who cared more for the vanities of the flesh than might have been considered becoming in God's Elect, had he not been a man of a bold speech, one also of much wealth, and who was very ready to aid the weaker of his own faith. It was his money that had done most to equip the brig. He might dress as he would. And when the oppressors were left behind for God to deal with in His own way, what use was there in distinction of dress, the meaning of which was a dead thing?

Hard they lived, and rough they dressed in the first days, but toil brought prosperity. Clothes were woven, and leather dressed. Character told as the generations passed. The descendants of Gabriel's God's-Truth were still first in the land. They had well-read Bibles and well-polished swords, which were two things with which the brig had been well-stocked, and which had remained when most of their owners died.

Michael God's-Truth was first in the land. Had you stopped twenty of its inhabitants, and asked who was the greatest there, they would all have spoken the same name. But to be first may be to be envied by many, hated by some. He might preside when the Elders met, but there were eleven votes to be told. Today his seat shook in a strange way, and there were those who counted that it would be overturned.

His three men were dressed in a more sober mode, but one of them had a sword, and the other two had quarter-staves of oak which they were skilled to use. For there had been acorns brought on the brig, from which three oaks had been grown, which were now of a great size, and when they had borne acorns in their time there had been many trees planted. Oaks sheltered all the homesteads. They made wind-screens for the fields. They made pleasant woods on the river-side. They gave good timber for many needs. There had been nothing that the brig had brought more useful than those acorns.

Michael God's-Truth stroked his beard in a thoughtful mood. It was a great thing, if it could be handled in the right way. But it would need care. He could see dangers both to right and left. And he must be quite sure. He asked again: "You are sure they did not come by the great river?"

"No. They say they came by the river that flows into the hills. Paradise has seen the boat. It is below the orchard still, if it has not been moved."

Michael said: "We will see that boat." He had another thought. "But the way under the mountains is closed with timbers, and a great chain. How could they have come through?"

"I know not. But so they say." He had a new fear. He knew why that cavern-mouth had been closed, though few did. It had been done more than eighty years ago. Five young men, saying nothing of what they had planned to any, had entered it in one of the old ship's-boats. Two of them had come back some days later. One was rowing, and one was mad. The one who rowed had been his own grandfather. He said that water-demons, which were like to men in their shape, had eaten the other three. He had scars on his arm till he died, but they were not such as would be made with human teeth.

This was not known to all, but it was the common tale that demons lived in caves under the frozen hills, where the river went. He saw the prejudice which would rise from the fact that his witnesses had come by that way. He had a worse fear than that. *Were they demons or men?* He was not one to be trammelled in Satan's net. It would be like the ways of the Old Serpent to get his daughter into this trouble, and then to lure him with lying witnesses to his own destruction. He asked: "Are they men in truth?"

"The man is young and comely enough, and of pleasant speech. They are fair women, and they say that they are unwed. They speak our tongue, though in a new way. The other man I have not seen."

"Do they come by shipwreck or storm?"

"They say they come of their own will, seeking strange sights."

"Two men and two women who are unwed? It is an unlikely tale."

"So it sounds. Yet a lying tale should be better made."

Michael saw that Abel was right in that. He said: "I will see this boat that has neither sails nor oars. They may come thus being angels of God or fiends of the lowest pit, but it is not after the manner of men. I will see first whether they can have come from the river-caves. And after that, I will see them."

He led the way to the place where the river entered the rock, and there was enough moonlight to show that the tale was true. He said: "But how broke they the chain?"

That was answered quickly enough. The chain had given way at one side. It trailed on the river-bed. It might have been thus for years. Looking at that broken way, the tale had a truer sound. They might have been guided of God, to give evidence at his daughter's need, or they might be demons come in the guise of men. How was it to be proved?

But one thing must be done at once. If they were angels of God, they would be in no haste to go back by the way they came, their mission being undone. If they were mortal men, they should not find it easy to do.

"Noah," he said, "I will go on with Ehud and Master Trustwell to see this boat, and do you stay here with the men, and stretch that chain again, securing all to the most you may. It is but a short swim to the further bank."

So he went on with Abel and his younger son to inspect the *Blanche*.

CHAPTER XXI.

FRANKLIN found Abel's room empty as he passed through it, as he had expected. His own door had been fastened on Abel's side, but with no more than a weak hasp which had given way to his first impatient pressure. Still, its meaning was the same, whether it were weak or strong. He made his way quickly to the door of the women's room. He called: "Are you all right? I am going down to the boat. I think Bunford's being attacked."

Eleanor's voice answered him, showing less excitement than his own. "I don't think I should do that. It's probably over now."

"Of course, if you'd rather not be left...." He had a previous doubt as to whether he ought not to stay beside them. But the danger did not appear to be here, and the boat was a vital need.

"It's probably over now," Eleanor answered again. "He's probably driven them off. I should think it would be better to stay here till we know more. But we'll come with you if you like. We're nearly ready now."

Franklin saw that that might be the better way. If an attack upon the boat had been repulsed, it might be possible for them to get back on it, and retreat without further difficulty. They must keep together for that. Had there been more shots, there would have been more reason for hastening to Bunford's aid, but the fight, one way or other, must be over now.

The women came out of the room together, and Paradise appeared also, bringing a lamp. Gwen said: "Eleanor's quite right. You'd better keep out of it till you know more. We heard men passing the top of the orchard an hour ago. Quite a lot. If Bunford's fired twice, he's killed two. You know he doesn't miss. You'd better have it quite plain that it's nothing to do with you."

That was one point of view, but there were others. He answered: "Bunford was quite justified, if they were attacking the boat."

"Or if he thought they were? You know what Bunford is if he gets scared."

"Well, it wasn't a good time to choose."

"I don't say it was. I'm not arguing for them. I say you'd better know what's happened before you butt in."

Paradise stood listening to this, quietly, but with a white face. Her eyes went to where her uncle's sword hung on the wall. The place was empty now. She asked: "You say there have been men killed? It is I who had better go. There is none will do harm to me. You should stay here."

She went out at the word, leaving the lamp on the table. They stood looking at one another, waiting for they knew not what. But there were no more shots. Whatever had happened must be over now.

Then there were steps approaching the house, and the voices of several men.

Paradise came in first. She said: "God has been good. There has been less hurt than was thought."

Then a large brown-bearded man filled the doorway. He looked at the three strangers keenly, but without speech. Abel Trustwell entered behind, and with him a younger man, who walked unsteadily, leaning on the other's arm. The right side of his doublet was streaked with blood.

The wounded man sat down on a chair, and as he did so Paradise was already beside him. Working swiftly and quietly, she uncovered a wound that looked no more than a small red puncture that had bled freely.

Gwen said: "Can I help you?" The voice, with its soft and different accent, turned the heads of all to the speaker, even that of the wounded man.

Paradise did not reply, but Michael God's-Truth said sternly, looking at Gwen as though in accusation: "A hack-butt-ball hath done this." And then: "It will be an ill business to cut it out."

"You won't need to do that," she answered confidently. "It won't be there." She turned to Paradise. "If you'll look, you'll see where it came out."

So she found it to be. There was a wound at the back of the shoulder, too, though it had bled less.

Michael God's-Truth came over to look. He said, wondering: "It was at many yards' distance." And then: "A little lower, it might have killed."

His tone was still one of accusation, and she answered it as confidently as before.

"It was not meant to kill. Bunford does not miss. He hits where he will. Where did the second shot go?"

"This was the second."

"Then he fired the first as a warning only. Why were you there in the night?"

It was a question at which anyone might pause to reply, and the wounded man, who had been waiting his chance, was the first to speak. He had been quite as interested as his father in the fact that the bullet had gone through, and in a more personal way. There was a certain crudity about surgical operations in Antarctica which rendered the idea of cutting out a bullet unpleasant for the one who supposed himself to have given it an uninvited hospitality. He may have felt an illogical gratitude to this attractive stranger who had relieved his fears. Anyway, if he could stop her quarrelling with his father to talk to him, he was disposed to do it. He said: "It must have been a small ball."

"It wasn't a ball," she answered. "It was like a pencil. I mean, long and thin. You must be very strong to stand it as well as you do."

He looked pleased at that. He didn't much care what was said, so long as he could hold her attention. His father saw that. Not with anger. Such a friendship might prove a good thing where everything was in doubt. He was cautious, watching the event. But his first purpose was to insist that there had been a wrong done. It held some truth, and might be an advantageous position to set up. He asked: "Must a man beg a stranger's leave when he walks on his own land?"

Eleanor was quick to answer that, for she saw that Franklin was about to speak, and she thought shrewdly that if this man, whom she supposed rightly to be Michael God's-Truth, was disposed to quarrel, he would do it less easily with a woman than with a man. "We are sorry that anyone has been hurt, but it was not the doing of any here, nor do we know what has occurred."

Her words drew his eyes. He looked at her with a bold and dominant glance, before which her own faltered, though it did not fall. He said: "Mistress, you have said well. Yet the wound came from one of your own part, and it was a shot fired against those who had meant no wrong. There must be more said when he who fired it is at hand. But we must know by what names we are called."

Introductions followed, with some formality. Then he prompted Abel to order a meal. "It will be light," he said, "in an hour's time. Let us sit in comfort to talk. And for Ehud you should find a bed. He has lost blood, and there is a wound to heal."

In all this, they were aware of a more vigorous personality than that of Abel Trustwell. One who was used to seeing others move as he spoke. They sat round the table as children are called to a class. Paradise was quick to bring food. Only, Ehud excused himself from retiring to bed. He leaned back in the armchair in which he had been placed at the first. His eyes followed Gwen. He said he felt too weak to move. At least for a time.

Michael waited only till the table had been supplied, and the confusion of service ceased, and then addressed Franklin in a way that held the attention of all there.

"Master Arden," he said, "I will speak in plain words, as men should. You came as strangers unasked, and no strangers are welcome here. If you should go back and tell of this you have seen, you may do us a great wrong. You can see that. We fled from your land, seeking a far peace. Are we to have none, even here? That is how we must feel, and it is a point on which more must be said. If you come here, bringing new thoughts, new inventions, new ways, it may even be a corrupt faith, it is the end of all that we are. I will say no more of that now.

"Yet is it also true that you come in a good time, and it may be that you have been sent of God. For you come at a present need.

"You come from the land from which our fathers fled. That is easy to see. You speak our tongue, though after a new way. You are of us, and yet apart. Seeing you, we may resolve that it is a land that remains, having been endured of God, be its sins what they may.

"And I must tell you this. There have been those among us (and I one) who have held that when our fathers fled from a world that persecuted the saints of God, and He brought us to this place, which is at the portals of Hell, but which has proved to be a secure haven, whether from demon or man (for what saith the Scripture? *The gates of Hell shall not prevail against it*), then we held that the Divine wrath would have blotted out a world from which the saints, being few, had been forced to flee. (For again, what saith the Scripture? Think not to find the Elect in a church which is great in numbers and power. *For many are called, but few chosen.*)

"This was my father's belief, and it has been mine. Three years ago, being so held by the whole church, it was made an article of our faith, which none may deny, but they find themselves at the mercy of the Elders, whether to slay or to keep alive.

"And, but five weeks past, it was reported that my own daughter is for trial for this in three days' time."

He paused a moment at that point, not as having ceased, but as having reached a climax, as he would do when he preached in the pulpit of Suffolk County, but Franklin answered him in the pause: "You would like us to bear witness on your daughter's side?"

"I doubt not, if ye be true folk, that it is even for that that you are sent here."

"I would take the risk for myself," Franklin answered. "But I will ask you something to which I would have truthful answer, as you value your daughter's cause. You say that this belief has been widely held and is an article of your faith. Witness against it may not be a thing that your people will be glad to hear. Can these ladies give such evidence with safety to themselves?"

"Our people care only for the truth, be it whatever it may." Franklin wished that he were equally sure of that. He thought, if that were so, he could convince them easily that the world existed today. Yet it was true enough, with a reason that Master God's-Truth did not say.

It was in his father's time that a heresy had arisen among them, some saying that the Christian miracles were not to be taken too literally, and pointing to the absence of such manifestations in their midst, true church as they were.

When this talk had gained ground, his father, Hush-Ill God's-Truth, had preached a sermon upon the text, *Be not deceived: God is not mocked*, in which he had reminded his hearers how they dwelt beside the pits of Hell, and who knew to what swift vengeance He might consign them, if the tempted their God too far?

The next day the volcanoes of Hell had blazed, as they often would, but no one had worried about that. Lava had never flowed into their land. It could not do so, for the volcanic cones were separated by frontier mountains which were higher than they. It flowed to the south, where there must be hell indeed. But who had passed the volcanic ridges to see that?

76

The volcanoes had been no nuisance at all, for when the hot fumes rose they drew inward the cooler air from the northern heights over the valley in which the saints of God dwelt, so that they saw the skies darken over the craters of Hell, while their own skies were cool and blue. But this time, when the craters belched, the wind blew from the south. It was a thing they had never known, either before or since. The air was black with scorching dust. The skies were hidden. There were hours when a man could not be sure of seeing his neighbour's face. But the Elders prayed, lying flatly before the face of their offended Deity, and at last the wind changed. But there was a thick layer of volcanic dust over all the land. There were some who died from the foul air they had breathed. The crops were scorched and ruined. There was starvation for many before the next harvest came, though, when it did, it was of a fertility which they had never known before, showing the forgiveness of God.

It was a lesson that they would not be quick to forget. They had looked into the very pit of Hell. It was a warning against heresy, and to deal faithfully with those through whom it might threaten again. God would not be likely to warn them twice. Master God's-Truth was right in saying that they only cared for the truth, but it was less sure that they would have good judgment to know it.

He was conscious of another thing that he did not say. He knew—all the Elders knew in their secret minds—that this idea of an ended world had been fostered from political rather than religious motives, to discourage further attempts to establish connections with it, which the Elders dreaded. In the end they had found, as priests have often done before, in every country and time, that they had raised that which they could not control. The belief had been formally added to the articles of their creed. And now Michael had to prove it false, or see his daughter handed over to whatever doom his fellow-elders might inflict upon her.

"If we do this for you," Franklin replied, "can you promise that we shall be free to go when the trial is over?" There was a silence which was as ominous as denial to those who waited, though it was but a ten-seconds' space, but when the answer came it had an honest sound.

"It would be for the Elders to say, of whom I am one in twelve. Yet I should be something more than a weak friend."

"And suppose we refuse, having no better pledge, and go now?"

"It is beyond your power, and it is more than I could allow. We are three to one. You have women with you, who cannot fight or run. I have four other men at the river-bank. You would find our friendship a better thing."

Franklin had a doubt of that. It was true that they were three to one, and they wore swords. But one was wounded; and they did not know that his hand was on the pistol in his jacket pocket. Three shots might be fired before one of those cumbrous weapons could leave its sheath. But they might not. Suppose the revolver jammed, or a shot failed to disable? If he were cut down, what of the women then? As to the four men on the river-bank, he did not care overmuch. He thought they would have too much respect for Bunford Weldon's rifle to be near the boat, and that rifle might be a powerful aid should the area of conflict approach its range.

But he was conscious of a greater difficulty. To shoot these men without warning was a thing that he could not do. It would require far more than a vague and distant peril to make it possible to his own mind. And to threaten would be a very foolish thing. He had a sure instinct that it would not succeed without being translated into action, for they had an aspect of resolution. And to let them know that he was armed would mean the surrender of his weapon, should he fail to use it.

The kitchen became very quiet as they waited for his reply. The men had no doubt what it would be. They thought him to be unarmed. They were between him and the door, and the women were on his hands. He appeared to have no choice. But the women saw more. They saw where his hand was, and they knew what his pocket held.

Eleanor made no sign. It was for Franklin to do as he would. She was alert to follow his cue.

Gwen reacted differently. She was disposed to think that they had come to a good place, and she felt that an appeal to force would be a foolish thing. She said lightly:

"We mayn't be able to fight, Master God's-Truth, but you'd be surprised if you saw us run." She looked at the ageing Abel, and at Ehud—well, he couldn't run like that, or she'd have been less certain of him—and added, "We'll give you ten yards start, and race you to the boat if you like."

Michael looked at her with some attention, but did not accept the challenge. Eleanor was the next to speak. She judged accurately that Franklin, if he had had a thought of resistance, had let it go. If they were to consent, it could not be too quickly nor too graciously done. It would come best from her. Seeing that, she saw also that the alternative would have been an ignoble thing. It was their first duty to aid this girl, so absurdly trapped in the bigotry of those among whom she lived.

"I don't think," she said, addressing herself to Michael as though ignoring the others that the room held, "we ought to think of going till we've seen your daughter out of this trouble. You can count on us for that."

It was shrewdly thought, and became sincerity as the words were spoken. It was alliance, not surrender.

Michael God's-Truth answered with a grave formality. "Mistress, I thank you, as my daughter will also." His eyes continued to dwell on Eleanor as he added, "It will be better that you do not stay here. You should come to my own dwelling while it is yet dawn. We must give thought to this, before any know you are here. I have more chambers than Abel, and Ehud must remain."

That, at least, was certain. Paradise had been busy in ministering to the wounded man, and his arm was now in a neat sling, but he sat half-conscious of the scene around him, aware only of a shoulder that throbbed hotly, and determination that he would not pass into an ignominious oblivion.

Gwen said: "He oughtn't to be sitting there." And then: "But he'll have a good nurse."

Michael, who was not given to frequent levity, smiled slightly at that. "Now if it were Noah...." he said, looking hard at the girl, who blushed vividly. Gwen guessed that Noah was his other son. She felt less reluctant to leave as she saw that blush, less unwilling that the wounded man should be in Paradise's charge. She thought, being accustomed to an unsentimental self-analysis, "What a fool I am!" She said, "There are quite a lot of things we shall have to get from the *Blanche*, if we're going to be away more than a day. We really must. If we're going to do everything before sunrise, we'd better go now." Eleanor agreed about that.

Master God's-Truth made no objection. He seemed to have taken Eleanor's word as a pledge which would not be broken. He had another reason for thinking that they would not easily escape, but, in fact, he was a good judge of men, and though these people were strange to him, he was confident that he was not being deceived.

Yet memory stirred of a precaution that he had resolved to take. It was a tribute to the personalities of these strangers that he had almost overlooked it. He asked: "The evidence that you give at my daughter's trial, you will answer its truth by the living God, and as you hope for the salvation of your immortal souls? *You will swear it upon the Book?*"

79

"Yes," Franklin answered, surprised at the solemn intensity with which the question was put, and the earnestness of the probing gaze that was fixed upon him. "Yes, of course."

Michael God's-Truth saw that, though Franklin might have been surprised at the sudden question, he had not been startled, nor had he flinched from reply. At least they were not fiends come in this guise to ruin him, either on earth or eternally. Franklin thought nothing more of the question. Had he understood it, he would have known more of the dark places of the mind from which it came. He was more alert to the remark that followed. Master God's-Truth's eyes, now that he was relieved from his superstitious doubt, dwelt on Eleanor for a time, and then moved to Gwen, as he said, not rudely, because unconscious of offence. "You say that they are un-wedded? Well, you have had your chance. It may be matter to mend."

None of them gave any response to that. They may have thought what they would, but they gave no sign that they heard. They walked on in silence.

CHAPTER XXII.

ELEANOR said: "This is the tree. I am sure of that." So were they all. That was the tree to which the *Blanche* had been tied, and it was not there. It was not tied to any of the orchard trees. It was not in sight.

They had all come down together to the water's edge. All except Ehud, and Paradise who was helping him to the bed to which he should have gone some hours earlier. They had been joined by Noah and the three servants.

Franklin looked at these men with a natural suspicion. They seemed genuinely surprised, and yet neither annoyed nor alarmed. If it were their real fear that their country should be reported to the outer world, then the going of the boat should have disturbed them equally whether it contained one or four. He was unwilling to sus-pect treachery, yet it had a queer look. There was also the question of whether Bunford had lost his nerve and fled. How would they be placed then?

Eleanor spoke confidently about that. "Bunny wouldn't slip off and leave us here. He'd sulk and grumble and stay." Franklin was inclined to the same opinion, but there was the fact of the missing boat. Suppose he had been misled by some circumstance into think-ing that they were dead, what else could he do but flee?

Michael read something of these thoughts, and spoke in a way which relieved a part at least of their fears, though it gave them a new warning that they had come to a place that might not be easy to leave. He turned to Eleanor, by whose side he had kept as they walked down the orchard path.

"I think you'll find that it has gone but a short way. I can tell you that it has not gone by the way it came, for I have had the river barrier repaired during the night, so that nothing should float down and be lost." He led the way up the river-bank. They came to a field of barley-stubble. It rose somewhat, so that a place came at which they could see up the river for half-a-mile, or perhaps more. After that, the banks were wooded, with groves of oak on both sides which had not yet shed their leaves.

"He may have gone under the trees," Eleanor suggested. She was not willing to believe that he would have left her thus.

Michael looked annoyed and perturbed. He said, "We cannot go on longer, not knowing how far it may be. I will have search made." He told his son to follow the river till he should find the *Blanche*. "It will be well," he said, "that he lie close under the trees. I would not have this thing known till I have thought more."

Franklin said, "He had better be careful how he approaches. We've had shooting enough."

"He'd better wave something white," Eleanor added. "And I'll write a note. That will be the surest way." She took a page from a pocket-diary, and pencilled: "We are among friends. Stay with the boat, and let us know where you are." She would not ask him to leave the *Blanche*, for it to be overhauled by these people more likely than not. Bunford would be most useful if he stayed where he was.

So they turned from the river-bank, and took the five-mile walk that led them to Master God's-Truth's house.

CHAPTER XXIII.

PATIENCE GOD'S-TRUTH was a woman of a different type from Paradise Trustwell. She had more of the physical and intellectual attributes of her father and brothers than of the small blonde woman who had given her birth. For Margaret God's-Truth had found sufficient mental occupation in her household cares. She knew her catechism, and went to meeting-house with exemplary regularity, but, beyond that, she left religion to men. Her daughter was of another mind. She had a tall, rather angular body, and a harsh-featured face, which became attractive only when it was animated by a spirit of unusual intellectual nobility. Patience was a woman of strong passions, most of which were held down with an iron will, but the strongest was the desire for knowledge, to reach truth, and to understand it.

Her channels of knowledge were the Hebrew literature of many centuries, which she had been taught to consider a single book, and a small collection of others of various types which had been the property of the seventy-six persons who had sailed from England three centuries ago, all of which had passed into the possession of Gabriel God's-Truth, and to his descendants after him. Some of them were of a somewhat incongruous character, and their existence was not generally known. The reading of these books may have helped her to a wider outlook, a more balanced judgment, than she would otherwise have gained, but she owed most to herself. Her occupation was the transcribing of parts of the Bible, for which there was a demand. The settlement had begun with many more of these books than there were men and women left alive to read them. But that was long ago. The people had increased, and the books had become old. Copies of favourite passages on goatskin parchment would bring a high price in whatever else of value the settlement held. One of the old books had a crudely-illuminated frontispiece, and Patience had stirred the settlement from end to end, with indifferent success, to devise colours which would enable her to illuminate her work in the same way, with the goat's-hair pencils with which she worked.

All this would have been well, and consistent with the standards of life and conduct for which Michael God's-Truth's family had an established reputation. But Patience, disadvantaged by circumstance as she was, had an independent mind. Gradually, unconsciously, it deviated in many ways from the orthodoxy of those around her.

There had been many arguments within the household, concerning which her father, sometimes stern in rebuke, sometimes willing to concede a private possibility, had warned her that such speculations must not be heard beyond the tolerance of his own roof.

She had never really believed in the destruction of the great world beyond the ice, the world from which her fathers came. She had always been aware of the political motive which underlay the suggestion. But she had not felt very keenly about it until, one day a few weeks ago, she had been transcribing the text, *I do set my bow in the clouds*, and looking up she had seen a rainbow across the blackness of an eastern storm. As she had looked, she had realized, not for the first time, the gulf which lay between the idealism of

Christianity, or even of the earlier Hebrew faith at its nobler moments, and the sombre religion which she had been trained to practise. She saw, with a convincing clarity, that the world was something much more, perhaps much greater, than these people of whom she came. She did not believe that it had been destroyed because their fathers had left it. It was an absurdity of egotism. And seeing this so clearly, she had said it to Mercy Pettifer, and to others with whom they were at the time, and not merely said it as a vague doubt, a casual speculation, but with the intonation of passionate conviction.

Coming from such a source, from one of Michael God's-Truth's family, and one who was of the intellectual reputation that Patience held, it was a thing which the Elders could not ignore. And there were those among them who had no wish to ignore it.

Patience had been challenged to make public recantation, and had refused to do so. She had out-argued her accusers in a way which would not easily be forgiven. But there was a fact that no argument could alter. The destruction of the world that the saints had left had ceased to be a matter of private judgment. It was a part of the church's creed. Was the heresy to be allowed to spread, and the hot dust of Hell to fall once more—to fall, and, perhaps, not to stop?

It was proposed that a day be set to inquire into this heresy of Patience God's-Truth, and the Elders were unanimous in assent, only her father, as their President, not recording his vote. She was to be tried, and, if found guilty, subjected to such punishment as might be considered adequate to avert the wrath of God. And such punishment was not likely to err on the side of mercy. It is always best to make sure.

But in the meantime she was under no restraint. That was not merely because she was not of a temper that would fail to meet her accusers: there was nowhere for her to go. Next to immediate death, the severest sentence that the Elders could pass upon her was that she should be expelled from the community. Indeed, it would be to condemn her to a death as certain and almost as swift, now that the days were shortening toward the winter night.

Where could she go? To the south there were the great hills, of which the heights were already frozen on their northern side. To cross their summits was to come upon the hotter slopes, where the Anabaptists dwelt in the caves, and which looked down upon the pits of Hell. If she could endure such a life, it was unlikely that they would receive her. Whatever they may first have been, they had become to her people savage, only semi-human, already tainted in mind and body by the fierce heat of the hell to which they would surely go.

To northward? To go once more toward the world that her fathers left? It would be to traverse, it might be, a thousand miles of the great tableland of glacier and frozen snow through the terrors of the Antarctic night. A thousand miles? It would be a feat of endurance to do ten. And at last what would there be but the barren frozen coast, with the frozen ocean beyond?

Westward there were lower hills that led at last to the level of the great ice field by which her fathers came.

Eastward, there was more of the valley than had been peopled yet. Much more. But even there, there could be no life when the winter darkness fell.

No. She was quite sure to stay in her father's house till the day of trial should come.

CHAPTER XXIV.

MICHAEL GOD'S-TRUTH led his guests by narrow beaten paths between fields that might have carried the aftermath of an English autumn, but that there were no dividing hedges, and that the soil was of a dark-brown and very powdery kind. There were no hedges, for there was nothing to keep out but the goats, and it had been found the simplest way to construct one single continuous barrier between the cultivated ground and the foothills on which they fed.

But the crops were of English kinds, and the weeds of a hundred familiar growths, the seeds of which had been mixed inevitably with those of the many cereals, herbs, and vegetables that the first colonists had brought. There had even been some young beech trees at one time, but they had never thrived, and had died during a winter of exceptional severity. There were some straggling hollies, and the oaks were everywhere. They grew low and broad, as though reluctant to rise too far into the icy winter air.

Beyond the cultivated land, on the lower slopes where the goats fed, coarse grasses and some of the hardier herbs had established themselves, and grew in a rank profusion for their short season beneath the unsetting summer sun. When the light died, the goats would be gathered in, and fed till the spring returned.

To his visitors, Michael God's-Truth's house was of a surprising size. It looked larger for being a one-storied building, with thick walls, partly of oak, and partly of rough stone.

There was a reason for this size, for here must be contained his own family, his three servants and their families, with food and fuel and all they valued that the cold would injure, for four months of every year. Here they must live through the long darkness, only venturing out, if at all, on the Sabbath day if there were some assurance of quiet weather, and the snowdrifts were not too deep, to the Suffolk meeting-house where Michael presided over the hundred and thirty people who inhabited Suffolk County, of which he was the preaching Elder.

The house stretched straight and long, with the apartments of his family in the centre, those of his dependents at one end, and the stores at the other, terminating in a stoutly built winter shelter for the poultry, which were the only livestock, except the goats, which the community possessed.

Beyond the stores were the tanning-yards, of which industry Michael claimed the monopoly. More than a third of the community were descendants of Gabriel God's-Truth on the male side, and all were more or less of his blood, but Michael was his direct heir. The three original acorns had been Gabriel's property. Michael did not claim every oak tree, but he claimed monopoly of the oak bark tanning which was one of the most important industries of the settlement. His fathers had fought out this contention in bitter controversy, in which many intrigues of conflicting interests had played their parts. In Michael's lifetime it had become a settled thing. And yet, if we were to turn aside to analyse the causes which had envenomed the accusation against Patience God's-Truth, we might find some of their strongest roots in the old-standing resentment of this monopoly.

They met no one at that early hour, on field paths which were no thoroughfare at any time, and Michael dismissed his servants to their daily tasks, with an injunction that no word was to get loose regarding the coming of the strangers, on the penalty of immediate expulsion from his house and protection—a threat too serious, in view of the organization of the community, to admit any doubt that his order would be obeyed.

He led them into a low-ceiled room furnished in heavy polished oak of a massive austerity. It was curiously reminiscent, in spite of some changes of design, of the Elizabethan tradition from which it derived. But it was something other than that. It was without vulgarity, but without welcome also. Bare and hard, it offered no compromise and no comfort. Coming from a civilization which may be past its flower, a world of evasion and flexibility, they felt a vague disquiet in the unbending bareness of the shadowed room.

They were presented to Mistress God's-Truth, and saw a small pale woman, whose blonde hair made little emphasis of the bleaching of age. She met these invaders from another world with a slight flutter of curiosity. She looked at the women's clothes, and a faint disfavour changed the lines of her mouth. Then her mind lapsed to the routines of hospitality. There would be two rooms to prepare. Her daughter Patience would wish to meet them. She went out.

Later, when she had realized what their coming might mean to her own child, they found her friendly enough in a cold way, but difficult, being without imagination, and of a dense stupidity if taken outside the radius of her experience or immediate interests. But she had little influence on the course of events at this time, except in negative ways.

They were left alone for a few minutes when she went out. Michael was with his daughter, telling her of the supernatural aid (as it might seem) that the night had brought. Before she came in to meet them, they had time to look round the room. Bare though it was, it had ornaments of a kind in the ancient arms which hung around its walls. A couple of hackbuts, kept polished, but looking the idle things that they were. Back and breast pieces also, and steel caps, as highly polished, but having a subtle difference, as though still in use. A couple of seamen's pikes, also looking as though they were not beyond the experiences of active service.

More interesting, there were a number of faded drawings around the walls. Three were of nautical subjects, two showing a high-pooped brig, which might very probably be the vessel which had brought Gabriel God's-Truth there. One, less successfully, attempted a memory of English woodland, perhaps before the first oak tree grew in the new land. Another, appearing to be by a different hand, and showing some vigour of execution, represented a regiment of Cavalier horsemen breaking before an Ironside charge. In the foreground two men fought. The Roundhead, leaning forward on his horse's neck, with hot relentless eyes on his opponent's face, made a fierce thrust, which passed the guard of the Cavalier's sword, and was sliding upward toward his throat. There was no doubt of what that picture was meant to be. *Richard God's-Truth on Naseby Field* was written beneath it, in a scrawl which was not probably in the artist's hand.

The drawing was one which might have been hanging without significance on any English wall, but as Franklin gazed at it here he felt the consciousness of a sinister warning, such as he had felt before and thrown aside, as he had gazed into Abel Trustwell's half-blinded eyes. To these self-exiled isolated people, things which were distant from the England of today were still alive and near. Was he Cavalier, they might ask, or Roundhead? Papist or Anglican or of the Saints of God?

Would it be the more natural that they should look upon him as friend or foe? Come from the land from which their fathers had fled, perhaps foe would be the more likely word. They would stir to a natural fear that if these unwelcome guests should be allowed to return, it would be the end of the isolation on which they considered that their freedom was based. How would they react to such fear? He remembered the fierce bigotries which had borne hateful fruit in New England villages, when such men as these, embittered by previous persecution, had found the power in their own hands. Did they burn for witchcrafts here? Even the engines of the *Blanche* might be sufficient evidence that they were leagued with supernatural powers. They might undo themselves at any moment by a heedless innocent word. And they were to be witnesses to prove that an accepted article of the religion of these people was a godless lie!

As he stood silent, gazing at the picture of civil bloodshed with these thoughts in his mind, and the two women beside him, Patience God's-Truth entered the room. Her eyes went to the picture. As they turned at her approach, she said with a simple directness, as though she might have known them from childhood: "Have you still the like in your land? To dwell among beasts of such a size, and to subdue them to your own use. It must be a strange world to see. And there are those that kill you if you go far into hills or trees?"

Gwen's eyes met hers, and she answered with an apparent readiness. "Oh, yes. We have horses still, but not so many as we did. We don't use them so much now. There have been many changes."

Franklin realized that she too was on her guard, saying no more than she need...feeling her way. Patience asked: "And the Men of Blood, sit they in the Seats of the Mighty still?"

What should they answer to that?

Eleanor, more at ease, more self-confident than her companions, whether by courage or obtuseness, gave a smiling reply. "They don't bother about our blood now. They think our money's more use." It turned the query aside more successfully than an explicit answer would have been likely to do.

Patience said: "There is much of which I would learn, but you should rest first. And there is food to be served. Shall we talk at a later hour?"

She went out again, and Gwen said: "I'm not exactly dying for the next meal. Do they eat all the time here?"

"We might do worse," Franklin answered. "The food's good."

"And the talk isn't quite so sure? Yes, I see what you mean. We've got to learn to open our mouths without putting our feet into them. And that's going to be a full-time job, if you ask me. What *has* become of the Men of Blood? Are they all dead, or is the Pope, or the Archbishop of Canterbury, carrying on the old firm still? We'd better the same."

CHAPTER XXV.

THE trial of Patience God's-Truth was to be held in three days' time. She had been given the intervening period in which to provide proof of her assertion, if she were able to do so. Time also, some may have hoped, which would be sufficient to change her resolution, and lead to a recantation which would mitigate the severity of the sentence which must be passed upon her. It had not seriously occurred to anyone that she could use it to her own profit in obtaining such evidence. It seemed an impossible thing.

During these three days, Franklin and the two women stayed in the house, being seen of none. Bunford had been located under the oaks at the waterside, as had been expected. An exchange of letters had resulted in his agreeing to remain in concealment there for the next four days.

In the house, it was a time of much talk. Franklin learnt many things about the modes of life and habits of thought of their new acquaintances, and he told much to Patience of the doings of the world he had left. But he avoided much that would have repelled or puzzled, leading the conversation to the larger outlines of history, to domestic habits, and to the development of inventions, such as high explosives, the beginnings of which were in her own tradition, and would not therefore be likely to take on a garb of supernatural terror. He saw always the danger that they might be charged on their own confessions with having come from a world that was possessed by demonic powers. If that were so, by whom would they have been sent so opportunely? The devil protects his own.

Might it not even be argued that they were fiends disguised to support a lying tale of a world that had no existence? Betraying themselves by the nightmare quality of the only kind of world of which a fiend could dream?

He spoke less with Michael, who showed little desire to engage him in conversation. He was out much of the time. When he was in the house, he had a look of preoccupation which was generally respected. Franklin observed that others seldom spoke to the master of that house, unless he first spoke to them. He noticed that Michael was more inclined to commence conversation with Eleanor, and, indeed, did so at every favourable opportunity. His eyes followed her with a sombre intentness. Had not the age and gravity of the man, joined to the fact that he was married already, and of a stern religious morality, rendered the idea fantastical, he would have thought that Michael was falling in love with the rich beauty of his alien guest. He remembered that remark as they had left Abel Trustwell's house: "It may be matter to mend," and a fierce unreasoning jealousy stirred within him—but no, it was absurd!

And then, on the third day, he learnt something from Patience which put a fresh doubt into his mind.

She had been telling him of the personalities of the first comers, and had mentioned the fact that almost everyone in the settlement was descended either from Gabriel God's-Truth or Ebenezer Clouts-clad. (The few exceptions arose from the fact that when the Anabaptists had been expelled, two of the children of Elisha Trustwell had elected to remain, and repudiated their father's heresy.) But she had distinguished between the descendants of the four women who had landed from the brig, so that Gwen had interposed with natural question:

"But whom did Hospitality marry?"

"Hospitality," Patience answered, "had been the wife of the mate, a man named Thomas Carvall, who died during the last year in the ice. It is said that he was one of the last to die. It was Hospitality's child who was brought alive from the ship. You may think by that that there should be Carvalls too, but he was killed when a young man in a quarrel. It is an evil tale, which is known of few, showing that Satan hath power, even over those who would flee from the dwellings of the unrighteous. It is best unsaid.

"But Hospitality, being widowed as I have told, was married to Gabriel God's-Truth, he thus having two wives, after the fashion of the patriarchs, as was seen to be the purpose of God, or He had not willed that there should be four women and but three men who survived the hardships of the way."

"Does this patriarchal custom still prevail?" Franklin asked, being most interested in the present position which they had to face.

"How did they decide that she should be Gabriel's wife?" Gwen enquired at the same moment, being more interested in the personalities of the suggested drama.

"No. Not now," Patience answered. And then to Gwen, "It was agreed by a majority, after a time of prayer, only Ebenezer Clouts-clad standing out, and, it is said, proposing that it should have been decided profanely on a cast of dice, or that they should have fought it out, which had been of a clear folly, as well as guilt, for, if one were killed, the evil (if such it were) had been worse than it then was."

"But there is no such custom now?" Franklin persisted.

"No. There could be no cause, and we hold such a practice to be an unchristian thing. It is the law that all may marry after their twentieth year, being of good health and of habits of work, and they may wed those of their own choice, except that a God's-Truth may not marry one of that name, nor a Trustwell or a Cloutsclad the like, except that there be no better choice, or that they will wait for two years. Yet, save with the Trustwells, this law is not over-strictly held. But they, being but few, have no cause to marry among themselves, and it is said that by marriages which are between themselves and us the children are of a hardier kind."

She added: "There is none unmarried in Suffolk County, king of a ripe age, except Noah and Ehud, and Paradise will have one of them, that is Noah, as I think." And then, as she remembered the exception which must be plain to their own eyes, she added steadily, "Except myself, who am sought of none."

CHAPTER XXVI.

THE whole area of the Puritan settlement was not more than sixty square miles, and this was not of a compact shape, but rather in that of an inverted L, the one strip facing the southern slope of the northern mountains, where the goats were fed in the summer months, and the other extending along the right bank of the warm river by which the four invaders had entered this secluded Eden.

The area might have been larger, had not the settlers been obliged to resort to intensive cultivation, whether they would or not, because, though there had been ploughs on the ship, there had been no horses to draw them, and they must break the soil with pick and spade, of which there had been good store, and in these days there was some working in metals, and new ones were made which were good enough, though of a rough kind.

The area would have been even less than it was, but that the ground was of an uneven fertility, and, there being no lack of choice, men avoided the shallower soils, leaving between their cultivated patches fallow wastes on which the rank weeds grew, and which were burned down when the weather allowed, before they could scatter seed.

The cultivation was, indeed, more of the nature of gardening than farming, except for some communal meadows which were mown to provide goat-fodder for the winter days.

The whole area was divided into eight counties, each having its own meeting-house, around which groups of dwellings had grown, inhabited by those who had developed trades other than agriculture, and who chose positions where their customers would come to them most easily.

The meeting-house in Suffolk County was not more than four miles from Michael God's-Truth's dwelling, and it was here on the third day (being Monday) that the trial of Patience God's-Truth was to take place. Michael had won his point over that, after some bitterness of contention, for it was a clear right, and so she would be tried among those to whom she was known, and among whom there was a majority of those of her own blood.

But even though this should obtain a more friendly atmosphere, it could make little difference to the result, for the judgment rested with the twelve Elders—the preaching Elders of the eight meeting houses, and the four lay Elders who had control of various phases of the civil life of the community—and from that verdict there could be no appeal, and there would be few to whom the idea of resistance would be likely to come, even as a possible thing.

On the day preceding the trial, being the Sabbath, Michael God's-Truth and his household attended the meeting-house, and he preached as usual. He chose the text which he had quoted a few days earlier, and which may then have been in his mind for this occasion. *The gates of Hell shall not prevail against it*. He was eloquent upon the Divine protection which had led the faithful to this remote and seeming repellent place, where the Church of His Elect might rest secure under the shadow of the very fires of Hell.

It was an orthodox sermon. No one could question that Michael would give no opportunity for any to doubt his fitness to sit in the seat of Judgment which would decide his daughter's fate. Indeed, no one, even in his own household, knew what he really thought, or what his attitude at the trial would be.

It might be that he would set his public duty, the sacredness of religious obligation, before his private affection, and be the first to condemn. It might be that his attitude was controlled by the resolution that no one should question his own orthodoxy, and that, through that attitude, he would have the more innocence in advocating her innocence; or he might regard her condemnation as certain, and think only to mitigate the penalty which would be inflicted upon her. No one knew.

Before the coming of the strangers, he had maintained this inscrutable attitude, and in the last days he had allowed no change to appear, beyond such as might be inferred, by the few who knew it, from the fact that he had received them into his house and concealed their presence.

Even Patience, sitting in the front seat with her mother and Noah—for she would have judged it cowardice not to be there, and her absence might have been brought against her as proof of Satanic possession on the next day—could not tell his thoughts as he announced that, *At a full Session of Elders, tomorrow, Monday, being the ninth day of March, 1931, at the noon hour, at this meeting-house in Suffolk County, Patience God's-Truth, spinster, being of full age, will be called to show in what manner, if at all, she can defend the accusation of schism and heresy, which, at the mouths of seven witnesses, will be brought against her; and to hear the judgment of the Elders, either to acquit or condemn, with or without penalty, they sitting in solemn and final judgment as the elect servants of God.*

The congregation listened with an expressionless gravity. Talk there must have been behind the walls of many houses, but there was little disposition to gossip at the meeting-house door over the approaching trial. They separated in a sober silence.

There might have been a similar reticence at the midday meal which followed the return of Michael God's-Truth and his household to his own roof, all the more, perhaps, because of the presence of their three guests, had not Ehud entered as the meal began. He had his arm in Paradise's sling, and was very pale, but walking firmly enough; and whether by accident or design, he found a place next to Gwen, from which position, after a few remarks had been exchanged with her of a trivial kind, he looked up to the head of the table, where his father sat, and said bluntly, "I came to know what we're to do if there's any trouble tomorrow."

Michael checked an exclamation of anger. He sat silent for a moment, stroking his beard. Then he answered: "You are free to be present if you will. That is the law. There may attend as many as there are seats to bear. Beyond that, you have no duties at all."

"But what if things go the wrong way?"

"It is not to be lightly thought. The Elders will be gathered in judgment, and so assembled they are of the counsel of God."

"Old Goat's-Beard?"

"It is an evil thing to speak of dignitaries thus. Malachi Trustwell is a man incorruptible, who would give judgment though it were against those of his own household, esteeming himself to be as the mouthpiece of God."

The fact was that Michael was angered that his younger son should try to force his hand in this public manner. For he was hardly sure of his own mind, and while he might be reluctant to see his daughter condemned to any serious penalty, and had welcomed the coming of these almost miraculous witnesses on her behalf, yet he was not insensible to the difficulty in which the Elders were placed, nor indifferent to the effect which his daughter's acquittal must have upon the prestige and organization by which the community was held together. He was, in fact, watching the position with a mind which was at once bold and cautious, waiting for the event to shape itself further, and alert for any chance which he could deflect to his daughter's advantage. But he saw that any talk which challenged the authority of the Elders beforehand, and suggestion that their judgment might be resisted, might increase the probability of condemnation, and array many who were friendly or indifferent into an active hostility.

Ehud felt differently. He was young, impetuous, and one over whose mind the religion which was so deeply rooted among his fellows had never had more than a superficial influence. He had barely observed its rituals, and sometimes with an open impatience. He was too indifferent to be regarded, like his sister, as a serious heretic, but there were few who would have engaged in political resistance to the Church's authority with as untroubled a conscience, and none who would have an equal influence in inciting such opposition among the younger and more headstrong members of the God's-Truth clan.

He was deeply attached to his sister, admiring her intellectual attainments without any desire to emulate them. He did not doubt that she was right in her present difference with her spiritual superiors, and had had little doubt, till the strangers came, that the Elders would wrongfully condemn her to some serious penalty. His mind had been seething with plans for her protection or vindication.

As he had lain impatiently nursing his wound under Paradise's gentle supervision, he had felt that the coming of the strangers had proved at once his sister's innocence and the Church's folly; but he had been less sure that the Elders would be prepared to admit their error. He saw also that to condemn her would involve repudiation of her witnesses also. What would follow from that? His mind turned from his sister's peril to the thought of a vivid dark-eyed face, to a voice that was soft and yet confident of itself, to a strangely-accented speech which was good to hear, to a woman seductively different from those that he had known till then. In short, to a girl that he had loved at the first sight, and that he would do much to win. Curse that wound! If those old hypocrites—! Everyone knew why they had pretended that there was no world beyond the ice. It might become a case to be argued with quarter-staves and swords. Curse that wound again! Well, it was time to know what his father meant to do. After all, he was the presiding Elder. And so he was here. And the girl of his two days' dream was beside him now. A hundred times more alluring than he had recalled her to be—and looking at him, he felt, with no unfriendly eyes.

Gwen's eyes were friendly enough. She liked the warmth of this championship, and may have guessed that it was not entirely a brotherly affection that had stirred its eagerness, but of its wisdom she was less sure.

She might be attracted by the physique of the man beside her, not less alluring for the pallor which had reduced the somewhat florid handsomeness of the God's-Truth pattern; she might respond to the admiration which was in every glance that he gave her, but it did not blind her to the possibility that the best brains in the room might not be in his head. She was considering the wisdom of a restraining word when Patience interposed with the same purpose.

"With the witnesses who have so strangely come to my help, I think not that we should doubt what the result will be. And, Ehud, we can trust our father to act wisely. Besides, I don't want any trouble about this."

She, too, saw clearly that the Elders could not acquit her without rejecting an article of their church, which had been issued with an assertion of Divine authority. When she had spoken first, it had been with the uncalculated purpose of expressing a truth that had become evident to her. Now she was inclined to shrink from the possible consequences—not to herself only—of the storm that her words had raised. She was not the first who had given a new truth to the world and seen cause to doubt its wisdom, when it was too late to recall it.

Franklin watched silently, reading the scene well enough, and judging that their position was even more precarious than he had already feared.

Eleanor, unperturbed, was talking to Noah with an air of slightly condescending graciousness, in a voice which did not reach across the table. Now and then her hands would move in some explanatory gesture, as though to help words which were inadequate for description. Noah was looking puzzled at what he heard.

"The session," Michael God's-Truth said, "will commence at noon, to the end that those who come by a far way may return ere the light shall fail. Speech is brief at such an issue as this, for it is held that we need but the facts, and that judgment should then be given unhindered by the clash of contentious words." ("That is to say," Franklin thought, "the Elders have found it best not to argue in public," but he had the sense to keep it unspoken.) "I know not how it may be now that there is your witness to call, but it was counted that it would be over by the second hour."

"Perhaps, if they called us first—" Eleanor suggested hopefully.

"The accusation must first be heard. I would that you reach the witness-room being seen of none. I had thought that you might go at an early hour, but it is the greater risk. There will be few or none who will come after the hour. They would not think to find space. It will be better that you come at a later time. You shall be led by a quiet way."

Franklin could make no objection to this. He did not mind being late, though the proceedings might be of some interest to anyone who could look on from a safe place. He would have been willing not to have been going at all. So he said when they were left to themselves.

Eleanor replied that he worried beyond any cause that she could see.

He said it would be different if he were alone. He was worried for them.

"We're not babes in arms," she replied, with some impatience. "We've done well enough alone before now. You make us feel afraid to go anywhere."

He felt annoyed in turn, conscious that it would have been more to his advantage in her eyes to assume the heroic attitude. And they had got to go through it, whether they might like it or not. There are positions in which sincerity may be dearly sold at a low price. He answered lightly: "Oh, we shall do all right, I expect, even though I am making a third. It's only that bigotry's always a dangerous thing. It's rather a new experience to people of our time. A kind of religious mania on a large scale."

"Yes," she said, her mind easily diverted from their own position to the more abstract problem, "the trouble is that we don't believe anything. Not really *believe*."

"I don't know whether trouble's the right word. It's the difference certainly. It just made me wish I were a bit clearer about the way back to the boat, if we should feel that we were outstaying our welcome."

"You needn't worry about that," Gwen said. "Ehud knows where it is."

"Is that going to help us?"

"Yes. He'll be sitting close to the witness-stand. He says, If they begin saying much about sons of Belial or Apollyon, or Beelzebub, or anything else that sounds as though they're not appreciating us at our true worth, we'd better make tracks for the door we've come through, which will be behind our backs, and he'll come the same way. And he says, if you've got six bullets, don't leave old Goat's-Beard off the list, even if he costs two."

"Then you told him I was armed?"

"Yes. Of course. I put him wise, in the language he'd be using himself if the *Morning Star* hadn't got a bit mixed, and decided it ought to set in the south."

"You're sure it was a wise thing to do?"

"I shan't lose any sleep over that. If you can't see that on our side...."

"There are possible questions of discretion, as well as loyalty. You seem to have found time to say a good deal."

"Oh, we said more than that. Quite a lot." Amusement at the recollection stirred in eyes and lips, but she offered no further word as to what those additional confidences had been.

CHAPTER XXVII.

WHEN the meeting-house in Suffolk County was built, the timber of the *Morning Star* had been long exhausted—it was all that had been available for a generation—and there was not an inch of wood, nor a bent nail, that had not been utilized from that stranded wreck. It had not been used as a starving wolf picks bones, for the bones themselves had been cleared away to the last fragment of metal or wood, the last strand of rope, till the place where it had grounded was as bare as though it had never been.

But the meeting-house of Suffolk County was built late. It was all of native oak, no stone having been used, and though it was without ornamentation, it had the dignity of solid simple strength, and of a single material. They had occasion to remark again that the things that these people did might be without allure, but they were without vulgarity. They claimed respect, though liking might be a more doubtful word.

That was from an outside view. They were led into a room which was normally the private vestry of Michael God's-Truth, but which was now occupied by Paradise Trustwell and another girl, Mercy Pettifer, whom they had not seen before, and who shrank with an astounded fear at the sight of these strangers, outlandish in dress and speech and come from she knew not where. They judged that these were the last of the seven witnesses, and that the other five had been called already.

As they were only a quarter of an hour after the time at which the proceedings were to commence, it seemed that the witnesses must have been dealt with as expeditiously as Michael had anticipated, and this was confirmed by the strange girl being called almost immediately, and Paradise Trustwell a few moments later.

Franklin supposed that his turn had come, but for some time he waited, while a murmur of voices sounded faintly through the heavy intervening door.

As the witnesses had gone in, he had caught an instant glimpse of benches crowded with sober-suited men and women, who watched the proceedings without interruption, but with a tense expectancy. He had seen no more, for he had promised that he would not expose himself to observation, but he gained an impression of humourless fanaticism that the Elders might be able to sway to their own will, by methods which doubtless would be familiar to them, being of the elementary science of the government of such a community. The door opened again, and a voice said: "Patience God's-Truth doth call her witnesses. Let him who is called Franklin Arden come forward." Feeling more as though he were himself an accused person than a witness to innocence, he stepped into the hall.

He saw an assembly of about three hundred people, men and women being about equal in number, crowding the ungalleried assembly-room. They were people of weather-beaten faces and toil-hardened hands, showing a general similarity of facial characteristics, as was natural from the inbreeding of centuries, and which was now intensified by the singleness of the feelings which possessed their minds.

There were surely individuals in that three hundred of every shade of temperament and variety of character, but as they gazed in a slow bewildered wonder at the unfamiliar and outlandish dress of the man who entered from the vestry door, they had a similarity of expression which, though from some of the baser impulses which degrade humanity, was yet of a sombre and perhaps sinister kind.

Franklin, entering with a resolution to retain his composure, and not be flurried by any manner of question into giving a hasty or foolish answer, looked around quietly at this assembly. Here and there he observed a girl of the candid comeliness of Paradise Trustwell, here and there a youth of whom he felt that he could make an easy friend, but there were few of the older people, either men or women, who did not have the same front of repellent fanaticism. They showed, at the best, the types of intellectual morbidity to which the human countenance settles when creeds of belief or codes of conduct have petrified in unadventurous minds.

He looked past them to where Patience God's-Truth sat solitary on the platform, a little below the Elders, on the side opposite to himself. She looked calm and self-reliant. He looked at the Elders, and was surprised to see that Michael was not in the high central chair. Surely as President....

Michael sat further to the right, among the row of the eleven Elders who supported the President on either hand.

That had been Michael's first surprise for the meeting; his first tactical move on his daughter's behalf; and it was one which was generally misinterpreted in a way which he had meant it to be.

The President had power in controlling the proceedings, which it might be thought that he would be unwilling to surrender, if he had come there to fight for his daughter's cause. Yet it could be understood that, if he regarded her condemnation as certain, he should not wish to be the one to pass sentence upon her.

But Michael knew that, be the talk what it might, it was votes that would decide the issue, and the President had no vote. That was their rule. The eleven voted, so that a tie was impossible. The President pronounced sentence only.

Michael knew that, of his seven colleagues among the preaching Elders, three would follow his own lead, and three others would almost certainly vote for condemnation. Among these last was Ebenezer Cloutsclad, the Vice-President, the eldest descendant of the original Ebenezer, a mild-mannered theologian, one who might be expected to control the proceedings with a careful equity, and might be merciful in imposition of penalty, but who had been most active in making the world's destruction an article of the church's faith, and would be intellectually incapable of condoning a heresy which denied its creed. By vacating the Presidential chair in his favour, Michael secured a majority of votes on his daughter's behalf among the preaching Elders, so that it was only necessary for the secular Elders to be equally divided to secure acquittal.

This had been his plan before the strangers came, and he saw no reason to alter it now. It was a manœuvre within his right, and was accepted without protest, even by Malachi Trustwell, who was the most likely to understand and resent its meaning.

After that, the proceedings had advanced rapidly. One by one the witnesses had been called, and had repeated the words of heresy which had been spoken before them. There was no custom of hired advocacy among these people, but Patience had the right to question the witnesses against her in any way that the President might not rule to be irrelevant. But she had asked one question only, the same to each witness, and it had always been answered in the same way:

"Said I this as one speaking lightly from a wanton mind, lacking reverence for the Church of God, or as one who speaks with sobriety, seeing a truth which should not be hid?"

It was a question which seemed foolish to many who heard it. It emphasised the deliberation of her guilt. It might make it more difficult for those who would have condoned the offence as a slight thing to continue to do so. Coming seven times, as it did, and each time drawing the reply that she had spoken in a sober and earnest way, it had the sound of a deliberate challenge of the Church's authority; a defiance, if not of God Himself, of the row of Elders sitting gravely impassive, who were the ultimate authority that these people knew.

When Paradise left the witness-stand, and stepped down to her six companions on the bench that had been reserved for their use, Patience would have risen to announce the calling of her own witnesses, but her father signalled to her to remain silent, and made the second effort which he had planned for her vindication. Should it succeed, it would avert the dangerous necessity of calling those witnesses from another world.

He said: "Before calling upon the accused for her defence, should we not consider, Master President, whether the accusation be well-founded according to our own law? We have listened patiently to the charge, which the accused does not deny, and the facts are without dispute. But these words, as we have now heard, dealt not with the foundations of our faith, or the salvation of the elect, but rather of a question of fact, of which we may say equally, whether God may have smitten the unbelievers, or reserved them for the doom of the Last Day, *Shall not the judge of all the earth do right?*"

The President inclined his head courteously in the speaker's direction as Michael commenced. He had the aspect of one who listens and weighs in an open and intent mind (he was, in fact, rather deaf, which he concealed with care), but at this point he lifted a thin hand of interruption. He could not have the proceedings delayed at this stage by anything like a general argument in the public hearing.

"Your motion is, Brother Michael?" he inquired courteously.

Michael had said as much as he expected to be able to do. He replied briefly: "I move that the words come not within the definition of heresy, and that the accusation is misconceived."

Malachi Trustwell; a small elderly man with malevolent eyes and a beard which explained Ehud's disrespectful nickname, began quickly: "As it is an article of our...," and was stayed by the President's uplifted hand.

"It is not a matter to debate, Brother Malachi. It is one on which each decides as his conscience guides, the facts being known to all." He paused a moment, seeing that it might be well that the issue should be avoided in this way, if it could be done with sufficient dignity. Then he turned to Patience. "If the accused will say that she spoke without due thought, and that she will submit her mind to the ruling of the Elders of the True Church," he suggested, in his quiet conciliatory voice, "it might be well that such submission be spoken before the vote on Brother Michael's motion be called."

So far as his influence or authority went, it was a clear offer of peace, and there were many hearers who thought that the drama which they had come to witness was being brought to a tame and early end, but Patience answered: "I am a humble member of the True Church, and will submit to it in all things that I may; but I cannot say that I spoke without due thought, who am more sure than I then was that God did not destroy the world when he guided our fathers here."

"That having been said," the President announced, in a voice which gave no sign of his thoughts, "I will call the vote."

The voting was by a simple and very secret method. Each of the Elders took two counters, a round and square, from small piles which were on the long table before them. Then a deep box was passed along the table into which each inserted his hand as it passed, and pressed one counter into the slotted centre of a smaller box that it contained, dropping the other into a kind of gutter which surrounded it. None could tell with which counter the vote was made.

The box came back to the President, who lifted out the smaller one which was within it. He shook out four round counters and seven square. He said: "The motion is lost. Patience God's-Truth, if you have any witnesses to call, they will now be heard."

Michael saw that his effort had failed. Only his three friends among the preaching Elders could have supported him. The secular vote must have been given solidly against the motion. Perhaps, after what Patience had said, it was not a surprising result.

CHAPTER XXVIII.

FRANKLIN stepped to the witness-stand. He was aware of the concentrated gaze of three hundred people, most of them in a stupor of astonishment. But the President gave no sign of any feeling. His face was inscrutable, and his voice had its usual quiet dignity, as he asked:

"Your name?"

"Franklin Arden."

"You will take this oath after me, holding up your right hand the while." The oath was taken.

"Now, Sister." The President leaned back, as he signed to Patience to examine her witness.

"Master Arden," she asked, "from whence come you?"

"From England."

"When left you that country?"

"I have lived there all my life, till last year."

"That is all I ask. I would call Mistress Gwen Collinson."

Franklin, glad that it should be over in so few words, would have stepped down to where Ehud indicated the vacant bench behind which he himself sat, but the President interposed.

"Wait," he said, in a tone of authority, though without discourtesy. "How long have you been in this land?"

"About three days."

The President turned to Patience, "Knew you of the coming of this man when you spoke the words which have brought you here?"

"No. I knew not that, till he came with others—it is three days since."

"That is well. It had been a levity beyond pardon.... Yet we need not speak of that. Though I see not that you are cleared. If it be three days since this man came, how may it be that no word hath gone forth? It is news that would travel fast."

"Because," she said boldly, "having been publicly charged, I would be cleared in the same way. Had it been common talk, it may be that we had not been here now. But I would have this man's testimony on oath, and I would be cleared by the verdict of those here."

The President made no comment on this answer, though he looked less than pleased. He said: "You have other witnesses of the party of this man?"

Franklin made haste to avoid the witness-stand. As he did so he observed that "Old Goat's Beard" was talking to the Elder next on his left with a whispered energy, which broke off as Gwen entered and took his place.

"Your name, Mistress?" the President asked.

"Gwendolen Collinson."

"Holding up your right hand, you will now take this oath."

Malachi Trustwell interposed.

"Mistress, how take you that oath?"

The question puzzled Gwen, and she answered cautiously, after a pause of thought, "With my right hand raised."

"I meant not that! Take you it in the peril of God, and knowing where you must stand at the Last Day?"

Did she know where she must stand at the Last Day? She felt that it would be an inopportune moment to engage in dialectic sophistries. She had the sense to say simply, "Yes."

The answer silenced Malachi for the moment. The impetuosity of the interrogation had, in fact, put his own words into her mouth, and there was no more to be said. The President signed to Patience to question her witness.

"Mistress Collinson, from what country do you come?"

"From England."

"It is a land which still endures?"

Gwen smiled confidently. "It was there last year."

The President was an honest man, and, apart from the prejudices of his theological bigotries, he was a good judge. Before the appearance of these alien witnesses, he had been prepared to condemn Patience God's-Truth and to inflict such penalty, even to death itself, as would assert the authority of the Church and avert the danger of a spreading heresy. But since he had heard Franklin's testimony, he had been considering the probability that the Church was in the wrong, and that it must be admitted in such a way as would be least harmful to its future authority. He was considering also—and the thought, in various forms, must have been in the minds of three-fourths of that silent, watchful audience—that the coming of these strangers might have other consequences, call for other enquiries, beside which this trial might seem a trivial thing.

Now, as Gwen answered, conviction came. From that moment he did not doubt that England was still there. But he sought confirmation in his own way.

"It is from England you come?"

"Not directly. We sailed from the Cape of Good Hope."

"The Cape of...?"

"It is the southern point of the African continent. We changed ships at that point."

"Know you New Amsterdam? Know you the lands of the New England, and those of the Spanish Main? How lie they by compass from this African port?"

"They lie west and northwest, the land which you call New England being the more northerly."

"It is true witness," he said honestly. He owned the crude charts which had been in the cabin of the *Morning Star*, and he knew more than any man there (except Franklin) of the conformation of the world which their ancestors had left.

"And is this—what call you the wider land?—this America"— Yes, that was the word on the chart. He recalled it now. It confirmed her evidence again—"Is it still a free refuge for the Saints of God?"

"Yes," she said, and Franklin, listening in some doubt of her reply, blessed her for the discreet monosyllable.

The President reminded himself that his question went beyond the scope of the enquiry on which he was now engaged. The Elders were strict on all points of procedure. It was by such etiquette that they maintained the dignity of office which had little spectacular assertion. He said: "That is enough."

And then to Patience. "Would you call further witness, or does your case rest?" His own judgment was that there was no need to hear any more evidence, but the votes were not his. She could call more if she would.

"I would call one more, and will then rest content," she answered. "Mistress D'Acre is the last witness I have."

"Let her be called," the President answered, and Eleanor entered the hall.

CHAPTER XXIX.

ELEANOR came in confidently. She was aware of her own beauty, and if any had told her that she was by far the loveliest thing, or at least woman, that the Antarctic held, she would have felt no gratitude for the mention of a fact so obvious. She knew that she had been equal to facing and overcoming more difficult, and certainly more menacing positions, both in Tibet and Arabia, than any which she supposed herself to be likely to be meeting here.

Her great wealth had eased the frictions of life, and given her an unconscious arrogance which might have become intolerable in one of inferior character, or without the charm of personality which renders forgiveness easy to grant. She knew that Franklin and Gwen were more concerned than herself about the possible reactions of these people among whom, and perhaps into whose power, they had fallen, and her own feelings had fluctuated in the same direction. But her dominant thought had been that they could contrive a greater comfort for the coming winter if they should stay here than would be possible in the wooden sheds which had been erected at the ocean-side. Her latest idea had been that Franklin and Bunford should go down and bring another boatload of their requirements. And it might include many things that these people would like to have. She saw herself distributing gifts. It was a pleasure which she often knew. Suppose she should promise them a shipload of many treasures next year? Horses, for instance. Horses ought to live here well enough. It was absurd that they could not plough. That they had nothing better for haulage than those little goat-sleds which had been shown to her, though she had not seen them in use.

As to this trial, if she had spoken her mind freely, she would have said that it was a silly business altogether, but not one about the result of which to worry, now that they would able to show its absurdity.

She had kept on the grey squirrel-coat which she had worn for the walk, for the waiting-room had been unwarmed, and what was comfortable enough for these people had been very cold to her. Warmly clad themselves, they sat in the unheated building without thought of the temperature. The real cold would come in the winter days. She came in still wearing the coat, but having opened it, so that it showed the perfect-fitting simplicity of the scarlet dress which she wore beneath it. The fur drew the women's eyes almost as much as the exotic beauty of the slender neck and small dark-gold head which rose from it. It was a style of beauty which they had not seen. They were a people of thicker build, of lighter hair, of less delicate features. But the fur was a wonder too. They did what was possible with the skins of goats and kids. Would it feel as soft as it looked? There were those who felt that such beauty must be an evil thing. They thought of the Scarlet Woman, who sits on the Seven Hills. Perhaps the dress helped them to that.

If there was admiration in many eyes, there was hostility also, and it did not lessen as she gave her name to the President's question in an easy manner, *Eleanor Blanche D'Acre*. It had a patrician, almost an insolent sound, however musically it might be spoken.

Franklin and Gwen had been self-possessed enough, had excited admiration and envy, as well as wonder in that silent three hundred who had gazed upon them, but there was a different feeling here. The other two might have been self-possessed, but they had taken the enquiry seriously. Subtly, Eleanor gave the impression to many who did not define it in their own thoughts that she regarded the whole proceedings with condescension, if not with levity. Bigotry could not easily be scourged with a worse whip.

Yet even Malachi Trustwell, surveying this scarlet vision from—where?—was silent while she took the oath with a graceful politeness rather than an appreciation of its solemnity, and it looked to Franklin as though things were going in the right way, after all (but Gwen knew better than that), as she answered Patience's first question, and then—just the little difference in the wording of the second, the little difference in the form of the reply.

"And when were you in that country last?"

"Last Christmas."

The answer meant little to most of those who heard it. They had no more than the vaguest ideas of the geography of the world which their fathers left, and their knowledge of ships was of a kindred quality. Folklore rather than fact. But the President had his charts. He, and others of the Elders, retained a more accurate tradition of that last voyage than was generally possessed. Ten weeks ago? It sounded an impossible thing.

"Mistress," he said, speaking without guile, "the witness which you now give should be of a careful truth, even in such matters as are not vital to the issue which we now try. Meant you not the Christmas of a year before, or is the time of that festival changed from the season when it was held of old?"

"I meant last Christmas…December…the twenty-fifth." And as she answered, she saw the natural astonishment that her reply might cause. With this realization came the memory of her companions' cautious attitude toward the ignorance of these people. She used the most natural weapon in her armoury, and one which would rarely fail, as she lifted her eyes to the President, and answered him with a personal intimacy, as though she honoured him with her private confidence. "I didn't want to leave until Christmas was over. We sailed on December the 28th."

Ebenezer Cloutsclad was, as had been observed before, a good judge of a truthful witness. He did not doubt that she was giving honest evidence, and he was acute enough to observe that it was not a point on which it was of any advantage to the accused that she should lie, but he was puzzled, and wished to clear the doubt in his own mind.

"How far is it," he asked, "from England to this land?"

Eleanor had to think. She supposed that they were now about as far as the South Pole, or within five hundred miles of that point. The circumference of the earth was—what was it? Thirty-six thousand miles. She felt sure of that. Halve that, and how far was England from the North Pole? She was far from sure. Say five thousand miles. That would be near enough. Then she had a disconcerting conviction that she had read somewhere (or learnt at school?) that a circumference is three times a diameter. And the diameter of the earth was eight thousand miles. She was almost sure of that. She said: "I'm not sure that I know exactly. It must be something between ten and fifteen thousand miles."

She looked at Franklin for confirmation, but he gave no sign. He thought that would do. His one desire was to see her come down from the witness-stand.

The President calculated. Others did the same. Vague as their knowledge was, it seemed an enormous distance to have traversed in so short a time. Even taking the lowest figure. Even with a fair wind all the day.

Aaron Cloutsclad, the preaching Elder of Lincoln County, a man with the eyes of a zealot and a sour mouth, broke out with a sudden question: *"Mistress, command you the winds of God?"*

It was unusual, but not strictly irregular, for other Elders than the President to undertake the examination of witnesses, but from whatever source that question had come it could not have been ignored, having once been spoken. It articulated all the speculation, all the doubt, as to the amazingly opportune arrival of these mysterious strangers, all the hostility that was latent among the three hundred that had watched and listened for a silent hour. It crystallized it in one dreadful accusation. The accusation of witchcraft. Could she command the wind?

There was something in the minatory tone of that question, something in the deep-breathed gasp of excitement which went over the audience as they heard and grasped its meaning, which would have warned anyone much less intelligent than Eleanor that she was walking a perilled way.

Seeing the danger, she rose to meet it with a fine courage. There was nothing for it but the truth, and to make it credible if she could. She answered readily, and with a smile of amusement: "We don't depend on the wind these days; we drive ships by other means."

"By what means," Malachi interposed, "that can be surer than the winds of God?"

"We drive them by steam and oil."

It is difficult to imagine what conceptions that answer gave to the audience which received it. They could scarcely have visualized a ship being driven by oil in any concrete way. Some of them may have known that oil will smooth the surface of water. Did they imagine such a surface that witchcraft smoothed, so that the ship glided over it? Or did they see a ship in full sail driven before a blast of pursuing steam?

The decorum of the assembly gave way before the astonishment or incredulity that the answers caused. There were murmurs among the audience, loud talking in one corner. Malachi and Aaron Cloutsclad were not the only Elders who attacked the witness with simultaneous questions. Eleanor tried to amplify her answer, and was conscious that she was unheard. Franklin's hand went to his pocket, and his eyes to the door behind them. It was close and unguarded. He saw that Ehud and Gwen were alert to the same idea. They would look after themselves. It would be his business to get Eleanor down from that stand, and get her clear. He did not doubt that the six bullets his pistol held would be sufficient for that. He felt the exhilaration of the approaching conflict. He was confident now. Confident that he would be sufficient for the event. This was better than the uncertainty of suspense.

And all this was in thirty seconds, before Ebenezer Cloutsclad proved his fitness for the position which Michael had vacated to him.

He rose, striking a loud note on the oak board with a gavel which was in his hand. "Know ye not," he enquired with a mild severity, "that ye are in the House of God?" And then, in a lower tone, addressing the Elders around him, yet so that all might hear in the silent hall: "Brethren, in this matter of Patience God's-Truth, she hath called witnesses whose testimony is such that, if it be taken as true, you may say that she hath sustained that which she said afore. Doth it not therefore become us, before we give judgment in this case, to make enquiry as to whether the evidence of these witnesses, which we do not impugn, be such as we can accept? That is not an inquest which can be made today. The sun sinks even now, and there are those of us who have far to go." He spoke lower, so that only the Elders heard. "There may be matters which are not for the public ear." He directed his attention to the audience again as he said: "We do adjourn this inquiry till the seventh day hence at the noon hour. You will go forth at once, and with the gravity which is meet."

Eleanor had left the witness-stand by this time. Franklin whispered, "If we make for the door, we can get away."

She shook her head in reply. "We cannot do that. How would Patience stand?"

Franklin did not see the issue to be as simple as she might think. If they got to the boat, they need not run away further than that.

They would have the support of Bunford's rifles. They could argue from a freer position. He could not tell what freedom might be left to them if they loitered now. But it was not a moment at which to differ. They could do nothing unless they were instant in action. Already people were moving toward the doors. Doubtless they would linger, talking in the freedom of the open air. They would block the ways. It was far better to stay boldly than to make gesture of fear, and then to give way.

He saw that the Elders were conferring in a group which was not without animation, though its words were low, and its members had a habit of dignity which they would not easily forget.

Eyes were turned in the direction of their alien visitors. The President spoke. "Master Arden," he said, "you have come at a strange time, by a strange way. Yet we would think no evil. We have appointed those of ourselves who would hear in private much that is still unsaid. We have the word of a brother, that of Master Michael God's-Truth, that you will not shrink from such inquest, having no cause for fear. Have I your word also for that?"

Eleanor was quickest to answer. She said, smiling: "Of course, we understand that there are lots of things that you'll like to know. We're quite willing to stay till next Monday, if you mean that."

Franklin said the same in his own way. What else could he do?

They went back into the vestry, Ehud accompanying them.

Eleanor said in a low voice, for Franklin's ear: "I hope I haven't got you into a worse mess than it looks now. You must forgive me for being a fool."

He answered with partial truth: "I don't think you have been a fool. I think you did splendidly." The sense of danger drew them together. Perhaps they had had no happier moment since they left England than they experienced then.

They overheard Gwen. She was teasing Ehud. "Oh, no. I can slip off if I like. *I* didn't promise to stay. I'm only the also-ran in this team." He may be excused if he did not understand her vocabulary, but he seemed content enough without that.

Patience came in. She looked wearied and troubled. She said: "Father thinks you'd better stay here for a time, till the folk have cleared." No doubt it was a wise thing to do.

CHAPTER XXX.

"STEAM!" said Malachi. "Hath it not the very savour and stench of hell?"

"It hath a strange sound," Ephraim Trustwell, a younger man, with a more alert manner than his companions, answered from a doubtful mind. "Yet she kissed the book, as I thought, with a good will."

"There is nought in that, as I fear," Aaron interposed in a tone of grave moderation, "for it is found that it was the copy which hath three leaves torn away. It may well be that there is no virtue in one that hath less than the full Word."

He spoke as one who stood apart from the fanaticism of Malachi, and who would judge all with an open mind. But his slow, hesitant words sank always at last to the same scale, and there was a cruel gleam in the small eyes which betrayed his satisfaction at the trail he hunted. He was known to be most implacable when he moderated his accusations thus.

"Yet I think not that," Ebenezer answered. "Were it not to treat too lightly that which remains? Hast thou warrant for that?"

Aaron must admit that he had none. Still, they all saw that it was a possible thing.

Yet Ephraim held to his doubt. "I see not," he said, "that the fiends should gain by a lying tale, such as is danger to them, and of no help to her that they seek to aid."

"It is the way of God," Aaron answered confidently. "So he bringeth their evil designs to nought."

But Ebenezer, being logician as well as theologian, saw that to accept such arguments was to convict on the evidence of their own assumptions. So he might have said, but Malachi broke out again.

"How know we it to be false? How know we it to be false? How know we not that the Devil may not rule indeed since the day that our Fathers fled? If the Lord hath destroyed the children of Moab and the Amalekites, may not fiends walk now in the garb of men, even in the streets that the godly trod? Is it not of steam and fire that the hosts of Hell would make a world to their own will? I doubt nothing if ye will question these three apart, that there will be more told of the same smell."

At this point a new question entered Ebenezer's mind. Suppose that Malachi's idea, in which there was nothing inherently improbable, should be the true explanation? Suppose that God had really destroyed the English Sodom after the persecuted saints had fled? *What then would be the verdict on Patience God's-Truth?* Would it not be possible (after having burnt these strangers for the fiends they were) to pronounce the article of the Church's creed to be true, and yet to acquit her? It was a straw-splitting of the kind that his mind loved. And he would be glad to see Michael God's-Truth's daughter cleared, if it could be done without loss to the authority of the Church, which was more to him than the lives of a hundred women. It was a thought to ponder. Yet he was an honest man, and he had thought that these strangers were of no evil kind.

"It might be well," Ephraim was saying, "it might be well to hear the evidence first before we decide what it may suffice to prove." Ebenezer answered to that: "It is well said," and they walked on in silence to Michael God's-Truth's house, where the inquiry was to be held. Michael was to be the fifth member of the tribunal. That had been conceded, fairly enough, when the Elders had talked together as the meeting closed. Michael had said that if these strangers were from the pit, it was of more moment to him than to any that the truth should be laid bare, for it was to his house they had come. If that were shown to be so, and he were not one of those to discover and condemn, might not the taint of that contact cling to his house forever? He wished to see his daughter acquitted, but not by such agencies as that....

His plea had been allowed; but he had been unable to object to the selection of Malachi and Aaron, whose verdicts were very probable, if not certain things, so that the decision would rest with Ephraim, the lay member of the tribunal, and Ebenezer Trustwell, who would be its president, and who would have a vote under the same rule which vetoed it at the full session of Elders—the rule that even numbers must be avoided, with their risk of an undecided verdict.

So they came to Michael's house.

CHAPTER XXXI.

BUNFORD WELDON was eloquent.

A hackbut lay on the table, and beside it the separated parts of one of his beloved rifles. He explained the differences, the immense improvements of three centuries, with an expert particularity, while Michael and his two sons surrounded him in a mental attitude of intelligent wonder.

This was at Michael's house. It had been Franklin's idea to make the enormous changes in modes and conditions of life, the astonishing inventions of the last century, such as they could not completely avoid revealing when questioned, natural to these people by illustration of the improvement which had taken place in things they already knew.

Immediately that Eleanor had committed them to another seven days' stay—a week which had been plainly indicated as one of inquisition into their own characters and credibility—it had become evident that Bunford could not be left longer in the boat, even had he been willing, which he was not. He said the solitude gave him the jumps. Either they must come back to the *Blanche*, or he must come to them.

In some ways, it might have been better that they should have retired to the boat, and remained there till the period of their promised stay should be completed. But there were objections to this. Michael opposed it strongly, and with a show of reason. It would display a lack of confidence, after having accepted the hospitality of his roof, the psychological effect of which might actually turn the scale against them, the committee of investigation being composed as it was. They could bring all their portable possessions up to the house. The boat would be safe. Theft in their community was almost unknown. The difficulty of both using and hiding, joined to the moral standards that prevailed, had rendered it an obsolete vice, of which, like some others, they only knew by their readings in the Mosaic law.

Without quite accepting this picture of innocence, Franklin recognized that the boat would be difficult for anyone to steal in a secret way. He said frankly that it was not that which he feared. He had more doubt that, if it were left without guard, it might be seized by the authority of the Elders to prevent their return. Michael assured him that this would not be. No one, apart from the order of a full session of Elders, had authority to take such action. No such session could be held without his knowledge and presence. He had the right to preside. The local authority also was his. They had landed in Norfolk County, which was under the jurisdiction of Malachi Trustwell, but the boat had been moved up the river into Suffolk territory, where he himself had the sole authority. Apart from the public decision of a full session of Elders, no one would act in such a manner in Suffolk County, except upon his personal order.

It was known that he had secured the entrance to the river-cavern against their return. He would tell them plainly that a watch had been set by Malachi at that spot as an additional precaution. There could be no objection to that. Malachi was on his own ground. Norfolk County was a long, thin strip of land between Suffolk and the northern hills. It was occupied mainly by goat-herding members of the Trustwell clan, and a few Pettifers. Pettifers were descendants of Gabriel's first wife. They were not numerous, and were called by her maiden name to distinguish their descent from that of the more numerous God's-Truths, who had descended from Carvall's widow.

111

If their whole party were at his house, no more thought would be given to the boat. It would be made clear that they intended to stay, at least until the trial of Patience was concluded, if not permanently. To retire to the boat was to bring the possibility of their return into instant prominence.

These arguments had a specious plausibility if Michael God's-Truth were himself to be trusted without reservation. The news that the mouth of the river-cavern was guarded had an ominous sound. It was becoming plain that it might not be easy to get away, either soon or late. But, on the whole, it did not appear likely that the *Blanche* would be an object of immediate molestation, if they should boldly empty it of their possessions, and show their confidence by the face that the last member of the party had come up to Michael's house.

Actually, the matter was settled after a conversation between Michael and Eleanor. He convinced her by his assurance, and his argument of the greater comfort of the house may have had its weight. Like other wealthy young women who have been fascinated by the adventure of exploration, Eleanor would endure hardship and privation very cheerfully under a sufficient compulsion, but she did not love them.

The Antarctic winter was approaching. Every day the hours of sunlight were lessening rapidly now. Even in this valley, the nights, so Michael told her, might become very cold. Already the goats were being byred through the long hours of darkness, and only let out to feed while the low sun was above the horizon-line. The boat might become very cold in the long nights. Eleanor had as yet experienced little of the severities of the south polar regions, which were to take an increasingly dominant part in the drama which was before them. Here the Antarctic cold may be said to have played its first card.

In the privacy of her own mind, she still had the idea that this thickly-built, well-warmed house might give greater comfort till the spring dawn came than could be hoped from the sheds that had been erected for them at the ocean-side. If she understood correctly, the temperature of this valley, even in winter, would be many degrees higher than on that glacial coast. If Michael God's-Truth caught any hint of this thought in the conversation mentioned, he showed no reluctance to encourage an invasion which might lead to such extended hospitality. He offered the services of his men to convey their possessions from the boat, and, under Franklin's supervision, the transfer was quickly made. This was on Monday. The next noon saw the coming of the committee of investigation whose conversation has already been overheard.

CHAPTER XXXII.

MICHAEL met his fellow elders in the square hall of his house. He addressed himself to Ebenezer Cloutsclad.

"I have thought much of this matter," he said, "and I am of a good will that you shall preside at this inquest, even as you did at my daughter's trial. I would not be first in this, either to speak or to judge, leaving it rather to you, for you must see that these folk are my guests, and their witness is on my daughter's part, and they appear also to me as of good conduct and a fair speech. Yet I would not have such help except in verity, and of a godly sort, and of those things I would that others be first to judge."

Ebenezer was pleased by these words. He had given much thought to the matter, and he had seen dangers of discord, even of disruption in Church and State, should Michael God's-Truth be resolved to support the strangers at any cost.

He said: "Brother Malachi is of a mind to say that they are witches' spawn, but I would judge all with an open mind. There be some things of an ill sound, as you know, and the coming of any here is an evil thing. Yet it would seem that they have cast no witchcraft on thee, or it hath been vain against one of a righteous mind."

Michael saw that he had taken the right line. He knew that Malachi and Aaron would vote for condemnation, whatever the evidence might be. If either Ebenezer or Ephraim should do the like, his own vote would be worthless. To win these two was a vital thing. If his own vote should thus be made of a decisive value, there was no doubt on which side it would be cast.

Meanwhile Franklin was saying: "If you will agree to leave the talking to me, unless you are directly addressed, and obliged to answer, it is the best chance. If we all talk, there's no knowing where it will end. Bunford, if you say a word about wireless or anything they can't understand, I shall just say that it's silly lies, and if they burn you after that, I hope we'll be looking on from a side seat."

Bunford said: "Why not call me a fool at once? I don't want to talk to the silly chumps. I didn't want to come here at all."

He spoke sulkily, having been lectured by Eleanor to the same purpose five minutes earlier. He knew himself to be the sanest member of the party, and the only one who could defend himself with a quick bullet correctly placed. Left to himself, he would have had too much sense to come here. He added: "Haven't I been telling Noah that I always shoot with a bow and arrows when I'm at home?"

Eleanor recognized that he was in a state of dangerous irritation, and tried to allay it by saying: "It wasn't meant for you, Bunny, any more than me. Gwen's the only one he trusts to say the right thing."

She said it with a smiling lightness, which did not entirely conceal a trace of underlying resentment. Franklin was aware that it held a larger measure of truth than he would be willing to admit. He said: "It isn't that, but I reckon there's always more danger of a fluke if two or three talk at once, than if one does it all. If you don't like to leave it entirely to me, I'm quite willing that someone else should take it on. But it's a one-man job."

"He only trusts me because I'm a professional liar, and one professional's always better than two amateurs," Gwen interjected.

"We'd far rather leave it to you," Eleanor replied seriously.

"Very well. Here they come."

The five Elders entered the room.

"Master Arden," Ebenezer began, "we would have you to know from the first that we would think no evil. Yet you have come by a strange way, from where it is an old tale (with some weight of proof) that devils dwell in the caves. And you have spoken strange words. It is matter to be sifted well, as you may see if you be true men. We would question you one by one, speaking first with you, while these others shall retire."

"Master Cloutsclad," Franklin answered to this unwelcome request, "I don't like to refuse, but do you think it is a fair thing to ask? You must agree that we are not on trial as citizens of this land. We came here by a wandering chance, and we are willing to go. Whatever may have been said has been no more than is true, and it was evidence which we were asked to give, at no gain to ourselves.

"We are still willing to give any further information you ask, and to prove our good faith, but we wish it to be clear that we do this not under compulsion, but in a spirit of good will. To submit to be separately questioned might imply more than we can allow."

"If your words be of a simple truth, I see not why you should so obstruct."

"But even that might be a possible thing. All of us might not be equal either in veracity or knowledge. I may prefer to speak for all. Yet I may fairly recall, and you will allow, that we made no objection to give separate evidence when we were first asked to do so in a friendly way."

"Master President," Ephraim intervened, "the sun is soon down in these days, and there may be much to ask. Would it not be well that these folk should first answer in their own way, and if their words be such that more inquest be needed, we can then so order it as we will. If we have fourfold queries today I see not at what hour we should cease, and there be those of us who have come by a far way."

Faced by Franklin's opposition, and with this objection from his own side, Ebenezer was not slow to give way on a point which had not been his own at the first, but that of Aaron and Malachi, as they had suggested it to him while on the road. He said: "There is good reason in that; and there may be justice also, Master Arden, in your own plea. We would not act with harshness to any."

They sat down on opposite sides of the broad and heavy table, Eleanor on Franklin's right, and Bunford on his left, with Gwen on Bunford's other side. The five Elders ranged themselves with Ebenezer in their centre, with Aaron and Malachi next to him on either hand, and Ephraim and Michael on the outside places to right and left. These positions separated those who were sympathetic, and placed the President with their enemies at either ear. Franklin observed this with dislike, but he thought that it might make little difference in the end. He thought that the contest would resolve itself into a duel between himself and Ebenezer, and if he could win him, there would be little further to fear. Ebenezer began with a question on which he had already decided. Nothing was written, from first to last. It was an amazement to notice how little this community, with its narrow intensities of interest and occupation, depended upon the written record, and how much was left to the collective memories of those concerned.

"Master Arden, not being shipwrecked, nor driven by stress of wind, why came ye to these parts?"

"We came on an expedition of discovery."

"Wherefore?"

"By the same impulse which has spread our race over a large part of the earth. The desire to see and to know."

Ebenezer pondered this answer. He had a thought that the wandering of men might usually have been impulsed by more urgent or more material causes. He asked: "Seeking wealth or land?"

"No."

"Being driven by persecution?"

"No."

"Nor flying from a wrathful law?"

"No."

"Ye came through the frozen ocean to this distant land seeking only to see and to know?"

"Being but two men, and two women to whom they say that they are not wed?"

"There were more for the most part of the way."

"Then why came they not here?"

"Our ship came to the limit of the land. It will come for us again when the ice breaks."

"How far was that from here?"

"I cannot tell you that with exactness I should say from five hundred to a thousand miles."

"And ye came by this far way with garments showing no rent, and hands showing no marks of toil?"

"We came by water from when we left the ship, finding it an easy way."

"How long took ye from the ship's side?"

"Between two and three days."

The President paused a moment, weighing these answers in his mind. Their direct brevity had had the effect of avoiding many explanations, such as the manner of Captain Sparshott's death. They also threw into relief the speed and ease with which this invasion had been accomplished. That is, if the answers were true. And that direct brevity had a convincing quality. He asked: "If ye came with such ease, will there not be others to follow in the same path?"

"If we should not return, it might be a likely thing."

"Why so?"

"Because, when the ship comes to take us off, they may seek us by the same path, if we are not there."

Malachi Trustwell had listened to these exchanges with a growing impatience. Now he broke in. "Say you so indeed? It hath the smack of a false end to a lying tale. If thy tale be true, it is a clear thing that there will be others here at speed if ye return by the way ye came, but if ye return no more, they will say that ye went by a devilled way."

Franklin looked at him in silence, and returned his regard to President, having the restraint to make no reply. It had been an outburst, not a question. It might be best ignored.

But seeing that he made no answer, Ebenezer asked, in his quieter way: "What say you to that?"

"Only this. As I know the arrangements which have been made, and the man who commands our ship, I may be the better judge of what is likely to happen. But if we should not return, it is a matter which the event will prove."

The President said dryly: "It would be a late day." He was disposed to believe the tale, and he saw the issues which it might bring. He had so many thoughts that his next question was slow to come. Michael God's-Truth was silent, as he had resolved to be. Also, he thought that matters moved in the right way.

Ephraim was silent also. He was seldom one of many words, but he would listen well. His eyes were on the disjointed rifle which still lay on the table, with the older weapon beside it.

The deadly slowness of Aaron's judicial tones interposed. "We have yet to learn how ye came at so great a speed, as though walking the winds."

Franklin knew that this was an issue which must be faced. "I would have told, had I been asked," he said readily. With a simple brevity, he reminded them of the rapid advance in the speed and range of ships which had taken place before the sailing of the *Morning Star*. He touched lightly on that, not knowing how little knowledge they might have. He pointed to the difference in complexity and in range between the two weapons which lay before them. He was as vague as he could be as to the present method of propelling ships. He said he was not himself either a builder or navigator. But he was willing to demonstrate with the *Blanche* how rapidly even a small boat might be driven by modern methods.

"So you might," Malachi said. "Yet should we not know but that the power cometh from below."

Franklin had anticipated this moment, and he had one argument by which he hoped to overcome it. He asked in turn: "From whence say you came the power of powder and ball?"

"Ask you that?" Malachi broke out. "It cometh from the very bowels of Hell."

It was a natural answer, under circumstances which Franklin had learned already.

When the *Morning Star* had grounded on the Antarctic shore, it had been well supplied with weapons, as was usual in those times, when a ship sailed through pirate-haunted seas to seek a settlement in savage lands, but there had been no use to which to put them, either against man or beast, until the quarrel with the Anabaptist descendants of Elisha Trustwell had led to the sound of shots disturbing the silence of the northern slopes of the mountains which must be scaled by those who fled to the pits of Hell. These firearms had been used on both sides, until their stores of powder were spent, which time was but a memory to those who now lived, but the Anabaptists had found saltpetre in their volcanic refuge, and there must have been a tradition among them of how gunpowder was made, for a day had come when the loud reports of their clumsy muzzle-loading weapons had greeted the saints of God once more when they had raided the mountain caves in reprisal for some successful pillage. The saints knew enough of the ingredients of powder to guess what had occurred, though they could not compete in its manufacture. The devil, they said very naturally, had helped his own. Of the fatherhood of black powder there was no doubt at all, even though its use had ceased again, probably because the ancient hackbuts were no longer serviceable.

Franklin saw that his opponent had fallen to the trap which had been laid to snare him.

"Though," he asked, "it be of the very fruit of Hell, yet hath it been used of the Saints, as yourselves will say. How much more, if there be a way found by which a ship can be moved even against the wind, may it be used by those of a good conscience, it being to the advantage and not for the destruction of men? Though I will not say, nor do I think, that this force is of Hell, as you have said that gunpowder was."

"It is shrewdly thought," Ebenezer said, fairly enough; and then changed the subject with a sudden probing question: "Master Arden, of what faith are ye four?"

"We are of the Christian faith."

"So ye would say. But of what church are ye called?"

"We are not all of the same name. There have been many changes since your fathers left our shores. New points of doctrine have arisen, and new names have been given. Perhaps the differences are less sharp than they were. And there are many who give little thought to these things, which I suppose was the same in the old days, in the England your fathers left."

"But not here," Ebenezer answered, with an asperity which he had not previously shown. "Nor would we have such a spirit beating against our doors. Master Arden," he went on in a graver tone, "for the first time you have failed to render a straight reply. You told me less than I asked, and yet more. What is the name of thine own Church?"

This was a question which he had feared, and hesitated how to meet. He had had no connection with any English Church since his boyhood, nor given much thought to their differences. But he had a confident feeling that the fanatic is more tolerant to those who are indifferent than to those who actively oppose his own creed. He answered carefully: "I am not at present a member of any of the churches in England. My fathers were called dissenters from the same Church which is established there, as it was in the old days."

He hoped that that reply might be sufficient to avert more detailed inquiry. The Anglican Church could not be popular with the children of those who had fled from the bitterness of its persecutions. He must avoid, if he could, the admission that Eleanor and her cousin were of that hated establishment—Eleanor with an active religious habitude, Bunford with no more than the perfunctory adherence that he would consider that his caste required.

As to Gwen, he suspected her of more definite beliefs and loyalties. But to what? He had thought that it might be as well that he should know. If necessary, she might be best able to do her own fencing, or make her own standing good.

Ebenezer took the reply well enough, but not as one that exhausted the information which he sought to obtain. It was evident that he was formulating a further query in his mind, when Malachi broke in again. "Were they of the Anabaptists, the fathers of whom you speak?"

Franklin had realized by this time that though Malachi might be intent to trap him, he was intellectually a less formidable opponent than, perhaps, any one of his colleagues, and that if he could overthrow him in argument, it might be of the first importance in establishing his own integrity. He answered, therefore, instead of giving a direct denial: "I am assured that they were not, but the fact is that the very word has died from the mouths of men, and I am not clear what the doctrines of the Anabaptists were. If you would tell me of them, I might give a more explicit reply."

Ebenezer looked at Malachi, and, for the first time, there was a gleam of something resembling humour in his expression. Whatever might have been the differences which had divided Anabaptists and Independents, as they had disputed for three years in the cabin of the *Morning Star*, while it drifted upon the ice, they had been forgotten for centuries. He was a student of theology, his learning only limited by the slenderness of the resources within his reach. Possibly he could have answered the question intelligently. He knew well that Malachi would be unable to do so.

But he was of no mind that an Elder of his church should be confounded before these strangers. He was quick enough in speech now, before his angry colleague could make reply. "It were but loss of time to pursue such inquiry further. Doubtless, if the name have died, so also have the errors which gave it birth. Master Arden, I will speak my own thought (though you will understand that I am one only in five) that you have answered in some part as a man should, and I would believe thee with a good will. Yet there is still much that is strange "

"Yes," Malachi's muttered interruption broke in, "as the reek of Hell."

"—that is strange to hear and to think. I see not yet that there was good cause that ye four came as ye did. And you must see that we probe these things with a double edge. We have to judge whether this tale be true of the world from which ye will have us think that ye came at so great a speed, for on that this trial of Patience God's-Truth may well depend; and we have further to think, if that be allowed for true, to what end will it come, if ye should go back with tale of the land which ye have here seen."

Franklin had a sense of relief. He felt, perhaps too readily, that the fight was won. He said: "The time of coming may seem short to you, but it was long to us, and it will be long before relief can come through the ice. It is a journey which can only be taken at a great cost, and for what? It may be that no others would come, even could they believe what we have seen, which they are not certain to do."

Ebenezer pondered this, but looked unconvinced.

Michael God's-Truth spoke for the first time: "Said you not, Master Arden, that your ship will not come till the next spring, and that the journey by water, your boat being of such speed, is but a matter of three days or of four?"

"Yes. But that would be...." He was about to say, if there were no accident to the boat, no breakdown of its motive power, but it was not an idea to give to these men. The danger was that they might think of it too easily for themselves! And he saw what was coming, and was resolved not to assent, if he could get away. He changed his words to: "But that would be a needless risk to take, we having our stores on the shore, and a good house built." He was not sure what he meant, or, at least, what he meant to imply. He had to finish the sentence as best he could.

Michael went on as he had expected: "Then might ye not remain here in comfort through the winter days, and there would be time for these things to be pondered at more leisure than is now ours?"

Eleanor looked at Franklin, and felt sure he meant to refuse. She did not want him to do that. She was disposed to stay, and she felt also that to accept was to avert the crisis, which might yet blaze into sudden violence should they show determination to leave. She may have been right in that. Her eyes went on to Gwen, who was leaning a little forward to catch her own. She thought that Gwen felt the same as herself. She may have been right in that too. She remembered that Gwen was not often wrong. She did not always remember that, but it suited her to do so now. All this was in a second's time, before she said, with her friendliest glance at Michael's bearded face: "Yes. We could do that."

Franklin started to speak, and stopped. They could not dispute before these men. And, after all, she was within her right. It was her expedition, rather than his.

Ebenezer looked at her intently. His questions had been seen already to be of a radical kind, for all their seeming simplicity, and the mildness with which he spoke. "Mistress, by what right do you rule thus?"

Franklin answered for her. "Miss D'Acre is a lady of great wealth, and this expedition is at her cost." He added: "I'm conducting it for her, and Mr. Weldon is her cousin. Miss Collinson is her secretary."

Ebenezer looked a mild displeasure. "That should have been made plain before now. Yet" (his sense of justice led him to add) "it was not asked." He turned his gaze upon Eleanor, and surprised her with a repetition of the question which he had asked before, but which he felt was unanswered still: "Mistress, to what end have ye come here?"

She answered him with smiling lips, and as one who recalls a jest which she would not refuse to share: "I think we came to find out whether the earth is flat."

CHAPTER XXXIII.

AS the words were spoken, Eleanor had a panic fear that, for a second time, she might have betrayed her companions to danger by indiscretion of speech, but it could not be unsaid. She had sufficient of courage and self-control to give no sign of perturbation, as Ebenezer, with a grave expressionless face, which had given no response to the merriment in her own eyes, asked: "Does the Christian faith, as it now is, deny then that the earth is of a flat shape?"

"A great many people think it is round," she answered cautiously.

"And ye were of different minds?"

"We thought we should like to find out. And we had heard from a man who had sailed in the frozen seas of the existence of the river-canyon by which we came."

"Then it is known of many?"

"No. No one believed him. It was only Mr. Arden and I who would listen to him at all. He is dead now."

"But why should it not be seen of any ship that sails by?"

"It is far apart, in a sea to which no man comes, even when the ice would let him through."

"Know ye now that the earth is flat?"

"We are still trying to find out."

"There is a Heaven above," he answered gravely, "and the Earth is His footstool. There is descent into Hell, which ye may yet see."

Eleanor had answered better than she knew. It was no part of the official creed of these people that the earth was flat, but it was so held by many, and it was a particular belief of Ebenezer Cloutsclad. He would have said more, but he knew that, as an Elder of the Church, it would be unseemly to do so at that inquiry.

Others of the five knew, with different feelings, the effect which that announcement would have on Ebenezer's mind. Aaron's small and cunning eyes were upon Eleanor in a considering way. By what method could he disclose her true character to colleagues who, he felt, were less sound in judgment than himself? Or less immune from the spells which a witch may cast? That it was witchcraft he did not doubt. We should be less than fair to him, if we do not recognize that. We have so few convictions ourselves. So few things of which we are quite sure, apart from the "scientific" facts of today, which will be contradicted tomorrow. It is hard to be fair to a mind that believes in Heaven and Hell

"Brethren," Ebenezer was saying, "if it be treated thus that these people will sojourn here during the winter dark, there is much more that may be learned in a leisured way, and there are matters of which we spoke as we came hither which may be left for the full session of Elders—and with which, of a verity, we have no warrant to deal. But in this matter only of Mistress Patience God's-Truth, I judge that vote may be taken without further words."

He passed the voting-box as he spoke, and the five Elders took up the counters, and inserted their hands into the box, o that none could see how they fell. It came back to Ebenezer, who lifted out the smaller box, and shook out the contents on the table.

"Brethren," he said, "there be three votes that the witness of these strangers is true, and two of those of another mind. I would that we had been of a more single thought." He turned to Michael. "Master God's-Truth, I see not that your daughter hath cause to stand trial more. I will do what is meet to that end." He rose up to go.

The other Elders rose with an equal alacrity. The sun was already low. They had no means of progress but their own legs. Some of them would not attempt to get back to their homes that night, but they would all wish to move as far as possible in those directions.

That was so well understood that Michael did not go through the form of offering a hospitality which he knew they did not seek.

"You will have food?" he asked. But they said no, even to that. They would feed at a later hour. The short daylight, the comparative warmth before the sunset came, were too precious to be reduced by dallying now that their work was done.

Patience came into the room as they left. She said simply to Franklin: "You have done much for me. I cannot think but ye are all of the true faith."

Eleanor came to Franklin. She felt that he was annoyed, though he would have said that he had given no sign. They had become quick to respond to each other's moods at this time. "Have I done wrong again?" she asked. The voice was almost humble—for her.

"No," he said. "It may have been the best way. But have you thought that someone will have to take the *Blanche* down to get our things? We have scarcely anything here."

They were interrupted by a stir of excitement in the room, which was now full of the God's-Truth family. Ehud said: "Yes, it is." They made a common movement to the door. Even Mistress God's-Truth showed some animation. Soon they were all standing outside the house, looking toward the darkness of the eastern sky. Their backs were to the setting sun, and the glow of the hells that lit forever the southern horizon deepened and spread as the daylight failed. They listened with straining ears to the faint sound of a bell.

"What is it?" Gwen asked Ehud, who was at her side, as he was apt to be.

"Hush," he replied, with a surprising curtness, and she saw that they listened not only to the sound, but for a message which must be spelt.

After a time they came in, having learnt all that they could. Michael answered the natural curiosity of his guests. "It is an Anabaptist raid. They would take the barley which is stored at Beth-El. But they are few and weak in these days. They will take little but their own deaths. There is no help needed from us, even could we be there in time."

They sat down to the evening meal. Franklin tried to conceal the worry that was on his mind. He would have given much to be back in the *Blanche*, running down to the winter-quarters where they would have nothing but the cold to face till relief should come. But he saw that he was alone in this. Bunford was making himself at home in his own way. Eleanor and Gwen had plainly resolved that they were not going back to those wretched huts, if they could stay in comparative comfort here. Gwen told him: "Ehud says, even in winter, it's often not too cold for them to go to church. It's nothing like it is on the hills." He saw that they were easy in mind, having lost their fears.

They might have felt less confidence had they heard the talk of the four Elders as they walked together till they came to a dividing way. Malachi was bitter in condemnation of the infernal powers which Patience God's-Truth had called to her aid. Aaron's mind worked in a quieter but perhaps deadlier way. He sought to influence Ebenezer. He quoted: "Thou shalt not suffer a witch to live." It was a command which allowed no exception. "Suppose the wrath of God should descend once more." He glanced apprehensively at the glare of the southern sky.

Ebenezer thought he had voted rightly, but he was not sure. Had he been misled by the lust of the eyes, and the glib lying of a witch's tongue? He went home a troubled man.

Malachi went some way with Aaron and Ephraim after Ebenezer had parted from them. He said: "As to this matter of Patience God's-Truth, I deem not that it can be left without further session, as Ebenezer's words may have been held to mean. Yet I think it might be allowed for a good defence had she been but a witch-ridden tool since the first words that she spoke to an evil end. Should we find these folk to be what they are, we might then acquit her, but not else. What would Michael God's-Truth say to that?"

"He would say," Aaron answered confidently, "what a father must. He would say, let the witches burn."

Ephraim said nothing. He was an Elder, but much younger than they. They may have talked partly to influence him, knowing how his vote must have been cast, but they had no fear that their counsel would be betrayed, let him think as he might. The Elders stood by themselves.

CHAPTER XXXIV.

THAT evening Michael told his guests more of the long strife with the Anabaptists, and the code of signalling on the old ship's-bell of the Morning Star by which the location of a raid could be given to all that heard, with other details by which they would know whether their aid were needed for its repulse. The bell was in Durham County now. It had once been nearer to the hills of the Anabaptists, and they had seized it in a swift raid, and it had not been recovered for thirty years. Even now, placed as it was, its sound would not reach through the whole land, though it was hanged high, and would spread far in a still air. Those to whom it would only faintly reach would spread the news further at a great need, both by swift runners, and by whistle and horn.

"Do they ever come thus far from the hills?" Eleanor asked.

"They have not done so for many years, for they are less strong than they were. There was a time when they would raid us every year, after the harvest was gathered in, taking such store of barley and flax and skins, and of a score of other things that we make or grow, that there were times when we were in want ourselves ere the next harvest could be gathered in. There would be fierce fights at such times, with slaughter on either side. So there are to this day, but on a lesser scale, for their numbers fail.

"That was because, when the evil grew, we would strike back with the coming of spring, seeking them in their own caves, which are over the pits of Hell.

"There were those who said that we should slay all, and so make an end, which had been easy to do at one time, for their children and women-folk, such as were too weak to flee, were in our hands. (This was when my father, Hush-Ill God's-Truth, was young.) I see not clearly that it had been wrong, for what said the Lord when the Amalakites fell before those of a truer faith? But there were some who said that though they were in the bonds of iniquity, yet they were still of our blood, so they took only the young to be brought up in a godly wise, letting the women go, to breed more trouble for us in later years."

"Wouldn't it have been better," Eleanor asked, "to make peace, letting them grow food on the land that you don't need, or bartering for such things as the mountains give?"

"Nay, had they but been of an alien blood. But to bring a false faith to our doors!"

"Yet," she persisted, "I thought Master Malachi Cloutsclad was less than sure what their errors in faith may be."

Michael commenced a reply in the stern tone of admonition which he would have addressed to one of his own household. But he looked at Eleanor, and the words changed. "Mistress," he said, "when you have been here longer, you will have learnt more."

Eleanor resented this reply, though she did not understand it, and the talk died. His thought was that if she should see an Anabaptist as they now were.

In the sudden silence, the clear low voice of Gwen talking to Ehud at the end of the room sounded plainly to all.

"Do you mean," she asked, "that your children are always born in the spring days?"

They did not hear his reply, but it seemed that Gwen was investigating the home life of this strange community with her usual thoroughness.

Michael resumed the conversation to tell of an attack upon the house which had been made when he was a boy, about forty years earlier. One end had been burnt at that time, and since restored. The objective of the Anabaptists had been the store of tanned skins which his father held, and though they had lost some of their spoils as they retreated, they had carried off so much of this leather that it was said that they had had little stint of covering from that day. "But I think," he added, "that there is little fear that they will venture so far again from the hills in which their safety lies, for they are now less strong than they were. They may take some corn and roots, or it may be garments or flax, from the southern farms. It will be nothing nearer than that."

Eleanor wished that she might see these strange wild outcasts with her own eyes. The insatiable lust of the explorer stirred in her heart. But she would not risk further indiscretion. She kept the thought to herself.

CHAPTER XXXV.

CONSEQUENCES may be logical enough: they may even, as the proverb suggests, be the Divine comments upon the actions of men, but they are no less difficult to foresee, and frequently of inconsistent or contradictory aspects.

Those which followed the inquisition of the five Elders, and Eleanor's decision to remain for the winter, were of no certain complexion. It seemed that the event paused, as though Fate itself were reluctant to decide its outcome.

Following a conference of the Elders, Patience God's-Truth had an intimation that her trial was postponed until she should receive a further summons. That might mean that it would be abandoned forever. It might be an adroit device to avoid the reflection upon the Church's authority which would be involved in a formal acquittal. But to Patience, it was not the same thing. The menace remained.

Neither was there any lifting of the deadly vagueness of accusation against the invaders of the godly kingdom. The Elders conferred among themselves. There were those among them who would have taken strong and instant action. They were restrained or delayed by the fact that Michael God's-Truth, the President of their Assemblies and their accustomed leader, was the friend and host of these aliens, and by the further obstacle that Ebenezer, his deputy, and the natural head of any opposition to his authority, was slow to move. He listened, he sometimes agreed, but he did not act. Against Michael God's-Truth alone, an opposition on ground well-chosen might have some chance to prevail. That had been tried, indeed, when his daughter had been accused. That had seemed a strong, even an impregnable case; and its result, so far, had not encouraged a further conflict, unless very circumspectly prepared. To attack the strangers again, without assurance either of his or Ebenezer's aid, was to invite defeat. For the time, Malachi canvassed his strength. Aaron was active with cautious words to draw waverers to his side. Popular opinion must be wooed also. The idea that to harbour these people was to invite the vengeance of God must be encouraged and spread. So a fortnight passed, and the night fell.

Meanwhile, there had been another trouble, of a minor kind, as to who should take the *Blanche* down to the ocean-side to bring up the necessities of the winter months. Michael had opposed this being done at all. There could be nothing needed, he said, which could not be supplied. Eleanor looked at him with amused eyes. She made it very clear that she must have her requirements fetched, or there would be no staying for her. She was inclined to think that she must go herself. She had come away thinking only of an absence of a few days. It would be a case of the opening of locked trunks, of rummaging among private things, of possibly difficult choices, should the *Blanche* prove unable to bring all that she desired to have.

She was inclined to think that she must go. But she could not go in a boat alone with men. Michael assumed that. No? Then Gwen must come too. With whom else? Franklin, of course. But Michael demurred from that. He may not have considered Bunford a sufficient hostage. Very well, then Bunford could manage. But then Bunford was difficult. He dreaded the amphibians of the caves. He did not mind trying a rush past, if it were to be for the last time. But to pass backward and forward! The creatures of the caves would get to watch their coming. They would lie await. There would be worse danger (he suggested) from these creatures in the dark winter days, they being confused in the light.

No. He would not go alone. Let Franklin go, if he were so confident in the boat's speed. At the least, let Franklin come.

"Then," Eleanor said, "we must all four go. Why not? We shall be back in less than a week."

But again and more emphatically, Michael would not agree. He might trust them himself, so he said, might have no wish to hold them against their wills, but he was responsible to others to whom his word was pledged. Suppose—well, suppose an accident occurred? Suppose they *couldn't* return? Where would he be?

Eleanor gave way so far as to say that if she didn't go, Gwen must. Michael agreed to that. But with whom?

He suggested that Franklin and Gwen should be accompanied by one of his own sons, and, resolute that the number of his guests should not be further reduced, and for the conventions that prevailed in his own land, proposed Paradise as a companion to Gwen. Abel Trustwell said no to that. His niece should not risk her life in the caverns under the hills. Demons dwelt there, as was known. Paradise herself was unsure. Had it been Noah who was to take the adventure, she might have offered a gentle opposition to her uncle's will. Hearing that it was to be Ehud, she submitted to the voice of authority in a cheerful way.

Gwen said: "What a silly fuss!" Eleanor agreed. Gwen could take care of herself. Michael recognized, somewhat late, that it was not his concern. Gwen could go alone if she would.

Franklin had meant from the first that he should be the one to go. If the bulk of the stores which had been landed were to be left to the spring, without any heating apparatus being set up, they should at least be secured very differently from how they had now been left. He imagined that they might arrive there at any time during the winter days in urgent flight. They might arrive without cover or food, to dig into snow and ice for the vital necessities on which their lives would depend. He must, at least, see that all possible protection was given to those stores, on which, apart from their present precarious hospitality, their security rested. It was not a matter to trust to others. Not to Bunford, anyhow

He had watched Eleanor's efforts to arrange that Bunford should go with a mixture of amusement and satisfaction. He saw that she would have preferred to keep him beside her, and was the more glad of that because Michael was increasingly monopolizing her society. But he knew that he ought to go. Eleanor would be in no danger here for a few days. Nothing from which Bunford might be less efficient than himself to guard her. Of Bunford's loyalty there was no doubt. No, he ought to go. And he had told Eleanor this, and she had had the sense to agree.

"I don't want you to go," she said, frankly. "I feel safer when you're about. But I know you think it's all my fault as it is. I don't agree about that. If I'd told those old devils that we meant to clear, we should have been having another trial before this. Gwen thinks the same about that. We've got to keep cool, and watch our chance to get away quietly when the spring comes. But if I don't want you to go, it doesn't say that it's not the right thing to do. If we lose the stores, it's not going to be said that it's because I kept you here."

"I suppose Michael will agree?"

"Yes. He'll have to. I've given way already about not going myself. I'll see to that."

She had spoken confidently, as being aware of her influence over the bearded giant, who was host and gaoler in one, and she had proved to be right. So long as she were not going herself? And Master Weldon staying moreover? Yes. That would be well enough.

CHAPTER XXXVI.

SO the *Blanche* ran down between banks lined with a fringe of amazed spectators, and disappeared into the low black mouth of the river-canyon, which had been opened to let her through.

She ran down at even greater speed than she had come up, being lighter now, and with the current to aid her. Franklin and Gwen steered in turns. Ehud, for the most part, was content to watch and learn. He asked many questions, but Franklin noticed that he asked nothing twice. His eyes were on Gwen continually. He was fascinated, if her fur hood were thrown back (for the cold was not intense in the depth of the narrow gorge), by glimpses of the glossy blackness of hair which was an even greater contrast than Eleanor's dark-brown curls to the light-haired women of his own kind, by an animation that seemed always alert and unhurried, by the alien charms of voice and manner which were unlike anything that he had known before.

Gwen observed and was well content. She had already decided to marry Ehud, in a clear and very resolute mind. But there was no need that he should know that. Not for a few days, anyway. After that, things might move rapidly.

She saw some definite difficulties: there might be others which she had yet to recognize, but she did not doubt that she would be able to overcome them. It was not if, but how. And while she planned this, in the intimacy of the little cabin of the narrow boat, she encouraged him with a capricious friendliness, as one who calls through a half-opened door.

And meanwhile, Ehud's thoughts, if less confident, were not backward to the same end. It may have been owing less to the hesitation of others than to the resolution of two converging wills that they were together now. Even Gwen might have been startled had she realized how stubbornly he had resolved to have her.

It was even darker in the narrow gorge, now that the summer daylight was fading, than it had been when they had come up at the beginning of the month. They depended for the safety of their speed upon the light in the bows, which could be thrown far forward, and upon the straightness of the narrow stream, which they had proved already.

It was colder also, and snow fell at times from the blackness of the distant sky. The stars were rarely visible.

There was no sign of the amphibious enemies whom they had feared to meet. Swiftly and without incident they came to the gorge-mouth, and out at a slackened speed to a blizzard that raged from eastward across its entrance

The comparative warmth of the out-flowing water kept it clear of ice for a long distance in the direction to which the current spread, and might have done much in a still air to mitigate the severity of the surrounding temperature, but it could have little effect against the icy rush of the blizzard which beat upon it. Warmly though they were clothed, they might well shrink from contact with that frozen tempest. To two of them, at least, far as they have penetrated to southward, it was their first intimation of what the Antarctic means. With their muffled faces bent aside from the stinging lash of the frozen snow, they peered forward where the searchlight struggled to pierce the storm.

Slowly, blindly, Franklin felt his way, steering outward for some distance, and striving for exactness of memory as to how wide must be his curve to gain the beach from which they had started, and avoid an outjutting of intervening rock.

Anxious not to turn too soon, he may have gone farther out then he should before he swung round to starboard, and faced the full fury of the storm. But it made little difference, if he did. As they left the direct line of the outward current, thin ice crackled before the bows, ice that thickened with every yard. The *Blanche* was strongly built, but she was not intended for icebreaking. Soon the ice held. Reversing the engines, Franklin had a difficulty in getting clear. Then she backed into ice again. He had lost the way by which she had broken through. He thought, "We shall be here for the winter, if I once let her get frozen in." His only purpose now was to get her back again into the unfrozen current. The storm could not continue forever. They must wait till they could see their way. So he shouted to companions who could not hear.

For some hours they lay thus in the current, driven at times westward against the ice, and beaten upon by the increasing storm. The water, which at first had not been very rough, became increasingly turbulent. It was easy to guess that they were being carried further out. After all, if the storm did not lift, would it not be better to regain the shelter of the canyon till it should be over? It could not sustain this fury forever.

Thinking this, Franklin put the boat round, and felt his way backward against the current. It was astonishing how far he had drifted while he thought he had held his position. And then there came a flurry of veering wind, and a sudden calm. The snow ceased. They saw the canyon-mouth, not three hundred yards away, and a snow-covered land which had no resemblance to the memory of that which they had left little more than a fortnight ago. Far outward as they could see, they gazed on a frozen ocean, broken only for some distance by the narrowing ribbon of the warmer current. Ocean ice and barren land were covered with the same mantle of snow, and it was hard to see where the sea ended and the coast began.

They looked for the sheds which had been built for their winter-quarters, and could do no more than guess them amid the snow-wrapped hummocks of the frozen land.

Gwen said, "They are over there. No, more to the right. I remember the way we came down to the boat."

Yes, Franklin agreed. There they were. It was best to gain them if possible while the light held. But how should they secure the boat on which their return depended? They found a place at last where it could ride in the warmer current, and be secured beneath a rock with land-anchors which would not drag. It would mean that everything would have to be carried for three times the distance of the previous loading, and over slippery and sometimes deeply crevassed rocks, but that was beyond avoidance. It was the first consideration that the *Blanche* should not be damaged, or frozen in.

They made a difficult way, not without some slips and bruises, to the frozen hummocks which were their security for life and comfort till the *Bergen* returned. They had with them no better tools than a boat-hook and shovel to dig them out. There were good picks a few yards away, but they were under the ice through which they must break to reach them. Ice which had formed as the ocean spray had blown over and frozen through the lengthening nights. They worked for half an hour to reach the door of the central shed, making slow progress, but deciding that they could break in before the darkness came. But they were uncertain of what they would be able to find readily, or what would still be buried beyond their immediate reach. If they should stay there for the night, it would be best to bring food and other necessities from the boat. Franklin said he would go back. Loaded as he would be on his return, it would be no easy task to make a safe transit of those slippery rocks.

Gwen said, "Well, be as quick as you can. I could eat a sheep. We'll race you whether we can break in before you get back."

He answered, "Well, here's the key, if you can. There's some loose wood inside near the door. I meant it for a first fire, while we were getting the stove to work. But you'd better look for the sleeping-bags first of all, if we're going to spend the night here."

He went off briskly enough, but he slipped on a snow-covered icy slope of rock when he was halfway to the boat, and got up with a bruised hip. It was not a serious hurt, but he limped for the rest of the way, and was obliged to move slowly, and with an increased care. The light was nearly gone, and he saw that he would have difficulty in finding his way back before it failed entirely. Yet he might have done it, had not the storm returned.

It came as suddenly as it had ceased before, a blast of icy wind and a thickening of the low darkness of the hurrying snow-cloud overhead; and he had scarcely regained the boat when its full force swept down in a driving blizzard of frozen snow.

So it was for two days. The *Blanche*, moored closely beneath its sheltering rock, and straining at sea- and land-anchors that did not break, rode it out well enough, but Franklin could not move from the boat. It would have been a feat of miraculous quality to find his way to the sheds through the denseness of the driving storm, had the way been along a straight and beaten path. Across the treacherous surfaces of snow-covered rocks, where the direction must be changed with every yard, it would have been an impossible thing, even could he have kept his footing on the unseen and slippery surfaces. Sheltered himself, he could only hope for the safety of those whom he had left, and watch for the storm to fall.

On the morning of the third day, there was a lull in the screaming wind, a thinning of the driven sleet of snow. A strip of blue sky showed overhead. Franklin emerged stiffly from the warmth of the little cabin, to look out on a world more thickly mantled than it had been two days ago. The thin line of the river-current, where it stretched out seaward, had shortened and narrowed. Everywhere the ice gained. The huts were more deeply covered—far more deeply covered—than they had been before. He made haste to land, carrying such things as would be most useful in an emergency which he could only guess.

Looking at the silent, snow-buried huts, he was disposed to blame himself that he had not made an attempt, however hopeless, to force his way through the storm. And yet reason told him that it would have been a foolish waste of his own life. What could he have done but stumble blindly about till cold and exhaustion would have overcome him, and he would have fallen and perished? Had he reached them (which he would not have done), it could have made no difference, except to where he died. Food without shelter would only have delayed their ends. Everything depended on whether they had been able to break through the icy ramparts that had blocked the door.

Living himself, he might still take succour if they were alive, in whatever extremity. There would still be one, at the worst, who could take the *Blanche* back, without which Eleanor would be deserted indeed.

So reason urged. but feeling is a different thine, and it was in a misery of self-reproach that he struggled towards the hut, from which no smoke rose.

It was rather by the mercy of God than his own care that he arrived with unbroken limbs at the snow-mounds which the huts had become.

The new snow had been deep enough on the open land, but against the huts it had been driven by the blizzard in a ten-foot drift. Remembering the slow progress of their efforts two nights ago, and with nothing but his gloved hands with which to dig, Franklin might well look with consternation at the depth of burial. And what better than literal burial could he hope to find?

But they had been chipping before on the hard ice that had formed from the spray that the wind had brought, before the surface of the ocean froze. Now the piled drift was of nothing worse than the powdered snow. He worked upon it as a dog digs, scooping the snow with his hands, and throwing it backward, till he was in a sunk hollow with walls of snow around and before him. As he burrowed, there came a time when he feared at each thrust of his hands into the snow that they would encounter the frozen forms of those that were now beneath it.

While he worked, the faint short daylight died, and the stars shone brilliantly.

He came to a time when he could feel the relief of knowing that there were, at least, no frozen bodies before a door which was closed now. Had it been opened? If so, why was there no sound of life from that dark interior?

When he felt that the secret which it held was near his finding, the snow fell in from the banked sides of his excavation, and there was a long renewal of labour. And then, as his hands scraped hard ground again, about two yards from the door, he came on a small dark object. There was a strange blue light on the snow, which he did not heed, but it was enough to show him what it was, even before he raised it. It was the key of the shed-door. The one that he had given to Gwen when he had left them to return to the boat.

It was an ominous sign. How could they have unlocked the door, and dropped the key at that distance outside it? It was beyond hope. As he held it in his hand a conviction came that he was wasting his time before an empty shed. Doubtless, they had realized that the forcing of the door was beyond their strength, and had attempted to return to the boat.

Doubtless, if so, they must have perished in the blizzard, probably falling in the darkness into one of those treacherous hollows which divided the slippery rocks. There would be little chance, indeed, of any life remaining after two days' exposure such as that. Yet he tried to persuade himself that it was not beyond possibility. The snow would have covered them in the hollow in which they lay. Was there not warmth under the snow? Had he not read somewhere of sheep surviving under such conditions? Not, it was true, under Antarctic temperatures. And that hope had been dwindling while he wasted his time and strength before an empty shed! Blaming himself beyond reason, he straightened stiffly, and stepped out of the hollow he had dug. The lights of the Austral aurora that had guided his hand to the key were overhead, but he gave neither glance nor thought to the magical wonder of their unfamiliar beauty.

Looking around, he saw the hopelessness of his quest. Even in the full light of day…. Even if he could have been sure that they had taken the right direction back to the boat…. Among those uneven rocks…. Beneath that mantle of snow….

Yet the search must be tried. Why had he made no effort to return to them when the blizzard came? He should have thought of this possibility. They might have called…have met. Why had he ever left them at all!

After that, he searched vainly for some hours. He searched till anxiety of mind and toil of body brought their inevitable end. It was with a blind instinct rather than a conscious violation that he found himself at last stumbling back to the entrance of the silent hut. It was there he had laid down the bags he had brought that he might move more freely in his search. But he did not heed them now. He should not have gone back to the boat.

But as he stood there in the misery of his ended hope, with sagging knees, and dimly conscious of the conquering cold, a thought came to him that, useless though it might be, he should not have ceased digging while he only encountered snow, for it was ice which the boathook had been chipping away, and while he only encountered snow, it meant that they must have penetrated further than that.

Well, he would end his work. When he came to the ice, it would be proof that he need attempt no more.

But he did not come to the ice. He scraped at the snow with his failing strength till the door was clear. It came open in his hand.

In the dim light he saw the dark shadow of two who lay closely in each other's arms. His hand encountered the side of a primus stove. It was not alight, but he felt through the torn glove that it was still warm.

He turned a flashlight downward. No, they were not dead.

CHAPTER XXXVII.

WHEN Franklin started for the *Blanche*, Gwen had taken the shovel which he had laid down, and, while Ehud worked with the boat-hook, chipping and levering at layers and blocks of the impeding ice, she assisted vigorously to the capacity of her indifferent tool.

Stimulated by the desire to force an entrance before his return, and feeling the necessity of effecting this while the light held, she did her own part strenuously, and realized no further significance in the fury of the blows that Ehud delivered upon the hardness of resisting ice. But he saw more than she. He looked up at the sky, and attacked his task with an energy which overreached itself, for the boat-hook broke in his hands.

He made no delay for that, throwing the broken stave aside, and working with the shortened tool, and with a vigour which had made good progress towards his goal when the wind came round the hut with a sudden violence which swept Gwen from her feet, and hid them both in a blizzard of blinding snow.

She rose unsteadily, struggling against the wind, and hardly conscious of the tattered rags that hung from her side, and of bruised and bleeding ribs. She was so confused by the fierce onslaught of the storm that she was actually moving away from the shed when Ehud's arm found her in the darkness and drew her back. Even in that physical extremity, they thrilled alike at the first closeness of contact that they had known.

He said: "There is some shelter here, if you crouch down. The door shall be open soon." He resumed his work in the darkness. She half rose from where he had placed her, in a desire to give further help, and sank down again, aware that her strength had gone. What had happened when the blizzard struck her? Her hands moved weakly, trying to discover the extent of injuries which were becoming painful now, and to draw together the shredded garments through which the wind came with a numbing intensity. From faltering consciousness she was aroused by Ehud's voice. "I can't open this door. I can't find the pin. Can you tell me how it is done?"

He knew nothing of locks and keys, but only of thong-pulled latches and twirling pins. He said, "It can't be barred on the inside."

She answered: "No. It's quite easy to open. Franklin gave me the key." And then, in a voice which she was too weak to control sufficiently to hide the terror in which she spoke. "I'm afraid I've dropped it. I haven't got it now." She began to attempt to crawl, feeling with hands which were numbed through the heavy gloves, along the frozen ground which the snow was already covering.

She could see nothing, but Ehud's eyes must have been better than hers. He reached down to her, and drew her back to the shelter which she would have left. He had only dim idea of what a key was, but he knew that there was little chance of finding anything which had been dashed from her hand when the storm struck her. He knew also that the door must come down. He drove his shoulder three times against it with all his strength.

But the frame-built shed which Eleanor's wealth had purchased to resist the severities of an Antarctic winter was not to be forced so easily. The close-fitting door did not even shake in its frame. Even in his desperation, he had sufficient coolness to see that he could not succeed by that method of attack, and the self-control to desist from a useless effort. He asked: "Is there any other way in?" But there was no answer from the girl who lay unconscious beside his feet.

He stood irresolute for a moment, debating whether he should take her up, and endeavour to make his way back to the boat, in which case they would have died together, and many things must have come to a different fruit. But he knew enough of the demons of cold and storm to see that it was a hopeless chance.

Yet he would not fail, with life and all it holds in the balance, and the woman he loved at his feet. He took off the heavy coat he wore, and wrapped it around her. Then he groped for the broken boat-hook, and strove to insert it between the jamb and the door.

Ten minutes later desperation and strength had triumphed. With broken bleeding fingers, and the snapping fragments of the boat-hook, flesh and wood and metal had done their parts to force open the stubborn door. Gwen waked in an utter darkness to feel that she was lying across his knees, and that his hand was chafing the numbness of her frozen side.

She was foolishly, absurdly weak, but her mind was clear, and her heart sang.

"Ehud," she said, "Are we in the hut?"

"Yes. I broke down the door. How are you feeling now?"

"Good for you! How do I feel? Right as rain, if you know what that means. So you broke it down? I didn't think anyone could. I half-thought that I wasn't going to wake again. So we've Bolivar'd fate this time, if you know what I mean again.

"'Euchred God Almighty's storm: bluffed the Eternal Sea.' But of course, you don't." She laughed with an hysteria of exultant weakness, and then suddenly regained her self-control and the poise of her normal manner.

"Ehud, what a fool, I am! Stop mauling and listen. There's a flashlight in the pocket of my coat—the left-hand side, if it's still there. Good. That's the style. There's a wood stove over there, and loose chopped wood behind the door. There's an oil stove as well, that won't take long to get working, and the big stove besides. We won't worry about that. A tinder-box? Yes, I suppose you have, but we won't wait for that. I've got matches. Let me move a little. No, I'll get them myself. I'm all right. Yes, of course. You can let me lie here. And put your coat on again, please. *Warm?* Nonsense. There's a thermometer over there. I expect you'll find it's thirty degrees below."

Ehud did not understand thermometers, but he was resolute not to resume his coat. He obeyed her instructions in lighting the unfamiliar lamp with a careful though clumsy accuracy. Soon they had all the comfort that food and light and warmth could give.

After a time, he said, with an awkward shyness, unusual with him, "We'd better see what we can do to that wound. We can't leave it like that."

"I was just wondering," she answered calmly, "how long it would be before you came to that conclusion. What about boiling some snow?"

He fetched snow from the inferno of tempest that raged without, and heated it over the stove.

Washed clear of the dirt and dried blood which had frozen upon it, there was no depth of wound, but black patches of bruise, and a wide space that had been scraped clear of skin, where a rib showed bare.

"Doesn't seem to be a case for a funeral," she suggested, as she tried not to wince from the pain of his gentle bathing, "but I shouldn't be much good for a hockey team for a week or two."

He listened with uncomprehending but satisfied ears. It was part of her fascination that she would tease him, consciously or not, by talking of things which were beyond his knowledge. "I shall have to teach those young women hockey," she went on. "It might make them almost human in time. And football for the men. They play that now? Well, that's good news, anyway. I hope Malachi's not too old. He ought to be somewhere where he'd get kicked. I should like to referee that game. Hockey's a good deal like football, only it's better for girls. I really will introduce it, after we're married. I am going to marry you, Ehud. But you may have guessed that already. You can kiss me, if you know how."

* * * * * *

They talked for a long time and of many things in the intervals when he was not waiting upon her. She would not be moved from the floor, which was, indeed, as warm as a raised couch, having been laid over a cemented cavity, and she soon had enough of fur and blanket around and beneath her to give no further excuse to Ehud for delaying to resume his coat.

They talked, but they could not sleep, or, at least, she could not. The reaction from physical and emotional excitement, and the effect of physical shock had left her mind in a restless activity, vividly conscious at once of the passing moments, and alert to anticipation of the life to which she had now committed herself. His slower though equally tenacious nature responded to her own mood, and to the triumphant crisis which had come upon them. Could he sleep while she waked? When all had been done which their comfort needed, he sat on the floor beside her, while she held his hand in caressing fingers, and talked and planned in a monologue which did not always call for reply.

But she dozed at last, and waked to see him sleeping on the floor a short distance away, and was in doubt as to how long she slept, and felt the need of action with a mind that had recovered much of its accustomed coolness. But her bruised side had stiffened, and to move was agony at first. Yet there were things that must be done, and she was soon standing upright, and found her way to a mirror which hung against the wall of the inner room, which was to have been Eleanor's and hers.

"What a sight I must have looked!" she said audibly, but in a low voice, for Ehud must not be wakened yet. And then, "I don't think I can stand straight now. I must have lost a devil of a lot of blood." The extremity of the expression was unusual to her, and may have indicated its quantity.

Through the selfishness of her own satisfaction, there came a belated thought. "I hope Franklin's all right. But he's sure to be. He'll be at the boat. There's no difficulty about getting in there. Ehud ought to make sure as soon as the storm stops." She paused to listen to the elemental fury that was still raging around the hut.

Reassured as to her own appearance, she came back into the kitchen, and stood for some time looking down with softened eyes at her sleeping lover. "I wonder what he'd say if I did," she remarked cryptically. And then: "No. It's the invalid stunt for me."

Amused at her own thoughts, but with a smile that failed at times as her movements sharpened the pain in her injured side, she lay down again. She arranged herself, not without regard to the appearance that would meet his waking eyes. "*J'adoube*," she remarked, and then, "I wonder if I talked French whether he'd be even better pleased than he is now. It's only another mile on the same road. But I'd be a sure witch if Brother Malachi heard. Probably even if he knew what it was. I expect they thought them a godless lot!" She spoke lightly, watching Ehud the while for certainty that he did not wake. But the next moment the thought sobered her mind to a realization of the severity of the struggle which was before her. She was sure of Ehud. Sure of him as she was of her own faith, of her own loyalty. Beyond that, what mattered? Well, quite a lot. There was the light of cool and merciless battle in her eyes, as she addressed an imaginary Malachi, "Perhaps you will. Who knows? But there'll be such a fight before that!"

It was a thought that brought her to the further realization that the present moment was hers, and should not be lost. She moved over toward Ehud, with an exclamation of pain, that was not entirely without reason, and he waked, as she had meant that he should. After that, she made good use of her time, planning and questioning, and making intervening love with a woman's subtlety of repulse. It was many hours later that she professed tiredness, but could find no posture of comfort except that which his shoulder gave, and so slept till she was wakened by Franklin's voice, and stirred to the sight of a sky made splendid with auroral light that showed through the open door.

CHAPTER XXXVIII.

IT was slow work loading the *Blanche*, a labour of several days, during which Gwen stayed in the hut. She could not make her way backward and forward across that rough and slippery way, being injured as she was, and she would not leave the control of what would be taken to Franklin's choice.

She might have walked on a good path, but the broken ice-covered rocks of the shore, with their worst treacheries half-concealed by the drifted snow, were a different matter. Besides, there was little light, little more than a long midday twilight now, though the auroral lights were an almost nightly marvel while the skies were clear; and Franklin and Ehud, struggling a burdened way, had bruises more than enough, and were fortunate to come through with unbroken bones.

The light, such as it was, showed the cause of her injury to be something other than the rocks on which she had blamed it. A heap of timber had been left near the door of the hut after its completion, and the jagged end of a broken board, projecting from the solid frozen mass, had torn along her side as she had been thrown forward by the first violence of the storm.

So she stayed in the hut, fighting some resolute battles with Franklin over the selections of what should be taken, about which three opinions clashed, without counting Ehud's, which went no further than to aid Gwen in the getting of her own will.

For Franklin had his own judgment of what would be most needed during the winter night, and would render them comparatively independent of their new acquaintances. Such things he had meant to take, and then to complete the loading with as much of Eleanor's things as the boat would carry.

Gwen might have thought it her first duty to see that her absent employer's wishes were not disregarded, and would certainly have considered herself a better judge than Franklin of their relative importances. It would be unfair to suggest that she was now oblivious of such considerations. But she had her own possessions also, and having resolved to make her home in these Antarctic solitudes, there was little that she was willing to leave.

Suppose that this should be the only journey that the *Blanche* could make before the spring? Looking out on to a sky in which the stars showed at midday, thinking of the severity of the weather which they had already faced, and of the time which was being taken, it seemed a likely, almost a certain thing. Suppose, when the spring came, that, for whatever reason, the *Blanche* could not come here and return again? Suppose it should be a case of final parting when it should start down the river? What she did not take now might be lost forever, and this thought, and the possibility of future isolation from her own civilization, transformed a hundred trifles into almost priceless things. And the total of her possessions, and Eleanor's requisitions, and a more modest list of Bunford Weldon's necessities, and Franklin's provision of requirements which Eleanor did not specify, perhaps because she assumed his attention to them, were far more than the *Blanche* could bear.

So wills clashed, and compromises were not easy to reach, even after Gwen had seen the necessity of clarifying the position between herself and Franklin, which she did when Ehud had started on a journey to the boat, and Franklin was about to follow with a suit-case of her own possessions which she had not quite finished packing—an absurdly small case, which he suggested should be sufficient for her private use.

"I suppose," she remarked casually, as she pressed down a reluctant lid, and then sat upon it—a position which effectually delayed him as long as she might desire the conversation to continue. "I suppose you know that I've got to marry Ehud?"

"Got to? No. Why? I had an idea that you were making up your mind that he'd got to marry you. I suppose that's about the same thing."

"Not in the least. It's because we were alone together in the hut for about a century. It's the law of the Church. I happened to learn that before I came. It's something about working folly in Israel. At least, that's what I understood. I didn't get a chance to look up the text. There's no get-out unless I can show that I'm a God's-Truth on both sides, and then something happens to Ehud instead. I don't know what. Probably he gets stoned."

"I don't see that those laws matter to you. You're not of their nation, and you're not bound by them at all."

"No. But Ehud is. That's exactly the same thing."

"If you want it to be. Yes, I see that."

"I thought you might."

"I suppose you know that you'll have to join their church?"

"Yes? Well it won't kill me, if I do."

He remembered the remark of Henri Quatre that a kingdom was worth a mass. No, he didn't think Gwen would jib at that, if it lay across the path of her happiness; but he noticed that her lips set firmly with a thought which she did not speak. He wondered, if she should disapprove of the faith or rituals of the God's-Truth tribe, with whom the victory would lie. He was inclined to think that the Church might find her an indigestible morsel which it would have been wiser to leave unswallowed.

It had had its troubles with Patience God's-Truth, but Gwendolen Collinson might regard its authority without her inherited respect, and offer opposition in more aggressive forms.

So he thought, as he made his way through the steel-blue dusk of the Antarctic night, beneath a heaven of stars that sparkled brilliantly in frosty air, and along a track that was becoming easier with every transit that defined it further.

What would be the prospect of happiness for an English girl as Ehud God's-Truth's wife? He liked Ehud, who said little but gave no impression of stupidity. Faced with unfamiliar conditions of life, he was intelligently interested, but without either hostility or subservience. In conduct he was considerate, always ready to help, and yet independent and somewhat reserved. He had shown the same independence of mind towards his own church, and some courage also, when he had challenged his father as to how far he would go in defence of his sister's cause. Of his feelings towards Gwen there could be no doubt, nor of hers to him, and Franklin was wise enough to see—at least, where others were concerned—that love is the vital factor in successful marriage. Yet, at the best, it was a hard adventure to take, even in that exhilarating, Antarctic air, where life reacts so buoyantly against the cold which is its final foe.

A hard adventure, in a land where, except in that narrow valley lit by volcanic fire, no life of animal or tree or plant had found existence possible against the iron severity of its winter night.

In that valley, what, year by year, would her life be? He saw that this must depend, in part, upon whether its isolation should continue. And that might depend upon whether its existence should be made known to the outer world. It depended upon Eleanor and himself—and Bunford Weldon.

This thought naturally brought him to the consideration of how they would be affected by Gwen's desertion. How would Eleanor take the loss of her only feminine companion? How would it affect the conduct and the intimacies of the remainder of the broken quartet? But, after all, would the question arise? Had Gwen announced a fixed decision, or would cooler analysis decide her to abandon it as too hazardous an adventure? When she considered all that must be resigned or forgotten, would she find the price to be higher than she was disposed to pay?

He was the more inclined to question this by the next morning, observing little demonstration of affection between his companions, for Gwen was not naturally demonstrative, and Ehud had a reticence which was partly his own, and partly that of a community that led sternly controlled lives, influenced both by religious discipline and the separations in which they were besieged by the Antarctic weather during the sunless winter months. Familiarities of speech or conduct, if they occurred, were not for his eyes.

So the next morning, on the first occasion when they could speak alone, he returned to the subject.

"You really mean to marry Ehud?"

"I thought I'd made that moderately plain."

"It isn't because...I mean you're not really meaning to do it because you were alone in the hut? Ehud didn't...I mean he wouldn't...I mean he doesn't seem to me that he would treat a woman with any lack of respect under any circumstances."

"The answers," Gwen replied, with an amusement which repelled the gravity of his own speech, "are in the negative. Ever been in a church?"

"Yes. Occasionally."

"Then you know what it was like. The reason Ehud and I are going to marry each other isn't because we had forty-eight hours too much of each other's company. We're not such fools as that. That's only a reason that he may find useful for home consumption. It's because...well, I suppose we both think it's a game worth playing."

"It may prove a rather serious one."

"Of course. Most good games are. You're not very complimentary."

"I only wondered whether you'd looked at it all round."

"No. Not half. There hasn't been time. But we're not going to change our minds, if you mean that."

"There's another aspect of the matter. It isn't really my business. It's between Eleanor and you. But is it quite fair to her?"

"Yes. There's no snag in that. I suppose you don't know how my agreement is worded?"

"No. I didn't even know you had one."

"Well, I have. Eleanor's lawyers saw to that. I don't even know that she's aware of what's in it. They signed it on her behalf. It says that either party hereto can give the other three months' salary, and call it off on the spot."

"Yes...I see." Franklin was not surprised by this information. It was characteristic of the way in which Eleanor used her money, or, to be exact, of the way in which she allowed it to be used on her behalf. The condition had a sound of equity, even of liberality, but in operation it would mean that she could rid herself at any moment of her companion, at a cost which was literally nothing to her, but which would be a prohibitive penalty upon "the other party hereto" should she desire to exercise a similar freedom. It was an additional warning which he told himself that he did not need, against bending his neck to the same yoke, however softly it might be padded. All the same, he felt that there were other considerations than those of a strict legality, which Gwen should have been more ready to recognize.

He added, after a pause: "That does seem to let you out, if you're willing to write the cheque. By the way, you'd better post-date it a few months, if you really mean her to get the money, or it'll be out of date when she pays it in! But are you sure it's quite fair? What should you have said if Eleanor'd done the same thing? I mean, if she'd suddenly given you a cheque for £75—that's the amount, isn't it?—say, just after the *Bergen* went? I don't suppose you'd just have signed a receipt and sat down in the snow."

"Yes. I know what you mean. I've thought of that, but it's not quite the same thing. I'm not leaving her here to starve. Besides, look what it means to me, if I'm making my home here. Suppose I go back to England, and Eleanor sacks me there, or I throw it up, as I should, how many years' salary would it take to pay the return fare?"

Franklin saw that. The ethics of the problem were certainly rather complicated, but he still felt that there was an implied obligation that they should hold together till the end of the expedition, or, at the least, till they should rejoin the *Bergen*, with its possibilities of wider companionship and ultimate return to civilization. But Gwen did not wait for him to resume the attack. She carried the war into the enemy's country with her usual efficiency.

"I don't think you've got anything to complain about. Rather the other way. It might just bring Eleanor to the point. Bunford's the one who might grouse."

"Why should it affect him particularly?"

"Only because he's the one that gets left. He's the odd man out."

"Do you mean that, if you stay here, Eleanor will be obliged to marry one of us, and I shall be the selected victim?"

"Not obliged. And I don't think victim's the word. But you're right on the main idea."

"Then you can put it out of your mind. Even if she would be willing, which I've not the least reason or right to suppose, I should

144

never marry a woman of Eleanor's wealth. No self-respecting man would, unless he'd got plenty of his own."

"I suppose you think that sounds noble, but it doesn't to me. It sounds silly and rather mean. You'd spoil Eleanor's life (and mine, just as an extra, only you can't) because you haven't got some money you'd never need."

"It's not as simple as that. The money may make a difference to the woman herself."

"You mean Eleanor's not worth marrying?"

"I didn't say that."

"You'd have been wrong if you had."

"So I should. But the price might be too high."

"You can't care for her much if you can say that."

"I haven't said anything."

"I'm not sure that I agree. But about what I'm going to do, there's another aspect of it that's worth looking at. How about sacrificing myself for the rest of the expedition? It's quite the proper thing to do on this continent. Like Dr. Oates walking out into the blizzard."

"I shouldn't joke about that."

"I'm not sure that I am. Ehud might be persuaded to help you to get away."

"Is that going to be necessary?"

"From what Ehud tells me, it might be awkward without. There'll be only one condition, and that is that you don't let anything out that'll bring other people crowding here."

"You mean you want us to promise not to tell anyone about what we've found?"

"I'm not saying that it's my stipulation, but I should quite agree."

Franklin fell silent, for the conversation gave matter for thought. He had been in doubt as to whether conditions, if not objections, might be made to their departure ever since he had realized the character and isolation of the community into which they had intruded, and that quite apart from the complications arising from the trial of Patience God's-Truth. That the marriage of Ehud and Gwen, if it should be welcomed, would strengthen their position, had been present to his mind ever since he had observed Ehud's infatuation, and the fact that Gwen accepted it with complacency. But he had been doubtful whether she would face the problems and renunciations that it appeared to involve, and fearful whether her final refusal might not exasperate the position at a later stage, by alienating those who were of a present friendliness. But it had not occurred

145

to him that the prospect of such an alliance might affect her own attitude towards the problems which were before them.

Yet that was reasonable enough, though it might be surprising that it should take the form of desiring to separate herself more entirely from the civilization to which she belonged. And it needed little thought to observe how absolute that separation might become. If the secret were kept, it might be centuries before any new contact would be established with the outer world. Even the knowledge which she possessed would make little difference to the possibility of such approach from her own side. A boat—even a raft—might be built which would drift down the canyon stream, and be grounded at last upon the ocean beach. But what would be gained by that, if there should be no ship to meet them there, in a place where but two ships had ever come? Was she content to be exiled forever in that sombre, firelit valley, knowing that whatever longing came, whatever trouble might arise, she could do nothing to rejoin her kind? He showed that he had ceased to think of his own position, or Eleanor's, when he broke the silence by asking: "Do you realize what it means?"

"Yes," she said, "I'm not sure, but I think I do."

She was not sure; though she was resolute to take the experiment. Her mind wandered to the two pounds of tea which was in her private suitcase. And the things that she had been obliged to cast aside to make room for that! There would be plenty of tea for this winter. That was one of the things which had been high on Eleanor's list. But afterwards…well, it must be a spoonful once a quarter, or perhaps less. She would have to calculate how long she would be likely to live. By a natural sequence of thought, her mind went to the case of whisky which Bunford had asked them to take for his own use. She had objected to finding space for that. It had been one of the objects of contention between Franklin and herself. It had been standing beside the door of the hut. She looked in that direction, and saw that it had gone.

"You haven't taken that whisky!" she exclaimed, rather foolishly.

"Yes. I felt I must. Bunford's asked for so little altogether."

"I suppose you know what he did with the bottle that he had with him?"

"No. What?"

"He gave some to Timothy—Abel Trustwell's boy. I don't know why. Perhaps you see why I think we'd better keep to ourselves."

146

"You mean you don't want your adopted countrymen to be contaminated with our civilization? I thought I'd heard you say that they were scarcely human."

"So I did. And so they are, or aren't. You know what I mean. They need shaking up more ways than one, and to drop some of the ghastly nonsense they call religion, but I don't say that cocktails and cinemas are the best way to go about it. Probably with some small-pox and a few other diseases thrown in."

"You mean they've got no diseases now?"

"I didn't say that. I believe they've got one all to themselves. Ehud says there's an isolation hospital somewhere. Something they get from the soil, if they wash vegetables without gloves. That's the best I could understand. But I think they've got enough diseases of their own, and probably enough vices too."

"Modern civilization isn't all vice or disease. The standards of health...."

"Yes. I know all that. But we both know what goods it offers when it calls to do business at a new address. Ebenezer thinks the rest of the world went to hell when the *Morning Star* sailed from Yarmouth Roads. Suppose you showed him a dozen Hollywood films, what would he think then? He wouldn't think; he'd know."

Franklin felt that denial was useless there. An average assortment of Hollywood's noble-minded drunkards and prostitutes might not convey an exalted idea of the sanctity of our civilization to Ebenezer Trustwell's mind. He fell silent again, imagining what would be the consequences of establishing contact between that isolated community and the complex confusions that had developed in the larger world; a civilization eager to open new avenues of knowledge, and resolute to take their control out of its Creator's hands, while dimly, disconcertingly, conscious of its own incompetence; doubtful in the multiplication of its own children, but confident in the multiplication of its machines; which built its homes of pines rather than oak, as though aware of its own impermanence. In imagination he saw it destined to the suicide which is the resort of so many of its component citizens, and then—in the fullness of time—might not this ice-bound colony prove to be the ark from which an all-ruling Providence would replenish a fallen world? He would have spoken his thought had not Ehud entered the hut.

The next morning they started on their return journey, leaving the black menace of a sky which might have burst upon them at any moment in such a storm as would have made that which they had already experienced seem no more than a summer shower. Even Ehud did not know what they might have faced, for the extremes of

elemental fury do not rage on the inmost glaciers, and over the remote Antarctic heights, but along its ice-encumbered coasts, a thousand miles from the mid-silence of its polar night. In the twilight of
the canyon, as the overloaded *Blanche* churned its way upward
through the warm river, with lifted bows and a stern that was a bare
three inches above the stream, they could be indifferent to the
weather that might be raging on the untrodden heights above them.

It was in the afternoon that Franklin, half-dozing at the helm—
for wakefulness was not easy when relaxing from the toils of the
previous week—was roused to instant wakefulness by the sound of a
loud splash beside the boat.

"There's nothing to worry about," Gwen said calmly. "I thought
we'd be a bit safer if we lightened the boat."

"What's gone?"

"Only Bunford's whisky."

"You shouldn't have done that. Besides there's no sense in it.
Don't they brew cider themselves? The principle...."

"I'm not worrying about principles. I'm facing facts."

Franklin said no more. What was the use? The whisky was gone
now. But he thought it a useless folly. The idea of Bunford distributing his precious beverage so freely as to create a party determined to
get more, even at the cost of abandoning their solitude, seemed fantastic, as perhaps it was. Certainly, had they been able to foresee the
future, it would have shown them the futility of such a fear. But he
did see that Gwen was of a resolute disposition to consider—and
control—the welfare of the country in which she aspired to be a ma-
tron—or, perhaps, a queen?

CHAPTER XXXIX.

MICHAEL GOD'S-TRUTH walked in torment, pulling his
beard. For thirty vigorous years he had ruled himself and the world
around him—the whole world, as he knew it—with an iron discipline. He had become the first of the Elders, though there were several much older than he, and seniority had always been held to give
the prior claim. Even in this recent accusation against his daughter,
he had felt the confidence of a strength which had always equalled
its test. When he had rebuffed Ehud's suggestion of violence, he had
done it in a spirit of self-reliance. He had not only aimed to win, but
to do so with the least possible religious or political disturbance.

There had been one black episode in his life more than twenty
years ago, when he had discovered the infidelity of the foolish un-

148

stable woman whom he had made his wife. But, even then, he had acted with discretion and self-control. There had been no public exposure. The woman had not been executed, as the levity of her conduct merited, both by human and divine law. She had stood beside him while Simeon Trustwell cast himself into the pit of hell. So Simeon had bought her life with his own, which was already forfeit. By watching, she had bought hers. No one else had even guessed the truth. It was her secret and his. He had done no more than thrash and forgive her. She had remained at the head of his household and in charge of his children. At least Patience and Ehud were surely his. Of Noah he was less sure. If he looked back, as he seldom did, he saw that he had acted well.

But now he was being tried of God or tempted by devilish powers, for the strange woman was in his thoughts both by night and day.

There were times, in his longing for her, when he planned impossible things. It was the custom to have no more than one wife, but it was less than a divine law. If he sought Bathsheba, he did a less wrong, in that there was no Uriah to be put in the forefront of the battle. Even if he should be punished of God, it had been shown what the penalty would be. Well, let the first-born die. There would be others to follow.

She was an unmarried girl of full age. She should, indeed, have been married years before now. It would not be policy to let her—to let any of these strangers—return to her own land. She must marry someone here. He was farsighted enough to see that the children of such a union might introduce new elements, a new vitality, into the interbreeding of their limited community. The balance of authority might shift toward the family which established such an alliance. Already there were foolish, futile attempts on the part of some of the women to imitate the fashion of her clothes, the dressing of her hair. Seeing this, was he to let her go to another?

It might be argued, as she was not of their community, that their marriage restrictions did not apply to her. She was extra, apart.

Then there was the fact that their first ancestor had had two wives. Much could be made of that.

Or if she were Hagar to his Abraham? A darker thought came. Suppose, after all these years, he should denounce his wife? There would be no doubt of the result. He knew her timidity, her cowardice. She would have no hardihood to sustain denial. And none could blame him, unless for the first concealment, and the weakness of human nature would be sufficient defence for that. After all these years, conscience had triumphed. And, after all these years, justice upon the adulteress would still be done. But he put the thought away with a firm will. He was not naturally base, even under such temptation as he now felt.

He did not avoid the thought, letting it linger and fret furtively in the dark rear of his mind. He faced it openly, imagining all it would mean, both of evil and good, and when he had done this it was no better than a dead thing. But he could not deal so decisively with the torment that possessed his soul. For he was doubtful whether his love was cast upon a human woman, or a fiend disguised to tempt him to eternal loss.

It was true that Eleanor had come at a good time. She had spoken on his daughter's part, which was a good deed. (Or, at least, it was good unless Patience had really blasphemed, in which case the fellowship of fiends was a likely thing.) But might that be for no other reason than to gain his confidence?

That was Hell's subtlety! Even to do a good deed so that a greater evil might follow. So she had crept into his very home, as she could have done in no other way. So she had been able to cast her spells upon him, and the devils laughed in Hell, seeing his feet caught in the meshes of the net she drew. Now Heaven and Hell fought for his soul.

And he had warnings enough! By the mercy of God, there are ways in which a witch cannot avoid the revelation of what she is. Out of the fullness of the heart the mouth speaketh. A witch cannot talk for long without disclosing some of the imaginations of her own place. There had been the absurdity, publicly stated, of ships driven at incredible speeds by blasts of pursuing steam. Only yesterday she had told him of a box which Franklin was to bring, by which voices would speak to her from the other side of the world. But Hell was nearer than that. How is it that when a witch moves among men she cannot do it as a simple guileless woman, but must say and do things which disclose what she is? All the wisdom of the controlling fiends does not prevent this. Doubtless, that is by the mercy of God, that temptation be not too subtle for His saints to see. For God deals faithfully with His own. *Thou shalt not suffer a witch to live.* There is no ambiguity about that. If we disobey, can we put the blame upon any except ourselves?

And yet, if he were wrong! Faced with this problem of what she was, angel or woman, witch or fiend, the rest seemed easy, if he could only know. Were she fiend, he would have strength from God to watch her burn, let him love her body as he might. Were she woman, he would find a way to win her, and together they would be greater than he had dreamed before. She had told him of her wealth, of what she could bring to transform this land. Could such things not be brought secretly, without establishing a dreaded intercourse with the outer world? But was not this the temptation of the wilderness? Satan's gift to those who will fall down and worship?

If he could only be sure!

And as he talked with Eleanor, sometimes when Patience was with them, sometimes alone, he fell under the spell of her alien beauty, and was fascinated by the new things of which she talked in a natural human way. And then he would walk apart, and again the torment possessed his mind.

Boxes that hold the voices and songs of men, and that will talk when they are told! Others by which you can learn what is happening twenty thousand miles away! *Thou shalt not suffer a witch to live*. What could be plainer than that?

Meanwhile, Bunford Weldon wandered abroad with Noah in the brief daylight hours, when the low sun moved above the horizon, or when the full moon, wonderfully ringed with all the colours of a repeated rainbow, shone down upon a whitened land, which doubled and returned its light from every crystal of the frozen snow.

Noah knew that Eleanor was a witch. He had known it beyond doubt since she had sat beside him at that first meal, when she had talked and he had listened with an inward trembling. Now he would save his father and sister. More than that, he would save himself, and the whole community if he could, from the wrath of God.

Every day he went out with Bunford Weldon, leading him into the company of others, and guiding the conversation to such directions as would disclose him for what he was. So, every day, new witnesses were provided.

Every evening Noah looked fearfully toward the red glow of the southern sky, and every night he prayed that God would regard his own efforts, his own integrity, and delay the doom that threatened an unrighteous city.

So the days passed, while the return of the *Blanche* delayed, and the confidence of Eleanor's outward demeanour concealed a sharpening anxiety. For, if they did not return, was she not abandoned here for a lifetime with Bunford Weldon, with all the restrictions and bareness of the life around her?

From their different angles, and with different anticipations, Michael and Bunford thought the same things. If Franklin and Gwen and Ehud had fallen victims to the creatures of the water-caves....

To Eleanor it was a frightening thought, and rather than endure it in solitude, she would talk to Michael as long as he would.

His gravity did not conceal from her, nor perhaps from others, the fascination which she had cast upon him. As to that, she was pleased. It was a flattery to which she was well used, which she regarded as no more than her natural due. He was married. A man twice her age. It did not enter her thoughts that there could be any danger from that.

And then Franklin walked in, and the anxiety was over. Ehud and Gwen came also. Ehud talked with his father alone for a long time. He wished to marry Gwen.

It was the last day of April, and that was the last day on which, according to their custom, marriages could be contracted until the next spring. Michael saw advantages in that marriage, actual and prospective. He acted with prompt decision. Gathering the necessary witnesses, he led a little party off to the Meeting-house, and there he married them himself, by the light of a rising moon.

CHAPTER XL.

MICHAEL'S house covered a wide area. It was massively built of stone and of solid oak. It had neither stairs nor windows. To be more exact, its windows were no more than unglazed squares covered by heavy shutters, which opened on a side hinge. The art of glass-making had not been brought to this land. These apertures were very solidly closed, for even in the comparative warmth of this volcanic valley, the Antarctic winter was to be treated with respect.

Gwen found herself alone with Ehud in a lamp-lit room, vaguely disquieted by a desire for an emotion which did not come. She had got what she wished, and that with an unexpected, almost unwelcome, suddenness. She did not call it unwelcome to herself, but she had a feeling that it should be a moment of exaltation, of emotion that should be a lifetime's memory, and that her mood was not equal to its realization. That vexed as well as disappointed her, for she liked to feel that what she did was beyond criticism, even of her own thoughts. Her mind was troubled by a line of half-forgotten verse. What was it? Swinburne? And from where?

"Love, sleep, and death, move to the sweet same tune."

Other lines came more dimly, all on the same rhyme. Some association of an emotion she must have felt when she read them first, that this night recurred. And then clearly:

"Oh, my sweet lord, I charge thee, leave me this,
Is it not better than a foolish kiss?
Nay then, take all, my flower, my first-in-June.''

Yes, she remembered now! *In the Orchard*. How absurd! And there was *Before Dawn*. How did it go?

"Between the bud and blossom,
Between your throat and chin...
To say of shame, What if it?
Of virtue, we can miss it.
Of sin, we can but kiss it,
And 'tis no longer sin."

What would Ehud think if she quoted that poem to him? Or, at least, as much as she could remember. She must rely on memory now, except for the half-dozen books that she had brought. And the things she had had to leave behind to bring them! It seemed that she had brought nothing except at the price of half a dozen possibly more needed things. Well, it was too late now for regrets. And she didn't regret! She was glad. It should be a success. At least, it should not be her fault if it failed. And she had a theory, that, if a marriage fails, it is the woman's fault in nine cases out of ten. As to the riches of English verse which had accumulated in the last three centuries, she had quoted to Ehud from memory, and been startled by the excitement of his reaction. After all, what did they know of each other? Well, she knew that his arms were coming round her now. "Oh, Ehud," she said, as she stood passively, feeling his kisses, "we mustn't fail. We must pull it off!"

Pull what off? Her idiom, as so often, had no meaning for him. But he heard the troubled note in her voice. His own consciousness was of delirious, amazing victory. He did not think of the future or recall the past. The moment was enough for him. But he held her the more tenderly for that note of inexplicable trouble, and when he answered, the words meant little to her, but the tone much.

In that first ten minutes, through that heavily-shuttered window, was it wonderful that they were deaf to the warning sound of a distant bell?

Actually, Gwen heard it first, though it had no meaning to her. Sound carried far in that clear frozen air. Perhaps her own ears, accustomed to collect their sounds from the din of a surrounding bedlam, were excessively alert to the few noises of this most silent land, which was without vehicle or machine, and where no bird called in

153

BEYOND THE RIM, BY S. FOWLER WRIGHT

the night. Its only voice was the wind, or the distant roar of an avalanche on the frozen heights. She said: "Isn't that the bell that we heard once before?"

Ehud unlatched the heavy shutter, and pushed it wide. He leaned out to listen.

After what seemed a long time to Gwen (was she not more important than the sound of a distant bell?), he drew in his head.

"It doesn't seem possible," he said, in a troubled voice. "I wish I'd heard it from the start."

With a hesitant hand, he drew the shutter, closing out the moonlight from the lamp-lit room. Gwen thought it was none too soon. They were still warmly clothed, but the night air held an icy chill.

Yet he stood in doubt, avoiding her eyes. Surely he need not leave her now—for so wild a tale?

A hand beat on the door. His father's voice called: "Ehud! Ehud! You must get ready at once. The Anabaptists are out."

Ehud unbarred the door, and his father entered without ceremony. He went to the closed window, and threw it open again. Faint but insistent, they could still hear the tolling of the distant bell.

"Hadn't you heard?" Michael asked impatiently. "They've been out six hours, and no one knows yet how far they've come."

"They could tell by the snow."

"Of course. They are following up the tracks. The wonder is that they've not been here before now."

Ehud saw that. Even without the explanation of the massacre at Naomi Trustwell's farm, and the words of the woman, dying and left as dead, which had told the hour at which they passed, it was easy to understand. At some urgent need, such as could not be satisfied by sporadic plundering along the outskirts of the settled land, they had planned a raid with their whole force, to penetrate deeply into their enemy's country. So they had done more than once before, but those incidents had been of earlier years. It was supposed that they were too weak and few for such an enterprise now. There must be something wrong about that. And such raids had always one main objective—Michael God's-Truth's tan-yards.

They looked out towards Abel Trustwell's farm, four miles away. It was further even than they from the mountains over which the Anabaptists came, the mountains that separated the valley from the slopes of Hell.

There was a slight rise of ground between them and Abel's farm. It was unlikely that they would see anything from that direction. Michael had opened the window to listen rather than look. But

154

now there was a glow over that low ridge, which did not come from the moon or the departed sun.

Michael said: "There is much to be done, and we may have no time at all." He turned hastily away, and it was Gwen's voice that stayed him, as Ehud was about to close the shutter again. "There is someone coming up the path."

Ehud said: "It's Abel's Timothy." His father and Gwen were already at the door. He stayed a moment to close and bar the shutter, and hurried after them.

Timothy came up the path at a stumbling run, showing haste but no speed. Before they reached him, he fell forward on his face, and did not rise. Michael raised him, turning him over. Where he had fallen there was a dark stain on the snow. *The sword,*" he said, choking on the word, *"the sword of the Lord and of Gideon."*

Michael lifted him in his arms, and strode backward to the house. His head hung loosely. It was clear that there was nothing more to be gained from him. Nothing beyond the message that had been on his tongue as he had run from the burning house: the message given him by Abel Trustwell, who now lay dead on his own threshold, careless of the creeping flames. After all, Timothy had proved true to his adoptive home.

Michael gave the wounded boy to the care of his wife and Patience. He looked round the living-room, crowded now with his sons and servants, with Franklin and Bunford, and the women. The largest man there, he seemed to be roused by the need for action to a new lightness, a new alertness, dominating the scene.

He looked on his visitors, and said curtly: "Can I count your help?"

He looked at Franklin as he spoke, but Eleanor was the quicker to answer. "We'll do whatever we can."

Gwen, standing back, cool and watchful, said nothing. There was no need. It was evident where her interest and her duty lay. It seemed that she would have no difficulty in remembering her wedding night—if she were destined to survive it. Having had the benefit of Ehud's conversation, she understood the peril better than her friends were able to do.

"Love, sleep, and death, move to the sweet, same tune."

Perhaps they did. But which was the nearest now? It seemed to have been an apposite line, after all.

But all this was an instant's thought, and did not distract her mind from hearing Franklin's cautious reply: "It's really a question of how we stand. If we're friends, we ought to help you, of course; if

155

we're no better than guests, it's not quite so clear; if we're prisoners, it's not clear at all."

She felt that he was remembering their conversation at the hut on the beach, when she had warned him that it might not be easy to get away. It was reasonable for him to make terms, if his help were wanted now. But he didn't understand.

Michael answered him plainly enough. "You can call yourselves as you like, and you can be friends if you will, but if you don't do what you can now, you'll be dead in an hour's time, it's more chances than not."

"Very well," Franklin said quietly, "if it's that bad, you'd better tell us what we can do. Bunford, I suppose you can spare one of your rifles? You won't want both."

Bunford looked his unwillingness. "It isn't them," he said. "It's the cartridges."

Franklin saw reason in that, though he did not know how greatly Bunford had depleted his resources while he had been out with Noah during the past fortnight, and encouraged to demonstrate his skill to different onlookers—itself to be a minor addition to the more damning evidence of an evil alliance which his conversation disclosed—for how could such unvarying skill be achieved except by supernatural aid?

He said: "I know I can't shoot like you. You'd better let me have just a handful, and one of the rifles. I won't use them, unless there's real need."

"Noah," Michael said, "Take Caleb, and go through the house, making it sure that every shutter is barred. Master Franklin, I shall thank your aid. Of a verity they will be here; it may be in less than an hour's time. I cannot tell in what force, but we can look for no help till the dawn."

As he spoke, he was drawing on a thickly quilted doublet, making his massive frame appear even bulkier than before. He belted on a heavy sword. The other men were occupied in similar ways. Swords, and pikes, and quarter-staves. Noah put on a steel cap, and the back-and-breast pieces which were too small for his father's wearing.

Franklin was a little puzzled as to where the greatness of the danger lay. They were a group of armed men, in a house that was very solidly built, and that was practically without windows. He had understood that the Anabaptists were little better than unarmed savages, and few in number. The whole settlement must be roused by now. In what, then, could the danger be? Why should help be delayed till the dawn?

156

He thought also that Michael might not allow sufficiently for the advantage of a rifle in Bunford Weldon's hands. He may have been right on this last point, but on the others he was to learn much before the night was over.

Ehud had gone to the still-open door, where he stood talking to Gwen in low tones, things meant only for themselves. While he talked, his eyes were on the snow-covered fields that rose slightly toward the west. "Father," he called, "they're coming now." Michael came out, and behind him men and women crowded to the porch to see.

Over the ridge, and down a field which the wind had cleared till the powdered snow lay scarcely deep enough to hide the barley-stubble beneath it, vaguely seen in the moonlight, there came a dark group of moving figures. They moved slowly, as though burdened. They were not coming directly to the house, but seemed as though they would pass across its front.

Seen in that ghostly light, they were weird and strange, rather than threatening, and a clearer vision might have shown them strange and repellent, but scarcely formidable.

They were about forty in number, all women, and not young. They were naked except for the leather coverings of their feet, and short skirts of the same material, most of which were so torn and shredded as to be of little use either for warmth or concealment. Their hair hung long and loose, in most cases smoothly combed, and in some extremely luxuriant. Their skins were hardened to fire and frost, with the baked aspect of those that Dante watched, who dodge forever the slow-falling flakes of fire. Each of them bore on her back a dead goat, its feet tied beneath her chin.

Eleanor said: "Oh, look, Franklin. They've got Paradise."

So it was. She walked in their midst. Like the others, she had a goat on her back. Her hands were not bound, but a woman walked on either side, gripping an arm.

Gwen said: "I thought you said they never take anyone alive when they're out like this."

"Yes," Ehud answered. "I wonder she's alive. It must be that she wouldn't run."

"Franklin," Eleanor said impatiently, "we can't leave her with them. Master God's-Truth, can't something be done?"

Franklin looked at Michael. He felt as Eleanor did, that they ought to attempt a rescue, but it was for Michael to decide. There was something vaguely sinister in the way in which this strange procession moved across their front as though unaware of their existence.

Michael shook his head. He pointed up the field. There was another larger group of men, coming at a faster pace, and directly toward the house.

Michael was no coward, but he understood the position as these strangers could not be expected to do.

There must be nearly a hundred of these half-naked, half-savage men advancing upon them, men who could run three yards to their two, men who were armed in primitive but deadly ways, men who, if they once started running away, would pursue and tear them to pieces in the sport and fury of the chase.

These men might have human virtues at other times, but when they raided their hated foes, and the lust of blood woke in their hearts, they became more savage than beasts. Ehud must have been right when he said that Paradise had escaped because she had not offered either to fight or run. And they had found her useful to carry one of Abel Trustwell's goats.

Seeing the number that were advancing upon them—a number larger than he had supposed to exist—Michael knew that he had been right when he said that they would have no aid before the next day. His neighbours would flee away, if they had time to do so. If any small group should show themselves, they would be chased and killed. There would be no attempt to relieve him till the whole force of the settlement had been collected. The women and children would be gathered in the Meeting-houses with sufficient garrisons of men to guard them, and the remaining men of robust years—perhaps three hundred and fifty—would then advance to his relief, or to interfere between the Anabaptists and their retreat should they have succeeded in plundering him of the stores of leather which were their main objective.

The goat-meat was an extra for the older women, who had been brought with them for that purpose, to carry to safety if they could. Probably they could get back through the night without meeting any opposition strong enough to bar their way. At the worst, they could drop their burdens and run, in which case they would not be easy to catch. It was a raid well planned, from the experiences of earlier years. Its success depended upon a speedy capture of Michael God's-Truth's premises; and the massacre of the inhabitants would be a mere incident of the enterprise.

Michael saw that, if they advanced to the rescue of Paradise, even if they could wrest her from the women, or if the women ran away, they could not regain the house before the whole horde would be upon them. They would not save Paradise. She would merely share their fate. In half an hour they would all be dead, and the raiders would be loading themselves with the bundles of tanned skins for which they had come, and which it was his part to protect.

It was Bunford, to whom she had not thought to appeal, who gave Eleanor what she asked. Nervous, restless, and frightened, he wanted something to do, above all something to shoot. He cared nothing whether they were women or men. They were scarcely human to him. They were things he hated and feared. He said to Franklin: "Can you get the near one, if I get the one on the other side?"

Franklin saw what he meant. If the two who held her arms were shot at the same moment, she would have a chance to run to them, and escape. But it was too great a risk. At such a distance, in such a light! No, he could not be sure. So he said.

Bunford lost no time with more words. The others were already drawing back into the house. The group of the goat-burdened women were immediately before him, about two hundred yards away. He fired twice. He made no mistake. The women on either side of Paradise collapsed to the ground. The group stopped in a confused way. Paradise showed no hesitancy in understanding the position. She may have been alert for any movement to rescue her as the house was passed. Hardly had the women fallen when she slipped her head through the legs of the goat with which she was burdened. She eluded the women round her, still burdened as they were, and got clear. She came running towards the house. Franklin had already started to run to meet her. He had dropped the rifle, but had his revolver in his hand. His action had the less merit in that he did not know the risk he ran.

Bunford became conscious that the group which had been around him had withdrawn, though they still looked out at the open door. He looked to the right, and saw the main group of the Anabaptists now running at their utmost pace toward the house. Coming down the slope in the moonlight they looked larger, nearer, more numerous than they actually were. He retreated hastily over the threshold, and made a motion to close the door.

Michael threw him aside, with a rough hand on his shoulder. He pushed the door wide again, and walked out, his drawn sword in his hand. He pointed it to the onrushing horde, and looked back at Bunford. "Shoot," he said, with impatient contempt.

He called in a great voice to Franklin. "Faster! Faster!" Franklin had reached Paradise now. She had run well. She was breathing hard. Running at her side, he would have slackened speed somewhat. There seemed plenty of time. He said: "We're all right now."

"Oh, but the stones!" she answered, running on, so that he had to spurt to regain her side. They were almost at the door, where Mi-

159

chael stood massively, sword in hand, as though in contempt of the wild horde which were rushing down upon them. Through the open door came the sharp reports and flashes of Bunford's rifle. He had regained control of the sudden panic which had possessed him, and was firing with deadly precision at the foremost runners.

Possibly he saved their lives. Possibly it was that their pursuers were running too rapidly to use their slings with their usual accuracy. The first stone struck Franklin when he was ten yards from the door. He fell next moment, struck on the head, and Michael dragged him in. He was none the worse for that half an hour later. Paradise, who had been on his further side, had nothing worse than a bruised chin, which, for an inch's difference, might have been a broken jaw, or even worse damage than that.

CHAPTER XLI.

MICHAEL GOD'S-TRUTH looked at Bunford in a speculative silence, stroking his beard, as his way was. He thought him to be a coward, but it was certain that he was a good shot—better than Franklin, by their mutual admissions. Besides, Franklin was still sitting half-dazed from the blow of the stone that had grazed his head. Bunford it must be, and it might be best to say nothing of the risk involved. That might be less than fair, but the position would justify much. Could he offer him Noah's armour, or his own quilted coat, without explanations which might result in refusal? Having the lives of all that were there in his keeping, it was a risk that he could not run.

The house was closed absolutely now, except for two shadowed slits which enfiladed the sides of the store-house. He had distributed his sons and servants in the various rooms, where they had nothing to do but to listen for any sound of attack, or watch for a sign of fire.

Fire was the greatest danger that they had to fear, but fire is easier to start than to stop. There could be no assurance, if the house were set alight, that their besiegers would be able to gain access to the stores it held before the fire should reach them. Still, they might risk that. If they did, it would almost certainly be attempted at the residential end of the house, which was the furthest from the stores they sought.

On the other hand, should they try to force an entrance, which he thought to be the more likely, it would almost as certainly be at the store-house end.

This store-house was at the north of the house, and somewhat narrower than the portion to which it was attached, so that, on either side of the end of the larger room which adjoined it, there were a few feet of wall, the windows of which looked along its sides. The shutters of these windows had had loop-hole slits ever since the house was rebuilt, following a successful raid in an earlier century, at a time when the old firearms were still in use.

Michael was in no haste. He calculated time. He wished them to settle down to their work before he should intervene. He calculated the hours of the night also. Every stage of attack and defence must be so handled that its course would be as slow as he could contrive to make it. When he thought that the right moment had arrived, he walked over to Bunford, who sat talking to Patience and Paradise.

Paradise, quiet and pale, making no trouble of her bruised face, was telling of the events of the afternoon, the destruction of her home, and her uncle's death. There was nothing for the women to do but talk—nothing, as yet, in that close-shuttered, silent house.

Michael said: "Would you take a shot at this hell-spawn from the loop-hole of a dark room?"

Bunford rose at once. He was restless for action. The account that Paradise had given had not been good to hear. But to shoot from a sheltered place—he knew he could do that. Give him the opportunity of a few more shots, and there would be fewer of these vermin to threaten their more valuable lives. The beggars might bolt altogether. He picked up both rifles. Franklin didn't need them now. It would save time in reloading. He followed Michael with a good will.

They left Franklin leaning back on a settle against the wall. Eleanor was beside him, having done what she could for his wound, which was not much. The stone had merely skimmed his head, but it must have been with a great force. He seemed dazed to those around him, and Eleanor said little, thinking rest to be his first need; but his mind had been clear for some time, though his thoughts came slowly, and there were blanks when consciousness loitered along the edge of sleep.

He heard what Michael said, and opened his eyes to see the two men go through the door that led to the rear of the house. He saw Bunford take his rifle, with a faint stir of resentment. But his thoughts were on other things.

There were only Patience and Paradise left in the room now. They were at the further end, talking between themselves. Neither was the kind to be watchful of Eleanor and himself, or to try to overhear what they might say. His first words showed in which direction his thoughts went: "I hope they won't get the *Blanche*. They won't be likely to look there."

"No," she said, "I shouldn't think that's likely." She had thought of the same thing. It would be disaster if the boat should be lost. And it had been only partly unloaded as yet. But for that, Bunford would have had more of the precious cartridges on which their lives might depend. Yet she saw that there was little reason for any fear. The *Blanche* was moored in a sheltered place, where the oakgrove came to the water's edge, as it had been before.

Franklin went on: "We don't know how things may go here. If there should be a chance to get away? You know what Gwen says, that they won't let us go later on, it's more likely than not."

Eleanor was slow to answer. She knew that there was reason behind his words, and it was easy to see that the accidents of this strife which was not theirs might give them opportunities to slip away which might never recur. As to their promise to support Patience in her trial, surely the very fact of its indefinite postponement was their release? And, besides, they would be leaving Gwen.

But, in spite of all this, she was reluctant to speak the consenting word which would have roused him to active planning. If this attack should be beaten off (and looking at the strength of the surrounding walls, and in that prevailing silence, she had no doubt of that), she would still feel that there was more here, both of security and comfort, than could be found in the huts upon the storm-lashed coast

She would have to go without Gwen. Alone with two men whom she recognised as her lovers, but neither of whom would dominate her, body and soul, as a man should. She would much rather have them here with the pleasant deference of Michael God's-Truth—she was secretly proud of that conquest—and many others around whom she would subjugate in the same way, if it should be useful to do so. She had little doubt that, before the spring came, she would have matters arranged to her own liking. She was used to getting her own way.

No, she was not going to spend the winter in those huts, with Franklin and Bunford for her only companions. Not that she was concerned for the unconventional aspects of such an association. But she was used to having Gwen with her. It added to her comfort in a score of ways, which were not trifling to her.

She said: "We can't go without Gwen."

"You don't want us to stay here forever?"

162

"No. Of course not. We can run down in the spring, when the *Bergen*'s due. We needn't go till we're sure she'll be there. They've been told to wait for six weeks."

"But you don't know that they'll let us go then."

"I don't suppose there'll be any trouble. Gwen ought to manage that for us. There'll be plenty of time to talk it over before then. It's far better to go openly, and be friends if we come again."

Franklin felt that he argued in vain. He felt too weak to press it further. Yet he made one more effort. "I think it's best to go when we can. There's too much at stake for a needless risk."

His persistence irritated her, all the more, perhaps, because she was not sure that he was wrong, and she was little used to meet resistance when she pressed her will.

"Considering what you've told me of the time you had at the huts, I should have thought you'd agree that we're safer here. It didn't sound as though we should get through the winter alive."

Franklin knew that there were answers to that, but he felt that they would be useless words. And he could understand that she didn't want to be alone there, alone with Bunford and himself, for the length of the winter night. And he saw that, at any cost, they must work together, planning with a single purpose to the same end.

At that moment he gave up definitely the thought of escape, and resolved, with a sombre courage—for the presentiment of evil was strongly upon him—that they must stand their ground here, and see it through.

Muffled by the thickness of the walls, but sounding clearly enough, there came the rapid continuous sound of Bunford's rifles, and then silence.

A few minutes later, Michael entered the room with Bunford in his arms. Franklin looked at the sagging form as the light fell on it, and knew that what he had proposed could never have been. Had he arranged to go with Eleanor—if he should ever go with her—it must be alone. Bunford's forehead was broken in, and a granite stone was still wedged in the wound.

CHAPTER XLII.

THE room to which Michael had led the way was in absolute darkness, except for two narrow horizontal slits at either side of the opposite wall, at which the snow-reflected moonlight faintly entered. Moving with a cautious quietness, he went first to the left-hand slit. Bunford, looking out beside him, saw the long side of the narrow storeroom, with its shadow stretching across the snow. Just beyond the limit of this shadow, a dark figure sat silent and watchful. He had an upright stick in his hand, from which hung a leather sling. Michael knew that, at the faintest sound, the slightest motion at the slit from which they looked out, the sling would have been whirling round the head of the watcher, and its missile would have shot, straight and hard as a bullet, toward them. He knew that these watchful marksmen were seated at short intervals all round the house, and it was against the deadly menace of their artillery that he had ordered every shutter to be tightly closed.

Bunford expected a request that he would shoot this solitary watcher, but he felt only a restraining hand on his arm as he was withdrawn quickly from the aperture, and led along the wall to that on the right-hand side.

Here the moonlight shone on the snow to the foot of the storehouse, and here was a more animated and more sinister scene.

Crouching in a little group against the wall, half a dozen of their enemies, their slings laid down behind them, were engaged in burning a way through the thick oak planks of which it was built.

The snow had drifted deeply against the side of the house, and they had scooped it away to right and left, so that, at first, it partly hid their operations from the two who looked out upon them. Michael's eyes went from them to a single figure who sat behind them with a ready sling, but showing no signs of suspicion. "Wait," he whispered very low into Bunford's ear.

Bunford looked at the slingsman who was most clearly in view. His hair, like that of the women, was long, but, unlike them, he wore it shaggy and rough, mingling with the luxuriance of an untrimmed beard. Like them, he wore a short leather skirt, and it was no better than a shredded rag. He sat in the snow as though his skin were hardened into insensibility either of heat or cold.

The group under the wall were becoming clearer now. Jets of flame would shoot upward from where they worked, and then they would scoop the snow toward them in their hands, putting out the fire with a great hissing of steam.

Michael knew what they did as well as though it had all been bare to his gaze. Their aim was to burn a hole through the planks by which they might enter, without setting fire to the building. Their instrument was something which he knew well as to its appearance and effects, but beyond that, it had a mysterious quality. The Anabaptists had not contrived a manner of life for two hundred years on the slopes of Hell without some discoveries of their own. Two of that little group had come armed with a hollow metal ball which glowed red-hot from an inner source, and which did not cool. Each was carried on a short chain, the heat of which would have burnt anything but an Anabaptist's hand.

Now these red-hot balls were being pressed again and again into the wooden planks, which charred and blackened and burst into flame, and were quenched in the hissing snow. The little group of the assailants kneeled in a pool of steaming water as the snow-piles lessened, till the whole of their operation was disclosed to Bunford's eyes.

"You want me to hit those red balls?" he whispered, in response to Michael's scarcely-articulate word.

"Yes. Quietly. Quickly. The men after, if there's time."

Michael did not know what the effect of such a shot would be. It was an experiment. He only knew that those fire-balls were the deadliest weapons in their enemies' hands.

The bullet hit truly enough. That was a certainty with the trigger under Bunford's finger. The fire-ball did not break, but the force of the shot jerked the controlling chain from the hands of the man who held it, and drove the ball into a neighbour's lap. The man screamed. Even his hardened skin could not stand the impact of red-hot metal. Bunford's second bullet, perhaps striking its objective more directly, shattered it so that it burst, with the upshooting of a green flame.

"*Quickly. Smash the other,*" Michael whispered urgently, but Bunford did not heed him then, nor a moment later, when he would have pulled him back in safety.

He had emptied the one rifle now, and picked up the other. The lust to kill was upon him: to kill safely from a sheltered place. He fired into that suddenly-astonished group, and each bullet was death.

It was the scream of the burnt man, the burst of the green flame, that gave him the needed seconds for these fatal shots. There was a moment during which they drew the attention of the slingsman. The next, he had seen from where the shots came, and his weapon was circling around his head.

Michael pulled Bunford from the slit, but it was too late to save him, for he was struck as he did so. He raised him in his arms. There would be five seconds while the slingsman adjusted another stone. He strode across the room to the door with his burden, hearing the loud crack of the missile that struck the wall beside him as he passed through. Life in that room, for some time to come, would be a precarious thing.

CHAPTER XLIII.

MICHAEL laid his burden down, and considered the dented skull. He saw that Bunford was a dead man. He turned to those who looked on to tell what had occurred.

Eleanor said no more than "Poor Bunny!" She felt no sharp emotion, and would be very unlikely to simulate anything which she did not feel. She took it coldly, as she took the danger in which, as she began to realize, they all stood. She was conscious that Michael addressed his account to herself rather than to Franklin, and with what, from him, was almost a tone of apology. But she could not see that he was to blame.

Franklin said: "I suppose you left the rifles there?"

"Yes. We should do ill to seek them as yet." Michael thought it would be some time before that room could be safely crossed again.

"Do you think they'll go on trying to burn away through?"

"I have good hopes. I would not have foiled them so far that they cease that trial. There might be a worse following watch over the hours."

He went on to explain that the worst anger was that they should attempt to burn the whole premises down, which it would be diffi-cult—if not impossible—to resist. But they would not be likely to try that method till others had failed. His aim was to delay the effort to break through the store-house wall, rather than to repulse it deci-sively. He counted hours till relief would come.

Franklin suggested that the rifles could be used against the first sign of breaching the wall, if they should watch from the inside, even more effectively than had been done from the loophole already. Stones could not be slung through the first cracks with the case or directness with which a bullet would penetrate. Michael agreed to that. He thought that, after a time, the intervening room might be crossed without great risk, and the rifles could be picked up. It might, indeed, be necessary to risk that crossing at any moment, if a call for aid should come from Noah, who was stationed in the store-house, where, with his mother, he prepared leather-coated screens, after a traditional pattern which had been used before, to set up against the entrance of missiles through any breach which might be made, and boiling compositions of objectionally adhesive kinds and red-hot weapons with which to meet any attack which might break through. The total garrison, men and women, was so small that there could only be one or two stationed in each room, and these must be withdrawn and concentrated as soon as any point of attack should develop dangerously. So—strangest of all wedding-nights!—Gwen and Ehud watched in their own room for the sound of violence on roof or wall, or the smell of the dreaded fire, alert for the call of danger elsewhere, at which he, at least, must be ready to hurry instantly to the threatened point.

But for the next half-hour nothing happened except that, in the store-house itself, after a time, Noah and his mother could hear sounds, muffled by the heavy timbers of the wall, which told that the attack had been resumed.

Noah had been placed by his father in the place where danger was likely to threaten first, as was a fit thing, for he was not only his elder son, and reputed to be of good courage and strength of arm, though they might be put at times to a cruel use, but he had the advantage of wearing the best defensive armour that the house contained. His mother was there because he was her favourite child.

She had his confidence also, as no one else had—certainly not Paradise Trustwell; who worshipped him in her heart for something that he could never be—and he had as much of hers as she could give to any.

There may have been no one waiting in the silence of that shuttered house for the attack which was sure to come who was not aware by now that they stood in a deadly peril, which each hour must increase till that of their rescue should come—if it ever came. But there may have been no one who did not think their chances better than they would have done had they heard the words that passed between the two who listened at the store-house wall. Who, indeed, scarcely seemed to listen, for Noah strode up and down the room with downcast brooding eyes that only gave an occasional apprehensive glance at the menaced wall, and Mistress God's-Truth, sitting at the boiler-side, followed him with a fear in her own eyes which did not arise from the faint outside sounds, and with words of protest which she felt that he would not heed.

"It is nought," she said, "nought save the veer of wind. The sounds were faint at the first."

"I doubt it nothing," he answered impatiently. "The bell sounds, as it must. There must be orders sent. But I would know what they are!"

"That you would not hear through the shuttered walls. It were faint sounds at the most."

"But I would hear! I would hear though I opened way!"

"That were a child's deed! We shall but die as the stones come."

"We may be marked for a sure death if I go not forth."

"You could never that. You would be chased and slain. It were vain to try."

"It is a poor chance or none. We shall but die here."

"But there I say you are wrong. You fret beyond reason or need. Will they let the skins go, for a witch's brood that they can roast at their own day?"

"But if they think that we burn? Must I say it ever again? Will there not be those who have marked the flaming of Abel Trustwell's farm?"

In fact, Noah fretted with some cause, as his mother might have been more ready to admit, had she not feared even more greatly the desperate remedy which was in his mind.

She had been in his confidence from the first. Had known the plots which were to end in the ruin of her strange and unwelcome guests. With a grim secret satisfaction she had watched events moving to an end which doomed them, and yet in such sort that even if other members of her household should be involved, there should be no shadow cast upon her favourite son. And she did not think that any would be so involved, beside a husband for whom she cared somewhat less than nothing. He had held her in scorn for too many years. Even Ehud's birth had done nothing to lift the shadow of mutual repulsion that lay between them. She saw Simeon leap to his death. As she looked, the fumes were hot in her mouth, and the depth of the pit was hidden by the glowing sulphurous vapours that seethed within it. *Vengeance is mine, I will repay, saith the Lord.* Perhaps it was. Yet was it a fitting thing that He should do it by the hands of Simeon's son?

But now the vengeance of the Lord was threatening in an unexpected way. Suppose it would have been better, after all, for them to have left Him to His own devices? Or suppose that Noah had been no more than a blind, foolish instrument of His will, who had been used to create such an atmosphere of apprehension that the children of Satan would be left to perish when, in His appointed time, the Anabaptists should fall upon them? Suppose that the blind instrument, having served its purpose, had been carelessly cast aside by an unregarding Deity, to perish with those whom he had betrayed?

These were possibilities which they both saw, though they reacted differently. Noah would strike a blow for his own life. He would break through the closing net. He remembered that he had done nothing to cause the countenance of the Almighty to be turned away. Might it not be by His far-seeing providence that he had the steel cap and the back-and-breast-pieces which would defy even the stones of the Anabaptists' slings? If he should wait until attack were concentrated upon one side of the house, and then make a dash from the other, might he not hope to get free? His mission would be to hasten the lagging rescue! Should it fail, it might still be the destined way of his own escape, as Lot was once delivered from Sodom before the brimstone fell.

So he thought and spoke. But his mother's courage was of another kind. It was her instinct to delay, to evade. To dodge consequences rather than to defy them. She saw that the idea that rescue would be delayed or refused was no more than a supposition in his own mind. Even so, the assault might be beaten off. The Anabaptists must be in increasing fear of attack as the hours passed. They might go off themselves, if their first hurried efforts should fail. She was for delay.

Through the wood there came the flicker of flame, and the hiss of the smothering snow.

CHAPTER XLIV.

THE cold dawn came, if dawn could be a seemly word to use of a sun that was never seen, nor had aim to rise to the heaven's height, but would move, mist-hidden, for a short space along the horizon's rim, and sink again, having given less light than came from the moon's full disc that was now descending in the western sky. Not that the moon showed clearly now, as it had done in the earlier night. For the wind had changed, and an ominous drift of cloud was hiding the cold splendour of the Antarctic stars. The dawn came, but the rescue on which Michael had reckoned as being due by then was a hindered thing.

In the meeting-house of Suffolk County, two hundred men, more or less, weaponed in their own ways, and including a little band of slingsmen as expert as any Anabaptist was likely to be, waited resolutely enough for the orders which did not come. And in the vestry where Patience God's-Truth's witnesses had once waited for her to call them forth, three Elders of the Church, Malachi, Aaron, and Ephraim, sat disputing with a bitterness which intensified as it continued.

"Brother," Aaron was saying, the smooth moderation of his tone concealing the venom that his words injected, "Malachi hath but spoken truth, though it may have been of an oversharpened edge. You cannot do that which is against the published will of the Elders who (except only ourselves) are assembled to guide the land."

"But it is a falsehood known," Ephraim protested impatiently. "They deem that Michael God's-Truth's house is no more than a burnt shell."

"Which is what it may be ere now."

"But we have no right so to say. And to loiter here as though it were a known thing…. Those of his nearest neighbours, having fled here, are at one that it was Abel Trustwell's farm that is burnt, and no more than that. How can they of the Bell-house have surer word, being as far off as they are?"

"That we might know, being there; but as it is, we can but heed that which is cast abroad for our guiding—and our control."

There was warning, even menace in the last word, smoothly and quietly though it was spoken, and Ephraim was not blind to the implication that it conveyed.

His position was not without difficulty. He was actually in command of the two hundred men who sat about the meeting-house, waiting his word, and he had no doubt what that word ought to be. They should be moving now at their utmost speed for the relief of Michael God's-Truth's household. But the news had been cast abroad by the distant bell, and was being sent by the system of whistling signals which prevailed to the furthest limits of population, that Michael God's-Truth's house had been fired and sacked, and that disposition must be made to obstruct the return of the Anabaptists, and recover the spoils with which they would be laden on their retreat. And this news, this order, had been sent out with the authority of all the Elders who were assembled together, excepting only they three who sat there and Michael God's-Truth himself.

Who was Ephraim to use his momentary power as military leader of the men who were gathered there to defy such authority? Malachi had answered that question with a discourteous directness less than five minutes ago. It was not merely that he was a lay Elder. He was unconfirmed in his office, and that meant that the hostility either of laity or Elders would leave him in twelve months' time a discredited and ruined man.

For the law by which Elders were elected was of a cautious kind, and, in itself, may be thought good. They were first chosen by popular vote, whether a lay, or preaching Elder, for a probationary period of three years. At the end of that time they had to secure a new popular vote, and also confirmation of office by the Elders themselves. After that, they were secure for life, in a position impregnable. Ephraim Trustwell had been first elected two years ago. The vacancy which he had filled had been that of the control of barter. (They had tried a tin currency once, manufactured with the limited and irreplaceable quantity of that metal which they had possessed, but it had been hurriedly abandoned after the bulk of it had been astutely cornered by a financial genius whose right hand was amputated in an excess of retributive anger, but who would have been Chairman of the Bank of France in a fairer world.) He had cause to believe that he had given general satisfaction, and was likely to be confirmed in that difficult office by the popular vote. But now, whatever the popular verdict might be when the events of this night should be reviewed and weighed in the privacy of five hundred homes, he knew that there would not be the faintest, remotest hope that he would receive the necessary confirmation of his fellow Elders if he should fail in the exhibition of an outward unity. For that, among themselves, was an unpardonable sin, and yet.... Nothing would ever alter the fact that this night he was in command of two hundred men who should be moving at their utmost speed to Michael God's-Truth's aid.

He said, vainly enough, for he had said it more than once already: "But the store of leather at stake! It cannot be thought that they would risk that, were the house witched in every timber and stone. Shall we heed an order issued in a belief that we know to be other than the fact is? Or would you have it thought that our Elders would spread a report which they know for a devil's lie?"

"We know it not for a lie. Neither you nor we," Malachi answered, in a cold fury of anger at the persistence of opposition. "We know not how the truth may be. And knowing not, we must needs bow to the voice of those who are ordained for the guidance of the Saints of God."

"Yet if we know that an Elder err?"

"They err not, as should be known to one who is elect of themselves."

"Yet what saith the apostle Paul? Even of Peter, who was an Elder, yea, of the very first. Saith he not in the Holy Word, *I withstood him to his face, because he was to be blamed*?"

"You may apparel yourself to Paul, if you will," Malachi answered sourly. "There may be similarities which we do not see, and Master Ebenezer Cloutsclad, for all his wisdom and age, may be no more than a Peter for your rebuke; and yet we are undismayed by a foolish word. For Elders may dispute and strive as did Peter and Paul, and as we do now, but the word which you would have us contemn is not of a single Elder, neither Master Ebenezer Cloutsclad or another, but of the assembled council, which is as the voice of God, for all men to obey."

"I would speak not lightly of Master Ebenezer," Ephraim answered, "who is of good judgment and righteous will, as is known to all. I say but that they at the Bell-house are misled by a false tale."

"And I say that is unproved, and it is not of your part to decide."

"Master Malachi," Ephraim answered, with the passion of one who was apt to be of few words and a controlled habit of speech, but now moved beyond his normal restraint, "It is none but I who am in command of those without, who wait but for my word. If I speak it not, it is on my soul that I shall answer therefore to God at the last day."

He rose as he spoke, striding the room. He added bitterly: "It is a thing not to guess, but to know."

"And how might that be," Aaron inquired mildly, "except you advance to an attack which is against the orders that all men hear?"

"I could send forward scouts, such as would return with a true word."

"Except they died, being chased by the Anabaptists, who are far swifter than we."

"They would not all die."

"Yet of a surety some would. You know well what will chance if the Anabaptists be approached by small parties or single men. If they stand they will be slain with many slings, and if they run they will be run down. It is for their lives that you would answer at the last day, they being lost by the stiffness of your own neck."

Ephraim stopped short in his stride. His angry eyes met the mild reasoning glance that Aaron directed upon him. "Is it," he asked, "of a truth that you desire the death of these witches, if such they be, of which I have a great doubt? Is it nothing but that? Nay, it is more! It is more, by the Living God! It is Michael God's-Truth's death that you would! It is you that would have his place when Ebenezer shall die. I tell you I will have no part in this thing, nor will I send men to a death where I do not go."

As he said this, he picked up the sword-belt with the heavy sword that he had cast on to a bench at the side, and began to fasten it on.

Aaron kept his mild gaze upon him, but showed no resentment at the accusation. He laid a firmly restraining hand upon Malachi's arm when he would have risen as though to bar his exit from the room.

Ephraim walked out of the vestry and down the aisle to the main door, followed by the eyes of his waiting men, but he spoke nothing and looked at none. They must not know of the quarrel which had been hidden by the vestry door, let them have guessed as they might, and wonder now as they would.

Inside the vestry, Aaron was saying to Malachi, as one who soothes an unruly child: "And what of that, if he will? Is it not the best end? It is such as he who will shake a state, be it large or small. But the grave is a quiet place."

CHAPTER XLV.

EPHRAIM walked fast, making no effort of concealment. He took no heed of the changing levels of ground, nor of the cover offered by fence or tree.

The sky had become grey and low, and there was a wind from the east, not violent, but very cold. He looked to the north, where, at this season, the dawn should be, and there was no sight of the sun, and little of its light struggled through. Nor did the low moon show in the southwest sky, nor were there visible stars in the heaven's span. He thought: "It is better for me. Yet if they plunder the skins, and retreat in a scattered way, they will be hard to foil if the storm breaks, as I think it may." He thought beyond that, seeking the truth in a mind which was courageous and clear, though it had been fed from birth on a strange food at once noble and base. It was from a field in which tares and wheat may grow with intermingled roots till the world's end, which was the parable, and may be the purpose of God.

They might be witches or fiends, though he thought not. God might have moved the Anabaptists to destruction of Michael God's-Truth's household with the blasphemers they entertained, though it was a matter on which they had no proof, and he doubted much. But there was the point. *They had no proof.* Having none, their duty of support and rescue was clear. If God would destroy, He was of sufficient strength, despite any motion of theirs.

He saw even beyond that. He saw that, whoever else might be right, it was not he. For if Malachi were in the wrong, then should he have come this way three hours ago, with every man that he had—with every man that should be behind him now. And if Malachi were in the right, then should he not be here at all, jeopardizing his own life because he would not submit to those who were older and wiser than he, and closer to the counsel of God.

With these thoughts, he came to a rise in the land, and looked down upon Michael God's-Truth's house, which was no more than two hundred yards away, or it might be three; and as he looked his sword came bare in his hand, though he was unconscious of what he did, and he cursed Malachi in his heart.

For there would still have been time! Still time for the saving of much. Of human life—perhaps of part of the house—perhaps of the stores it held. And now that hope was no more than a lost thing.

The store-house, which had been first attacked, was a guttered wreck, over which the Anabaptists swarmed. It had been torn down in part, and in part fired, but the change of wind, it being at the north end of the house, had held back the flames from the middle buildings. Bales of skins, dragged from puddle and fire, showed in the flickers of evil light, darkening the snow.

More ominous than that sight was the fire that had been newly set to the house at its southern end, which the wind fanned to its destruction. Ephraim understood that the Anabaptists had secured as much of plunder as they could bear, and now they would but linger till they had completed the destruction of the house and those it held, which would need but a short delay. He knew that there was no way in which those that the house held could put out the flames—none, surely, that would not expose them to a swift destruction at their enemies' hands. There was no hope at all.

It came to his mind that those who were still living in that dark-shadowed, flame-lit house would soon be standing at the bar of God to account for what they were, whether evil or good, and of how their lives had come to that common end. (In this thought he showed some unsoundness concerning the Doctrine of the Intermediate State, which had, in fact, been the point on which the first Ebenezer Cloutsclad and Gabriel God's-Truth had quarrelled with Elisha Trustwell two hundred years earlier, and which had caused Elisha to be driven out, to become the ancestor of the savage horde that was now before him. But that was the thought he had.) He thought that there would be Michael God's-Truth, and a dozen others, women and men, who would want to know why they had been left to die thus, and he felt that Michael would not lack words at such an issue, even in the presence of God. And it seemed to him that, if such an accusation were made, it was his place to be there too, to make such reply as he might, which would not be much.

As he thought thus, he saw a door open in the dark centre of the house, making an instant oblong of light, and a man issue therefrom and come running swiftly toward him. The next moment it opened again, and a woman called frantically to the man to come back, and seeing that he did not heed, she ran after him into the snow, leaving the door open behind her.

Whether he would have escaped had she not appeared is beyond knowing, but her cry, and the sight of the open door, drew the eyes of all the Anabaptists who were at that side of the house's end, making up their burdens by the faint light of the dawn, and the failing flames of the store-house wreck.

Noah God's-Truth, running with his head crouched in his neck, so that the rim of his steel cap was close to the back-piece collar around his neck, heard the rush and shout of pursuit, and the whiz of a stone that passed beside his ear. Another smote him on the back with such force that he fell forward and must struggle to regain his feet, but the good steel held, and he was no worse when he rose. Yet, knowing the speed of foot of those who would come behind, he thought of himself as little better than dead. And the next moment he came upon Ephraim Trustwell, who advanced toward him with a drawn sword in his hand.

Ephraim, having looked in the right way, had seen more than he. He saw a woman's figure that lay face down in the snow. He saw that the door she had left open had attracted the attention of the Anabaptists to the advantage of the flying man, so that there were no more than three who were now active in his pursuit. He saw that the Anabaptists had actually gained the threshold of the door before those who were within had perceived their danger. Now there was a fierce hand-to-hand strife being waged in a narrow space between those who would close it again, and those who would force entrance at that unlooked-for chance.

As Ephraim advanced, the three who were in pursuit halted and drew back. They might not have done so from him and Noah alone, but they did not suppose that he would have come single thus. They ran back with a warning cry that their enemies had arrived.

Ephraim looked at Noah, and understood something, though not all. He said: "It was a thing worth to try. Run with all the speed that you have, taking word from me that I do that which I may here." He told where the gathering was. He had no time for more. There was a door to be closed, and he would be inside when that should be done. Yet he paused for an instant's space to look where a woman lay, and to be sure that she was beyond human aid. The next moment he was at the back of the group that strove round the open door.

"*The sword of the Lord,*" he cried, seizing the nearest of the Anabaptists by the mane of his shaggy hair, "*and of Gideon,*" and he cast the man aside as his sword-point pierced him below the ribs. Right and left they broke, the naked, many-weaponed savages, from the rush of the armoured man, and the stabbing blade that had broken upon their rear.

He stood breathless within the door, as the great shoulder of Michael God's-Truth drove it back into its place.

Michael God's-Truth was black with smoke, and his face was streaked with blood that had run and dried at its own will. He had in his hand a broken sword, from which half the blade had been snapped away. Behind him were a group, women and men, of whom we know most, but at whom it might not now be seemly to look, they being as they were, and we not having seen the ordeal through which they came.

"Master Ephraim," Michael said, "you do come in a good time, as a true man will. I said but an hour back that when this house shall fall, Master Ephraim will not be far off, even though we see nought of our own kin."

That was better to hear than that the same voice should impeach him at the bar of God, but he did not answer directly. He said: "Heard ye that? It may be that we shall still live." For above the screaming of the Anabaptists, above the crackle of flames, there came the wailing cry of a great wind. They knew it well for the first voice of the coming of Antarctic storm.

CHAPTER XLVI.

NOAH slackened his pace as he passed out of danger of the pursuit which had been delayed by Ephraim's appearance. It was twenty-four hours since he had had rest, and the night had been spent in anxiety and some violent exertion, so that he might well be tired, as he was. Beyond that, haste had little use. Suffolk meeting-house was four miles away. He considered that, let him hasten as much as he liked, the fate of his father's household would be decided before any rescue could reach. He was sorry for that. Sorry for his father, for whom he had some affection. Sorry for Paradise Trustwell, who had the good sense to value him for what he supposed himself to be, and whom he had intended to marry next year, if he should be quite sure by then that Salvation Pettifer was beyond his reach. Sorry for all that were within the fated walls, even for the supercilious witch, Mistress Eleanor D'Acre, who had conveyed to him in some subtle way that he was too far down for insolence to annoy or even reach her. Even for her, and the lesser spawn of hell that he had betrayed without malice, as the godly should.

Yet any sorrow he had did not blind him to the discriminating justice of God, which had loosed him free from the Gomorrah on which His vengeance fell.

When he hastened his pace again, it was not with any foolish thought that he could interfere with the predestinations of the Eternal, but because he felt the sudden buffet of a screaming wind, and looked up to a sky in which the snow-clouds drove so low that it seemed that a man might reach them with a lifted hand.

He came to Suffolk meeting-house dragging heavy feet that sank in the deepening snow, and breathless with the violence of a wind that strove to fling him sideways from the path he followed in a deepening gloom. He found that the most of the assembly that Ephraim had supposed to be waiting his word had already scattered.

It would be hard to blame them for that. They had received the orders of the two Elders there, and Aaron Cloutsclad had been with the first party to leave. They knew the signs of approaching storm, and many of them had far to go. Should they be stayed by blizzard too fierce to face, there was no farm-house in the land that would not give shelter, and be stored with food sufficient till the skies should clear, but to be weather-held in Suffolk meeting-house, which had no food at all, and no drink but the sacramental cider, would have been evil indeed.

As for the Anabaptists, they could not chase them or be chased in such weather as the skies would be scattering now. They must make their way back to their native hells, or perish as best they could. Having been the instruments of Divine punishment upon a roof which had given shelter to the sorcerous and the ungodly, it might well be that protection ceased when they had fulfilled the purpose for which they came.

Noah found none but Malachi and a score of those who were also of Norfolk country, and whose homeward way led southward, too near to Michael God's-Truth's house for them to be in haste to start till the storm deepened, or they had certain news of the movements of the Anabaptists there.

Noah told what he knew. He added what he supposed. He may not have made the distinction clear. He would have it plain that he had not left while a hope stayed. He said, truly enough, that he had escaped from the dark middle of the house, when it was alight at its two ends. There could be no others who had got clear, for the Anabaptists had closed between him and the opened door.

Ephraim? He had no doubt he was dead. Hearing that, Malachi saw the wisdom of the counsel that Aaron Cloutsclad had given. He saw also that, if Michael God's-Truth were dead, Ebenezer Cloutsclad would be President, and he was an old man and reputed frail. After him, Aaron might be a good choice. A man of wisdom, and one whom he could understand and respect. He felt that the day had gone well, and faced the storm stoutly enough, being of a quiet mind, and winding a goat's-hair muffler around his throat.

CHAPTER XLVII.

THERE are few things that unite men more closely than a common experience of dangers faced and vanquished, few things which test and reveal more nakedly the weak or heroic elements which make up the composite individualities of the majority of mankind.

The little group of the defenders of Michael God's-Truth's home gathered, blackened and bloodied from a night of such strife as comes to few unless in a nightmare dream. They were still alert for unsuspected danger or renewed attack, but yet triumphant with a sense of security which they had scarcely hoped to know ever again. The tempest screamed without, and the fire that was eating into the thick timbers of the southern end of the house died hissing like an angry reptile beneath its mantle of descending snow.

In that hour of relief, they felt a closeness of fellowship such as might not have come with a dozen years of more trivial living.

And, curiously enough, with this sense of comradeship and of life lived on a higher plane, life itself had become a smaller thing, so that there was less of grief, less of regret, for Patience God's-Truth or Caleb Cloutsclad, whose broken bodies lay on the floor of the living-room, to which retreat had been made when the northern portion of the house had been abandoned to the assailants, and for whom the hot fury of the strife which had raged hand against hand, after the Anabaptists had broken through the collapse of the store-house wall, would be the last of human emotion that they would ever know.

They had held the store-house for several hours—might have done so for a longer time if there had been more than a dozen cartridges left for the two rifles which Franklin had retrieved from beneath the loop-holed wall, and which he had used well enough, though with much less than Bunford's skill. But the time had come when a large part of the western wall had fallen in, though the roof still stood on its massive smoke-blackened beams, and Michael, seeing that further resistance was vain, and that they must abandon such of the stores as the fire would spare, for a spoil to the sons of Anak, had cried, "*Back! Back!*" in a great voice, and the invaders, scrambling over the collapse of the charred and smouldering planks, would have come to no more than a deserted interior, with a barred door at its southern end, had not Ehud delayed a moment at his wife's need. For Gwendolen God's-Truth stumbled with the agony of a burnt leg. "You'll have to help me," she said. Ehud saw that her dress was burnt away at one side. He had not known when it had happened or how it had been put out. He stooped to pick her up, when the most of their friends had already disappeared through the narrow door. As he did so, they heard the yell of the Anabaptists swarming upon them. Gwen did not know why Ehud loosed her, and sank gently to the ground. She heard Caleb's voice as he turned back, "Master Ehud's down," and the next moment there was a fierce and mortal struggle above the spot on which she tried to cover his body from kicking feet, and vainly to regain her own. She saw the sweep of Michael's sword over her head, and the countering stroke of the ancient bill-hook that broke its blade, and went on to strike his head with a lessened force. But Michael did not seem to notice the blow.

He seized the man's arm in his two hands, as one might take the handle of an iron pot, and lifted and swung him round. With this living flail he beat the Anabaptists backward, and right and left. He stepped forward, clear of his son's body, shouting as he did so, though without turning his head: "*Patience—Patience—drag him in.*"

Gwendolen struggled to her feet in a clear space. The moment—it could be no more—but the moment was theirs. She saw that Franklin was at Michael's side, using the revolver that he had withheld so long. He had allowed the rifle ammunition to be exhausted, but he had felt that the six shots that his pocket held were for the private use of those whom it was his first duty to guard, and that only at a last need. But he was using them with deadly deliberation now.

Patience was beside her, and Paradise and Eleanor also. They were dragging Ehud toward the safety of the door which was no more than twelve feet away. Then an Anabaptist ran behind the fighting group that covered them. Patience rose to meet him. "Quick, Eleanor," she said, as she faced the danger with unweaponed hands, and clutched the raised arm of the advancing savage. Gwendolen forgot her injuries as she bent to take the place that Patience had left. She did not see what happened beyond that. In another moment they had Ehud inside the door. The others crowded in after them, Franklin's revolver sounding again. Michael was the last to enter, thrusting backward with his broken sword. His daughter was on his other arm. He looked round as the bars were driven home. "All here?" he asked, and then: "Where's Noah?" But Noah entered from the farther side of the room. He said he had been round to see that the other parts of the house were still secure.

Michael said nothing to that. He saw that the tale of those whose lives were in his hands was complete. They had left no one on the wrong side of the door. But Patience hung limply, and as he laid her down he saw that she had a broken neck. Caleb was bleeding from a mortal wound that they could not staunch.

It was then that Noah had seen that it had become time to go.

CHAPTER XLVIII.

THE storm raged for ten days, with a severity which was exceptional even for that Antarctic valley, and especially so at a time when the winter had scarcely come. Before the wind fell, and the snow-laden landscape glistened in the light of ten thousand stars, the last glimmer of daylight failed, and the three months' night closed down upon the ten million miles of desolation which is the Antarctic continent. A desolation to which the earth has no likeness, and the Arctic pole has the gentleness of a summer night. Northward, beyond the narrow range of this lava-heated valley, rose the bleak heights that led to an interminable tableland, where glacier, crevasse, and moraine broke perilously the long monotony of the frozen snow.

Even in the Arctic wastes there is life of snowy owl and fox and bear, fierce and hardy and defiant, but here, even in its summer of unsinking sun, there was no sound but of the screaming wind or the falling avalanche, no life of mammal or bird or insect that had braved it for a million years. Even in its summer days…and when the iron night closed in, its cold was beyond the knowledge of man.

In the sheltered valley, lit forever by the hell-fires that blazed beyond the caves where the Anabaptists dwelt, the storm raged from the eastward (from which quarter the worst tempests would always come) and piled the snow to the very eaves of the stout-built farmhouses. Then it fell and the stars shone, and men and women looked out and began to cut paths, and to tread with wide flat footgear a hardened path, where they knew that the drifted snow would lie most thinly from the experience of earlier years.

From Michael God's-Truth's house, where there had been nursing of many wounds, and where their dead had been laid out in the snow to freeze, as the winter custom was in that land when they were house-bound by continuing storm, men and women looked forth, and seeing hope of quieter days, they commenced with vigour to break down the isolation which the storm had inflicted upon them.

There was no moon now, but they worked in a clear, star-lit air, and as they did so they heard the cheering sounds of whistle and goat's horn, and the distant bell by which men were commencing to exchange greetings and news, and to re-establish the communal life which did not usually submit so early to the monotonies that the season brought.

Gradually the news spread, and was built up item by item, till it was known to all that Michael God's-Truth lived and his house stood. Of the Anabaptists, there was some reason to think that the women, starting back with their burdens in the earlier day, had regained the security of their familiar heights, having cast off the dead goats they carried for a swift flight at the first sign of approaching tempest, to which they may have been more alert than were those who were actively occupied in besieging the store-house. For these last, there was little hope. Their secrets would be revealed when the spring came and the snow melted away, and they would be found scattered over the land in the places where their strength had failed.

There were others missing, of more importance than they. Among these were Malachi Trustwell and the little party of Norfolk people who had set out with him, for whom the sudden fury of the storm must have been too great, or they may have wandered from the path on which their lives depended. With these had been Noah God's-Truth, though this was for some time an assumption rather than a known fact, and was not proved till the spring came; for, like the Anabaptists accursed of God, those of the godlier race who died in that storm must wait for Christian sepulchre till the thaw of the covering snow.

But five days later there was a funeral at Suffolk meeting-house of those who died at Michael God's-Truth's house: Mistress Margaret God's-Truth and Patience and Caleb Trustwell and the stranger, Bunford Weldon.

The weather, as though exhausted by its own violence, remained clear and calm, though of a cold more intense than was often known in that valley, and its severity was not sufficient to prevent the assembly of a congregation that filled the straight oak benches, and crowded porch and aisle with a standing throng.

Michael preached himself, as his custom was. He took for text, *Greater love hath no man than this that he gave his life for his friend*, and if it had little application to Bunford Weldon's end, and one to Mistress God's-Truth's into which it might be foolish to probe too far, it was true enough that Caleb had died for the rescue of his master's son, and had been the quickest to see his peril, and the first to turn back for his protection. But of Patience God's-Truth, whether she gave her life for the friends who had borne witness for her or for the brother whom she most loved, it was no less than a naked truth.

Michael said little of his dead wife, which we may see some cause to excuse, but he spoke of his daughter with a moving eloquence, and for the first time, he did not allow his position as Presiding Elder to silence his own assertion of her innocence of the charge which had been brought against her. It is true that he did not directly attack the actions of his fellow-Elders nor the authority of the Church, but he made it so clear on which side he stood, that there would be no resort but silence for his opponents in future, unless they were themselves prepared to exhibit the Elders of the Church in open conflict.

He alluded to the strangers who had been sent by an over-ruling Providence from the outer world to his daughter's vindication, showing that the Almighty would ever shelter His own, nor would He permit His Church to err. He reminded them that these strangers had fought, and one of them had died beside him, when the machination of Satan had spread a lying tale whereby the rescue was withheld for which he had a right to look.

But the Lord had shown that His arm was not shortened! He had but breathed, and His enemies were scattered. They had become as the crackling of thorns under a pot. When the spring returned, and the frost broke, they would see the evidences of the Wrath which descended upon those who lifted impious hands against the elect of God.

In all this he made no allusion to the fact that Malachi Trustwell and the Anabaptists must be shown at last as lying in equal graves. Men could think that out for themselves, if they would. Nor did he mention his elder son, who was supposed to have fallen to a like end. Men must think about that as they would, too.

They saw that it was his hour of spiritual triumph, even though he spoke at the side of a wife's and daughter's grave. They saw also that he was handling the position with a certain largeness and magnanimity characteristic of the man at his best. They saw the folly of those who had intrigued against him, even of those who had held back the help on which he should have been able to rely confidently, at his greatest need. It had but increased his triumph. The defence of Michael God's-Truth's house might be an epic of future centuries.

The dissensions of the Elders, which they foolishly supposed to be concealed behind a public front of sufficient unity, were the common talk wherever men might meet, and had been so since the accusation against Patience God's-Truth had been first made.

Men recalled incidents of earlier years when Michael's authority had been assailed or his conduct challenged. Long ago, there had been the disappearance of Simeon Cloutsclad. There had been other—quite different—incidents. But always he had shouldered his way through the opposition, equally ready with hand or tongue. Ready also, it had been noticed, to let such incidents die. He went on contemptuously, seeking no revenge, as though he had remembered nothing, or as though his enemies were beneath regard.

He had triumphed, as he always did. And this triumph must be shared by the strangers that were within his gates. They had become already as members of his own household. One of them had married his son. The latent hostility evident from many glances in the crowded church did not lessen from that cause, even among those who were Michael's friends.

Franklin was not unaware of that feeling around them as he sat, with Eleanor beside him, in the seats which were reserved for Michael's household, aware that they were freed from the threat of any instant danger, but no less apprehensive of the future than he had always been, and conscious that the pistol his pocket held was now no more than a useless toy.

He was conscious also of an increased isolation, irritating and depressing, which had developed in spite of the close companionships of the last ten days, when he had been one of the dozen people shut up together within the narrow limits of Michael God's-Truth's house. Not that there had been any personal antagonisms, except with Michael himself, and perhaps that would be too strong a word for the mutual reserve which had risen between them. With Ephraim, he had even established an actual friendship, as he had done with Ehud earlier. But they were of a different world. Their interests might be diametrically opposed to his own wishes and plans, and there was no one there to whom he could speak with an open sincerity to whom he could reveal his thought. He supposed that Eleanor must be more or less acutely aware of the same problems, but even of that he was less than certain, for she had avoided him, or—at least—she had avoided opportunities of any private conversations. Of that he was sure. In any case, they would not have been easy in that crowded house, which had been reduced to little more than half its previous size.

And he could not talk to Gwen, even if she were not always with Ehud, who had been little worse on the next day for the knock-out blow he had received. It was Gwen who had been the real invalid, having burns that were still unhealed, though she had managed to walk here today. But she and Ehud were always together now, and, if he should talk to her alone, how could he tell that Ehud would not hear what had been said half an hour later? Gwen might be good friend enough, but her interests were no longer his. She was a God's-Truth now. And she had already said that she did not desire to establish contact with the outer world. *If* Eleanor and he were to return, they were to promise that. Well, such a promise might be given by Eleanor, might be accepted by her, but would it be accepted by her new friends? Would Eleanor give it? *Did Eleanor mean to come?* It seemed absurd to doubt that. Yet she did not seek opportunities of conversation, and she was disturbed in mind. Of that he was sure.

He was sure of another thing also. Michael did not want— probably did not mean—Eleanor to go. With the jealous instinct of love he read Michael's mind well enough on that point, though others might be less quick to do so. And Michael's wife was dead.

He was quite sure of what they ought to do. Certainly, of what he would do if he could have his own way. Eleanor and he would have slipped away at the first chance. They would get back to the *Blanche*. Once on the river—under the hills—who could stay, who could even follow them?

But Eleanor showed no sign of desiring his counsel or of planning flight. She might—naturally—dislike a programme which would make him her sole companion in those desolate huts on the barren coast till the ice should break and the *Bergen* appear again. Under most circumstances it might be too great an audacity to propose.

Did she plan to stay here till the spring, confident that she could control the events of the winter days, and then find freedom to leave, or means of a secret flight? He could not tell. But it seemed to him to be a desperate risk.

And though he said nothing to Gwen, he felt, when she looked his way, that she was reading his thoughts: that the problem was clear to her. Did she see its solution too? Had she planned, in her thorough, efficient manner, what that solution should be?

He was right about Gwen understanding him, though he might have been less than flattered had he known the criticism to which such understanding gave birth. Eleanor was Gwen's difficulty. Curiously, the perturbations of Eleanor's mind were more clearly perceived by Franklin than by her. They were like two explorers each surveying a different part of the same territory. What they saw they knew, but they saw different things, making explorations that did not meet, and that left much unseen, and perhaps unsuspected by either. Gwen, thinking of Michael, of Franklin, of the difficulty and perhaps sinister powers that might yet move against her without Michael's will, or which he might even call to his aid in confidence that he could control them—thinking of these, and of other obvious things, and looking at Eleanor in her serene aloofness, asked herself: "Is she a fool?"

It was because Eleanor was not a fool that there was in her heart an inward panic screened by natural courage, a self-confidence that had justified itself in previous difficulties, and a pride which was partly of her own nature, and partly of the environment of wealth which for twenty-five years had given all, or almost all, that she had asked, as though it were her natural right...the wealth that had brought her here.

She had always meant that it should bring her to strange places, to strange events. That it should be a power in her hands, a power that should buy fame, as well as the softer, ignobler things which all women desire, which is all, to most, that money can ever mean.

Confident in the power it gives, she had come here, where she supposed that they would be the first to penetrate. She had come with her three companions, confident in their ability to serve and shield her. With the pleasant consciousness that she was the first among them. Bunford was her dog, grateful for a stroked back, or a gracious word. Gwen was her paid servant, whom she had gracefully made her friend. Even Franklin had come only by the power of her own wealth. And now Bunford was dead. And Gwen was married, independent of her. Even one who might have to be asked.... And Franklin.... *Why did not Franklin act?* Do something. It was a man's part! What if she had said that she would stay here till the spring? If it were a foolish thing, he should have said so at first. He should have refused to give way! Anyway, he should do something now. Had she not shown him in instants of revelation, such as she would never have given even to Gwen, never admitted to any other, the fear that was like a shadow that would not lift? If it had been Michael, she thought bitterly, Michael would have found a way! And this thought forgot its anger as it increased her fear, for it was Michael—ultimately, it must be Michael—against whom she fought. And Michael would find a way!

Not that Franklin lacked courage or self-possession in danger (she would be fair in that), nor had he failed, as yet, in resource or judgment. And he had told her from the first hour that it would be wiser to come away. Perhaps even now, if they were to talk it over together.... But she saw the danger of that. Michael overlooked little. It had been a wise prudence on her part which had kept her at such a distance from Franklin as had been possible in their narrow quarters. Besides, in the altered conditions, now that they had lost Bunford and Gwen, the proposal must come from him, not from her. He ought to see that. (There might be two opinions on that point, but that was hers.)

She had other causes for irritation. The unloading of the *Blanche* had only been commenced when the Anabaptists and the tempest came. Since then it had been said that nothing more could be done. Nothing till more urgent matters had been accomplished, more urgent pathways made. She had agreed, of course. But there were things in that boat of which she was very badly in need. Above all, there were the cigarettes!

The last thought brought back to her mind the full absurdity of the idea that she should marry Michael and live forever in this frozen wilderness with these impossible people. Of course, she saw what was in his mind. She had known his feelings from the first—what woman wouldn't?—but they had seemed no more than a pleasant flattery, had lacked objectivity until Margaret God's-Truth died. Now she knew what Michael planned as surely as though it had come to the spoken word...and he was of those who will win their way.

She had not exactly disliked him. He had been pleasant to talk to, at one time. To talk to, *but not to touch*. Now, with this fear in her heart, she hated him with a fierce loathing. There were other matters, petty though they were, which had united to vex her mind.

There were the ugly, ill-fitting clothes that she must wear for this day. Clothes that had been Patience God's-Truth's once. Black clothes that had been pressed upon her with a polite insistence. For these people, who had lost or forgotten so much of the civilization from which their fathers came, had retained that ugly, repulsive custom of wearing black for the dead. That she should go to the funeral wearing either of the two dresses that were all she had till the cargo of the *Blanche* should be unpacked had seemed to them an impossible thing. Even her furs, even a squirrel coat, had seemed to them an indecency to suggest. So she wore Patience's clothes, and thought it cause enough for annoyance, and Patience, who would have worn them very willingly, was in the coffin before her. Did the impatient thought show in its comparison how petty, how mean she was?

Vividly, there came back to her mind the vision of the Anabaptist rushing upon them as she had lifted her eyes to him, stooping still, with her hands under the shoulders of the unconscious Ehud. He had a weapon flourished over his head. Curiously, she could not recall what it was, though she must have seen. But she saw Patience rise to meet him. She heard again that quiet, insistent call, *"Quick, Eleanor,"* as she grappled with him, to give them the seconds which would enable them to drag their burden to the safety of the open door. They were the last words she would speak before those horrible, fire-hardened hands would be round her throat. But that Eleanor had not seen. She bad bent to her task, and when she had looked back a few seconds later, it was to see Michael's broken sword come down upon the matted head, while his free arm caught away the body of his daughter which still clung to the trammelled savage, whether in life or death.

She recognized that she was among a people who could do noble things, as she suspected they might do others, of opposite sorts. Be that as it might, they were not her people. Their ways were not her ways. She looked at Michael, now stirred to peroration in which his own eloquence and that of Isaiah were about equally mingled: *"There was noise of a multitude in the mountains."* There were worse men, both in England and Antarctica. Smaller men. She admitted that. But all the same, she would be no Ruth for that bearded Boaz. Franklin must see her through.

There was a stir of relaxed tension as the sermon ended. She looked round at the hundred of alien faces. She looked particularly at the women, as they at her. She saw little friendliness. Even in the clothes she wore, she was so much fairer, and not merely that, she was so much more vivid than they. She felt herself to be of a finer breed, and contempt faintly altered her face, lessening its charm. She might possibly have won them had she had a more and different experience of life. It would have been a nobler thing to attempt. But she had no such thought in her mind. She was conscious only of their envy, of their dislike, which was returned in a colder way. For what were they to her?

Even the women, the wives of Michael's servants, with whom she had spent the last ten days—they were a dull lot. Even Caleb's widow, Miriam—she looked sad enough, but she had seemed to Eleanor to take her loss in a dull way. But she must except Paradise. Paradise had lost her uncle, and the man she loved (it might be too much to call him her lover) was almost surely dead. But Paradise had a serenity of soul that seemed too great to be overcome by any earthly sorrow. Not that Paradise was dull. Eleanor admitted that. No one would call her dull. When she looked at her, a text entered her mind, *The peace of God that passeth all understanding*. That was it. It was that which had saved her life from the Anabaptists, when she had declined to run, and they had seen that unless she ran, she was one that they could not kill. Paradise was the one woman there that Eleanor could not despise—the one also whom she felt did not despise her. Doubtless there would have been others, had she gained a more detailed knowledge, but her perception of the general feeling was correct enough, and of the dangers which were around her feet.

CHAPTER XLIX.

THE long night continued cold and clear beneath its procession of brilliant stars. Franklin's thermometer told him that there were thirty or forty degrees of frost, but to those who were warmly clad there was no menace in the dry, still air. People began to move abroad, as they would do when such weather shortened the winter night, while the snow was not too deep to be cast aside or flattened to a solid depth.

Michael God's-Truth took prompt advantage of these conditions to summon a meeting of Elders, primarily to fill the gap in their number occasioned by the disappearance of Malachi Trustwell (in the temporary manner usual in such emergencies), but also to deal with any other business which might have arisen. As to which, there was the disposal of Abel Trustwell's farm, concerning which he had a proposal to make, and there was the policy to be adopted toward the aliens within his gates. He had decided what this policy should be, and he saw that the more swiftly he should act, the more easily he should prevail. There was no sense in giving others time to get together and make up their own minds and each other's before they met. It was better that they should assemble in confused uncertainty, not knowing what others thought. If he were prompt and bold, he saw that the hour was his, and these were not qualities in which he was likely to fail.

The Elders were to assemble at the Bell-house in Durham county, that being a more central point than his own meeting-house. It meant a walk of thirteen miles, but he thought little of that, the weather being as it was. He would do it in seven hours, allowing for two calls for rest and food at farm-houses he would pass on the way.

He set out at the hour he chose, taking Ehud for company, and so that his son should have opportunity of knowing his mind, as they should talk on the way. The stars gave sufficient light for their need, and a persistent aurora drew swiftly-changing curtains of green and gold across the southern sky. Sometimes they were edged with crimson or purple light, sometimes they were peacock-blue, sometimes of a rainbow complexity, but they were never consistent or still. They danced and flickered and died in a procession that never failed. Their heads were in the highest sky, and their feet on the red volcanic glow that rose from the pits of hell.

There was a stillness in the air through this windless pause of the winter night, very strange to an English ear, but to Michael and Ehud it was the world that they had always known. It was a silence that was emphasized rather than broken by the boom of a distant avalanche, falling in the northern hills.

Michael spoke of Gwen. He thought well of her, that she would make a good wife. Did Ehud think her resolute enough to forget the past—the godless country from which she came?

Ehud said yes to that—with a reservation which he thought to keep to himself, but which turned his own words to the wonder he felt at the dimly-imagined marvels of that abandoned world, as her conversation had suggested it to him. He mentioned the strangeness of an existence in which men were only among many thousands of varieties of animals and birds. Gwen had described—had drawn—some of these creatures, of which there were many millions in England alone, some of them much larger than men. There were wild creatures in many parts of the world (as she had said) which disputed with men the territories in which they lived. There were smaller animals, some of which actually shared the dwellings of men, crawling about their floors. Small black animals—much smaller than goats—lived in this way, and hunted and killed still smaller creatures which lived in the houses of men against their wills, and robbed them of their food. These scenes of fighting and killing might go on around the feet of people seated at a meal, but would more frequently disturb the night hours with scuffles and screams of death.

Michael listened thoughtfully to this account. It was a fact more or less clearly evident from the Hebrew literature which was their principal mental food, but it became more real as it was related by the mouth of one to whom it had been a living experience.

To these men who had been born in the isolation of Antarctica, the world of biblical history was as remote as Heaven.

Michael saw the significance of the fact that the Almighty had not permitted any other creatures (except the goats and fowl which were necessary to their use) to enter the ice-bound sanctuary to which He had guided His elect. The swarming of inferior creatures, some of them in active rebellion against the authority divinely conferred upon Adam and his descendants, was significant of a condition of life where heretics, atheists, and witches walked with a blasphemous boldness. Probably some of the horrible creatures around the feet of the impious were no better than the incarnate fiends.

So he said to Ehud, who agreed very readily. Gwen had audaciously told him, with a rare lapse from her deliberate caution, that the black cat (the creature that hunted and killed in the houses of men) was reputed to be the familiar spirit of whose who practised witchcraft. What else would you expect? It was at a later date that Eleanor, knowing nothing of this, mentioned at the meal-table, in the hearing of all, that she had a black cat at home of which she was extremely fond.

There was a full assembly of Elders, and Michael God's-Truth took the President's seat without question, as his right was.

He made it the first business of the meeting to consider the vacancy caused by the disappearance of Malachi Trustwell. In that land, at that season, disappearance meant death. That was too well understood to need words, It was their duty to make a temporary appointment, which would continue till the elections next midsummer. Michael proposed the name of Ezra Pettifer. There was a subtle wisdom in this nomination which, after the exchange of a few discreet words, was generally recognized. The Pettifers were few, and had developed aptitude in one or two special trades which caused them to have interests which might clash with those of larger sections of the community. It was a ceaseless grievance with them that there was never anyone on the Council of Elders who bore the Pettifer name. The truth was that they had failed to produce a man of commanding personality, but they attributed the position, very naturally, to other and meaner causes. And having this feeling, they had developed a practice of using their votes *en bloc* in disconcerting ways, as minorities can.

The nomination of Ezra Pettifer by the Elders would show that they, at least, were above such prejudices. Ezra was a lay preacher residing in Norfolk County. As a successor to Malachi, he was a natural choice. Michael thought that nine months of him (he being what he was) would be sufficient to insure that his election would not be confirmed by popular vote. Even Pettifers might decline to support him.

So far, the Elders saw into Michael's mind, and approved its shrewdness. They failed to guess that he had a further thought, going beyond that. He had resolved upon nominating his own son at the next election.

Ehud was young beyond precedent, but the God's-Truth vote was strong, and he was generally popular. Yet it would not have been prudent to propose him now. It would be to invite defeat. There was much to be done before that. Meanwhile, Ezra Pettifer would be an excellent stopgap who could be displaced more easily than a stronger man.

Michael was not the only man who had thought of Ehud for the vacant office. In the privacy of the marriage-chamber, in one of those interludes of affectionate demonstrations which astute women know how to use, Gwen had proposed the same thing.

Ehud said it was absurd. The men elected were almost always of mature years, twenty or thirty years older than he.

Gwen countered with the question: "What about Ephraim?"

It appeared that he was an exception.

"Well," Gwen asked, "why not two?"

Ehud thought that the fact that his father was on this Council vetoed such a possibility.

Gwen said she didn't see that. She added: "Twenty years! I mean to be on it myself long before that."

Ehud stared and laughed. "We don't elect women."

"Then it's time you did."

"You'd better not mention such an idea, except to me. They might think you were serious, and there'd be more trouble than we've got now."

"What have we got now?"

"Nothing, of course. Only there might be. I didn't mean to say that."

"No, but you meant it all the same. I know what you mean."

"Well, anyhow, don't talk about women Elders again. It isn't—well, decent. It's against the Word of God."

"Not it. What about being a Mother in Israel?"

"Meaning Deborah?"

"Yes. And a few others."

"That was different. She was…I mean, she wasn't…."

"It doesn't sound very clear. I suppose you mean she bossed the show and did it off her own bat? Well, there might be worse things than that."

Ehud was silent, avoiding even the obvious reply that Barak contributed a useful score. Perhaps he was intrigued with the curious idioms by which Gwen conveyed her thoughts. Perhaps he knew that he had said enough to ensure that she would avoid giving her ideas any perilous publicity. The understanding between these two was becoming a rather wonderful thing.

Gwen added, after a pause: "What's wanted here is a few good Sunday Schools. 'Specially for the girls. They ought to understand

191

what they believe. But I suppose you'd have to start with a class for teachers first."

Ehud thought they probably would. He turned the conversation to a matter of more immediate importance—the locality of their home.

That conversation had been a week ago, and this question of their new home was the second business which Michael was bringing before the Council, and had been an additional reason—or rather excuse—for bringing Ehud with him. His first reason was the desire to have his son as much as possible before the eyes of men, in view of his purpose of nomination.

Now he said: "There is a proposal in respect of the farm of Abel Trustwell, which has been approved as equitable by our brother Ephraim, as he will testify to you, but I would not that it should be settled unless our full Council shall approve, it concerning one of my own house."

He put forward the proposal. Paradise was the legal heir to her uncle's property, which was still of value, though his goats were dead, his home a blackened shell, and his slave slain. She could not farm it alone, even had she so desired. She could not restock it without help. He offered that the house should be rebuilt, and a new herd of goats assembled as his own charge. The property should pass to his son, with the condition that Paradise could live there while she remained single, on her old footing, and receive a substantial dowry should she marry, as she naturally would.

Aaron Cloutsclad asked smoothly, "Was there any proposal as to that?"

Michael answered him with a formal courtesy. He might have a suggestion to make, even before they should separate, but he would like the basis of this arrangement to be approved, irrespective of such possibilities.

Ephraim gave details which it would be wearisome to set out. They were of an obvious liberality, and his office would have entitled him to approve them without this formality.

Ebenezer Cloutsclad said that they were such as would be anticipated from Michael. He moved their approval. No one dissented. Aaron may have seen that by this punctilious attitude toward a bargain in which he was financially interested, Michael had obtained the formal assent of the Council to the grant of land to one who had an alien wife. But if so, he was too cautious to give any sign. He saw that he must wait his time.

Michael might have closed the meeting with the transaction of other routine business, and many would have considered it the more discreet method of procedure, but he had resolved upon a bolder course. He said: "There is a matter which must be faced, if not now, then before the spring shall come, and it is one on which it may be well that we should be of a settled mind. Should it be a winter of storm, we know not surely when we may be fully assembled again, as we are now.

"I speak of these strangers within our gates, of whom one is dead, and one is now of ourselves. But there are yet two who may seek to leave, and, they being now in my house, I would have it clear. Can we permit it to be?"

He paused on that question, as though he would have others show their hands before they could do more than guess at that which was in his own mind. But those whom he most watched were as wary as he.

Seeing that others were slow to speak, Ebenezer Cloutsclad replied. "Brethren," he said, "there are those among us, as all know, who have judged these strangers to be of an evil seed, and I will tell you in open words that it is a matter on which I have been in doubt, though I have prayed much.

"Yet we have this to face, that the wrathful purpose of God fell not upon them (though it be true that one died in that strife, as a man may without shame), but rather upon the devil's spawn that were spewed up from the mouths of Hell. Being leagued in verity with the angels of darkness, had they fought as they did against those who were the comforters of their evil deeds?

"And we must face this too, if we would weigh judgment in equal scale, that there was one of us who was most forward and sure in all accusation which has been made against them, as he was also in that on which Patience God's-Truth was tried, and—we would judge not one who is beyond answering now, but he—is not here."

He spoke as one still in a troubled doubt, being an honest man, as all knew. He was as one who sought truth in a shadowed place.

Aaron, following him, took the same tone, though from a lower temper of thought. "It is a doubt," he said, "which has been anxious in all our minds, and there is much force in that which is now said. Yet is it a known thing that (whether for trial of faith, or for other cause, which it were presumption to seek to know, it being of the hidden counsel of God) there are times when the devil hath power to protect his own, even to the confusion of the saints of God."

"Brother," Michael answered him, with something as near to contempt as he thought it well to show in that place, "you do well to look at all sides; yet had the end been that of my own death, with the loss of all that was mine, I may have a doubt as to the words which

193

you would have then said. And I will say here that it might so have been, save for the high comfort of God, I being left unsuccoured of all, except only that Brother Ephraim came and passed unscathed through the hordes of the unrighteous, wetting his sword with their blood. In that was marvel enough, on which you may ponder well in a quiet hour. Nay, for I have not done!" For he saw that Aaron would be prompt to speak, should he give but a second's pause. "If you be in doubt, as you say, I can give you peace, stilling a vain thought, which has no substance on which to stand.

"For you will see, if you will face this thing with a straight glance, that the devil did not protect his own, unless you will say more than that they were his which my house held, whether of my own kin or the strangers that were within my gates, but you must say that the Anabaptists were of another sort, and where will you then be?"

There was a subtlety here, even beyond his own, by which Aaron was stayed from speech for a minute's space, seeing not what to reply, or, it may be, not comprehending as instantly as he would have liked to do; and Ebenezer, to whom it was but a simple thing, he being the theologian he was, had the first answer again.

"Brethren," he said, "it is a point which it were easy to miss, yet, being seen, it hath a forehead of truth. For, of a verity, it was urged against the strangers that were in our midst that they were accursed from God, even as being fiends in the likeness of men, and had the devil sustained his own, as our brother would have us think, had he sustained them only, and not those also whom he sent forth from the caves of Hell? And for what did he send them forth, if our Brother Michael was at that time in the hands of the angels of night? And to what end fought they as they did, if they were all of the same brood?

"For we must see that when the tempest came, which is the very garment of God, and His right hand was outstretched therefrom, the devil had little power to protect his own, that is the Anabaptists, as we know them to be."

"I would say nought against any," Aaron replied, in his mild perplexed voice, "being one who seeks only the truth for the land's good. Yet is it a thing which we cannot wink that Patience God's-Truth was of those who died, she being the one in whom this trouble had birth."

There was a murmur of protest from several of the Elders at the implication which underlay this suggestion, and which could not be hidden beneath the mildness of Aaron's speech, but it died before the sudden fury of anger which blazed in Michael's eyes, as he half-rose from the table, bringing his hand down with a force beneath which the heavy table shook.

"Now may God—," he began, and then checked himself. He sat down again, and in a voice which was strangely quiet after that outburst, he went on. "All men die. There are those who will never die as she died. Yea, there be some here."

He looked round a table which had grown still, as is the air when it waits a storm, and his manner changed again. "Brethren," he said, "we go far from the point which I would have raised. It was not of that on which there were those who erred, nor would I have said a word as to the way in which I was left to die had it not been teased forth, but we have a plain issue to face.

"Let us say that these strangers who have come here are no worse than an honest folk, yet is it well that they go back, taking word of a fertile land which we do not fill? Is there no jeopard that there will be others who will then come of a different breed? Do we seek bloodshed and losing strife, or to see the land taken by those who will reject our rule, and, it may be, lead our young men and our maidens to the worship of other Gods, even to their souls' cost? Here is question to be faced without heat or feud, as we should know how."

Judah God's-Truth, a man large and bearded as Michael, but of a more placid countenance, being one who had repute of good humour and good sense, but all in a slow way, spoke for the first time.

"Brother Michael," he said, "you will not have brought us here to debate this without thought given thereto. We would have your own counsel in this, and the more so that you know these folk better than others can."

"It is fairly asked," Michael conceded, "and I will answer it in the same way.

"The woman is young and fair, and of a good wit. She is also of a great pride, thinking herself to be somewhat more than she is, but that is an ill not beyond cure.

"The man is of prudent speech, and one to trust if his word be pledged, but not else. He is quiet and cool. He has much knowledge of the forces of God, and how they can be bent to the use of man...I mean not in evil ways. Of this knowledge he makes little boast, but it is there, and might be used to our gain.

"I say that they would be well to hold, but might bring much evil upon us being set loose. I say that they should not go."

Ephraim asked: "Would you hold them by force?"

"I said not that. I would have them to stay of a good will. There is this to be seen, that they cannot go except by the way they came, for which a boat is a needed thing."

"If we should take the boat," Ebenezer asked, "how think you that there will be goodwill to be gained?"

"There is one way that is sure. They are both unwed."

"But why, being wed, should they be of a good will to settle here?"

"I meant not that they should wed one another, but that they be joined to those of this land. To be wed together they are clearly of no mind, or it had been seen ere now."

Ephraim asked: "Are you so well assured?"

Michael looked the surprise he felt, if not more. It was an unwelcome suggestion, coming from one who saw more than he would always say. It was a thought which he had put out of his own mind, feeling that reason was on his side, but instinct can be restive, even when reason has closed the door.

"Had they willed to wed," he replied, "had they not done so before they set out on a wandering way, they being of full age and having wealth beyond words, as themselves tell?"

Ephraim thought "She having wealth," making distinction in an exact mind, but he said no more.

Michael went on: "As for the woman, I will tell you in plain words that, if we be of one mind that they shall stay here, I will wed her myself when the spring shall come, I being yet in the vigour of life, and Mistress God's-Truth being dead, as you know."

There was no comment on that. The Elders looked at one another or at the board, as their natures led them to do. Margaret God's-Truth was but just dead. Few were clear as to how she had died, beyond that she had fallen to an Anabaptist's sling. To the elder men there came memories of more than twenty years ago, when things had been whispered which were not fitted for open speech. It was known to some that there had been little love between Michael and his wife in the later years. Well, it was his matter, not theirs.

There might be other aspects of the case which were unwelcome to some, but they could not speak them beneath his eyes, and so they could not gain the strength of that which is spoken aloud and has the common assent. But the thought that the two alien women should both be wed to Michael's household might be a matter on which to debate at another time.

Ebenezer, who, by the dignities of office and years, must be looked to for speech when a pause came, answered in his own way, "And what then of the man?"

"It is that which we might not force, yet it might come in a natural way. Paradise is a fair maid, and they will walk in the same paths."

Ebenezer said: "All this may be as it will, for no woman may wed by our law except at a free choice. It is less than that which we must decide now, and yet more. Shall we permit them to go, if they should prove of a stubborn will?"

The question roused the Elders to speech. It was easier to discuss that point than to say whether Michael God's-Truth should wed whom he would while he sat by.

There was quick talk which was soon done, for they found that they were of one mind. Having come unasked, the strangers must stay, whether they would or no. How was it best to make sure?

There was little doubt as to that. They could not go without the boat (that was agreed). Then let the boat be destroyed.

But there was some reluctance to face that solution. The *Blanche* was recognized as a very valuable thing. Even the metals and timbers of which it was built. But they would not break it up for their own use without its owner's consent. They were not thieves but God-fearing men. In fact, the elect of God. Let the boat be hidden away.

Michael suggested that which had been in his mind from the first. Hidden things may be found. They could take a surer course. Let it be sunk. A sunk boat could not be raised by Franklin in a quiet way. Next summer, if all went as was planned, it might be raised with his own co-operation and transported to the great river, where it would be useless now, for that water only thawed for a few weeks in the later summer, and then not always for its whole length. Meanwhile, the *Blanche* could be sunk in the stream where it now was, which did not freeze, being fed with water hot from the heart of Hell.

They knew little of what damage such submersion might mean, but it was a middle course, which seemed both safe and good. It was trusted to Michael to do this, for it was clear that it would be in safe hands, his plans being what they were. He mentioned that it was still loaded with the strangers' goods. It was agreed that they should be first rendered to them. Michael undertook that Ehud should oversee that. Then he would sink the *Blanche* in a quiet way. None would know that it had been debated by the Elders at all. None would know how it had been sunk. Men might think as they would.

They broke up without haste, not being vexed by shortness of time, as they were in the autumn days, for what are hours in a winter of changeless night? They looked only at the weather, which was still clear. They went home by their separate ways, feeling that they had done well, but there were some who felt that there would be more to do at a later day.

On the way home, Michael told Ehud of the part which had been chosen for him. Michael thought it a good omen but he should be brought into the secret counsel of the Elders thus, but he was silent on this, knowing that it is easy to speak too soon. He thought that Ehud would welcome any course which would close a final door against thought of return to the alien land from which his wife came, or of connection therewith. Be that as it might, it did not enter his mind that Ehud would fail to carry out his own order or the instruction of the Council, which all must obey. He spoke freely, but that not to test his son, but from an open mind, when he said, "It is to your gain that there should be no lingering thought of a left life."

Ehud answered frankly to that, "My wife will not look back. Her hopes are all in this land. It were evil, indeed, that more should come of her kind. We have grown too far apart. We two are of one mind about that. It would be the end of all that we are."

In the following days the *Blanche* was unloaded under Ehud's supervision, and its cargo was drawn on goat-sleds, and rendered to those to whom it belonged. It took time, for Ehud said (with truth) that it had been found impracticable to unload it at the place where it had been moored, and it had been towed up the river to a spot where there was a track running near, which was already made through the snow. He contrived that the unloading should be finished before Franklin was aware, so that he should not know where the boat now was. That might have been cause for resentment, but some excuse was made, and there could be no complaint that the work had not been thoroughly done. Even some of the furnishings and fittings of the boat had been brought away. Ehud said that they had not known what might be spoiled by the winter cold.

After that, the wind rose again and there was more snow. At that time, and for many weeks, it would have been death to go forth. The cold might not be so intense in the valley as on the northern heights, and the endless tableland that stretched beyond, but the nearness of the volcanic range to the south may have caused the precipitation of the almost continuous snow. Fierce winds raged from the east, often rising to a blizzard's strength. Snow-clouds stretched over all, heavy and low, and beneath them the darkness was night indeed.

When there came a break, and the stars sparkled over the frozen snow, it lay in drifts so deep that Michael's house was buried to the roof on its eastern side, and the cold grew deadlier as the wind moved beneath an open sky.

Men and goats stayed where they were, thankful that life was sustained with fodder and stove and lamp behind the thick warmth of their wooden walls. But the heavy snow was a blanket to the fallow land and the myriad seeds it held. It covered the dwarf-grown apples, and wrapped itself high around the boles of the stunted oaks. When the summer came, the valley would owe much to the thick warmth of the snow.

And so the long night passed, and there were no outward signs from the far-scattered, close-shuttered houses, so firmly closed against the unfriendly night that there was often no glimmer, through any narrow crack, of the flickering light within, no outward signs of the dramas of life and death that must have been passing within them. Only here and there, a door would open widely for a little space, and the dead would be put out to freeze till the spring came, beneath the mantle of descending snow.

That was the custom of the land, for which there was cause enough, and they lay quiet and secure. No prowling bear would find them, no wolf would burrow. Corruption itself would have no power upon them. The land was too dead for that.

But the house of Michael God's-Truth, so much as the Anabaptists had left habitable, remained silent and closed. It had no more dead to put forth. Beyond that, it was like the others. It gave no sign.

CHAPTER L.

THE northern hills rose steeply toward the stars. They rose fold above fold, higher than the goats could feed, even in the brief warmth of the summer that had no night. They rose to ten thousand feet, but at the last there were no bold outlines of peak and ridge, but a level edge, beyond which, it was said (but few had climbed that height within the memory of those who now lived), there stretched stark fields of everlasting ice, over which such tempests beat as no man might endure and live.

Eleanor looked up at these heights. The long night had not ceased, but there was a change which had opened doors, and caused many to toil at the making of paths, which was a first necessity for the resumption of open life. It had brought Eleanor forth, and Franklin beside her, to watch a sky in which the stars paled. Over the northern heights it seemed that the dawn came. The dark sky trembled into olive green, and then into an exquisite rose, which was of a beauty beyond words, for there is nothing like it except in the polar cold. It moved far up the sky. Surely the dawn came.

But even then it grew less, and the stars resumed.

It was the seventh day now that they had watched that light in the northern sky. Every day it grew more. To Eleanor, it was the light of a great hope. It was like a rainbow after rain. Soon there would be a day when the sun—the actual sun itself—would show above the northern height. Only for a moment perhaps. Perhaps only a part of its golden disc. But every day it would grow more. It would move along the northern sky. It would increase its arc. The time would come when it would circle around the sky, and would not set at all. But by that time they must be.... Ah, if she knew where. But they must be far from here. There could be no doubt about that.

Yet she was not without hope, not even without confidence, as she looked at the trembling dawn. There was hope in the very quarter from which it came. It was to the north they must go. It was from the north that her rescue came. Even now (she thought) there would be activity in the Cape Town dock where the *Bergen* lay. Soon it would be steaming toward them, buffeting the ice-cold seas, feeling through the mists that lay over the glacial fields that broke at the coming of spring into a million of jostling floes. It would come at last to the frozen beach where their huts would be standing. And she meant that they should be there too. What though the *Blanche* were sunk? She did not doubt that, for she had Michael's word, and she knew that he did not lie. There must be other ways! The sun beckoned them to a sunlit way.

She turned to Franklin with sudden passionate speech, and was not rebuffed even by his silence and the misery in his face. Was he to fail her now? To fail her in every way, as servant, friend, and lover? She would not believe that.

Her servants had never failed her. Never till now. They had been too competent, too well-chosen. Her friends had been swift to content her whims. Of lovers, she had accepted none.

But she had learnt to know herself during the long watchful purgatory of those winter months, to know her feelings at least. Franklin could have her, if he would. She had made that clear, if not before, yet very plainly in these times when they had come out together to watch the approaching dawn. And the price was to get her clear of this hateful place. Surely he would do that?

There were times when he felt the same—when he felt that he could not fail. For the old barriers were down now, the old values gone. He thought little of her distant wealth. What, indeed, did it avail her here?

He knew her now as one who might be his, as he had feared to hope. Not the Eleanor of a too arrogant pride, but the Blanche of his dreams. His to carry away. *Beyond the utmost purple rim*. He knew now from where that line came, and it had a mocking sound. For he had thought—how he had thought!—he had thought for a winter's length. And he knew that they were in a trap which he could not break.

He had thought of a secret raft. How or where or of what he could construct it he did not know, but he had imagined so often what would happen when it was launched already done.

It would float down of itself. Would blunder through the dark caves while they lay flatly upon it and felt it striking the rocks, now on one side, now on another. But the force of the current would bear it on.

If it did not take them where the rocky roof was too low and would scrape them off, or press them to a drowning death, they would come out to the light at last.

And they would drift down, swiftly enough, though not at the rate that the *Blanche's* engines had brought her up. They might be a week—or two. They might be a prey, long before that, to the tearing teeth of the fish-men of the caves. That was a likely thing. They would have no force to defend themselves, no speed for escape.

And if they came out at last to the frozen sea, unstarved of hunger and cold, to what landing would the warm stream bear them, where the ice began? How could he hope that it would be where they would be able to reach the huts on which their lives would depend? What weather would they drift out to meet, either on sea or land?

It would be a desperate, hopeless chance, not one to offer any, except at a final need; yet it might have been tried, only—how could such a raft be built, be launched, among those by whom his every movement would be known? And it must be done in these first days, if it were to be of any avail. It was not a sane thing to plan.

And yet—something must be done now, or the last chance would be gone. It had come to that.

They were not to be allowed to return. Michael had told them that in plain reasonable words many weeks ago. It was a decision of the Elders, from which there was no appeal. And they were to remain at a peril which he was at no pains to obscure. There were many who would have their blood, if they could. Many who would attribute any adverse circumstance which might arise to their presence among them.

Franklin saw that such a position might occur at any moment. A scatter of volcanic ash, and their lives might not endure for a day.

Michael went further than that. He made it clear that the attack upon them was, in part, an intrigue against himself and the God's-Truth clan. If he were to give them the support without which they would not be safe for a week, he must know that he could depend upon them for a corresponding loyalty, and for conformity with the Elders' requirements.

He had not wooed Eleanor in any personal way, but he had indicated her destiny by implication, and sometimes by open words. He let her get used to the idea. But it was clear that, when the spring came, there would be the necessity of a prompt decision.

But it was not that alone. Had it been only that, there might have seemed a faint vague chance that she might have refused, even defied him, and still won sufficient tolerance from the community to make life endurable. Michael had a certain largeness, a magnanimity of character, which made anything possible. But Eleanor knew in her heart that he regarded her already as his, with a restrained passion which might be terrible in defeat. It was incalculable at the best. He was a man who was not often thwarted at a light cost.

But it was not that alone. There was a condition which he had made it clear that they could not evade, a decision which they would not be allowed to delay.

At the first meeting after the snow should melt—at the celebration of spring—they must join the Church in an open and formal way. The old errors of unregenerate days might be forgiven—might be passed over without a too-perilous probing—but there must be no seed of heresy planted here. The Elders were the theological conscience of the community to which all must conform.

To make a difficulty of this would be to produce a crisis which even Michael (so he said) could not control.

It was a point about which Gwen made no difficulty. She had agreed that with Ehud from the first. Franklin had been right when he had thought that she would consider that a kingdom would be worth a mass. Discussing it with Eleanor, she had defended herself with ability. Was she to set up an opposition Church with a single member? Was there any Church with which you could agree, if every doctrine which you professed to hold must be endorsed in detail? What about Eleanor's own Church, and the incongruous elements which it contained? Did Bishop B. accept the Thirty-Nine Articles, except with his tongue in his cheek? Did Dean I.? They would say that they reformed the Church from within. Well, what about that?

But while Gwen defended her conformity with her usual competence, she said nothing to persuade Eleanor to a similar attitude. Rather, she accepted the fact that, Eleanor feeling as she did, she would be obliged to refuse. She did not argue the position nor offer any suggestion. She stood aside.

Eleanor was puzzled by her attitude, and then resentful. It seemed that, having married Ehud, her first concern had been that they should not reveal her hidden land to the outer world, and now that that fear was removed, she left them, with little sympathy, to get out of their difficulties as best they could.

She was, in any case, obviously absorbed with her own affairs. Already, with the help of the snowshoes that were made to a local pattern, there had been several expeditions to the ruin of Abel Trustwell's house. The fire had done less damage than had been supposed. One or two of the lower rooms could be made habitable with little repair. Ehud and Gwen were both eager to take possession of their new home. Preparations were pushed forward with such haste as the conditions allowed.

In fact, these conditions were more favourable, in spite of the meagre light, than they would be at a later date, when the snow would begin to melt. The thaw came with a north-western wind, and was usually very rapid. While it lasted, the whole land was in flood. It drained mainly toward the east, where was the great river of which Franklin had heard much, though he had not seen it, but there would be enough water poured into the warm stream that came from the southern hills to raise its level beyond its banks. This was told to Franklin as a condition that hindered all outdoor operations till the floods fell. He thought of it as one that would make it impossible for boat or raft to escape under the hills, for the water would choke the passage, rising to the low roof of the caves. Neither Franklin nor Eleanor was of a deeply religious temperament, nor of theological convictions of very decided patterns. Probably Gwen could have stated what she believed, and why, in a more coherent way than Eleanor, if not Franklin, could do. But it did not follow that they were equally ready to conform to a creed to which they gave adherence neither by individual conviction nor the family tradition which may be its equivalent.

To Eleanor, in particular, by pride, by tradition, and by an individual fastidiousness, it was an impossible thing to which she did not give the tribute of a moment's consideration. It only demonstrated the inevitability of that of which she was resolved already. It was an impossible place in which to remain. She had made a mistake in staying here at all. She was willing to admit that. Franklin should have been firmer. What are men for? Especially when you engage them as leaders of expeditions. Still, she would admit that she had been wrong. Now she saw her fault. She wished to go home. The method was for Franklin to contrive. The road was that which called her by the retreating dawn.

CHAPTER LI.

THEY stood again in the same place when the next dawn flushed and trembled over the northern hills, making a promise which it did not keep. It lasted longer than before, fading at last to a lucent dove-grey quietude, with one primrose bar that lingered under the returning stars. There had been things said since yesterday in that house, of which she hated every timber and stone—words said by Michael which had been hard to endure with silent lips, though he may have been unaware of offence—words which showed them both that any freedom of decision that might still be theirs was a very fleeting thing.

"We cannot stay here," she said. "You can see that. If we cannot go by water or air, we must go by land. There is no other way."

He looked up at the black basaltic hills, rising to a glacial pallor which darkened now beneath the retreating dawn. He thought of the thousand miles of pathless desolation that separated them from the ocean's side. The iron cold, the certain roughness of the frozen way. To walk it on a beaten path, even if the sun shone in a windless air, carrying all the provisions that they would need till the journey's end—it was not a difficult, it was an utterly impossible thing. And on those blizzard-beaten heights, over drift and glacier and moraine....

"If I thought there were the least chance," he said wretchedly. "But it would be to lead you to death. We have not even a sleeping-bag."

"But we have the tent."

It was true that they had a tent. A small portable one which had been part of the *Blanche's* cargo, and which Ehud's thoroughness had included in the total of its contents which had been brought to the house. It was very light, very strong, very well-made. The best of its kind, as all Eleanor's equipment had been. Yet its weight would be a serious item on such a journey, a serious reduction of what might otherwise have been carried of the food which would be life itself.

"Yes," he said, without enthusiasm, "we have the tent." After all, suppose they did try? They had nothing to hope for here. At the worst, they would die together. They would go where no life had dared to be, perhaps, since earth had shuddered and rent and given birth to this barren continent in the Polar seas. It would be a royal tomb. If she could see it as he did—if she regarded it as the suicide that it surely was! But he knew that she did not regard it in that way. She looked impatiently across the intervening distance to the spot where the *Bergen* would surely come, and where she was determined to be. The endless intervening distance was no more than a difficulty to be brushed aside. To let her go with this thought in her heart was to entrap her to a suicide which she did not mean. Let her think of him as she would, it was a thing that he could not do. He added, as in explanation or apology, "Perhaps, if I loved you less. But I know that it is an impossible thing. We mightn't live for a day. It is a plateau where no life has endured from the dawn of time."

"You cannot tell, if it's never been tried," she answered obstinately. "It might be easier than you think."

For the first time her unwavering courage caused the sanity of his own judgment to falter. In the vigour of health, in the beauty of her imperious youth, she looked so far from death! And what she said was true. It might be easy in some unexpected way. After all, who could have guessed the existence of the valley in which they stood? Suppose that it were true that they had only to climb those frozen forbidding heights to find some relief, some rescue, that they could not dream? And it was his cowardice that held them back! Besides, what else was there to weigh against it? They did not face the future here with any hope, even with any plan, because her determination to escape prevented discussion of such issues. But he knew that that was only half the truth. He had thought for many hours, and if she should ask him, he had nothing hopeful to propose. He understood too well the temper of the people among whom they had come like a strange disease. If they would conform to their Church, if she would marry Michael, they might have at least a hope that they would escape or overcome any active hostility in the future days— but these were things that they would not do. So his mind wavered toward the insanity of assent, and then hardened again as he remembered the distance that must be traversed.

"You mustn't forget," he said, "the distance we should have to cover. I daresay it's not less than a thousand miles. Even with sledges...."

She looked at him with an anger that was near contempt. "You talk of love!" she said bitterly. "And you won't help me to get away. Do you *want* me to marry that man?"

"I only don't want to kill you. It's certain death to try that."

"Then find another."

Alas! What way was there that was not equally hopeless, equally mad?

"If you'd read more about what's been done in these regions, and what it's like on the high ground."

"But you don't believe all you read, do you? Of course, they make it out worse than it is. That's to make more of themselves. A child could see that. Look how easily we got here!"

Yes. He saw that that was where the trouble lay. They had got here so easily. On the *Bergen* she had had every comfort that money gives, even in Antarctic seas. And then there had been the three days on the *Blanche*, with no real hardship to face; and then the winter in this sheltered volcanic valley. Hard enough it might have seemed to her, but it was, in fact, almost miraculous that she should have come to this remoteness of the Antarctic wastes without experiencing its more sinister possibilities.

"If I could see a chance," he said, miserably, "the faintest, smallest chance...."

She answered impatiently, "How can you tell till you try? It isn't as though you've been there before. It's just that you don't dare. Do you think if there were anything like a man I could turn to except you? Do you think I should be talking here now? *Do you mean to go alone?*"

He told himself that he must keep sane, and not give way to the madness with which she would infect his mind. "You don't seem to realize," he said, in a tone that he tried to keep clear of emotion, even against the impact of her contempt, "that we couldn't carry food for such a distance. We should be starved to death after the first few days."

"But of course we could carry that. It would be heavy at first, but it would get lighter at every meal."

"Have you calculated...?"

"Of course I haven't. How could we, when we don't know how far it is? Not by hundreds of miles. Nor how rapidly we could get on. It's a chance that we've got to take. It's the only way. Calculating wouldn't do any good. It wouldn't make us able to carry a pound more. We've just got to take all we can."

206

"It can't be much less than a thousand miles, even if we find the nearest way—if we strike the coast at the right point, and that's expecting a good deal."

"It's not expecting too much. There'd always be the river on our left hand. We should keep close to that. You're just making difficulties."

"Well," he said, "I won't make any more."

"You mean you'll try it?"

Yes. He meant that. He had given way. After all, it might be the cleanest way out, to die a frozen death on the heights of snow. When she said there was no other way, she was so far right. He could see none that he could imagine that she would stoop to take. It might end in a witch's death.

Anyway, the moment was theirs. She showed him that, as they went back to the house, till he felt that, with such a prize at the end, there could be nothing that he could not do. Might there be a chance after all?

CHAPTER LII.

HAVING once accepted the plan of escape which she had thrust upon him, Eleanor could not complain that Franklin showed any lack of energy or skill in preparation for the adventure. He made an offer to help Ehud and Gwen in transporting their various possessions to their new home, which was readily accepted, and by that means he got some useful practice in walking a burdened way. More important than that, he contrived to load himself in part, on each occasion, with his own requirements, and to cache them at a place between Ehud's new home and the hills. By this means, he was able to accumulate all—and more than all—that they could hope to carry at a point five miles nearer the hills than Michael's house. It was a trifling difference, when considered in relation to the total distance that was before them, but it was a difference on the right side. Beside that, it was an essential part of his plan for getting a long start before their flight would be guessed, for Eleanor could make some excuse to visit Gwen's new abode in his company, making the time of their return indefinite. Ehud, if he thought of it at all, would suppose that they were returning to Michael's house. So would Gwen. Michael, as it became prolonged, would suppose that they were delayed in helping his son or his son's wife. There would be the maximum of time before their absence attracted notice, and, perhaps, pursuit. This time was the more important, because Franklin

planned to start with a greater load than Eleanor and he could hope
to bear as they ascended the hills—which might prove sufficiently
difficult, even for unburdened climbers. When they had found a way
of ascent, he would return for a second load…perhaps a third. Even
if he made double journeys for the first few days, it might be their
salvation in the end. It was not speed in itself which would save
them, but only speed in relation to their stocks of food. Once on the
heights, he thought that he could soon baffle pursuit by choosing a
course where their footmarks would leave no trace.

Now that he was committed to the attempt, he put its folly resolutely outside his mind. With the tent and the warm clothing that
was theirs, he supposed that they would not die of cold. There was
no fear of thirst, which is worse than hunger. They had only to con-
serve food, and they would go far. They knew nothing of the insatiable hunger which comes to those who toil all day in the Antarctic
cold. That which he took was mainly pemmican, and other preserved and concentrated foods that had been part of the six weeks'
provisions with which they had loaded the *Blanche* for her first voyage. He thought, with care, that it should go far.

His plans worked with absolute, even ominous, smoothness. It
was only a few days after he had yielded to Eleanor's importunity,
and the sun was rising no more than its own breadth above the
northern hills, when they turned their faces towards its golden disc,
in the hope that, whether for life or death, they were leaving that
valley forever.

CHAPTER LIII.

"JUST you go back?" Eleanor asked, and knew the folly of the
words she uttered.

After many hours of exhausting and burdened toil, they had
gained the great height at which they aimed. The sun was down, but
the long twilight of the Antarctic spring showed them a vast white
plain that sloped downward for miles which they could not guess,
and then rose again to the distant skyline. That must be the first
stage of their journey. The snow was frozen and firm. They might
make good progress with the snowshoes which they had used to get
to the foot of the hills, and which were part of the load for which
Franklin must now return. If the land beneath that frozen surface
were firm and level, it looked a safer, easier way than they could
have reasonably hoped to find. If there were hidden, snow-bridged

crevasses, as was a likely thing—well, they would have such hope of life as a rope gave.

Franklin looked back on the wide shadowed valley, and across to the further hills, which glowed, as ever, with volcanic fire. Would they overwhelm it at last? Pouring down dust and lava till it would be buried with all it held? Men might come after, surveying desolation, and not believing the tale that they would have taken back. If they should ever take it.

But he must not think that. It was too late for doubts. It must not be if, but how. He turned his eyes again to the white roof of the world on the edge of which they stood. He had set up the tent beneath a wind-sheltering rock. Eleanor would be safe there till his return. But he could see no break in the downward slope of snow that stretched for—how many?—miles. If the wind rose, and it was strong and bitter now at this height if he stepped aside from the shelter of the protecting rock, it might be impossible to set the tent up on that plain. Suppose it should be blown away? They must endeavour to cross that great expanse at a single effort, not camping till they came to the further ridge. Or perhaps it might not be as smooth as it looked, nor as far. Perhaps, in a better light....

Eleanor's question broke through his thought. "Yes," he said, "you know that." And then, "Are you afraid?"

"No," she answered, "there is nothing to fear. There is no one here—except God."

She spoke in an awed tone, which was echoed by a feeling which was not far from the surface of his own mind.

Life teemed over the wide earth, and in ocean and air. Even its Arctic centre was full of life of a thousand sorts. Life was everywhere through the temperate and tropic zones. It was active in every one of the myriad, million drops of the great oceans that stretched round the southern pole. It struggled upward against the outer edges of the Antarctic barrier. Seal and penguin, snow-petrel and skua-gull, fought for tempestuous life against the blind violence of its blizzards, the iron severities of its frozen night. That was along its outer edges, over which the east winds screamed, from which the icebergs broke. But, beyond that, far inland where no life could come—was it not really the outer rim, with which God had girdled the earth He made? Beyond which no life could endure?

Standing there, it was easy to think, even to believe. Yet as to that, he saw that, far as they had come, they had proved nothing. If they had come straight inland for a thousand miles, it was no more than—it was not as much as—is left uncharted on the Antarctic maps.

What did it matter? Here, where no life would dare, they were alone—with God. Alone, where it seemed that no life had a right to be. Eleanor need not dread being alone, for her life had nothing to fear—nor to hope.

Life must endure, if at all, by feeding on other life, as all life does. Here, there was nothing on which to feed. Nothing to destroy. Nothing, either, to destroy them. And because destruction is the law of life, they could not themselves endure beyond the limit of the food—the fruits of violence and death in other lands—which their hands bore.

So his thoughts wandered, as they will when the body is at rest after exhausting toil. Eleanor asked him twice if he would not have some food—at least, some longer rest—before he should start downward again. But he said "no" when he heard her. He spoke from a resolution which he had made at the first, that he would not reduce the little stock of food which they had already brought up, but would endure till he could regain the cache, where he had more (as he saw now) than he could carry up those final cliffs in less than half-a-dozen journeys. No, he would eat what he could while he was down there. And by holding to this resolution, he nearly ended the adventure before it was well commenced. For he had overestimated the time that he could endure in that climate without food and while continuing in sustained activity.

He had lain down more than once, in a lethargy which it had been hard to conquer, before he arrived at the cache, and then he was no more than half-conscious, in a mechanical way, and it was not until after a long interval of food and sleep that he was able to load himself for a second climb. Then, when he came to the steeper cliffs, he found that it would not be possible to scale them with the load which he had attempted, and had to lay down part for a return journey. In the end, he had to make three further descents before he was satisfied that he had brought up all that would be necessary for their existence, and which there was any hope that they would be able to bear across the frozen wastes.

The last climb was the most difficult, being made in the worst light, for the wind changed to the west, and the landscape below him, which had been thawing for many hours, no longer reflected upward the light of stars and crescent moon from a garment of sparkling snow. Yet he thought, as he looked on the dark vision of the flooded country, that there would be no present danger of pursuit, as was, indeed, the case. For the snow had become too soft and treacherous for safe journeying upon its surface many hours before the land was flooded by a thaw of exceptional violence. As confidently as Gwen supposed that they had returned to Michael's house, so was it concluded there that they had stayed with her, rather than adventure return till the thaw should have become complete and the floods fallen. To Franklin the changing weather had made no difference. The winter blizzards had blown too strongly along the steep hillsides to allow the snow to accumulate upon them, nor did the thaw rise high enough to alter their frozen surfaces. It was only when the landscape darkened beneath him, and he climbed among the shadows with an added peril, that the change of weather was any hindrance to him.

On the height where the tent stood and Eleanor waited, the wind was still bleakly bitter, and the cold almost as intense as before.

CHAPTER LIV.

"YOU'D better have a good rest now," Eleanor said, "There's no hurry about starting."

Franklin saw that. They had reluctantly agreed that he had brought up more than they could possibly carry, and that some of the food must be left.

"They won't trouble about us," she went on confidently, "even if they know we've gone, which they probably don't. They're too busy being drowned out. We've got to take the tent and the stove, and enough fuel to keep it going for meals, if not more. We don't want to start sucking icicles before we're obliged. And we must have an ice-axe, and we've got to allow for the fact that we may have to carry the snowshoes when we can't wear them. Beyond that, it's just a question of how much food we can hang round us, and stagger along. We can't take all we've got here, so if we stay a week to eat it, we shan't be any the worse off, and it might mean—"

She left the sentence unfinished. Her thought had been that it might be a week more of life, and perhaps it was best unsaid. But she had had leisure for thought while he had been engaged on the toil of that repeated climb, and had faced the deadly folly of the enterprise that they had undertaken.

Not that she admitted an earlier error. She told herself, and it may have been partly true, that she had always known that it had been a desperate, if not hopeless effort. But while she had been in the hateful prison of Michael's house, she had seen one supreme necessity—the necessity of escape—to the exclusion of every smaller issue. She had felt that they must go, at whatever cost, and that Franklin must be made to see it. She did not regret it now. She told

211

herself that she would never regret it. Was it not better to die, if die they must, in this severity of desolation, rather than to endure the kind of life which was offered to them in the valley below?

She still looked steadfastly ahead. She still saw, in imagination, the *Bergen* with Captain Ericson on the bridge, its bows pointing toward them through the sea-mist and the jostling floes. But she was more conscious of the immensity of the barren wilderness that intervened. To cross it was no more than a faintest hope, to be faced for the thing it was, but no less bravely for that. All men die. If death must come, is it not better to be of those who meet it with quiet eyes, than to go through life dodging it desperately toward a blundering end?

She did not speak her thoughts in open words, but they were implicit in much which was said, and in the growing closeness of the intimacy that united them. The wealth which had held them apart was reduced by distance to its true insignificance, as though it were weighed in the scales of God. The unconscious arrogance, the impatience of opposition, the resolute self-will and self-confidence which had brought her here, fell away before the high austerity of that frozen waste.

They started with the first promise of light.

They halted at last, looking back on a wide expanse of whiteness, the extent of which it was hard to judge, and forward to one which seemed no less than it had done when they started in the morning light.

"I'm glad," she said, "that we've got nothing to measure how far we've come. It would be a weary thing counting how many miles we'd done each day—or how few—and it wouldn't mean anything, not knowing how far it is."

"Yes," he said. "It'll be better just to feel we've done the most we can, and leave it at that. I did hope we should have finished coming down before we halted, and begin on the upward slope after our first rest, but you can't judge these distances when there are no landmarks at all."

Eleanor looked to their left hand. "The ground slopes further town that way than it does ahead."

"Yes. You'll remember that the cliffs were quite low where the river goes underground. I suppose, more or less, we shall be at that point when the level begins to rise again—though, fortunately, we shan't have had to go so far down as the ground must sink at the canyon edge."

Yes. It was fortunate. She saw that. There's no use in going downhill, when every foot has to be climbed again. And they were fortunate that the weather continued calm. It would be poor camping in time of storm on this open plain—and perhaps impossible to continue struggling forward. She felt that she needed all the fortunate things of which she was able to think to sustain her now. To look at the interminable slope, and to think that when they ceased the gentle descent they would be "more or less" where the river entered the hills! Practically, not started at all. And Franklin made her eat as much as himself, and she wasn't sure it was fair, as he carried so much more, but she could have eaten ten times as much. And so she rose, and straightened aching limbs to resume her burden, and the onward way.

"I'm so glad," she said cheerfully, "every time I think that I shan't see it again."

CHAPTER LV.

IT was the thirteenth day. The weather had been marvellous. They knew that, though they could not tell how different at that season it might often be. It held back its strength, as though in derision or contempt of these atoms of conscious life who had dared to enter its desolations. Every hour they wandered further into an interior where no life endured, every hour they made their fates more certain. There was no need for the storm to strike them. Their doom was sure.

Once or twice there had been sharp icy gusts of buffeting wind, and the stinging lash of a frozen sleet had blinded them where they stood, but in a moment it had blown past, and they had looked up again to a sky of stars, or the daylight's frosty blue. And each day the sun rose higher, and gave more light, and even a little warmth as it shone in the northern sky. Heavily loaded though they were, they made good progress over the frozen snow. The level of that white expanse sank slowly and steadily before them, and the bitterness of the pursuing wind was somewhat lessened. They took some comfort from that, and from the clearness of a dawn which showed, first gold and rose, and then a vivid crimson which spread upward to the central sky. They did not know that the wind they thought so bitter was the gentlest zephyr that that desolation would ever know, that it might have been a pursuing fury, or a cross-buffeting fiend against which they would have had no force to fight, that they were favoured with weather such as was seldom equalled, even beneath the unsetting circle of the summer sun.

On the second day the sun had fronted them with an hour-long curve above the northern horizon, in a glory of golden mist. Then it failed, and the half-faded splendours of dawn became the glow of a sunset sky—a sunset which seemed to move westward with the passing hours, rather than to fade away.

They had spoken little except that Franklin would ask at times if she were not too tired to go on, and she would answer, "No, I'll tell you when I feel that. No, we'll wait a bit longer. Think what we ate at the start!" So she spoke, for courage she would never lack, though she was aching in every unaccustomed limb, and felt a hunger and weariness which would have gladly sunk with all she carried, even into the unfriendly snow. As it was, she knew that Franklin had shortened his pace to hers, and that his burden was nearly twice as great.

In that cold serenity they had progressed well, and after the first two days Eleanor had found no difficulty in keeping pace, had, indeed, thought at times that Franklin was more quickly exhausted than herself. Her fine vitality thrived in the clean keen air, and, besides, she was having a larger share of the precious store of food than would have been allotted by a more impartial hand than Franklin's was likely to be. Not that she was aware of this or would have consented to it. And the hunger of both of them was a craving that never stilled.

They had made good progress, as they owned, and yet the hope of ever reaching the distant ocean had grown fainter in the hearts of both.

For one thing, the endless immensity of the great tableland on which they wandered had sunk into their hearts. Its landmarks might be few, but they would be the same at night as in the morning hours, as though they had made no progress at all. It was an enormous land.

For another, they had been obliged to turn eastward, many miles out of their course, to avoid a fissured glacier over which they could have made laborious progress of a few miles a day, or less than that, and which stretched its green transparencies beyond the limit of sight. (Why was there so little snow upon its uneven surfaces? Could the scourge of the winter wind sweep it as bare as that? What terrors of Antarctic storm might there be, such as they had not yet seen?)

So they had kept to a surface where their snowshoes could still be worn, even though it turned them far from the direction in which they sought to go, and, one by one, the miles that were so hard, and meant so little, were left behind, with nothing of incident or difficulty to remember, beyond a few falls, a few bruises. And on the thirteenth day the storm came.

They were making slow progress at the time across a depressed plain, having a very rough and broken surface, on which huge granite boulders had been scattered by some old convulsion, whether of ice or fire. They would have avoided it if they could, but it had stretched across their way to the horizon's edge, and did not appear to be very broad. The great boulders lay in a scattered string in this shallow depression, which lay, east and west, like the dried bed of a gigantic river.

The snow was deep and hard underfoot in some places, and others were as bare as the windswept boulders themselves. It was hard to guess where the snow went, or why it was not of the depth of a hundred feet. It seemed that, on those frozen heights, it could never melt. Falling so often, must it not increase forever? The sea-drawn moisture that the snow-clouds scatter must return at last to the sea from which it came, in the form of the bergs that the great ice-barrier sheds forever from along its edge, as the glaciers push it outward. But how does the snow become less in the absence of summer thaw? So Franklin wondered, and thought the answer might be, in part, that the blinding tempests of snow, of which he had seen enough already to understand their fury, might not always be scattered from descending clouds. Did not the wind rather catch up the snow from where it lay, and dance with it in its arms, as it might have done with the same rakes perhaps a thousand times before?

It was coming now, from whatever source, in tiny frozen flakes that did not fall, but drifted along the wind. And the wind was rising fast.

"We'd better camp somewhere," he said, "while we can. We shan't be able to see a yard ahead if this thickens."

"Well," Eleanor answered, "what about this? We shan't even need the tent here...not while the wind's as it is."

They looked up at two huge converging blocks that roofed a space which they protected also from the quarter of the advancing storm. There could be no better place, unless the wind should change. It might soon be over. But they were glad to set up the little tent, for such comfort and warmth as it was able to give.

An hour later, they looked out and could see nothing. In the black darkness, they heard the blizzard rave across the entrance of their granite cave. So they endured for five days. They lit the stove only at long intervals, sufficient to make a drink of the tea that was almost gone. They lay close for warmth, which, even so, was not easy to get, thickly clad as they were. They ate sparingly of the concentrated foods they carried, which were so ominously less burden-some than they had been at first. Their hunger remained insatiable, but through hunger and cold their lives endured, and they learnt to know one another in these days, they learnt knowledge and love, as they might not have done in a year of the life of crowded routines which had become so distant now.

On the morning of the sixth day, the storm ceased. They crawled out to the blinding light of the risen sun, over snow that had been piled halfway to the summit at the entrance of their granite cave. They stretched stiff limbs, and shivered in a sunlight that gave no warmth. Through fur and leather and wool, the cold pierced as they had never felt it before. The Antarctic played with them still, but it tested them with a cold that they had not yet known, as though it grew impatient that they did not die.

Franklin said, "There's one thing certain, at least. "Nobody'll find us now." Was there regret in his voice? Had he always had a faint unacknowledged hope that some pursuit, some rescue would follow?

He could hardly have answered that, but the fact was plain that the storm would have covered their tracks, or blown them a hundred ways. Surely, no one would find them here.

They looked at their store of food, feeling that they could have finished it then, but with care—perhaps for three days? Perhaps—even for four.

Eleanor said, "Suppose we leave the tent and push on?"

He answered: "Yes, if you like." His tone was indifferent, and she responded quickly: "You mean it's no use going on at all."

"No. I didn't mean to say that." But he had said it, whether meant or not.

They looked back at the tent. Why not stay where they were? They could sustain life without exertion for some days longer with the food they had in that sheltered place than if they should toil in the deathly cold. The hours would be longer there. They might be happier when they had resigned themselves to a fate which must surely be, rather than to die in a futile struggle. They looked back at the tent, and then into each other's eyes.

CHAPTER LVI.

MICHAEL said: "There is no need for such words, for on this matter we are at one. They must be followed and brought again."

Aaron answered "You will not learn, even now. Will you lay a flown witch by the heels? Can you travel with fire and steam, as you have heard that she doth from her own lips?"

Michael countered that with: "Then it will show that she is no witch, if she be brought here again?"

"I said not that, for the devil will fail at times, being no more than he is."

"Brother," Ebenezer interrupted. "We waste words, where we should be acting with speed. Brother Michael, whom would you to send?"

"I have charged Ehud that he make ready with comrades who can travel fast."

Aaron said: "Aye, you would send God's-Truths alone. You would send your own son."

"I may send him to his death," Michael answered gravely. "For myself, I am too old." And then, with contempt, "You can go, if you will."

Ebenezer interposed again: "If Brother Ephraim were in charge, with Ehud also...."

"It is a good thought," Michael answered readily.

Ephraim said he would go, though in a slow way. "How far would you have us seek?"

"I would have you seek till you find," Michael answered, with energy. "A woman's steps are short, and they must be laden, or they are already dead."

"Well," Ephraim said, "we shall soon know." Ehud had lost no time. He had prepared all while the Elders met. Ephraim and he started off a few hours later with twenty of the strongest of the younger men who could be persuaded to go.

They travelled fast, some drawing the light sleds that were made for the goats. Every ten miles they cached food. From time to time, men turned back, their burdens lightened to no more than they would need on their return. They may have gone twice as fast as those they pursued, and though they lost their traces at times, it was not for long. That was till the storm came. At that time they were not more than fifteen or twenty miles behind. They made the best camp that they could, and waited till they could move again.

When the sky cleared, Ephraim sent back the men that remained, for they had used up most of the food that they still carried. He went on alone with Ehud, who would not go back, for so he had promised his wife. When they were alone together, Ephraim and he, he told much that had been secret to his own mind, for they were good friends, and had become better as they had been together at this time.

"So," he said at last, "it is our fault, or so she will have it, that we thought it wise not to speak at a sooner time, and they may be dead from this cause. But I have promised her that I will not return unless I have found them, whether alive or dead."

And this promise he kept, for there came a day when he stood with Ephraim in the presence of the Elders and said: "That was how we found them at last. They lay dead in each other's arms."

Ephraim confirmed that. He described the stone cave in which they died.

Michael walked apart after that, having sombre thoughts. Yet he was not one to waste life on a lost hope or a broken plan.

After a time he said: "Yet Paradise is a fair maid." He would be as a god to her, and he would be good to her, in his own way, as it is easy to guess.

CHAPTER LVII.

FRANKLIN and Eleanor looked in each other's eyes, and they were conscious of a thought that had come to both, and that was not easy to cast aside. Yet they knew it for a thing that they could not do without shame.

They had set out to the conquest of this iron waste, and they might fail, for failure is a thing familiar to men, but to give up while their hearts beat as they did, and while there was food for three days (or it might be four) was to defeat themselves, as men often do, but it would not be a good tale to take together to the throne of God. They might do badly enough, but they could do better than that.

Franklin said: "No, we won't take the tent," as though the question between them had been no more than that. "We'll push on as fast as we can while the food lasts. We can't tell what we shall find."

So they went on for that time, making rapid way, though the cold had become a cruel thing in the still bright air, and they understood why there is no life in that land, better even than they had done before.

The days were longer now, and there was twilight, and moon and stars on the sparkling snow, and the aurora made a splendour of the next night, as it had done in the autumn days. They were not hindered from going forward by darkness or evil weather, but only by the deadening cold, and the weariness in their own limbs, which they felt all the more now that they had lost any hope they had that they would come to a good place.

It had been foolish to leave the tent. Even clad as they were, they could not rest in comfort, though they found such shelter as a rock gave. They could not go on for weariness, and they could not rest for the cold. Surely it would have been better to stay in the tent, where they could have talked and thought in a peaceful way?

That was how it seemed at the dawn of the third day. Men may make the nobler choice when the roads of life fork, and the issue is hard and clear, yet they may have later times when they will say, "Was it worth it?" or "Did we do well? We had trodden flowers in a fairer field." They may ask themselves which is Heaven and which Hell, and have a fear that they have guessed wrong. So if we should search to every thought that they had as the hours passed, and they trod the hard smooth surface of the endless snow, we might find that it seemed to each a useless effort to which they were drawn by a companion's folly, but one about which they had been too tired to argue, too weary to resist. What did anything matter now?

In fact, they went on with thoughts that wandered further from where they were, into memories of earlier days, or a mist of dreams, as the body weakened, using itself to sustain their way, in place of the food that it did not get.

Eleanor thought, "If I stop now, I shall fall. It will be the end. If I speak, I shall say, 'I can't go on,' and that will be the end too. I don't want to fall in the open snow."

She wanted a corner, a cave. It is the instinct of all men, and of most other creatures, to have a shelter in which to die.

Franklin's voice broke into the lethargy that possessed her mind. "That isn't the sunrise. It's too far to the west for that."

The long twilight of dawn made a glory of gold and grey in the northeast sky that would move northward until the sun should come. Beyond that colour and light, there was a space where the horizon was of a more sombre grey, and more westward yet there was a high flicker of fire.

No, it wasn't the dawn. It was a light for which Franklin had looked almost from the day when they set out, and now that it came, it was no more than the assertion of a defeat that they already knew.

When they had come in the *Blanche* so swiftly up the narrow canyon, there had been a time when the strip of distant sky had flushed to a fiery red. He had thought then that it might be the reflection of volcanic fires, and subsequent experience had made this little less than a certain thing. He had thought of this volcanic region (if such it were) when they set out, with a vague hope of its possibilities. There might even (he dreamed) be other life there, such as they had found in the valley which was behind them. Yet he knew that to be a wild, even an absurd hope.

Still, it had been something to which to look forward. Something nearer than the coast. Something with other possibilities than the leagues of eternal snow.

And now it showed on the sky line, telling them what they already knew well enough, that they had made little progress toward the distant sea. It told them also how far they had wandered from their course. It should have been ahead or on the right hand.

"I don't see any help in that," Eleanor answered, "we can't eat fire." And yet, as she said it, a faint hope flickered through the weariness which delayed her mind. *Warmth—rest*—to rest in a warm place! It was an instant's hope that died as it came. How far might that distant beacon be? Perhaps a hundred miles. Perhaps much less than that. She had no more than the vaguest idea of how far such a light might show over this snow-white plain. But it mattered nothing. If it were twenty miles, it was a distance that she would never cross.

They couldn't eat fire. Franklin knew that. The last fragment of food had been eaten an hour ago. He had no more hope than she, being in an even greater extremity of exhaustion, for he had contrived with difficulty during the last two days that she should have almost all the food that remained. Now he was determined not to give way while her strength should last. Like her, he did not wish to fall in the open snow. But if she should fail, he could do no more. It would be a place where they would both lie.

Now he was stirred to a moment's life, which was a pain to feel. When we have resigned the torment of hope, it is no pleasure for it to wake for the pang of a second death.

They knew that there was no hope in that distant light, yet their feet turned toward it in a blind way. They were so dimly aware of what they did that they did not notice that they turned toward an expanse on which the snow did not lie flatly, but that rose and fell in uncertain curves, as the sea swells after a storm.

They did not even turn or look back when the frozen surface of snow, which had trembled slightly beneath their feet, fell behind them into the crevasse which might have given them a quicker death than would come from the patient, relentless cold.

Yet they must have known it, for Franklin said, about half an hour later, but not knowing that there had been any interval of that length: "We should be safer here with the rope."

Eleanor made no answer, and he made no motion to untie it from around his waist.

Then they came to where the level fell. It was only a fall of a few yards, but it was too steep in places for the snow to cling. They saw black igneous rock.

They chose a place of descent where the slope was least steep, but Franklin slipped on to his knees. He tried to rise, but he was dizzy with exhaustion and the deadly cold.

She reached a hand to help, but it leaned on him rather than raised. She said: "Not here. We can find a better place." She looked on a scene which was no longer level. She thought that they could find some shelter, some hollow in which to die.

Then she knew that he had sunk unconscious. She was alone indeed. And a sound of the falling of water was in her ears. Surely she had gone mad?

She knew that there could be no falling water in that frozen land. Yet the sound persisted. It seemed to be quite near, though she could not see from whence it came.

She looked at Franklin, who lay face downward in the snow, and did not move. She said aloud: "Nothing matters now. If I am mad, I am mad. I will see what it is." She went forward toward the sound.

She came to a cavity in the rocks into which water fell. It had a canopy of ice, grotesquely shaped, which was forming ever from the ascending stream. As she looked, a piece broke off this canopy, from its own weight, as must have happened often before, and fell into the water with a loud splash.

Up to then, she had looked on the steaming fountain as one who walks in a dream, but the sharp sound of the fall waked her to a clearer mind.

She knew nothing of fumaroles, or of the nature of a land completely formed by volcanic action in some time of primeval violence, as that must have been; but she knew that there was heat here, which was one of their two vital needs, and she saw the dark entrance of a cavern ahead, as was likely enough in such a land, of which the surface had once been lava that had flowed out, not from a local cone, but from a crack in the earth's side. It might be of a hundred leagues in its length.

That was an old tale of the earth's youth, of a time, it may be, before men were; and the lava had cooled and contracted, cracking in places, and in others, making tunnels within itself; and had changed into the black rock that she now saw, but the turmoil that was deep within still forced upward a thousand jets of heated water or steam, and the cold besieged them, but could not kill.

She went back to Franklin a different woman, being awake and alert with a new hope. It did not go far, for it gave no prospect of food, without which they could live, at the most, for a space of days, but she knew that he would freeze where he lay, and that she could bring him to a better place.

She wondered, as she went back, if she would have strength to drag him to the cave she had seen, but that was not tried, for he waked to the note of hope in her voice, and after some delay for a broken thong, for he had damaged a snowshoe when he slipped—a little thing, but much to them as they were—they made way together to the cave.

As they went, they noticed that which they had not seen before, a place where there was a hummock of snow that heaved under pressure of water, or rising steam, but was too heavy to be thrown off, seeming like a demon holding it down by the power of that frozen land. Yet it was clear that the heat fought for life at a hundred points, and would not be slain.

The cave was of the shape of a black funnel, running far into the earth, and having a temperature which was heat to them, after what they had come through. They could rest there without danger of death, and there Ephraim and Ehud found them two days later, as they told truly enough, except only that they were asleep, and not dead.

CHAPTER LVIII.

FRANKLIN said: "You have saved our lives, and we must be grateful for that, but it is no more than a doubtful gain, unless we can go on."

"You cannot do that," Ehud said, "for I have promised that it shall come to a different end. Besides, we have no food we could spare. We should start now to return to the last store we have made, for we may be no better than dead if the weather change before we shall be there. But as to how we found you after the tracks failed, we made wide circuits on either hand, so that we crossed them again. Had you stayed where you first were, it is a likely thing that we had not found you at all."

Eleanor asked: "You mean you had promised Gwen?"

Ehud said yes to that. He added: "We may have been wrong, but we had taken a great risk, and we had agreed that it was the surest way. How could we think that you would come out thus to a certain death?"

"I don't know what you mean by taking a risk," Franklin answered, "and you may call us fools, if you like, for having come here—I suppose most people would—but unless...."

"That," Ehud interrupted, "is a tale that I would tell, and it is not without hope, though it is less simple than it once was. When I was ordered to sink the boat that was yours, my wife was of a fixed mind that it should not be done. She said you must return when the spring should come. After we had considered it well, we were agreed, and I hid the boat where it would not be found till the spring, and then not as a likely thing, if it be left in that place.

"We were agreed that you should have it for secret flight, asking one thing in return, that you should tell of this place to none."

"And if we didn't agree to that?"

"The boat being hidden—"

"Yes. I see that. It was fair enough. But why not let us know what you had done? We weren't likely to give you away."

"To give—" Ehud was still puzzled by the idioms of a strange speech, even after a winter of his wife's examples. "We saw, when we found how you had done, that we may have been wrong. Yet it had seemed the safest way. You must see that you could not have reached the boat while the snow lay on the land, nor could you have gone through the water-caves till the thaw had been, and the water fallen again. We said one to another...."—Ehud was too loyal to say that it had been Gwen's insistence, when he might have taken a simpler way—"...that if you thought the boat to be sunk, you would so speak and act that no doubt could arise that you had a plan of escape at hand. That there should be no doubt, and no watch kept, was to your gain, and for it to be found that I had not sunk the boat was ruin also for us, as it may yet be.

"Then a day would have come when you would be gone, none could say how, and there would be flurry and search which would die down, whether after a short time or a long, and men would dispute how you had left, but there would be no proof, and each might think as he would."

Eleanor said: "Gwen meant to make sure that we should clear out. She meant to have no risk about that."

There was a faint note of resentment in her voice, which Ehud observed, and by which he was puzzled, as well as by the words themselves. He understood "clear out" as little as "give you away," which he had had from Franklin before. He said: "There was heavy risk, whichever way it were done, and we meant it to be your gain."

223

He added: "We have come here also at a risk which you may think to be less than it is, for the storms that come to these parts, and which may endure for many days, are what you have not yet seen, though you may think that you have had enough as it now is. It will be well if we can return while this calm shall last. But I was charged that I should not go back, leaving you unfound."

Eleanor saw that she might have been less than fair. She had no doubt that Gwen would be glad for them to go. Having decided to make her home here, she preferred to manage matters in her own way, with no desire for the competition of another Englishwoman of superior attractions, who might occupy the position of her father-in-law's wife. Neither would it have suited her plans at all for discord to arise, possibly in acute and dangerous forms, in which she herself might have been involved, and by which Ehud might have been placed in very difficult positions of conflicting loyalties. It was in every way best that they should go, and, seeing that, she had acted with her usual efficiency and thoroughness, prevailing upon Ehud to save the boat, and resolving to keep the knowledge that it would be available secret from them till the time should arrive when they would be able to use it. Indeed, the thoroughness of her efficiency had almost over-reached itself.

But these facts did not alter others which were of equal importance. They had wanted to get away, even to the point of this desperate venture. She had planned to make it possible for them, at a great risk, both to Ehud and herself. That it might not have been unwelcome to herself, hardly lessened the value of the vital help that she had proposed to give. There was no proof—and it was ungenerous to suppose—that she would not have done the same had it been to her detriment that they should go. She had sent Ehud here, at a risk which was not light, when it would have been a simple thing to have let them die in the snow. She had been urgent that the pursuit should not turn back till they were found. Who could say, but for the impulse of her mind upon his, that Ehud would have come so far?

She said: "You could always trust Gwen." And then reverted to the vital question which Franklin had raised. "But how will it be now?"

She looked at Ephraim, wondering somewhat that Ehud should have spoken so freely before him, but he said nothing, and Ehud answered again:

"It may still be that you can escape, if the boat be not discovered before our return, of which I have a good hope. We have talked much of this, Ephraim and I, and are of one mind that it will be best for all that you should go in a quiet way.

224

"As to not having sunk the boat, it was my own doing, to which he could have given no countenance, he being an Elder, but it is a thing done. It was my deed, not his.

"If it should be known now (and you have returned to our land), it might be that my father would take my part, even against the Elders' wrath, and there might be those who would be of the same mind. It is hard to foresee. There might be strife that would wreck the land.

"But if you will stay behind on the last day, we will go forward alone, Ephraim and I, with a tale that we found you, but that you were both dead, which will be doubted of none, they knowing how far we had searched in vain, and the storm that did then come. And on the next night, if you will come down secretly to the water's edge, to the spot where you landed first, it may be that the boat will be there, and that you will be away while the darkness endures.

"Against that we ask but the one thing, and that you shall swear by a binding oath."

Ephraim spoke for the first time. "There is no need for oaths. It shall be requital that we have saved you here. We will give you trust that you bring not the ruin to our land that must be if more of your kind should come. Your life may be good to those who are reared in your own ways, but to us it would be no less than a slaying plague."

Ephraim thought that there would be little risk that they would break this condition, if it were left in that way. But he had much practice in settling the differences of men over matters of barter and land, and he knew that, if there be no honour in a man's heart, his oath will break like a soaked straw.

CHAPTER LIX.

IT was three hours before dawn. The sky was starless and dark, being covered with a light mist, as it often was at that time of year. Franklin supposed that the moisture rose from the thawed land till it froze in the upper air. Let that be as it might, it was a troublesome thing to those who had climbed far down the side of the hills in the long evening twilight, when they had lost the fear of being seen from below, and now had to find a way which they had only once trodden before. It was something for which they were not prepared, for, except in time of storm, though there is little of light in the Antarctic winter, there is little of dense night in a land that is white and sparkling with the frozen snow. But it was different here after the thaw.

They were to be at the foot of the orchard which had been Abel Trustwell's six months ago, and was now the property of Ehud and Gwen, at the spot where they had landed first, an hour before the long dawn should commence to lighten the land. But now they would not be there till it would be broad daylight again—not unless they could make better progress than this. Even if they could find the way at all!

Suppose that they should wander till the light should come, and then find themselves far from the waterside, and in view of those who would denounce them? To be so near escape, and to be stopped by this blinding mist!

Eleanor said: "Do you think we ought to go on? It's not fair to Gwen."

Franklin had the same doubt. It might not be fair to Ehud either, or to Ephraim, both of whom had declared that they had seen them dead. What savage penalties might it not mean to those who had been their friends, even to the secret defiance of the half-political, half-religious tyranny under which they lived? Or what extremities of civil warfare might it not mean if they should decline to submit themselves to such judgment? *The beginning of strife is like the letting out of water.* Who can recover it or restrain its course?

In a few hours they might be free forever of this gloomy land, or they might be involved in conflict which they could no longer honourably leave. Worse than that, their boat might be seized, their last hope of escape gone, and they themselves in peril of death from the charge of witchcraft which had hung over them, an unlifting shadow ever since they had landed here. And all this as the result of a spring mist!

Franklin hesitated, but he had a natural reluctance to turn back to the difficult climbing of those frozen hills. It would be doubtful how far they could get. The higher slopes might be lighter, but could they get so far in the night hours?

Already they had crossed the barrier which divided the cultivated land from the open hills where the goats ranged. If Ehud had not failed in his own part of the plan, they must be within three miles of the place where the *Blanche* was tied. And the *Blanche* meant safety! They thought nothing now of the perils of storm or ice, of difficult landing on the frozen beach when they should run out of the narrow canyon on the strength of the warmer current which would strive to hurry them onward toward the besieging floes. (And in what condition would the *Blanche* be now to do more than drift at the water's will?) Let them only get clear of this, and let the rest be as it would!

But ought they to go on? The argument was not all on one side. If Ehud had brought the boat down, it might be a terrible risk for it to remain there for another night. He might wait in hesitation till it would be too late to take it back to any certain hiding.

"I think," Franklin said, "we ought to make an effort. After all, if we once get to the riverside, it oughtn't to be hard to find that."

A voice answered them out of the mist.

"It will, if you go that way."

"Gwen!" Eleanor exclaimed. "Oh, Gwen, how did you find us?"

"I didn't till I heard you talking. I started out as soon as we saw the kind of night it was likely to be. We're not grumbling at that. Ehud said it couldn't be better, if only you could find your way. So I thought I'd better come and make sure."

"You think you can lead us right?" Franklin asked. It was a natural question. She was not likely to have been over that ground more than they had themselves.

"I'll take you there if you'll come quiet, as the police say. But you mustn't talk as you were doing. There's Malachi's house half a mile on, the way we shall have to go, and Aaron's living there now. We shall have to pass it quite close, if we keep to the only way that's safe in this fog, and you know how sound carries in such an air."

"Need we go so close?"

"We've got to follow a ditch. That is, when we find it. I've got to trust my footmarks for that, and that this torch won't go out for the last time. Fortunately, there's enough mud."

She flashed an electric torch, carefully conserved during the winter months against such an emergency, upon the way she had come. Certainly the marks showed.

They showed also that, after their pause of hesitation, Franklin and Eleanor had been starting off in the wrong direction.

Franklin said: "Go ahead. We won't spoil Aaron's sleep." Silently, in single file, they made their way through the mist.

CHAPTER LX.

THE *Blanche* strained at the mooring-rope on a stream that ran fast and high. The bulk of the flood-water did not drain in this direction, and the worst of the floods was over now, but the river was still much higher than it had been when they came up. Franklin looked down on it with a doubt which he could not still. With the water as high as it was, how would they get through the cavern beneath the hills?

What he said was: "What about the barrier? Hasn't that been secured against us?"

Ehud answered: "You'll have no trouble about that. We have it lifted when the floods come, lest it be burst asunder. There is only the chain, and I have had that slackened."

Gwen said: "I think you'll find one of the engines will work. I couldn't make anything of the other. Of course, it may be simple to you. But you'll find it doesn't leak, and the steering's all right, and I've fixed up the light. There's plenty of carbide for that. You'll find some extra wraps in the boat and lots of food. You won't find much else. I know it's theft, Eleanor, but the temptation was too strong."

"Of course you've kept anything that could be any use," Eleanor answered carelessly, "As though we should mind that!"

"But we don't want the boat to ride higher," Franklin said, with an anxiety which he could not entirely conceal. He remembered how they had tied it up when they landed first at the same tree. The water must be a foot higher now

"We've thought of that," Gwen answered. "We've put some stones in for ballast. You can throw them out, if you like, when you've got through the cavern."

They stood in a last moment of silent awkward hesitation, feeling the finality of that parting, and shrinking from any exhibition of feeling with the reserve of their race.

Gwen said: "You won't give us away? We both trust you for that."

"We shan't do that," Eleanor answered "But suppose we look you up in a few years' time. We might just come to the door, and turn back if it wasn't a good time to call."

"Of course, we should be glad to see you again," Gwen answered. And then: "Oh, I don't know!"

She had a sinking of heart at this finality of separation from all her past, when the boat would slip from the shore; but the thought that she might still step into it if she would did not enter her mind. Perhaps it was best that she should feel that it had ended here. She had put her hand to the plough, and she had no mind to look back. No, it would be best that she should have no secret thought that they might be coming again, that there might be a time when she could still escape if she would. She thought of the child that would be hers. Even Ehud had not been told of that yet. No, her future, for good or evil, was in this land. "Oh," she said again, "I don't know. Perhaps it's better not."

Eleanor was kissing her now, with words which were more emotional, though not so deeply impulsed as her own. Franklin had drawn up the *Blanche* for Eleanor to step in. He had a secret thought that if the water should be too high, they could delay for a time at the cavern entrance. Every hour it must be falling now.

Ehud stood somewhat aside, aware of emotions that he could only partly share. Eleanor's voice roused him. She had Gwen in her arms. Being so much the taller, her eyes went over her into the mist. She saw Aaron Cloutsclad a few yards away. "Look behind you, Ehud," she said, with a quiet insistence. The next moment the two men vanished into the mist together.

"What was it, Eleanor?" Gwen said sharply. "*Aaron?*" Her voice rose as she called. "Ehud, don't let him go. *Oh, don't let him go.*"

They heard a scuffle, and a choking cry. Ehud called: "Where are you? I can't see the way."

Guided by their voices, he came back, dragging the spying Elder, with hard fingers around his throat.

They looked at one another in a common uncertainty. They had caught something that they had no wish to keep, and that might only be loosed at the cost of their own lives.

"Gwen," Eleanor said quietly, "you'll have to come, after all—Ehud and you."

"No," Gwen answered, "we're not going to do that." She looked at the frightened, trembling man in Ehud's powerful grasp. She thought of him—Ehud, and of all the plans for the future that they had made together. She thought of the coming child. The eyes of Jael were not harder when she looked on the sleeping Sisera. "Franklin," she said, "please go. We want that chain back in its place in an hour's time. Every moment's an added risk. No, we've got to deal with this in our own way. *Please go.*"

She spoke with a passionate energy that bore down the doubts in their own minds. Franklin and Eleanor were in the boat now. Gwen bent down quickly, and cast off the rope. The current caught the boat, and hurried it onward.

A loud splash sounded behind them. Franklin, busy in getting the boat under control, said: "What was that? He hasn't escaped, has he?"

Eleanor answered: "No. I think they're holding him down." Her voice trembled a little, but Franklin's mind was full of his own problems.

"I hope they are," he said heartily. "There've been better rats drowned than he. We shall have to risk the cavern now."

He thought that Aaron Cloutsclad might not be the only one who would be drowned that night. If the flooding water rose at any point to the cavern roof.

The searchlight shone into the low, black mouth, and upon the rushing water beneath it. There might be a foot of clearance, perhaps less. Well, it was the only chance.

CHAPTER LXI.

FROM the *London Courier*, Tuesday, February 2, 1933:

TRAGEDY OF THE ANTARCTIC

News has been received by wireless from Captain Ericson, of the *Bergen*, the rescue ship which was dispatched from Cape Town about two months ago to bring back the members of Mr. Franklin Arden's Antarctic expedition. The *Bergen* is at present frozen in, and there is some doubt as to whether it may not be obliged to winter in the South Polar regions.

Captain Ericson reports that he has picked up Mr. Franklin Arden and Miss Eleanor Blanche D'Acre, who, it will be remembered, was financing the expedition. They are both in good health, but it is deeply regretted that the remaining three members of the party, Mr. Bunford Weldon, the well-known sportsman, Captain Sparshott, and Miss Gwendolen Collinson, succumbed to the rigours of the Antarctic winter.

Captain Ericson reports that they had been buried side by side by Mr. Arden. He has conducted a burial service, and erected crosses above their graves.

So another chapter is added to the records of Antarctic heroism and disaster. The scientific fruits of the expedition cannot be fully known till Mr. Arden is able to return, but it is already evident that the Enderby quadrant has maintained its reputation, and is likely to be avoided in the future, as it has been for the last three centuries.

ABOUT THE AUTHOR

SYDNEY FOWLER WRIGHT (1874-1965) penned over seventy volumes of science fiction, fantasy, classic mysteries, historical novels, poetry, and non-fiction, many of them being published by the Borgo Press Imprint of Wildside Press.